Carl Weber's Kingpins:

Oklahoma City

Carl Weber's Kingpins:

Oklahoma City

Clifford "Spud" Johnson

www.urbanbooks.net

Urban Books, LLC
97 N18th Street
Wyandanch, NY 11798

ISBN 13: 978-1-62286-979-4
ISBN 10: 1-62286-979-6

First Trade Paperback Printing June 2016
Printed in the United States of America

10 9 8 7 6 5 4 3 2 1

*This is a work of fiction. Any references or similarities to
actual events, real people, living or dead, or to real locales
are intended to give the novel a sense of reality. Any simi-
larity in other names, characters, places, and incidents is
entirely coincidental.*

Distributed by Kensington Publishing Corp.
Submit Orders to:
Customer Service
400 Hahn Road
Westminster, MD 21157-4627
Phone: 1-800-733-3000
Fax: 1-800-659-2436

Carl Weber's Kingpins:

Oklahoma City

Clifford "Spud" Johnson

Prologue

Four People. Two meetings. The same location. The same topic. Drugs. On the far right side of Charleston's restaurant, Toni was smiling at Flamboyant. Toni liked the confidence he seemed to possess. Everything about him suggested success to Toni. *But can he withstand any pressure?* Toni wondered, and continued to listen to Flamboyant speak confidently of his operation.

"There's nothin' that I can't move in this city. So, as long as you keep me properly stocked, I will bring you that paper. Guaranteed."

"Would you have a problem if I set a certain timetable on the delivery of my money?" Toni asked, with that smile still firmly in place.

"It depends. Shit may fall differently from time to time, so I'd have to see how well my team is rockin' before I'd accept terms like a time limit and shit."

"That's understandable. I'm in no rush; as long as I get my money in a timely fashion I'll be satisfied. I told you when we first met that you fit my qualifications as a moneymaker. That's why we're here today. I have a few more questions I need answered before we get to the next phase of this meeting."

"Ask away," Flamboyant said in his normal cocky manner.

"I can tell that you're confident in your team. That's a good sign; it shows me that there's loyalty in your camp."

"No doubt. No one on my team would ever cross me."

"What if you found out that there was an informant within your camp? Or, worse, someone was planning on trying to take you out? How would you deal with a situation like that?"

Flamboyant sat back in his seat, sipped his flute of Krug Rosé champagne, and said, "If any member of my team ever crossed me in any way they'd have to be dealt with."

"How?"

He stared at Toni momentarily and answered, "Severely."

Toni smiled and said, "You don't strike me as a man who tends to resort to violence."

"Violence is a tool of our trade. When a certain tool is needed to get the job done that tool is put to use. Period. Don't let this smooth taste fool you, Toni. I do what needs to be done in order to maintain a strong team."

"Understood. So, tell me something. Which would you prefer: to be loved or to be feared?"

"In what, my personal relationships or business?"

"Both."

Flamboyant smiled brightly and said, "I'd rather be loved."

"Why?"

"As long as my team loves me they'll continue to do what it takes to make sure that I'm happy. As for relationships, I have only one and I don't plan on havin' another, so that's pretty much the same as with my business. Wifey knows the love is real on my part so she'll continue to love me just as much as I'm lovin' her. Real talk."

"Interesting. I've always thought the streets had no room for love."

"The love is out there in them streets. Some niggas just don't know how to use it to their advantage."

"And you do?"

"We wouldn't be havin' this meetin' if you didn't already know the answer to that question, Toni."

Toni laughed and said, "True."

On the opposite side of the restaurant, Charlie was telling King exactly what was to be expected of him. "I have complete confidence in your ability to move the ya-yo. What concerns me is everything else. I'm about to be supplying you with everything from X pills to PCP. If you want pounds of that potent California weed, then that'll be available to you also. Are you positive that you can handle that much product?"

"When we first hooked up you asked me if I was ready to get some serious money. I was fresh outta the pen for the second time; that was five months ago. Since that time I've gotten my squad as well as myself in order. I've been waitin' for an opportunity like this my entire life. I have a plug now and I plan to take full advantage of that. Makin' money isn't new to me, Charlie. True, I've fallen a few times in this game, but who hasn't? I will move whatever you give me. The more you have the better it is for me and my squad," King said convincingly.

"Good. Before we get down to the specifics of how we'll be conducting our business, I want to ask you something."

King didn't say a word. He stared at Charlie and patiently waited.

Charlie grinned and asked, "Which would you rather be: loved or feared?"

Without any thought or hesitation King replied, "Feared."

"Why?"

"As long as niggas out in them streets fear the King, they gon' respect the King and never try to do the goofy."

"The goofy. Hmmm. Okay, what if someone in your immediate circle did do the goofy? How would you handle it?"

"If I even thought someone on my squad was on some stupid shit they'd quickly become a mama's memory. I don't play games, nor do I withhold this information from those around me. Every member of my squad knows how the King gets down. This ain't no TV or make-believe shit crackin'. I've stressed that to my squad so they know what to expect from me."

"What are some of your weaknesses, King?"

He stared at Charlie for a moment before replying, "I don't have any."

Charlie started laughing and said, "Okay, let's get down to the particulars."

"Let's," King said, and for the first time during their meeting, he smiled. It was finally time for him to get some of that serious money and, man, was he ready.

Forty-five minutes later Charlie watched as Flamboyant left the restaurant, just as Toni watched King as he strolled toward the exit. Though they were only a few steps from one another, both King and Flamboyant were now tied to the same plug in the game. Charlie smiled, pulled out a cell phone, and sent a text message to Toni, who was still sitting on the other side of the restaurant. It read: Let the game begin!

Chapter One

It had been six months since his meeting with Charlie. Since that time King and his squad had been extremely busy. Not only had they surpassed all of Charlie's expectations, they actually shocked the shit out of Charlie.

Toni was all smiles because, on the other side of Oklahoma City, Flamboyant and his team were equally impressive as King and his people. "Looks like we've picked two winners, huh, Charlie?"

"Just because they've started out well doesn't necessarily make them winners, Toni. Let's sit back and continue to monitor our newly crowned kings of the streets. It's still early in the game."

"True, but our money is coming faster and stronger than even we expected it to. That should make a certain person very happy, don't you think?"

"That greedy mothafucka will stay happy as long as we continue to bring in the meal tickets. It is what it is! I got to go. I'll holla at you later."

Toni smiled and said, "See ya, Charlie."

"The block is wildin' right now, dog. Ever since we got that new batch, shit has been crazy! They lovin' that shit!"

"That's cool, real cool. But you got to make sure that niggas don't be slippin', 'cause the money is rollin' way faster than usual. Keep 'em on their toes," Flamboyant said as he continued to stare out of the window of his Mercedes-Benz S-Class 600.

"Don't worry about it, Flam. We got this for ya boy," Prince, Flamboyant's right-hand man, replied.

"A'ight, make sure that everyone continues to eat, my nigga. I'll get back at ya later."

"Gotcha," Prince said as he watched as his man, Flamboyant, pull away from the curb and left the block that was making them so much money. The south side of Oklahoma City was theirs and it seemed like so was the entire world. *It feels real good to be on a winning team,* Prince thought as he went back into one of the several trap houses they had running on the block.

On the other side of town, King sat on the porch of his main trap house and watched as the many fiends came to spend their money. Tippi, his most trusted soldier, sat next to him and watched the fiends as well as the other squad members as they got that money. Everyone knew that Tippi was not to be fucked with. Not only was she King's number one, she was the top killer of the squad.

Tippi was a damn fool and everybody on the north side knew it. When she got hot there was no telling what she'd do to a nigga. For that matter, niggas on the north tried their damnedest to stay on Tippi's good side. She was a fairly small woman who had deceptive strength. Though she looked and acted like a tomboy, she was very attractive, if one took the time to really pay attention to her looks. Her light brown complexion and her long sandy brown hair that she kept braided in several French braids gave her a kind of distinct look. She chose to keep her hair braided straight to the back and held tightly in a ponytail, or had crazy Allen Iverson–like braids all over her head. Though she was small, she was thick when it came to her thighs and ass. She stood about five three and normally could be considered a dime. But to those around her Tippi was considered a damn fool and was not to be fucked with.

Tippi was extremely nimble for her size. She was even more accurate with whatever weapon she chose to use to do a nigga. She was known to carry several different types of pistols on any given day. It was also another well-known fact that Tippi had killed men with her bare hands as well as with knives. Her murder game was definitely up to par. For that reason alone the word all over the north side of Oklahoma City was, "Do not fuck with King or his squad." The north, northeast, and the northwest sides of Oklahoma City belonged to them. Every penny that was made illegally on them streets from cocaine, X pills, weed, and PCP, you best believe that King's squad got a percentage.

King was loving the fact that all seemed to have fallen right into place for himself and his squad. So far there had been no wrinkles in his game plan. He chose to stay hands-on at all times. That's why he was on the block so much. He wanted those around him to understand that this was a team effort even for the star and the captain of the squad. Tippi hated the fact that he exposed himself so much. She felt that he should play in the background more and let her handle the day-to-day hassles of getting their money. He knew how Tippi felt but still chose to play the block daily. He was more comfortable around his own. No amount of money was going to change him from being where he felt he belonged. The block was his kingdom, so the block was where he'd be. Period.

"Here comes 'em two funny style–ass niggas, Trey and Vaughn," Tippi said as she lit up a Newport cigarette.

"Where have 'em fools been? I haven't seen them for a minute!" King said.

"They went to Tulsa to see if they could set up shop down there with some of their cousins or some shit like that. You gave them the green light, remember? Or has Lawanda got you slippin' now?"

King grinned at Tippi. He knew she hated his kids' mother. He also knew that she was madly in love with him. That gave him an advantage over her wild ass, 'cause he knew if he ever pissed her off for real he'd have to kill her before she killed him. That's why he chose to keep their relationship strictly business.

"Oh, yeah, I forgot about that shit. Thanks, baby," he said playfully.

"Baby? Nigga, you gon' make me do you somethin' for playin' wit' me. You know how bad I want that dick."

He laughed and said, "After we get about fiddy million and retired from the game I'm gon' take your ass somewhere and fuck you for as long as you can take it."

"Promises, promises, nigga! I'll be right back. I don't like these fake-ass niggas," she said as she stepped off the porch, just as Trey and Vaughn made it to the first step.

"What up, Tippi?" asked Trey as she passed him. Tippi ignored him as she went across the street and started talking to another member of the squad.

"What it do, King?" Vaughn asked.

"What's up? You niggas get that shit crackin' out in Tulsa?"

"Kinda. 'Em Crip niggas down there were hatin' and shit, but once we told them some of our prices they told us they'll think about fuckin' wit' us. So we left it at that for now."

"Yeah, wasn't no use in pressin' the issue," added Trey.

"Is that right? So, what's what?"

"We're 'bout to hit the northwest side and get with Keko and see if he needs any help over that way."

Shaking his head no, King said, "Nah, I need y'all to stay out this way. Y'all can go over to the North

Highlands and check with Damus over there. See if they're good. If they ain't, tighten 'em up."

"That's cool. So, have you thought about what we talked 'bout?" asked Trey.

King stared at them for a moment then said, "If that thing works out in Tulsa for y'all I'm gon' let y'all have it full time. So that way y'all will have y'all own spot to run and maintain. As long as you understand that you are to never, and I mean never, get any work from anyone but the squad."

"That's fa' sho'. You know we ain't tryin' to go against the grain, baby," Vaughn said.

"Yeah, we know what side our bread is buttered on," added Trey.

For some strange reason Trey's corny statement made goose bumps pop out all over King's arm. He smiled and said, "A'ight, then, go on and check on 'em niggas in the Highlands for me. Get back at me after everything is good over there." King pulled out his cell and started dialing. Their meeting was over.

As the phone was ringing, King watched as Trey and Vaughn got into Trey's Chevy Avalanche and left the block. King closed his phone and smiled, then jumped off the porch and called Tippi. When Tippi came back across the street he asked her, "You hungry, boo?"

"'Baby,' 'boo,' damn, I must really be gettin' close to gettin' me some of that dick I've yearned for all of my life, huh?" she asked with a smile on her face.

He laughed and said, "Maybe. Come on, let's go get our eat on. We got some shit to talk 'bout."

Her smile quickly faded as she asked, "Am I needed?"

He shrugged his shoulders and said, "I'm not knowin' yet. Come on, let's go talk about it." Tippi followed King as he led her toward his black Dodge Magnum.

***

Trey and Vaughn stopped at 7-Eleven right outside of the neighborhood called North Highlands. Trey needed a pack of cigarettes and Vaughn wanted a bottled water. When they walked inside of the store, three Bloods from North Highland were inside, harassing the store's cashier. When they saw Trey and Vaughn they walked over to them and spoke. Trey stuck out his chest as if he was the big man and asked, "Y'all good over there in y'all hood, or do we need to hook y'all up?"

B-lo, one of the main go-getters in the Highlands, said, "Yeah, we need to holla. When can we get down?"

"Check it, let me make a few calls then I'll meet you on Eighty-third over at Pimpin' Steve's niece's house," Trey said as he grabbed a pack of Newports.

"That's straight," B-lo replied as he led the other two Bloods out of the store, much to the cashier's relief.

After paying for their purchases, Trey and Vaughn stepped out of the store and saw two white men standing next to Trey's SUV. Fear gripped them both instantly. *Ain't no cracka got enough nerve to be around my shit unless he's the Ones,* thought Trey as he stared at the two white men.

"Excuse me, is there a problem, Officer?" Trey asked sarcastically.

"No, as a matter of fact, there isn't, Trey," answered one of the white men.

Before they could say a word, the other white man pulled out a badge and showed it to them and said, "FBI. We need to ask the both of you some questions."

"Are we under arrest?" asked Vaughn.

"Not at the moment, Vaughn, but if you don't hurry up and get into Trey's truck you might soon be," said the FBI agent who had spoken first.

"What?" asked Trey.

"The both of you need to get inside of your truck and follow us. If you don't follow us and we have to come find you, neither of you will be seeing the streets for a very long time. Now move it!" the agent said with authority.

They did as they were told and climbed back into Trey's truck. They watched as the white men got into a navy blue Tahoe that they hadn't paid any attention to previously. The FBI agents pulled out of the parking lot, followed by Trey and Vaughn. B-lo, who had forgotten to ask Trey if he could get fronted some sherm, had decided to come back real quick and ask him, but stopped short when he saw Trey and Vaughn talking to some white dudes. Once he saw one of the white men flash a badge, he quickly turned and got the fuck away from that 7-Eleven. *Hope them niggas ain't dirty,* B-lo thought as he headed back into his hood.

The FBI agents led Trey and Vaughn to a Motel 6 right off of I-35. Once there one said, "My name is Agent Bullock and this here is my partner, Agent Van Horne."

"Man, what the fuck is this shit about? We ain't done shit!" said a nervous and frustrated Trey.

Agent Bullock smiled and said, "Now, Trey, you know as well as we do that the both of you work for King."

Vaughn's eyes grew wide as saucers when he heard the agent mention King's name. "What . . . what do y'all want from us?" Vaughn asked nervously.

Agent Van Horne smiled and mockingly said, "You ain't know? We know you two are small fish. We want the shark. We don't have any time for negotiations so let me tell you how it's going to be. Either you help us get King, or you remain loyal to him by doing a minimum of twenty in Leavenworth."

"For what? You ain't got us with shit!" yelled Trey.

"We're the FBI, son. Haven't you ever heard of conspiracy? Or, better yet, we can get the both of you for distribution."

"Distribution of what?" asked Vaughn.

Both of the agents laughed, then Agent Van Horne said, "Of anything we want to put on ya, son. Cocaine, weed, sherm, X. Hell, we could even hook you up with some crank. So, what's it going to be, guys? Are you going to help yourselves or are you going to remain loyal to King?"

Trey was sitting on the edge of the bed slowly shaking his head from side to side. "I ain't doin' no dub for no nigga. What up with you, Vaughn?"

Vaughn shook his head and said, "This shit ain't cool, Trey."

"What other choice we got?"

"Nigga, do you know what King's goin' to do to us if he ever finds, no, when he finds out we got down on him? Better yet, what he gon' have Tippi do to us? I ain't wit' it, my nigga. I'd rather take my chances in the pen."

"Did you hear what this cracka told us, fool? They talkin' 'bout giving us a dub, nigga! I can't do no number like that there. Fuck that shit!"

Vaughn sighed heavily as he stared at his closest homeboy. "Are you positive you want to go out like this, dog?"

"Like I said, what other choice do we got, Vee?"

"This is some real fucked-up shit." Vaughn turned toward the two FBI agents and asked, "What y'all wanna know?"

King and Tippi were enjoying their meal of catfish and French fries when King's cell rang. He wiped his mouth and answered the phone. "What it do?" He shook his head in dismay as he listened to whoever was speaking to him on the other line. "A'ight, I'll get at y'all in a li'l bit. Good lookin' out," King said as he ended the call.

"Was that the call?" Tippi asked.

"Yes."

"And?"

"Your services are needed."

"Good. I never did like 'em niggas," Tippi said as she started back eating her catfish.

After they finished their meals they left the restaurant and went back to the block. As soon as King's Magnum came to a stop several members of the squad came over to his car. King and Tippi got out of the car and led the other members of the squad toward the trap. Once King got to the porch he sat down on the top step and said, "I've already called Keko. He's on his way over here now. When he gets here we're goin' to take care of some thangs. I already told y'all what was what, but I want y'all to see for yourselves so y'all will know fa' sho' what went down and why. I can't afford to shut down the block so some of y'all are gon' have to stay here and hold it down. So, who's it gon' be?"

There were seven squad members present in all. Three out of the seven chose to stay on the block while Flex, Nutta, Cuddy, and Boleg decided to go with Tippi and King. Ten minutes after that decision was made Keko pulled in front of the trap in his 1970 Impala. His twenty-four-inch chrome rims shined brightly as he climbed out of his old-school Chevy. He stepped quickly to the porch and said, "Let's do this shit. I'm missin' mad money on my side of town."

"What, Spook ain't takin' care of shit for you while you gone?" asked Tippi.

"Spook can't be everywhere the way I can, Tippi," Keko replied sarcastically.

"Whatever."

King smiled and said, "Load up and follow your boy." They all followed as King went and got back into his car with Tippi. The other squad members climbed into Keko's car.

As Keko followed King he said, "Man, 'em niggas done fucked up!"

"That's putting it lightly, son. Did you peep the look on Tippi's face? That broad 'bout to be on some murda shit fa' real," said Cuddy.

"Man, I ain't tryin' to see none of that crazy-ass shit Tippi be into," said Nutta, the youngest member of the squad.

"Why the fuck did you wanna come for then?" asked Flex.

Nutta shrugged his slim shoulders and answered, "I dunno."

"Now that's some silly shit right there, youngsta," Keko said as he continued to drive.

King pulled into the parking lot of the Motel 6 and parked his car right next to Trey's Avalanche. Everyone got out of Keko's car and came and stood next to King. King pulled out his phone and made a call. When the other line was answered he said, "Yeah, we're out here now. We're on our way up, y'all good?"

"Yes, we're fine, sir," answered Agent Van Horne, who actually wasn't really an FBI agent at all. He was a friend of Charlie's who became a friend of King's. When King got hit with those goose bumps during his conversation with Trey and Vaughn earlier, he took that as a warning. So he decided to give Trey and Vaughn a little test. He wanted to make sure that they were loyal to him as well as to the squad. If they passed it would be all love. But if they failed then, well, they had to die.

King led the way upstairs to the room where Trey and Vaughn were telling two fake FBI agents everything they knew about King's illegal operations on the north side of Oklahoma City. When they made it to the room, King knocked on the door lightly and smiled at Tippi. Tippi wasn't in a smiling mood but she returned his smile anyway; he had that effect on her. *Damn, I love this nigga!* she thought. The door to the hotel room was opened by Agent Van Horne and King entered the room followed closely by Tippi and the rest of the squad. Trey and Vaughn both looked as if they were about to have a heart attack. Both of the fake FBI agents started laughing as they watched Trey's and Vaughn's reactions to King's entrance.

"Look at them. They're scared shitless," said Agent Van Horne, laughing. His name was really Mike Webb. He was a car dealership owner out in the city of Bethany.

"Yeah, that look is priceless, fucking priceless!" Agent Bullock laughed too. His name was actually Ted Johnson, one of Charlie's many accountants.

"So tell me, guys, did my two friends here have a lot to say about me?" King asked as he stared hard at Trey and Vaughn.

"Let's just say that we now know everything there is to know about your operation, King," said Mike.

"That's right. We even know about your plans to go legitimate in a couple of years," added Ted.

Boleg, Cuddy, Nutta, Flex, and Keko stared at Trey and Vaughn with looks of disgust and hatred on their faces. Tippi had murder in her eyes but King was as calm as could be. His facial expression showed nothing. Though he was very angry he chose to remain extra calm about this situation. A point was about to be made. A show of sorts was about to be given to his squad members that if they ever chose to cross him, this would also become their fate.

Trey stared nervously at King and said, "King, man, we didn't—"

"Shut the fuck up, nigga! Say another word and you're goin' to die real slow, homie," Tippi said menacingly.

"You two were a part of some real shit. I was goin' to let y'all earn all you could make, but I guess that wasn't good enough, huh? You had to go and try to cross the King. For that y'all gots to pay with your lives." He turned toward Mike and Ted and said, "Thanks, guys, I really appreciate your help on this, especially with such short notice."

"No problem, King, you know we hate snitches too." They both laughed as they left the hotel room.

After the door closed, King turned back toward Trey and Vaughn and said, "If I don't test those around me whom I deem loyal, how will I ever truly know if their loyalty is true? You two failed my li'l test miserably. I want you both to know I get no pleasure out of hurtin' someone I considered my own. But y'all aren't a part of the squad. You never were. Y'all was fakin' wit' us."

"Can you please save all of this drama and let me take these two bitch-ass niggas down?" Tippi said angrily, staring hard at Trey and Vaughn.

King frowned and silently gave himself a reminder that he would have to check Tippi for her fucking slick mouth. With a nod of his head he gave Tippi the go-ahead to do her. Neither Trey nor Vaughn saw it coming, even though they were expecting an assault. Tippi moved with lightning speed. No one inside of the hotel room saw her when she reached down and grabbed both of her stilettos from the holster she had strapped to each of her calves. That's why everyone was shocked when they saw her damn near decapitate Trey with one swift swing of her right arm. She severed every major artery in his neck. Before a gasp could be made, Tippi, with a backhand motion, stabbed Vaughn directly into his heart. He arched his back hard as his last breath left his body. Tippi pulled her knife out of his heart and smiled as his body fell back onto the bed. Blood was gushing out of Trey's neck like a fire hydrant. To say things were messy would be putting it mildly; blood was every-fucking-where.

"Daaaaaamnnn, look at that shit!" Nutta said as he stared at the gruesome sight.

"Damn, Tippi, now we gotta have somebody come and clean up this mess. Why didn't you blast 'em two niggas?" King asked as he stepped away from the bed where blood was slowly spreading all over the carpet.

"I used these because I wanted to make sure your point was made." She turned so that she faced everyone inside of the room and continued. "You cross the squad or any of its members and this will be your fate. Real talk." She then calmly stepped into the bathroom and began cleaning her weapons.

King shook his head and said, "Y'all go on and bounce. Me and Tippi will take care of this shit. Get at me later on and let me know what's what out in 'em streets."

Keko laughed and said, "You got it, massa. We gon' make sho' everything is in order."

Cuddy, Boleg, and Flex laughed at Keko's joke but King and Tippi's point had definitely been made. Do not cross the squad. If you do, death will definitely be yours.

Chapter Two

Flamboyant walked inside of his four-bedroom home out on Sky Island, a neighborhood mostly full of white people. With his new connections he was able to acquire his dream home. Now that he was making the type of money he knew he would one day make, he felt it was time for him to live up to his name, so he went all out; brand new expensive Italian furnishings were all over his home. Nothing but the best was inside of every single room. From the kitchen to the backyard, everything was top of the line. He smiled when he saw his lovely wife-to-be sitting at the dining room table, nibbling on some cashews as she read the latest *Sister 2 Sister* magazine.

"Hey, babe, what's really good?" he asked as he gave her a kiss on the cheek and joined her at the table.

Shayla smiled at him and said, "Nothing much, bored really. How was your day?"

"You act as if I've been at a fuckin' job or something. All I've been doin' is pickin' up money, babe."

Shayla frowned and her extremely cute features showed her displeasure in her man's answer to her question. "Just because you were out there in the streets doing what you do doesn't mean that I can't ask how your day was. You irritate the hell out of me when you act so fucking immature, Marco."

"Sorry, babe, but you act like you don't be knowin' what time it is. You know how I get down and you know I'm no Huxtable-type nigga, so why you trippin'?"

She slid out of her chair, shook her head from side to side, and went into their bedroom without answering his question.

Shit, he thought as he followed her. Once they were inside of the bedroom he said, "Come on, babe, don't be mad at me. Why don't you get dressed so we can go out somewhere for dinner. I'll make some reservations real quick down at that spot you like in Bricktown."

"I'm not hungry. Why can't we stay home and cuddle and watch a movie or something? Or is that too Huxtable for your ass?" she asked with much attitude as she went into the bathroom.

"Nah, we can do that. As a matter of fact, we can watch Netflix all night," he yelled as he sat down on the bed and started to take off his shoes.

Shayla came back into the bedroom and asked, "What do you wanna watch? And please don't tell me no gang-sta, shoot-'em-up stuff, Marco, 'cause I'm not trying to watch any of that shit tonight."

He reached out and grabbed her around her small waist and pulled her onto his lap. He nuzzled his face in her firm, D-cup breasts and said, "Well, you better choose a movie real quick 'cause you definitely ain't tryin' to watch any of the movies I wanna see."

She laughed and said, "You are too predictable, boy!"

"But you love me, right?" he asked as he stared into her pretty, light brown eyes.

She laughed and said, "Sometimes. Now pick something decent to watch for the evening. While you do that I'll make you something to eat."

"You mean to tell me that you're going to cook for Flam?"

"No. I'm cooking for Marco."

"You know what I mean," he said sheepishly as he walked out of the bedroom.

Shayla went into the kitchen and began to make her man a quick meal. While she was preparing a steak with a can of mixed vegetables she was thinking about her life and how things had turned out so different from what she had originally planned. She shook her head and smiled as she thought about her past. "That was then; this is now," she said aloud as she put the steak into the oven.

Shayla and Flamboyant seemed to be a perfect match. They were both extremely good-looking and that was a definite plus to Flamboyant. He was not only borderline conceited, he was a walking fashion show. No matter where he went or who he was with, he had to shine. When he entered a room with Shayla on his arm he felt as if he owned the world. His six foot frame was solid and he kept himself in tiptop shape. He worked out regularly so he could maintain his near-perfect physique. He kept his hair cut short and tapered on the sides. His light brown skin seemed to match Shayla's crisp bronze tone. Her short, naturally curly hair gave one the impression of Halle, but one look at her firm, voluptuous body and one screamed, "Melyssa!" Ford, that is. People not in the know swore that her D-cups had been paid for by Flamboyant, but they were just as natural as her pretty face. She was the real deal and a real beauty. Flamboyant knew that he had, hands down, the best-looking woman in Oklahoma City. They were royalty and he was determined to make sure that his queen had everything she ever wanted. And more!

The next morning when Flamboyant woke up he saw that Shayla was not in the bed with him. He climbed out of the bed and went into the living room. As he headed toward the kitchen he was thinking of the tasks that he was going to have to tackle for the day. *Another day of gettin' more money.* He smiled when he saw the note left for him from his queen.

After reading it he went back into the bedroom so he could pick out his gear for the day. The summer had just started so he chose a light linen shorts set with a pair of alligator sandals. As he set his clothes onto the bed he wondered why Shayla had chosen this morning to go and enroll in school. He knew she'd been talking about taking a few classes at the junior college, but why today? *Is she that bored at home? Hell, I give her everything she wants. She can't be that fuckin' bored,* he thought as he went into the bathroom to take a shower.

After he was dressed he grabbed his cell and called Prince as he went inside of the garage and got into his 600. "What's up, my nigga?" he asked when Prince answered the phone.

"Ain't shit."

"All is well?"

"Oh, fa' sho'. As a matter of fact we need to talk. When are you comin' through?"

"I should be over that way in 'bout thirty. Do you need me to make a stop or are you good?"

"We need to chop it up first, but you will definitely have to make that stop sometime today."

"I feel you. What's up with Wave and Ken? Have you heard from 'em?"

"Yeah, they're the reason we need to have a sit-down. Hurry up and get your ass over here, boss, then all of your questions will be answered."

Flamboyant laughed and said, "I'm on my way, clown."

After he ended the call he made another one. When Shayla answered her cell Flamboyant said, "Good mornin', babe."

"Good morning to you, sleepyhead. Where are you?"

"On my way over to Prince's spot for a minute. You still at Rose State?"

"Mmmm hmmm. I should be finished in a hour or so. Have you had anything to eat yet?"

"Nope."

"A'ight, after I'm done here let's meet at Jimmy's Egg."

"I don't know how long I'll be with Prince, so call me when you're done and I'll let you know what's up, okay?"

"A'ight, bye," she said as she hung up on him.

"Oops," he said, laughing as he pulled out of his garage.

Prince was smiling as he watched Flamboyant get out of his car. *That is one flossy nigga,* he thought as he stared at his man. When Flamboyant entered a room everyone around paid close attention to him, and he loved every minute of it. It was as if he was a famous movie star instead of a local hustler.

"What's up, Flam?" asked Prince as they shook hands.

"Same old same old, my nigga. Now what's the deal?"

They sat down in Prince's living room and Prince began giving Flamboyant the rundown on how everything had been going down.

"So, everything is good," said Flamboyant. "What's up with Wave and Ken, though?"

"Wave, with his cowboy ass, got into it with some brand new niggas at Club Déjà Vu. Before Ken could calm him down Wave pulled heat and blasted one of the niggas."

"What? Did he get popped?"

"Nah, he good. 'Em New York niggas who own the club are slightly trippin', though. They like they ain't havin' that type of shit pop off in their spot. Basically, a lot of rah-rah shit."

"Check it, get at 'em and slide 'em some change and let 'em know that Flamboyant sends his apologies for my man's behavior and that it will never happen again. My word."

"Never say never, Flam, you know how that nigga Wave is."

Flamboyant sighed and said, "Yeah, I know. Call that fool and tell him I said to get his ass over here like yesterday."

Flamboyant then went into the kitchen to get something to drink while Prince called Wave. When he came back into the living room Prince told him that Wave and Ken were on their way over.

"Good," said Flamboyant. "Now, tell me, do you need some more work?"

"Yeah, I was gettin' to that. Wave told me that them youngstas out on the southeast side want some gallons of that sherm. Since we normally don't be slangin' them by the gallons I wanted to get at you first with it."

"How much are they tryin' to spend on a gallon?"

"I'm not knowin'. Wave will have to answer that one there."

"That's cool. What else is poppin'?"

"That's about it really. Everything else is on point. The ya-yo moving lovely and so is the X. Them Kerr Village niggas been buyin' all of the bud so that's cool, too."

Flamboyant smiled and said, "A'ight, then, let me make a few calls and I'll get the stock resupplied. Where's the ends for this last round?"

"Counted and put up."

"Have you bagged up the others' pay yet?"

"Yeah, everything is ready. I was waitin' on you to give me the green light to drop everyone their ends."

"Go on and handle that shit later on. Let everybody know that I said since we've been doin' so well, everyone gets a bonus on the next payday. On top of that, I'm planning on taking the team on a weekend trip to Miami. You think they gon' be wit' that?"

Laughing, Prince said, "You damn skippy! When are we gon' make that happen?"

"I was thinking about doin' it on the Fourth of July weekend. I'll have Shayla set it up for me and get back with you with the details."

"Don't tell me you're goin' to bring sand to the beach, dog. That shit ain't even cool right there."

"This trip is for y'all to relax for a weekend and get y'all clown on. As for me and Wifey, we'll do us. I ain't tryin' to be with no other broads. I'm completely satisfied."

"Flam, we're talking 'bout the MIA, baby! Do you know how many bad Cuban, Puerto Rican, Haitian, hell, bitches period are goin' to be out there? You'd be straight trippin' if you took Wifey out there with us," Prince said seriously.

"Call me a trip then 'cause Shayla is comin' with me when we hit the MIA, baby!" He laughed. "But let's get back to this BI for real."

"A'ight. For the last few months we've been clearing close to two hundred Gs a month from the ya-yo bud. The sherm has been bringing close to three hundred Gs a month alone. We're clearing another hundred Gs with the X pills. So, all in all, we're clearing half a ticket a month. After payin' the bills and the team we're looking real good, baby. Real good."

"That's what I'm talkin' 'bout!"

"But, peep this out, I think we need to be tryin' to look at settin' something up out there in Del City and Midwest City. I've heard that it's a lot of ends over that way."

"'Em grimy northeast niggas ain't got a hold of that yet, huh?"

"Not to my knowledge. From what I've been hearing, that nigga they call King got all of the north on lock, but they ain't fuckin' wit' Midwest City or Del City. We might as well get a hold of that shit while we can. That can only add to our monthly profits."

"Let me think about it. I'll get back to you in a day or so."

"Cool. You won't mind if I send some of my peoples out that way to start scouting for traps for me, will you?"

Flamboyant laughed and said, "I guess you already know what my answer is goin' to be, huh?"

Prince smiled and said, "Pretty much."

"Go on and do you, my nigga."

"Fa' sho'."

Before either could say another word there was a knock at the front door. Prince went to let Wave and Ken inside of the house. As soon as Wave saw Flamboyant sitting on the couch he smiled and said, "My bad, Flam. I already know what you're going to say."

"If you already know what I'm goin' to say then why in the fuck do you be on some rah-rah shit all of the time, Wave? This don't make no damn sense. Here we are all eating good, damn good, and you're trippin' the fuck out, shootin' niggas in clubs and shit."

"It was only one nigga, Flam."

Flamboyant gave him a look that said, "Don't fuck with me." Wave sat down next to Flamboyant while Ken stood next to Prince and watched as Flamboyant went off on Wave's ass.

"You've got to stop this rah-rah shit, Wave! Sooner or fuckin' later you're gonna cost all of us our position in this game. Before I let you fuck up what we've built, I'd put an end to your ass, dog. Do you feel me? You know I don't get down on that violent shit unless it's absolutely necessary. Believe me, when it comes down to all of us eatin' good, then it's absolutely necessary that I do what needs to be done."

Wave stared at the man who had made it possible for him and his family to have more than he'd ever imagined having. For that he felt ashamed of his actions the other night. "My bad, Flam. I won't force you into doin' something that's not cool. It won't happen again. My word."

"Wave, I'm not asking you to bow down to no nigga. I just want you to use more caution before you go off and start bustin' your gun. I love you, nigga, and this money will never change that fact. But it's a must that we continue to eat as good as we have these past six months."

"I got ya, Flam."

"Good. Now, what's up with you and Ken?"

Ken smiled and said, "Money, baby. M-o-n-e-y! All is well on our side of the south. Did Prince get at you about them young'uns who want some gallons of that water?"

"Yeah, he told me. How much are they tryin' to spend?"

"They'll pay up to twenty-five a gallon."

"That's cool. Since we're gettin' them at five a gallon that's a crazy flip for real. But will servin' 'em this much affect your sales on your side?"

"Nah, 'em young niggas want the gallons so they can take them to the country and sell it for close to forty a gallon. They won't be in our way at all."

"Okay, go on and make it happen then. If we run low, make sure you get at Prince so he can get at me and I'll make the call to keep you right."

"That's what I'm talkin' 'bout," Ken said, with his smile still in place.

"A'ight, then, gentlemen, I'm about to get somethin' to eat with Wifey. Y'all know how to reach me if needed. Prince will be gettin' at y'all with y'all's ends for the week so everything should be good. I'll holla at y'all later," Flamboyant said as he stood, shook hands with his team members, and left Prince's home in a very good mood.

Flamboyant met Shayla at Jimmy's Eggs restaurant for breakfast. While they were waiting for their food to arrive, Shayla told him about the three classes she decided to take at Rose State junior college.

"Babe, you never told me you were interested in fashion designing before," he said as he sipped his glass of orange juice.

"It's always been something that I wanted to try. Since I have so much time on my hands now, I thought, why not? Maybe I can start my own clothing line one day. What do you think?"

"I think if that's what you want to do then go for it. You know I'll support you on whatever. If you want to start your own clothing line then we'll start your own clothing line. I want you to know that no matter what it is that you want to do, I got your back. I love you, Shayla."

"Awww, come here. That was so sweet," she said, and then kissed him tenderly. Their kiss was interrupted by the waitress with their orders. They smiled as the waitress set their food onto the table and left them alone to enjoy their meal.

After they were finished eating Flamboyant asked her, "So, what are your plans for the rest of the day?"

"I'm going to get my nails done, then I'm going back home to relax and chill. What about you? What do you have planned?"

"I have a couple of runs to make then I'll be free to do whatever. You want to hit the mall up and spend some of this easy-earned bread?"

"Now, you already know I'm with that," she said as she gave him a cute smile.

"Okay, I'll give you a holla after I'm done. Come on, let's shake this spot." Flamboyant walked Shayla outside to her Mitsubishi Eclipse Spyder, a cute little convertible that fit Shayla perfectly. After she was inside of her car, he bent and gave her a kiss. As he pulled away from her he asked, "Can I have some of you when we get home later on?"

"Don't ask, baby; take what you want." With that said she closed her door, started the car, and smiled as she pulled out from her parking space.

Flamboyant went and got into his car and grabbed his cell to call Toni. Toni answered the phone just as he turned into the midmorning traffic. "How you doin' today, Toni?"

"Just fine, Mr. Flamboyant. How about yourself?"

"All good on my side of the world. Check it, we need to meet. I have an order I need to place."

"Where are you?"

"I'm out south; where are you?"

"Okay, meet me at Quail Springs Mall in about twenty minutes. I'll be parked right outside of the Dillard's entrance."

"See you in twenty," he said as he ended the call.

Twenty minutes later Flamboyant was sitting inside of Toni's brand new Jaguar. "So, what do you need, Mr. Flamboyant?" asked Toni.

He smiled and said, "The usual. I got all of the ends for some more ya-yo as well as for some more X. I should have the ends for the sherm in another week or so. My team has just hooked up with somebody who wants to get heavy in the water game and buy some gallons. So be expecting that to pick up dramatically."

"No problem. Whatever needs you have will be taken care of. I'm glad to see that everything has worked out so well. I must admit, you've surpassed my expectations."

Loving whenever he was complimented, Flamboyant's smile brightened as he said, "I told you I can move anything that you give me. I'm lookin' into spreadin' my wings a li'l more and covering some more ground in town. If my next move comes across like I think it will, I'll be movin' even more work."

"Good, very good. Now, if that's all, I have some other things to take care of."

"Yeah, that's about it for now. When you gon' holla at me?"

"Within a couple of hours."

"That's cool. I'm goin' to hook up with Wifey and do a li'l bit of shoppin', but I'll be ready when you call."

"I know you will, Flamboyant," Toni said with a smile. Flamboyant got out of Toni's car. Toni watched him as he strolled confidently toward his car. "Make that money, hustla," Toni said aloud and continued to smile.

After several hours of shopping at two different malls and a few local urban gear stores, Flamboyant was shopped out. "Come on, babe, can we head on home now?" he asked Shayla as she led him into yet another store inside of Penn Square Mall.

"Let me see if they have some of that new Baby Phat stuff. You know I'm lovin' me some Kimora Lee Simmons. She is the shit!"

Flamboyant shook his head but chose to remain silent as he followed his woman inside the store. After another thirty minutes in and out of stores inside the mall, Shayla finally had enough. "Okay, baby, let's go get something to eat and head on home so I can take care of you for taking such good care of me," she said sweetly.

"Now that's what I'm talkin' 'bout." As they were leaving the mall he got the call that he hoped and prayed wouldn't come until later on. He was anxiously thinking about his upcoming sex session with Shayla. When he saw Toni's number on the caller ID of his cell phone, he automatically started to think of an excuse to give Shayla. As much as he wanted to get freaky with his queen, business had to be handled first. He answered the phone and said, "Your timin' couldn't have been worse."

"Sorry about that. I got tied up longer than I thought. I'm ready now, so let's move quickly because I have another appointment and I'm running late as it is."

He stared at Shayla as they walked toward his car, and said, "A'ight, when and where?"

"The Toys 'R' Us across the street from Crossroads Mall. Be there in thirty minutes."

"Gotcha." After putting their bags inside of the car Flamboyant told Shayla, "Babe, I got to make a stop and take care of some business real quick. Do you want to ride with me, or do you want me to take you home first?"

"Where do you have to go, Marco?"

"Out south."

She sighed heavily and asked, "How long is this stop going to take? I'm hungry."

"Not long at all. I have to meet somebody real quick and then we can go get something to eat out that way. You know you love some Pearl's, so let's hit Pearl's on the south side."

"Humph. Pearl's on the north is better, but I guess I can make an exception; this time. Come on, let's go get this over with."

He leaned over and gave his woman a kiss on the cheek and said, "Thanks, babe." He then quickly sped out of the mall's parking lot and got onto the highway headed toward the south side. He had some money to drop off and some drugs to pick up. *Once again it's on.*

Chapter Three

The block was jumping and the squad seemed to have everything well under control, King thought as he watched everyone on the block making that money. He pulled out his cell and called his children's mother. When Lawanda answered the phone he said, "What it do, girl?"

"Girl? Nigga, now you know it's nothin' but a grown-ass woman you're talkin' to. Where yo' ass at?"

"On the block."

"Should've known. Are you coming through or are you hangin' out with that dyke bitch killa of yours?"

"Gone wit' that shit, L. Tippi don't even get down like that. Why can't you cut my girl some slack? She don't have shit against you."

Lawanda laughed and said, "Nigga, if you believe that shit then you're not as smart as I thought you were. Anyway, are you comin' through or what?"

"Yeah, I'll be through there later on."

"What time? I want to be ready when you get here."

"Ready for what?" he asked with a smile on his face because he knew the type of answer he was about to receive.

"Ready for some of that big ol' dick of yours."

He laughed and said, "I should be there between eleven and twelve."

"That's good; the kids will have been long asleep by then. You better go see Dr. Bombay and get you some of those last-long pills."

"See who? For some what?"

"Whoever be sellin' them Viagra pills or whatever else they be callin' them pills that keeps your thang hard all night."

"Now, what the fuck am I goin' to need some shit like that for?"

She laughed and said, "'Cause when your ass gets over here me gon' love you long time! Bye, nigga," Lawanda said as she hung up the phone.

King shook his head from side to side as he put his phone back into his pocket and went across the street where Flex and Tippi were talking. "What's good?" he asked them as he made it to where they were standing.

"The same old shit over here, my nigga," answered Flex.

"It looks like it's time to make some more shit happen over here. You make that call yet?" asked Tippi.

"Yeah, but I won't be able to hook up until the morning. Check with that nigga Keko and see if he still has some work left. If he does, go get a bird or whatever he can spare and bring it over here for the block. I'll hit up Cuddy and Boleg to see if they have anything left. If so, that should last until I can get us hooked back up."

"A'ight. What are you gettin' into for the rest of the night?" Tippi asked as she lit up a Newport.

King smiled as he thought about what Lawanda had just told him and said, "After I make a few stops I'm goin' over to Lawanda's to chill with my shorties."

"Whatever."

"What's that supposed to mean?"

Before Tippi could respond Flex said, "Excuse me, y'all, but y'all gon' have to hold up for a sec, 'cause I'm not trying to hear y'all's lover's spat."

In unison they both yelled, "Fuck you, Flex!"

They both started laughing as they watched Flex cross the street and start talking to one of the many workers on the block.

"Why you be trippin' out every time I have to go spend some time with my kids?" King asked.

"It ain't the kids, and you know damn well why I be trippin', King. Nigga, it ain't no fuckin' secret, I love yo' ass! Shit, I get tired of watching you go over that tramp's house and give her what belongs to me, for real."

"Oh, so this dick belongs to you, huh?" he asked with a smile.

Tippi stared directly into his brown eyes and said, "You damn skippy. If you wasn't on so much fuckin' bullshit you would have been done got with me."

"Look, we've been through this shit before. You know how I feel about us mixin' and shit. I know the love is real with you, just like I know the love is real on my side. If I give in to my emotions shit will get fucked up business-wise. And that's something that I can't let happen. We got chips to make and until we reach our goal we gon' keep this shit purely on a business level. So back your sexy ass off and cool the fuck off."

Tippi smiled and said, "Damn, I love it when you on some big man time. That shit gets me wet as fuck. I feel ya, though. Just do me one favor later, okay?"

"What?"

"When you're over Lawanda's fuckin' the hell out of her dried-up coochie, just as you start nuttin', think about me."

"Yo' ass is crazy!"

"Yeah, nigga, crazy about your fine ass," Tippi said as she turned and went and joined Flex across the street with the others. Tippi watched as King went and got inside of his car and left the block. His solid six two frame was definitely diesel. He had muscles everywhere. With the combination of his smooth, dark brown skin and his near-perfect physique, King was all of the man Tippi ever wanted in her life. Twenty-six years old and soon to be one of the richest street niggas in Oklahoma City. *And to top it off, that nigga is super fineee!* Tippi thought as she watched the man who possessed her heart leave the block.

After stopping at a few other trap houses on the north and northwest side, King decided to check on Keko before he went over to his baby mama's house. When he pulled in front of Keko's main trap he noticed that Keko was having some words with a couple of guys, and from Keko's body language, King could tell that someone was about to get hurt. Keko was a relatively small nigga, but he was a damn fool when he was upset. As King got out of his car he heard Keko tell one of the guys he was talking to, "Nigga, if you don't get the fuck outta here I'ma have to do you somethin' for real!"

"Come on wit' that shit, Keko. All we tryin' to do is eat around this mothafucka too," replied the guy Keko was yelling at.

"Eat? Eat? Nigga, you can't eat on this side of town unless you down with the squad! You already know what time it is, clown! So back the fuck off my block. If I see you again then we won't be havin' any words, real talk!"

Before either of the two guys could respond, King intervened and said, "Check it, if you niggas want to eat around here all you have to do is get your work from Keko. As long as you move our work, we ain't got a problem with y'all gettin' some of this paper."

"Damn, King, what if we got our own plug with some better prices than y'all got? You still expect us to get down like that?"

"Karlo, you and I both know y'all got some wack-ass work, probably some of that blow-up shit them Cali niggas been bringin' out here. Just because you get that shit cheap don't mean we gon' let y'all move it in the north. We got a reputation of keepin' the best work and it's gon' stay that way. So, either you and Frank get down with us, or y'all can get to steppin'."

"We was raised in this hood, King. How you gon' tell us what we can and can't do in our own hood? That shit is crazy!" said Frank.

King smiled and said, "It's simple really, 'cause this hood, this block, is my block. Everything on the north belongs to me. I don't give a fuck if you killed niggas for this hood, all of this shit is mines. You tryin' to test the King, Frank?"

"It ain't like that, King. I'm just sayin' we want to eat good too."

"Then fuck with the squad and get money, nigga. That's the only way you'll get to eat on the north side."

"Give us a couple of days and we'll holla at you, Keko," Karlo said. He turned toward his partner and said, "Come on, Frank, let's raise up."

"A'ight, then, King, holla back," Frank said as he followed Karlo to his car.

"Fuck them niggas. They actually been tryin' to get their grind on down the street. When I found out they been on some short-stoppin' shit I sent Mack and Juan down there to get them fools for me. Then they had the fuckin' nerve to tell me that stupid shit about not eatin' and shit. I got a feelin' I'ma have to lay them niggas down," Keko said seriously.

"If they try you again, do what needs to be done. We can't be havin' these niggas gettin' fresh out the pen thinkin' they can come and interrupt our groove. What's that shit Beanie Sigel be sayin' on that one flick?"

"What, you mean 'get down or lay down'?"

King started laughing and said, "Yeah, that's it. Get down or lay the fuck down!" They both laughed as King followed Keko inside of his trap.

Keko led King into a backroom where there was an assortment of drugs and money spread all over a dining room table. Keko grabbed some of the money off of the table and put it into a small duffel bag and gave it to King. He then yelled, "Hey, yo, Spook! Come here for a minute, nigga!"

Spook was Keko's right-hand man as well as head of security for all his traps. Spook's sole purpose in life was to make sure that Keko and the money they made were kept safe at all times. Spook was a stone-cold killer and no one in their right mind would ever fuck with him or Keko.

Spook entered the room and smiled when he saw King standing next to his main man. He shook hands with King. "What it do, big homie?"

"It's all love, my nigga. I see you're still in good shape, fool. I thought you'd get all fat and flabby fuckin' wit' this nigga, Keko," said King.

"Nah, I got a nice stack of iron out back. I got to keep this diesel look; plus, the hoes love a nigga on swoll."

"I know that's right."

Keko gave Spook the last few stacks of money that were left on top of the table. "Take care of the crew. Let 'em know that we slammin' this bitch for the rest of the night."

"What you doin' that for?" Spook asked as he accepted the money from his man.

Keko smiled broadly and answered, "We out of work, nigga! We won't be back on until tomorrow, so you know what that means, huh?"

"Yeah, I know what that means. It means I got to watch yo' tricky ass fuck off some more chips on them strippa hoes!"

King laughed. "You already know!" They all started laughing.

They were interrupted by Keko's cell phone ringing. "What up, Bolo?"

"Dog, didn't you just have some words with Karlo and Frank?" asked Bolo, one of Keko's best clients on the northwest side.

"Yeah, 'em niggas was tryin' to get they serve on down the street. What up, though?"

"Dog, them niggas over here on Thirty-ninth doin' the same thang to one of my spots. My nigga Skip just called and told me that he saw you checkin' them a li'l while ago. So, I wanted to get at you before I got at them, feel me? They can't be over here fuckin' wit' my money, dog."

"That's right. Peep this, don't even worry about it. I got this for you, my nigga," Keko said as he got off of the phone. He smiled at King and said, "You're gonna have to excuse me and Spook; we got some work to put in real quick, dog."

"What's up?" asked King. After Keko told him what he had just learned about Karlo and Frank, King became infuriated. "'Em niggas think this shit is a game? Come on, I'm rollin' with y'all," he snapped.

Keko shot a sideways glance at Spook and smiled. Spook shook his head from side to side as he followed them out of the back room.

Karlo wasn't going to let Keko nor King stop him from getting his money. He convinced Frank to ride along with him. They went and got their guns and were prepared for whatever, to do whatever, for their money. In truth, though, Karlo knew he was way out of his league fucking with King, but he couldn't back down in front of his man, Frank. His pride was about to cause him a whole lot of trouble.

As soon as King saw Karlo and Frank standing on the corner of Thirty-ninth his anger took complete control over him. He quickly parked his car, jumped out, ran over to where Karlo and Frank were standing, and yelled, "You niggas think you can just say, 'fuck the King'? What the fuck y'all doin' over here? Huh? I know you ain't servin' shit 'cause you ain't bought nothin' from the squad! What the fuck is poppin', Karlo?"

Before Karlo could respond, Spook and Keko came by King's side and stared menacingly at both him and Frank. Keko shook his head sadly at them because he knew without a doubt they were about to die.

"I gave you niggas a heads-up simply because y'all from the north. I told y'all I ain't got a problem with y'all eatin' 'round here, but you got to get your work from my peoples. I thought you had more sense than this, Karlo. You too, Frank."

"Come on wit' that shit, King. You can't dictate how a nigga get his money, dog. We men too, nigga; don't play us like that shit," said Karlo.

King inhaled deeply and asked, "So, y'all over here tryin' to get money, Karlo?"

"We doin' us, King. And we gon' continue to keep doin' us," he said defiantly.

"Fool, you gon' take food off of my plate and eat it right in my fuckin' face? Right after I gave you my rules for the north? You bold, nigga! A dead nigga, too!"

Before either Karlo or Frank knew what happened to them, King whipped out his 9 mm from the small of his back and shot both of them right between their eyes. "Call your man Bolo and tell him I said to close his spot for the night and to get at me tomorrow so I can give him a blessin'. I'm outta here. I'm 'bout to go get me some ass."

Keko started laughing as they casually strolled away from a double homicide.

***

It was a little after midnight when King pulled his Magnum into Lawanda's driveway. By the time he made it to her front door she was standing in the doorway looking extremely sexy. She was wearing a sheer nightie with a pair of four-inch stiletto heels on her small feet. Her light brown skin was practically glowing. She had her long weave pulled tightly back into a ponytail. She didn't want to sweat out her new hairdo during what she knew was about to be a very intense sexual encounter. It was always that way when they were together. She loved this man's body and the way he made her feel when he was inside of her love walls. Just thinking about it made her moist down below.

When she focused and saw the look on King's face she knew instantly that something was wrong. He walked right past her without a saying a word; then she knew for sure that her late-night freak session was in jeopardy.

After closing the door, she followed King into her bedroom. She stood at the foot of the bed and watched as he silently took off his clothes and went into the bathroom. She sat down on the bed and listened as he took a shower. She didn't know whether to join him. Ten minutes later he came out of the bathroom with a towel wrapped around that gorgeous body of his. He came and stood right in front of Lawanda, who was still sitting at the foot of the bed. He let the towel around his waist fall to the floor and whispered, "Suck it." Lawanda stared lovingly at his ten-and-a-half-inch dick for a second and then proceeded to do as she had been told. *Looks like my late-night freak session is still a go,* she thought as she continued sucking her babies' daddy's dick.

Tippi grabbed her cell phone and made a call. After she was finished she went and told Flex that she was out for the night and for him to make sure he held down the block. She got into her H2 and quickly sped off the block. As she was driving she fired up a blunt of some Indo and got her smoke on. By the time she arrived at the Skirvin hotel she was nice and high. She parked her truck and went inside of the hotel. Once she was standing outside of the designated room she knocked softly on the door. The door was opened by a tall, slim, but handsome man. He smiled at Tippi and said, "Hey, you."

Tippi rolled her eyes at him as she entered the room. After taking a seat on the bed she said, "Come here, Mondo." Mondo did as he was told. When he was standing in front of her she smiled at him and said, "Strip." As he was taking off his clothes Tippi slid back onto the bed and watched with an amused smile on her face. Though she was staring at Mondo, she was thinking about King. Oh, how she wished this man in front of her was King stripping instead of Mondo. When Mondo had finished stripping she told him, "Now get on this bed and take my clothes off."

Mondo climbed onto the bed and gently pulled off her white tee and her DKNY sports bra. Her firm C cups stood at attention while he undressed her. After he pulled off her baggy jeans he smiled at her as she slid off her black thong. When she was completely naked she said, "Now eat me." Once again Mondo did as he was told. As his tongue gave Tippi tremendous pleasure her thoughts were still on the one and only man she knew who could truly satisfy her every need. *King.* King. That's all she thought about as she came over and over on Mondo's face. After her fourth orgasm she felt somewhat obligated to let Mondo have some of what she knew he loved most: her pussy. She pulled him from between her legs and turned him so that he was lying flat on his back. She grabbed a condom out of her pants pocket and slid it onto his average dick. Once it was secure she mounted him and gave him a twenty-five-minute ride of his life. She squeezed her pussy muscles tightly as she rode Mondo hard. During the entire ride her thoughts were still consumed. *King! King! King! This is your pussy, King, and you don't even want it. Damn!*

Chapter Four

Life can't get any better than this, thought Flamboyant as he chose which expensive piece of jewelry he was going to wear for the day. Conservative he wasn't; it was all about the shine with him. After a few more minutes of contemplating, he finally decided on his twenty-four-inch diamond and platinum chain with a diamond capital "F" pendent hanging from it. After securing his chain he put on his diamond Aqua Master watch and two heavy-looking diamond pinky rings for each of his pinky fingers. He was definitely bling-blinging.

Since Toni had restocked his drug supply, Flamboyant felt that it was necessary for him to make some rounds today around the south side of Oklahoma City. Instead of his 600, he decided to drive his boy toy. He climbed inside of his new GMC Denali with the big twenty-four-inch chrome rims and all of the trimmings, everything from TV screens to DVD players, and an extra-loud sound system. He even had an online PC with e-mail capabilities, though no one ever e-mailed him. As he pulled out of his garage he smiled. Flamboyant was in full floss mode today.

When he pulled onto the block he saw Prince talking to some of the team. He parked his truck and went and joined them. Though he really didn't care to be seen in any drug area, he knew it was important that he occasionally came through and kicked it with his team. The entire south side of Oklahoma City was his; how would it look if he didn't show his face to his peoples from time to time? That's what Prince had drilled inside his head time after time until it finally sank in.

"What's good, my niggas?" Flamboyant asked as he shook hands with Prince and Gunna, the young man standing next to Prince.

"Same old shit, new day, Flam," Prince responded.

"Yeah, just makin' this paper," added Gunna.

"I know that's right. What's up with Ken? Did he get at them youngstas yet?"

Prince shrugged his shoulders. "I don't know. He hasn't come through since we got back on."

"Text that nigga and see what's what."

Prince pulled out his cell and sent the text:

> Ken, baby, what it do?
> What's poppin', Prince?
> Flam wants to know what's poppin' with them young'uns.
> Tell him everything is good. I'll get at y'all later with the details.
> Fa' sho'.

After putting his cell back into his pocket Prince smiled and said, "And the money keeps on rollin' in."

"I know that's right. Okay, what's up with you and that Del City or Midwest City thang?"

Prince smiled at Gunna and told Flamboyant, "That's what me and my mans was just talkin' 'bout. Tell him, Gunna."

"I got a cousin who stays out in Midwest City. He gets down with the ya-yo a li'l bit. He told me that if we plugged him proper-like he'd hook us up with some of his homeboys out that way."

"That's cool. What they be spendin' for a zip out there?"

"'Bout nine an ounce. But the real money will come from the weed and the X pills. 'Em niggas be gone on that shit out there. I got this female who stays on Sycamore over in the Panic Zone. She told me that we could make a killin' over there 'cause all of the young gangbangin' niggas over there be shermed the fuck out all of the time."

"The Panic Zone?"

"Yeah, that what they call they hood on the backside of Midwest City. The Bloods hood is called the Murda One and the Crips turf is the Panic Zone."

Flamboyant shook his head and laughed. "That shit is crazy. A'ight, y'all go and make some moves. Keep me posted."

Prince smiled and said, "Nigga, you'll know how good we're doin' by how much more work we gon' be needing."

"I know that's right. A'ight, then, I'm outta here. I'm 'bout to go over on the southeast side and holla at Milo. I'll get at y'all later."

"What's up with hittin' the strip club for lunch?" asked Prince.

"That's straight. I'll meet you there around one. I'll holla," Flamboyant said as he went back to his truck and left his block.

As soon as Flamboyant pulled in the Southeast Fifteen Street apartments he saw his man Milo beating the shit out of somebody. He quickly got out of his truck and ran over to see what the hell was going on. When he made it to where Milo was stomping on some dude he asked, "What the fuck you doin', Milo?"

Without stopping his beat down Milo said, "This. Nigga. Beat. Me. Out. Of. Three. Zips. And. For. That. He. Has. To. Pay. Flam," Milo replied as he continued to stomp the hell out of his victim.

Flamboyant let Milo do his thing for a few more minutes then said, "A'ight, dog, your point is made. Let that nigga live so he can get you your money. A dead nigga can't pay no debts."

Milo laughed and said, "You right!" He then kicked the poor guy one last time and said, "Get my money, nigga, or the next time I swear to God I'm finishin' yo' ass! Fuck the money. I'll pay for my losses out my pocket!"

Flamboyant shook his head from side to side and said, "Come on, crazy man. Let's go chop it up a li'l."

Milo fell in step with Flamboyant and said, "What got you on my side of the south this morning?"

"Just makin' sure that everything is good. Wifey went to school so I thought I'd get out and about."

"Right. What's up with this Miami trip I been hearin' 'bout? Any truth to the rumor?"

Flamboyant smiled and said, "Yeah, it's true. When I get everything sorted out you'll be notified."

"How we all gon' bounce out to Miami and keep this machine runnin'?"

"Everybody ain't rollin' with us. Just the capos of the team. You, Prince, Wave, Ken, Gunna, myself, and Wifey."

"Wifey? Damn, nigga, you in mad love for real! You takin' Wifey to Miami where some of the baddest hoes in the world live? That's got to be some deep love."

"You sound like that nigga Prince with that shit. It is what it is, dog. I ain't givin' a fuck 'bout no other broads as long as I got Wifey with me. 'Em Miami hoes ain't got nothin' on Shayla."

Milo shrugged his shoulders and said, "Whatever. But, still, how is everything going to be handled while we're out?"

"What, your soldiers can't keep the block up and runnin' over a weekend?"

"That won't be a problem. As long as I got plenty of work for them they'll make that fuckin' money."

"You already know you won't have to worry about that. I'll make sure that everyone is properly stocked."

"So when is the trip jumpin' off?" Milo asked.

"Fourth of July weekend. Like I said, I'll notify you when everything is everything. Now, how's shit over this way?"

"Good. The traps are clockin' more during the late night so I shut 'em down during the day. Ain't no need for all of that traffic during daylight hours."

"Ain't you missin' money by doin' that?"

"Nah, 'cause I have my boys out here handlin' all sales. I ain't missin' no money that comes through here. Them X pills are fuckin' hot! I can't seem to keep 'em bitches. As a matter of fact I'm gon' need you to slide me some more later on."

"Hit Prince when you're ready and he'll come through and hook you up. What up with that Indo? Is it bomb?"

"Is it? Nigga, I'm 'bout to roll up some of that fire now. You tryin' to get high with me this mornin', Flam?" Milo asked and started laughing, knowing damn well that Flamboyant didn't smoke weed.

Flamboyant ignored Milo's silly question and said, "A'ight, then, dog. I'll holla." He shook hands with Milo and jumped back into his truck, heading over to Ken and Wave's block.

Ken was sitting inside of his Navigator with its Lamborghini-style doors, talking on his cell phone when Flamboyant rolled up on the block on the southwest side. Wave was holding court with a couple of females who looked as if their young asses belonged in high school somewhere. Flamboyant jumped out of his truck and strolled over to Ken's Navigator. "What it do, my nigga?"

Ken set his cell phone on his lap. "Everything is good. We dumped four gallons to them young niggas. They told me they'd be back in a couple of weeks for four more," he told him.

"That's sweet."

"Ain't it, man? Let me get back to this call, though. My bitch is straight trippin'," Ken said as he put his cell back to his ear and frowned, listening to his girl yell at him some more.

Flamboyant smiled as he went over to where Wave was still talking to the young females. When Wave saw Flamboyant coming toward him he smiled. "My nigga, what's up?"

They gave each other some dap and Flamboyant said, "What the hell you doin', robbin' the cradle, nigga?"

Wave laughed. "Hell nah, they of age, fool." He turned toward the two young ladies and said, "Ain't y'all?"

In unison they replied, "Umm hmm."

"Yeah, right. Come holla at ya boy for a minute, though," Flamboyant said.

Wave excused himself from the teenyboppers and stepped out of their hearing range while he spoke with Flamboyant. "What's poppin', my nigga?"

"I just came over to check on y'all. How is thangs over this way?"

"Ken told you 'bout them young niggas?"

"Yeah."

"Shit, with that hookup we way ahead of the game. As for everything else, it's all on autopilot, dog. We got these chips comin' in from every fuckin' angle. We ain't missin' a thang. The traps is rollin' with the yay and the bud. The X pills are a li'l slow but that picks up for us on the weekends on this side of town. You already know what we doin' with the water, so all in all we good on the southwest side, baby."

"That's what I'm talkin' 'bout. A'ight, then, I'm about to roll. You ready for the MIA?

"You fuckin' right! That shit gon' be crazy right there, my nigga, real talk!"

Flamboyant laughed and said, "Yeah, I know. Tell Ken I said to send his girl a dozen red roses to her job. I don't know what he did to get her hot at his ass, but that'll get him outta the dog house for a minute."

"Gotcha."

"Oh, and Wave?"

"What up, Flam?"

"Leave 'em young bitches alone before you get yourself into some shit."

Wave smiled and said, "Call me R. Kelly!"

Flamboyant shook his head and laughed as he climbed back into his truck and left the block.

By the time Shayla's class was over she was eager to get something to eat. She called Flamboyant and asked him if he wanted to have lunch with her. He pissed her off when he told her that he was having lunch with Prince at some damn strip club. *How in the hell can you have lunch at a strip club?* she wondered as she walked to her car. She decided to get something to eat on the northeast side. It had been a minute since she'd been over to her old stomping grounds. She put her bags in the back seat of her car and climbed inside. *Yeah, I'm in the mood for some good old soul food on the east side!*

Shayla felt nostalgic as she entered Stells. It had been a long time since she had a good soul food meal at one of the best soul food restaurants in Oklahoma City. She shook her head and smiled as she thought about how old her boyfriend and first love would bring her to Stells every morning for breakfast. After she was seated a waitress came over to her table and asked her if she was ready to order. When Shayla told her what she wanted the waitress said, "Shayla? Shayla Carter? Girl, how you doin'? It's me, Shavonda!"

Shayla smiled and said, "Hey, girl, what's happening?"

"The same old thang; just working and trying to finish school so I can get the hell out of this boring-ass city."

"You know you need to quit it, girl. You ain't trying to leave the city."

"Humph, when I finish school and get my mom right, I'm out of here."

"Where you gon' go?"

"Either Dallas or Atlanta. Most likely Dallas 'cause you know I ain't trying to go too far from home!" They both started laughing. "So, how have you been? Better yet, where the hell have you been?"

"I'm fine, just going to school, trying my best to get something going for myself. I stopped coming around and hanging out when Trevor went away. Things wasn't the same when he left."

"Shayla, Trevor has been home for two years now. Don't tell me that you two haven't spoken to one another?" The shocked expression on Shayla's face answered Shavonda's question. "Oooh, girl, that means you don't know, huh?" she asked excitedly.

"Know what?"

"Girlfriend, Trevor is major, and I do mean major, out here."

"Stop playing! Trevor's gangsta attitude always gets in the way whenever money is involved. I'm surprised you didn't tell me that he was in jail again, for murder this time. That man is c-r-a-z-y!"

They laughed and then Shavonda said, "For real girl, Trevor is ballin' big time."

"Does he still come here for breakfast every morning?"

"Yep. If you would have come in here three hours sooner you would have seen his sexy ass."

"He still looks good, huh?"

"Good? Girl, that man has a body out of this world. How come you two stopped talkin'? What, you couldn't wait for him while he was in the clink?"

Shayla frowned and said, "It wasn't like that. He didn't want me to wait for him. He told me to go on and live my life 'cause he didn't want to get hurt. So, that's what I did."

"Do you want me to get a number for you so you can holla at his super-fine ass?"

"Uh-uh, that's cool. If I want to get in contact with his ass all I have to do is call his aunty's house. I know Doris May's number is still the same; she's too old school to ever change it."

"All right, girl, but if you do decide to get back with him you better let me know 'cause I be in here flirting with his ass every single morning. A bitch got bills!" They started laughing.

After Shavonda left to give her order to the cook Shayla's thoughts were of her ex-boyfriend. *A baller, huh? So you finally made it to the big time, Trevor,* she thought as she let her mind drift back to the past. She thought about all of the good times they shared. Her first time ever having sex and how gentle he was with her. How he supported her when her parents died in that car crash back when she was in high school. His strong hands and how soft they'd become once they started to make love. She realized just as Shavonda returned with her food that she has never stopped loving that man. Trevor was her everything. But now she had Marco. *Oh, shit, let me hurry and get the hell out of this place. What the hell am I thinking about? Marco's my man now. I have to leave the past in the past,* she thought as she wolfed down her food. There was no way that Shayla and Trevor could ever get back together. Or was there?

Chapter Five

King woke up early the next morning and helped Lawanda get his kids ready for school. It seemed odd to him. *This is some family shit for real,* he thought as he helped his daughter, Tandy, tie up her tennis shoes. Tandy was seven years old and smarter than he was at her age. She smiled lovingly at her father and asked, "Can you come pick us up from school, Daddy? I like riding in your car. It goes so fast."

"I don't think I'll be able to make it this afternoon, Tan, but I can take you to school if you want me to."

"That's fine."

"What about you, li'l boss? You want Daddy to take you to school too?" King asked his five-year-old son, Trevor Jr.

Trevor Jr. smiled and nodded his head.

"Well a'ight, then, you can go on and do you this mornin', Lawanda. I got these two for ya."

"Good. That saves me some time. I have a few things that I can take care of before I go to work. Will I be blessed with your company anytime soon?" she asked as she led the kids into the dining room to eat their breakfast.

King followed them into the dining room and said, "It depends if I'm needed around the way. Give me a holla when you get off."

She smiled and said, "Whatever."

"Why you got that funny-ass grin on your face for?"

She laughed and said, "I was wondering if Shelia knew where you spent the night last night."

He frowned and said, "Tippi don't be all in my mix like that. Why you on some messy shit this early in the mornin'?"

"You know damn well that girl is in love with you. I don't know why you be tryin' to fake it with me. It's written all over that he/she's face!" She laughed.

"You are real lucky that Tippi knows how I feel 'bout you 'cause those last two statements you made could get your ass hurt real bad if Tippi didn't care about me. So you need to back the fuck up and leave that shit alone."

"How do you feel about me, King? I'm curious; you've never told me exactly."

"Stop playin'. It's too early for this shit." Before Lawanda could say something else slick he told his kids, "Come on, y'all, let's hit the road. We can stop by Stells and have breakfast there." Tandy and her little brother got up from the table and followed their father.

Lawanda sat back in her seat and smiled as she watched him take their kids to school. She didn't know why she liked messing with King; she knew that it could be hazardous to her health if she chose to play too hard. But, for some reason, she enjoyed living on the edge with him. She wanted him to be her man full time, but she knew that King was not a man to be pressed. So, she continued to be patient and hoped her patience would pay off. She was determined not to lose him to that dyke bitch, Tippi. *I hate that bitch,* she thought as she sipped a cup of tea.

After having breakfast at Stells, King dropped off his children at school and went to his home out in the city of Edmond. After showering, he changed his clothes and was back inside of his car within thirty minutes. As he was driving toward the block he pulled out his cell phone and called Tippi.

"What's up?"

"Shit. 'Bout to hit the block. Have a nice evening with that dragon bitch?"

"Fuck you. Have you talked to Keko?"

"Nah, what's up?"

"I'll put you up on it when I hit the block. I'm on my way now."

"A'ight. Did you enjoy yourself last night?" Tippi asked sarcastically.

King smiled and answered her question with one of his own. "Since you're in the mood for games this morning, I'll play. How was your night?"

"What's that supposed to mean?"

He started laughing. "Come on with that shit, Tippi. You got to know that I know everything 'bout those around me, especially you. I wouldn't be the King if I didn't."

"And?"

"And what?"

"You still ain't told me what you meant by that question."

"Girl, stop playin'!"

"I ain't playin', nigga, you are!" she stated angrily.

"Since you bein' all sensitive and thangs this mornin' I take it that Mondo didn't break you off properly last night, huh?"

"Fuck! You! Nigga!" Tippi yelled and hung up the phone.

King laughed and shook his head as he turned onto the highway.

By the time he made it to the block he saw that Tippi was in a real foul mood and that wasn't cool; someone could get hurt. He quickly stepped over to the trap where

Tippi was standing with the tip of one of her sharp stiletto knives pointed directly at a crackhead.

"Nigga, I don't give a damn how much you spent last night. We don't do credit, so get the fuck on!" Tippi said in a deadly tone.

Before the crackhead could say something stupid and get himself cut, King stepped in between the two and said, "Come on with that, Tippi. Let him make it. It's too damn early for this shit." King saw Tippi's angry glare and knew that this was going to be one hell of a long morning. He turned his back to her and faced the crackhead. "You need to go on and raise up outta here. Ain't no credit poppin' off." The crackhead turned and left, mumbling about how much money he spent last night and how fucked up it was that they wouldn't give him any credit. The game was definitely a cold one.

King turned to Tippi. "What the fuck is wrong with you?"

"You already know the answer to that shit so why the fuck you askin'?"

Shaking his head from side to side, trying his best to make some kind of sense out of Tippi's actions, he said, "You on some way out shit this mornin', Tippi. Come on, let's take a ride."

"I'm not tryin' to be ridin' with you right now."

"I didn't hear myself ask you a gotdamn thang! You ain't got a fuckin' choice. Now bring yo' ass, Tippi!"

He left her standing there as he walked back toward his car. Tippi let him take about five or six steps before she began to follow him. Once she was inside of the car he said, "Listen, I don't like the fact that you have to get yours off with a square nigga. Fuck, any nigga for that matter. But it is what it is until our money is so long that that shit won't matter anymore. There's only one female other than you who's ever held my heart and you already know she's long gone. I've told you this shit over and over. I will not mix business with pleasure. I'm not goin' back to the pen for doin' some stupid shit that will jeopardize this money. We're finally in the position to make some serious paper and you're trippin' more and more! I won't let you fuck this up for us, Tippi. I can't. So you got to get a hold of ya feelings and this jealous shit you be on 'cause that shit is detrimental to all of our goals."

Though Tippi was a stone-cold killer, she was putty in King's hands. Her heart belonged solely to him. "I can't help it, King. I mean, damn, I've been in love with you for years. It seems so fucked up that I can't even have the dick that I want when I want it! Then to have to accept you goin' over to that flabby-ass Lawanda's fucks me up even more. I understand the game plan and I know what's what. But you're not feelin' me and how I feel about this shit. This is like the second time around, King; how much more do I have to take?"

"Don't do that. Look, I feel you, but you have to put those feelings aside for this money and continue to run this shit like it's supposed to be run. You are a very important piece to all of this shit, but if you keep on I won't hesitate to replace your ass. Nothin' and no one will stop be from becoming one of the richest niggas that the streets of Oklahoma City has ever seen. So get with it, Tippi, or get to fuckin' steppin'. Real talk. This will be our last time speaking on this shit. Do you hear me?"

"Yeah, I hear yo' ass. But before we dead this, I got to know one thing."

"What?"

"How long have you known about Mondo?"

He laughed and said, "Now you know damn well the King can't give up privileged information like that. I can't have my number one involved with anyone without havin' a full check made. Don't worry, though. I know that nigga is a square and knows nothin' 'bout you or what pops off with us. That's why I fell back and let you have your li'l boy toy. I won't front; that shit fucked me up at first. The love is real, Tip, so to say that I don't be gettin' jealous when you're with that nigga would be a straight lie. I accept it because of everything we've been through but, more importantly, this fuckin' money. Like I've promised you over and over, once we get this money and got mad cash stashed, I'm gon' take you somewhere and make crazy love to your sexy ass for days and days."

"Make love? Sexy? Where are those words comin' from, King?"

He touched his heart and said, "From right here, girl, you know damn well I love your wild ass."

Tippi felt herself about to become emotional and she didn't want to show the man she loved more than anything in this world that side of her. Not yet anyway. She regained her composure quickly and asked, "So what's up with this Keko shit you was gon' get at me with?"

King gave her a replay of the events that took place the night before on Thirty-ninth Street. Afterward he said, "It's been a minute since I had to murk a nigga. That shit was wild."

Tippi grinned devilishly and said, "Gets the old juices flowin' though, huh? Nigga, you know you a killa, just like me. Don't let the money blind you to what you really are."

"Nah, I know what it is and I know what it's gon' be. I'll do whatever for the sake of this money. You already know ain't nothin' soft 'bout the King."

Tippi laughed and said, "G'on wit' that shit, nigga! Look, Cuddy and Boleg wants to holla at you about opening a spot out in Midwest City. They say they been checkin' it out for a minute now and they feel it'll be profitable."

"Who's goin' to run their side of the north while they're out in Midwest City gettin' this shit jumped off?"

Tippi shrugged her shoulders. "I guess you'll find all of that out when you holla at them niggas."

"Call them fools and tell them I said to meet us at Keko's spot on the northwest side." While Tippi was doing as she was told, King was thinking about the profits that would come from opening a trap out in Midwest City. *Unchartered territory. Yeah, more money. The more the better.*

Keko, Cuddy, Boleg, Tippi, and King were all seated in the back room of Keko's main trap over on Northwest Twenty-seventh Street. King smiled as he listened to Boleg and Cuddy as they told him their plans for Midwest City.

"My mans out that way tells me that it's all lovely. Them Midwest City niggas hate havin' to drive all of the way into the city to get work. It would be a plus for them to be able to have us on deck like that. Less risks for everybody," Boleg said as he fired up a Black & Mild cigar.

"Yeah, plus them niggas be lovin' that water out that way. Them fools some straight sherm heads for real," added Cuddy.

"What about the X? Did y'all check on that?" asked Tippi.

"Nah, we was more concerned with the yay and the water. We already know the bud gon' pop off. Everybody and they mama smokes trees. We wanted to get the main shit established first; then we'll bring the X into play," said Boleg.

"That's straight, but who is goin' to run y'all shit out north while y'all are out in Midwest City?" asked King.

Cuddy smiled and said, "Dog, we got this. We've already put together a nice li'l plan. Check it: me and

Boleg will take turns goin' back and forth out there. The north is basically runnin' itself anyway right now so it won't take much for us to keep this shit on and poppin'. If it does get too hectic we have a small crew already on deck once we get our feet all the way in. They'll take care of the day-to-day shit out in Midwest City."

"That's cool. A'ight, roll with it and let's see how shit pops off," King said as he stared at everyone in the room. "Anything else?"

"Yeah, I've been checkin' out some shit in Del City. I think we could set up shop over there, too," said Keko.

"Midwest City, Del City . . . What, y'all tryin' to take over the entire state?" King asked with a smile on his face.

"You fuckin' right! Let's get this fuckin' money! It's still touch and go right now. I've been sendin' a few of my niggas out that way to check shit out for me. So far it looks promising. I'll get at you with more when and if I decide to make a power play over that way," Keko said seriously.

"A'ight, then, get at me or Tippi if y'all need anything. Everything should be everything in a li'l while. We're about to head back to the block."

"Tell that nigga Nutta I said to get at me. I know he's gon' want a part of this Midwest City thang," Boleg said as he inhaled deeply on his Black & Mild.

"Gotcha," Tippi said as they left the trap.

During the ride back to the block King received a phone call from Charlie. "How ya doing this morning, Mr. King?" asked Charlie.

"I'm good. All is good in my kingdom. What's up, Charlie?"

"I thought we'd get together this afternoon for lunch. I have a few things I'd like to discuss with you."

"That's cool, 'cause your services are needed. I was just about to call you."

"Good, that way we can kill two birds with one stone. How about some Red Lobster, say, one o'clock?"

"Which one? The one on the Northwest Expressway or the one out by Quail Springs Mall?"

"The one on Northwest Expressway will do. I'll see you later," Charlie said and ended the call.

By the time they made it to the block King noticed that Flex had everything under control. He turned toward Tippi and said, "I'm 'bout to go get everything ready so I can get with Charlie, so make sure you let everybody know that we'll be back fully operational within a couple of hours."

"A'ight. Be careful, nigga."

He gave her a smile and said, "Always." Tippi got out of King's car and watched him leave the block. She smiled as she went across the street and joined Flex. Together they maintained the block and watched as the young squad members got that money.

King turned the volume up on his sound system and was bumping the rapper Rick Ross's hit single, "Hustlin'." He sang along with the Miami rapper, feeling real good about how everything was going for him and his squad. "'I know Pablo, Noreaga, the real Noreaga/He owe me a hundred favors,'" King sang along. He was interrupted by the ringing of his cell. He turned the music down and smiled when he saw his Aunt Doris May's face pop up on the screen of his phone. "What it do, Aunty?"

"Not much, boy, just thought I'd give your ass a call 'cause you seem to have forgotten about your aunty."

"Nah, you know I can't do no shit like that. I've been caught up doin' me, that's all. You know you can never be forgotten by the King."

She laughed and said, "Boy, you are somethin' special. Are you too busy doin' you to stop by here and kick it wit' your aunty for a li'l while? I needs me some more medicine. I done ran out."

Now it was King's turn to laugh. "Yeah, I'll be through there this evening. I've got a few thangs to take care of first. You know I got you, though."

"All right, I'll see you later. Be good out there, boy."

He laughed again. "Aunty, I'm twenty-six pushin' twenty-seven. Why do you still insist on callin' me 'boy' like I'm still some snotty-nosed li'l kid?"

"No matter how old you get or how much money you make, you will always be my favorite nephew, boy. So I'll call you 'boy' as long as I damn well please."

"I'm your only nephew, Aunty."

"Bye! Boy!"

After getting off the phone with his aunt he started thinking about all of the good times he shared with her. If it weren't for her, only God knows where he would have ended up. Both of his parents ran off and left him when he was seven years old. He remembered that day as if it was yesterday.

He came home from school and saw his Aunt Doris May sitting in the living room, watching television. He smiled when he saw her because she always showed him so much love whenever she came around. He ran over and gave her a hug and kiss and said, "What's up, Aunty?"

She smiled a sad smile at her only nephew and said, "Hey, boy, you have a nice day at school?"

"Mmm hmm. Where my mama and daddy at?"

Tears swelled in Doris May's eyes as she told her nephew, "They gone, boy."

"When they comin' back, Aunty? My daddy told me he was taking me to the mall to buy me some shoes today," he said innocently.

Doris May sighed and said, "They not comin' back, boy. They done ran off somewhere."

"Wha . . . what do you mean, Aunty? I don't understand."

"Your mama and my no-good-ass brother done ran off and left you with me. I'm not goin' to hide or sugar-coat nothin' from you, boy. I loves you and I'm goin' to raise you so you can be a much better man than that so-called father of yours."

Tears fell slowly down King's face as he listened to his aunt. While she hugged him tightly he asked her, "What did I do to make them leave me, Aunty? What did I do?"

She grabbed him lightly by his little face and stared directly into his innocent eyes and said, "Nothin', boy. You didn't do a damn thang and don't you ever forget that. One day they gon' realize and regret leavin' you like this. Until then, we got to make do the best way we can. So, are you with me, boy?"

He smiled through his tears and said, "Uh huh. I'm with you, Aunty." They hugged each other tightly and cried some more.

That pain seemed unbearable, but his aunt's love made everything a'ight. *Damn, that was twenty years ago. I wonder whatever happened to them bastards.*

Chapter Six

"Why would you wait until the night before we're supposed to leave to throw this at me, Shayla? This is really fucked up," Flamboyant said as he stared across the dining room table. Shayla had made dinner of catfish and rice. While they were enjoying their meal she decided to tell Flamboyant that she wasn't going with him and his friends to Miami. She knew he was going to be disappointed, but she didn't expect for him to be as upset as he obviously was.

"I don't want to be around you and your friends for an entire weekend. You are too arrogant when you're around your crew. I'll stay here; that way you can act out and have all the fun you want."

"You don't understand. I won't have any fun if you're not by my side, Shayla. I want my queen next to me when I'm out there. This shit ain't about no flossin' or nothin'; it's about spending a nice weekend with you and my team."

She shook her head slowly and said, "You can't have it both ways, Marco. Go on and have fun with your team. When you get back then we'll plan something for us to do. I'm not with sharing my man and I'm not about to start."

"You're serious? You don't want to go with me to the MIA?"

"I'm dead serious. I'm not going with you and your friends to Florida," she said with finality in her voice.

"This is some fucked-up shit!" he yelled as he left the table and stormed into the bedroom. Before Shayla could put a forkful of fish in her mouth he came back into the dining room and asked her, "What are you goin' to be doin' while I'm in Miami?"

She swallowed her food and answered, "Most likely nothing. I know I'm going to get some studying done. That's about it, really. I don't have any plans. I might call Taj and see if she wants to get together or something."

"Do you love me, Shayla?"

She frowned and said, "Yes, Marco, I love you. Don't let me not wanting to go to Miami with you put any silly thoughts into that fat head of yours. Nothing has changed between us. You're still my boo." She smiled sweetly at him and he returned a relieved smile her way.

"You know I'd lose my mind if I lost you, right?"

"The only way you'll ever lose me, Marco, is if you cheat. If I ever catch you cheating on me there will be nothing you can do to stop me from walking out of that door. I mean that shit. Now sit your butt back down and finish your food." They both laughed as he did as he was told.

The next morning after Flamboyant had left for the airport, Shayla lay in bed thinking, thinking about someone she had no business thinking about: Trevor. The real reason she'd changed her mind about going to Miami. Ever since she had that talk with Shavonda at Stells she just couldn't get her former boyfriend off of her mind. Curiosity had taken control of her and there was nothing that was going to stop her from seeing him. "It's not like I'm going to fuck him or nothing. I just want to see how he's doing, that's all," she said aloud as she climbed out of the bed she shared with Flamboyant.

***

After they were all aboard Flight 116 to Dallas/Fort Worth, Flamboyant and his team were in an excited state. Wave was flirting heavily with every flight attendant who was within his arm's reach. Prince was laughing and playing with Gunna while Ken and Milo laughed at all of them. Even though Flamboyant wasn't really in the mood to be clowning around, he had to smile at his team and their antics. *Fuck it, might as well have some fun. I still can't believe Shayla didn't want to come with us. I ain't trippin', though. I'm gon' have a ball when we get to Miami without her ass.*

After they arrived in Dallas/Fort Worth, they boarded another plane and were on their way to sunny Florida. Once the flight was airborne Flamboyant asked Prince, "What's what with those moves y'all was supposed to make out in Midwest City?"

"Gunna set up shop in Del City first. He got two apartments in the Candlewood apartments. He told me that it already started clockin' like a mothafucka."

"That's cool, but I thought y'all was gon' be workin' out in Midwest City. Where did this Del City shit come from?"

"If you let me finish puttin' you up on everything all of your questions will be answered."

"My bad, my nigga, damn."

They laughed and Prince continued, "Gunna's cousin has been havin' his Blood homeboys hit him off somethin' lovely. They gettin' that work as well as the bud somethin' crazy for real. On top of that, that female Gunna was talkin' 'bout hooked him up with some of the Crips over in the Panic Zone and they gettin' that money too. 'Em niggas are heavy into that water so the money is lookin' nice, my nigga."

"That's what I'm talkin' 'bout! Who does Gunna have taking care of thangs while we're out?"

"He got eight of his soldiers from Kerr Village over on Scott Street at the apartments doin' their thing, and he got two of his men posted with ol' girl in the Panic Zone. He dropped them a nice load last night and told them that he'd get back at 'em on Monday or Tuesday. They should be good until we get back."

Flamboyant smiled as he relaxed back in his seat and said, "A'ight, then, looks like shit done fell together real smooth-like."

Prince smiled as well and said, "Yeah, I know."

Since it was Friday and she didn't have to go to class, Shayla decided to go get her hair and nails done. She called her best friend Tajanaye, or Taj as everybody called her. "What's up, Taj, what you do, girl?"

"Girl, I was just about to call your ass. You want to hang out this afternoon or you got plans with Mister Man?"

"You too stupid. Remember I told you he was going to Miami this weekend?"

"Stupid? No, you didn't just call me stupid. If my memory serves me correctly, Ms. Thang, you were supposed to be accompanying your man to Florida this weekend, so how in the hell am I stupid?"

Shayla laughed and said, "Whatever! Look, let's get our nails done so I can tell you what's been goin' on."

"What's been goin' on? Shayla, what have you done now?"

"Nothin' yet. Meet me at Images in an hour."

"Images? Why you want to go to Images all of a sudden? I thought you let them chinks out there on Shields do your nails?"

"I do. But I want to see if Stacey can squeeze me in real quick. You know with this short-ass hair she can do me something real nice, real fast."

"Your hair is naturally curly, Shay. Wet that shit and style it your damn self and you'll be just fine, girl."

"Whatever. Are you meeting me at Images or what?"

"Yeah, I'll be there. Can't wait to hear about what you got going on now."

Shayla laughed and said, "Bye, girl. I'll see you in an hour."

After she hung up the phone she went into her closet and pulled out her outfit for the day. She pulled out a pink and yellow shorts set. She grabbed a pair of pink sandals and set them by the bed. She smiled as she went into the bathroom and stepped into the bathtub. The hot water felt so good as she reclined and let her head rest at the end of the tub. The smile never left her face as she continued to think about the past. *Trevor, hmmm.*

By the time they arrived in Miami the entire team was amped, Flamboyant included. The weather was warm and addictive and there were women everywhere they looked. Flamboyant rented two Lincoln Navigators for them to get around in for the weekend. Each was equipped with twenty-four-inch chrome rims as well as a booming sound system. They had rooms reserved for them at Hotel Victor, a hypermodern Asian water-themed hotel in South Beach. Flamboyant spared no expense for him and his team. They were about to go all out.

After they were checked in at their hotel, Flamboyant led the team out to the beach. Prince wanted to go Jet Skiing while Gunna and Milo wanted to go parasailing. Wave wasn't interested in any of that stuff; his mind was on all the lovely ladies who were all over the beach. He couldn't believe his eyes. There were women of all shapes, sizes, and colors everywhere he looked. As far as Wave was concerned, he was in heaven and he wasn't trying to do anything else but mingle with and get to know as many of these beautiful women as he could.

Flamboyant and Ken watched as Wave got his mack on with two Hispanic females. "That nigga gon' catch something this weekend, watch." Ken laughed.

"Nah, that clown may be crazy but he ain't no fool. He'll strap up if he gets lucky enough to get some ass." They both started laughing. Flamboyant pulled out his cell and said, "Excuse me, my nigga. I got to check on some shit back at the house for a minute."

Ken grinned and said, "She's good, dog. Don't sweat her. It'll give her the impression that you're on some weak shit. She chose to stay at the pad so enjoy this shit. Give her the impression that you're havin' the time of your life without her ass. That'll give her some act right on the indirect tip."

"Nigga, wasn't you just havin' problems with your girl a few weeks ago? How you gon' be givin' me some advice?"

Ken shrugged his shoulders and said, "It is what it is, dog. You live and learn, my nigga. Come on, put that shit up and let's go kick it."

Flamboyant stared at his cell for a few seconds and then said, "Fuck it, let's do this shit."

Back in Oklahoma City, Shayla was sitting down getting a manicure and pedicure at Images Hair & Nails when Taj entered the beauty shop. Shayla smiled at her and said, "What's up, girl? Damn, you lookin' good today."

"I look good every day, you already know," Taj said with a smile.

"If I would have known that your conceited-ass friend was comin' up here too, I wouldn't have made room for your ass, Shayla," joked Stacey, the owner of the beauty shop.

After setting her Chanel purse down, Taj gave Stacey the hand and said, "Anyway. Now what's the deal, girlfriend? You know you got me real curious with this all of a sudden let's hang thang. I know your man is gone, but what's really good?"

"Damn, I can't call my girl and hang for a minute without something going on?" Shayla asked as she let the manicurist put her feet into the warm water.

"Now you know damn well I'm not going for any of that, so you might as well cut that shit out and spill it right about now." Taj sat down next to Shayla and smiled. If one were to use one word to describe Taj that single word would simply be "Gorgeous" with a capital G. She was top-model slim; no matter how much she ate she couldn't gain any extra weight. Her almond-shaped eyes seemed to see right through a person when she stared at them. Her perfectly sized C cups were every man's dream. And her onion was another one of her gifts from God that brought men to their knees when she walked by them. Taj stared at her friend and again asked, "So what's the deal, girlfriend?"

Shayla smiled and told her best friend everything that had been on her mind since she found out that her ex, Trevor, was home. After she was finished she said, "I mean, damn, I can't get him off of my mind. It's like he totally consumed my every thought."

"Why haven't you called his aunt yet then?"

"I don't know." Shayla shrugged.

"I can tell you still care about dude, but don't forget that he's your past. Marco is your future. Or is he?"

Shayla stared at her friend before answering. "If Marco is my future then why in the hell am I thinking about my past so much?"

"You're the only person who can answer that one, girl. I say after we finish gettin' hooked up we go out and hit the mall up for a little bit, get your mind off of that nigga for a minute. Before the day is up you should give his aunt a call so you can satisfy that curiosity that's eating at you. Or, better yet, you should just pop up over there to say hi since you're in the neighborhood."

"Girl, we're on the east side. I'm not in her neighborhood."

Taj grinned and said, "You will be when you pop up over her house."

After spending a couple of hours and a couple thousand dollars in the mall, Shayla and Taj decided to get a bite to eat at the Cheesecake Factory. While they were waiting for their food Shayla had made up her mind. She pulled out her cell phone and told Taj, "Girl, it won't hurt if I called Doris May and ask how that boy has been doing."

Taj smiled. "Nope, it sure wouldn't." She continued to smile as she watched her friend dial the number on her phone. Shayla inhaled deeply as she waited for Doris May to answer her phone.

"Hello?" answered Doris May when she picked up the line.

"Hi, Aunty, how are you?" Shayla asked nervously.

"Shayla?"

"Yup, it's me."

"Now, where in the hell have you been hidin' your damn self? I haven't heard from you in years!"

"I know and I'm sorry about that. After Trevor went away and did me the way he did, I kinda faded away from everybody."

"Faded away? Li'l girl, you disa-fuckin'-ppeared! That boy has been home and done went back to jail since you've been gone."

"He . . . he's back in jail?"

"Not now he ain't. That was about a year and a half ago. He's home now doin' real good. Real good," Doris May said with emphasis.

"I'm happy for him. Could you tell him I said hello?"

"Why don't you call him and tell him yourself? Take down his number and give him a call."

"I . . . I can't do that, Aunty."

"Why not?"

"I . . . I'm involved with someone at the moment."

"So what! There ain't no harm in callin' an old friend."

"Now you know good and well me and Trevor are more than just old friends."

Doris May laughed and said, "Well, hell, there still ain't nothin' wrong with you callin' that boy. What, you got yourself one of them jealous types?"

Shayla laughed. "Something like that. I just don't want to cause any problems. Plus, I know Trevor's moved on with his life. He's probably forgotten all about me."

"You may be right. But, tell me, why did you really call me? I know it ain't because you missed old Aunty Doris May and decided to give her a holla. 'Cause if that were the case I would have heard from you li'l ass years ago."

"To be honest with you, Aunty, I heard that Trevor was home doing extremely well for himself. After a lot of debate with myself I finally decided to give you a call to see how he was doing. I won't lie. I do miss y'all."

Doris May laughed and said, "You're something else, girl. Now write down this boy's number." After she had finished giving Shayla King's cell phone number she said, "I won't tell him about this call. You can do it yourself if and when you decide to give him a call."

"Thanks, Aunty. So, how have you been?"

"You know me. I'm gon' always be a'ight. As long as I have my medicine every day I'm A-okay!"

"Ooh, Aunty, I know you ain't still smoking all of that weed?"

"Humph, I don't see why not. Shit, my medicine helps me deal with the day-to-day problems of the world." They both laughed.

A waiter came with Shayla's and Taj's food so Shayla told Doris May, "I'm about to eat and think about what I'm going to do about calling Trevor. I'll give you a call again soon, Aunty, I promise."

"You do that, girl. You know you was always my favorite."

Shayla frowned and said, "You sure? I could have sworn you liked Lawanda more than you liked me."

"Lawanda? No, you didn't sit there and say that craziness to me! You know damn well I never could stand that silly li'l girl. And now that she's had those kids I still can't stand her ass!"

"Kids?"

"Oops. Girl, g'on and call that boy and let him tell you what's been goin' on in his life. Bye now!" Doris May yelled as she hung up the phone quickly.

Shayla was truly in love with Flamboyant. They had been with each other for close to four years now. After she had broken up with Trevor she went into a deep depression. That depression ended the day she met Flamboyant. She knew that she loved him, but she didn't know why she was feeling so jealous about the fact that Trevor had gone and gotten that witch Lawanda pregnant. More than once, too. *Doris May did say 'kids,'* she thought as she nibbled on her food. *I can't believe that shit.*

"Earth to Shayla, can you hear me?" Taj asked from the other side of the table.

Shayla shook her head and said, "My bad, girl, I was gone there for a minute."

"A minute? Girl, you have been gone for the last five minutes. What did she say that got you so lost like that?"

Shayla gave her a replay of the conversation she just had with Doris May. "Ain't no way I'm callin' that nigga. Fuck that! If he's had kids with that ugly-ass bitch then he don't need to be hearing from me," she stated angrily.

Taj stared at her friend. "Don't get mad at me, girl, but can I ask you something?"

"What?"

"Why are you so mad at the fact that he has some kids by Lawanda?"

"Because I can't stand that bitch! She used to be all up in our mix tryin' her best to take Trevor away from me. That's why!"

"Calm down, girl, before you give yourself a heart attack. I understand how you feel, but what I don't understand is why you're so angry. Your ex has moved on with his life and so have you. He has Lawanda and you have Marco, one of the richest niggas in the city. You have absolutely no reason to be this upset. Unless . . ."

"Unless what?" Shayla asked, obviously agitated.

"Unless you're still in love with Trevor."

Shayla was stuck. She sat there and stared at her friend because she couldn't think of a response to what Taj had just said to her. *Oh, shit!*

Chapter Seven

"Dog, I'm tellin' you that shit is crackin' like a motha-fucka out there!" Nutta said excitedly.

Boleg and Cuddy smiled at each other as they listened to Nutta explain how much money he was making out the Midwest City.

"Do you need some more work or are you tryin' to chill for the rest of the weekend?" asked Cuddy.

"Chill! Nigga, is ya crazy? I'm 'bout to hit up King now and get at least another bird or two. Them niggas is spendin' like crazy! You know I'm the number one trappa on the squad, and after this weekend my position and title will be upheld!" They all started laughing.

"G'on wit' that shit, fool. You ain't clockin' more than me and Cuddy," said Boleg.

"Check it, my nigga, just like my nigga Hova said, 'Men lie, women lie, numbers don't.' In less than two days I've dumped over a bird and a half. Ounce for ounce. That means I've clocked close to forty Gs for myself as well a nice chunk of change for the squad. So don't sit your big ass over there and tell me that I ain't the number one trappa right about now. I'm 'bout my dollars fo' real," Nutta said proudly.

"A'ight, fool, you got that. But I heard that Keko and his niggas got that Del City shit poppin' off too," said Cuddy.

"That's good. The more money he makes the stronger the squad becomes. I ain't no hater. We're all rockin' together and our goal is the same."

"Yeah? What's our goal, li'l nigga?" asked Boleg.

"Get this fuckin' cake! Act like ya know, fool!"

"I know that's right, dog. When you get at King tell him that I said we're goin' to be out in Midwest City with you. We might as well dump some of this load we have over that way since it's kind of slow out this way."

"That's straight. I'll get at y'all later," Nutta said as he jumped into his truck and sped off of the block.

Boleg and Cuddy were like brothers; they'd been best friends for years. The both of them grew up with King on the north side and they all attended the same high school. They were the same height, standing a little over five ten, and were considered heavyweights. Combined, they weighed close to 560 pounds or more. They were each other's yin and yang. Cuddy was the one more prone to use violence, whereas Boleg chose to be more laidback. They were both hustlers to their core. Getting money the illegal way came naturally to both of them. They could smell a dollar miles away. That's why Boleg was confident that this move they made out in Midwest City was going to pay off big time for them.

"I told you, Cuddy, we 'bout to get chipped up for real out there. Them niggas is lovin' our shit. Nutta just confirmed what I knew all along: Midwest City is a fuckin' gold mine," Boleg said as he leaned against his Suburban.

Cuddy, who was sitting on the passenger's side of Boleg's truck, said, "Yeah, it's sweet right now, my nigga, but shit ain't over wit' yet."

"What you mean by that shit?"

Cuddy shrugged his broad shoulders and said, "Shit don't stay sweet all the time, Boleg. We gots to get this money, but we also got to watch our asses at the same time. We can't afford to get rocked to sleep, my nigga."

"I got you, dog." Boleg smiled.

***

Tippi and King were sitting on the porch of the trap on the block watching as the youngsters on the squad made that hand-to-hand money. King frowned when he saw a police cruiser turn on to the block. The police car was spotted immediately, and three shrill whistles came from the lookouts who were strategically posted on each corner of the block. The squad members who were on the block serving hand-to-hand sales all slid into the cut and got out of sight of the police car. The police officer inside of the car stopped in front of the trap where King and Tippi were sitting.

"Looks like today's a profitable one for you, King," said the officer.

King smiled and said, "Every day is a profitable one, Officer Don. How may we be of service? Do you need anything?" King laughed at his joke and so did Tippi and a few other members of the squad who were in hearing distance.

Officer Don frowned and said, "One day, one day, I'm going to have the pleasure of either locking your ass up, or watching the city medical examiner zip a body bag over your ass, King. I don't know how you done it, but for some reason you've kinda become untouchable. Nobody remains untouchable for long. Remember that."

"Have a nice day, Officer." He stepped off of the porch, strolled to his car, and hit his alarm button. As he opened the door he turned and faced Tippi. "I'm 'bout to go over to Doris May's. I'll be back later. You good?"

She shook her head yes. "Tell Doris I said hey."

"A'ight, then," King said as he slid into his car and pulled away from the curb. When he passed the police car he noticed Officer Don make a quick U-turn and hurry to pull right behind him as if he was about to pull him over. He smiled because he knew that he was going to trail him for a little bit. That was exactly what King wanted him to do. "Yeah, come on and ride with me, clown. I don't need yo' ass on my block slowin' up my money," King said aloud as he grabbed his cell and gave his aunt a call.

When Doris May answered her phone she said, "Where you at, boy?"

"I'm on my way over to your house. What's up?"

She smiled into the receiver and said, "I'll tell you when you get here. Hurry up." She hung up the phone before he could say another word.

King was smiling as he turned onto the highway. Officer Don was still following about three car lengths back. Ever since he hooked with Charlie his life had become extra smooth. *Charlie is one hell of a plug,* he thought as he continued to drive. Not only was he able to get the best drugs in the state for the lowest prices, he also got police protection from Charlie. Charlie made sure that, no matter what, King would be able to make that money for the both of them. The game was good.

By the time King made it over to his aunt's house, Officer Don had chosen to leave him alone. King hopped out of his car and went inside of the house he was raised in: a three-bedroom, two-bath neat little house in a neighborhood called Creston Hills on the northeast side of Oklahoma City. After his parents left him with his aunt, her home became his home and he loved her so much for that act of kindness. There was nothing in this world that he wouldn't do for his aunty.

As soon as he stepped inside of the house Doris May said, "Guess who called me a couple of hours ago?"

He stared at his aunt as she inhaled deeply on her neatly rolled blunt and blew out the potent marijuana smoke in a thick line of her mouth. "Who?" he asked.

She frowned at him and said, "I said guess, boy!"

He sat down on the couch and said, "Come on, Aunty, I ain't got time to be playin' with you now. I got some shit to do. Who called?"

Doris May took another drag of her blunt and said, "You ain't no kinda fun. Shit, I know you gon' be happy when I tell you. Why you got to take away my fun?"

"A'ight, a'ight, let me see. Was it my mommy and daddy?" he asked sarcastically.

She gave him the finger and said, "No, boy, but it was the one girl who loved you more than anything or anyone, except me, that is."

His eyes grew wide as saucers when he asked his aunt, "Shayla?"

Doris May was in the middle of taking another deep pull of her blunt so she gave him a nod of her head to answer his question.

"Where is she? Where has she been? Did you get her number for me? What did she say?"

"Damn, boy, if you slow yo' ass down I'll answer your questions. First off, she's still here in the city. She didn't tell me where, though. She did tell me that she chose to fade away after you went to jail. I told her li'l ass hell, she fuckin' disappeared! I gave her your number and told her to give you a call. I told her I wasn't goin' to tell yo' ass but you already know I can't keep no secret," she said with a smile.

With a smirk on his face he said, "Yeah, I know. So what did you tell her about me, Aunty?"

"I kinda mentioned that you had some kids with Lawanda."

"You did what? Aww, damn, Aunty! Shay's not goin' to call me now. You know how bad she hated Lawanda. What you go and do that shit for?"

"It slipped, boy. I didn't mean to. Don't worry; if she doesn't call you, you can call her. Here's the number where she called me from. I think it's a cell phone number," Doris May said as she passed him a slip of paper with a telephone number written on it. "I got it off my caller ID. Ain't you glad I let you talk me into gettin' that shit?"

King smiled and said, "You damn skippy!" He got up and kissed his aunt on the cheek and said, "Everything happens for a reason. Shay's come back into my life for a reason and I know it can't be nothin' but a good one!"

"Hold on there now, boy, there's something else she told me."

"What?"

"She told me that she's involved with someone."

"She got a nigga?"

"Unless she done switched sides, I assume so."

"That's nothin'. You know how she feels about me. Why else would she call if she didn't want to get back with me?"

"Why don't you take this one step at a time, boy? Don't take anything for granted. Wait a day or so to see if she calls you. If she doesn't then give her a call and see what the deal is."

"You know what, that's the best advice you've ever given me. I'm gon' do just that, Aunty." He gave Doris May another kiss and happily left her home and headed back to the block. *Yeah, shit is goin' my way for real! And I love it!* He turned up his music when he got in his ride.

When King made it back to the block he saw Tippi talking to Nutta. Nutta was telling Tippi about how much money he was making out in Midwest City as King came and joined them. "What's up, big homie?" Nutta said to King.

"What's up with you, young one?" King said as he gave Nutta a pound. "Tell me somethin' good."

"How 'bout I've been servin' my ass off out there in Midwest City at Boleg and Cuddy's new spot. That shit is rollin' nonstop. I need some more work 'cause I'm done.

Boleg and Cuddy are out that way now doin' 'em while I take a break, but I'm tryin' to get back out there before the late-night shift. That's when it really pops off. Feel me?"

"Fa' sho'." King turned toward Tippi and said, "Go get him a bird and a half. That should hold you for the night."

"Yeah, if not then I'll snatch whatever Cuddy and Boleg got left."

"Cool."

"Have you gotten at Keko? I heard his thang is jumpin' off proper out in Del City too. Looks like it's more than firecrackers poppin' off for this Fourth of July weekend."

"I haven't heard from that fool in a few days. I'll get with him later on though. I was thinkin' 'bout hittin' the club tonight, though. You tryin' to roll with me before you head back out to Midwest City?"

"Nah, I'm gon' chill at the pad and relax for a li'l bit. I'll get at y'all tomorrow, though."

Tippi came out of the trap carrying a brown Louis Vuitton knapsack with a kilo and a half of powder cocaine inside of it. She gave the bag to Nutta, smiled, and said, "Just like T.I. say in that song, 'What You Know 'Bout That.' Here your Louis knapsack; where the work at?"

Nutta accepted the bag from her and said, "You got jokes today, huh, Tippi? At least you ain't out here stabbin' nobody today. That got to count for somethin'."

"The day's not over with yet."

"You need a role model. I'm outta here," Nutta said as he shook hands with King. He smiled at Tippi and said, "Be nice out here." He was laughing as he climbed inside of his truck and left the block blasting his music.

Tippi shook her head and laughed when she heard Nutta's extremely loud sound system bumping the same T.I. song that she was just talking about. "That li'l nigga is somethin' else."

"Yeah, I know. And he's a young hog when it comes to gettin' this paper," King added as he stepped over to the porch of the trap.

Nutta was the youngest squad member; he was only twenty-three years old. He earned his respect among his peers with his moneymaking skills and his knack of always finding good moneymaking spots around the north. He, Boleg, and Cuddy made a formidable squad within the squad.

"What's this shit 'bout you hittin' up the club?" asked Tippi as she sat down next to him on the porch.

He shrugged and said, "I don't know, it ain't shit else to do. Might as well go out and get a li'l bent. It is the Fourth of July."

"Since when did you start givin' a fuck 'bout a holiday?"

Before he could answer her question his cell rang. He checked the caller ID, frowned, and answered his phone. "Hello?"

"Hi, Trevor. How are you?"

King stepped off the porch and started walking toward his car before he answered. Once he was inside of his car he said, "Shay, is this really you?"

She laughed and said, "Yes, it's really me, silly."

"Where are you? Can we get together or somethin'?"

"I just called to see how you were doing, Trevor. I heard that you were home and doing quite well for yourself."

King smiled from ear to ear as he remembered how Shayla always refused to call him by his nickname; she preferred his government name instead. "Yeah, you could say that. But, look, I'm not really tryin' to get into all of that on the phone. Why don't you meet me somewhere so we can chop it up for a li'l bit?"

"I . . . I can't do that, Trevor. My . . . I mean, it just wouldn't be right if I met you."

"What are you talkin' 'bout, Shay? It's me. What's not right about us meetin' each other somewhere?"

She took a deep breath. "I have a man, Trevor. He wouldn't like me meeting with my ex-boyfriend. I have to respect that."

With a slight edge in his tone, King said, "Yeah, I feel you. So tell me, why did you really call me? I mean, what's on your mind, Shay? Obviously it's not me."

"You're wrong, Trevor, and don't you dare talk to me with some attitude in your voice. Don't forget that you're the reason why we're not together anymore. I would've waited for you. You're the one who told me to move on with my life, remember?"

"Baby, I remember every last mistake I've ever made. Believe me, I'll never forget that one. But, on the real, I thought I was makin' the best decision for you. I didn't want to be a selfish nigga and try to lock you down. Yeah, I had other reasons, too. I didn't think I would have been able to deal if you started out riding wit' me while I did my bid and then fell off along the way. That would have hurt me too much, Shay. I couldn't take that chance. Can you understand that?"

Shaking her head from side to side as if he was there and could see her, she said, "No, no. I was your woman and I had the right to choose, too. You took that right away from me. You hurt me, Trevor. But, hey, that's the past. You're doing well, I'm okay, and life goes on."

"That's right. You got my number. If that clown nigga you're wit' fucks up give me a holla," King said as he hung up the phone. He got out of his car and went back and joined Tippi on the porch of the trap.

Tippi could tell by the look on his face that something wasn't right. "What's wrong with you? You look like somebody done pissed you the fuck off."

He shook his head and said, "No matter how good I do or how much money I make, it seems like my past always comes back to haunt my ass."

"Stop talkin' in riddles and tell me what's up."

He stared at Tippi for a few seconds and then said, "Nothin' is up. It is what it is. So, you tryin' to roll with me to the club or what?"

"Might as well. I ain't got faded in a minute. The Patrón and Grey Goose is on you, nigga," she said and started laughing.

"Fa' sho'."

Shayla sat down on the bed and stared at her cell phone as she held it tightly in her hand. *I could have met him somewhere. It would have been harmless.* Just as she was about to call King back her cell started ringing. She checked the caller ID and saw that it was Taj. "What's up, girl?"

"Nothing much, bored as hell. Let's do something we haven't done in a long time," said Taj.

"What's that?"

"Let's go to the club. I heard that Club Déjà Vu is off the chain on Saturdays. They always have someone performing and the drinks are right from what I heard."

"You know what, I'm with it. I don't want to be up in this house all night bored outta my mind."

"That's right, you need to get your mind right anyway."

"What's that supposed to mean?"

"Come on, Shayla, I'm your girl. I know you have the wrong man on your mind right about now."

"Is it that obvious? Damn."

"Only because I know you and I know how much you still care about dude. Don't trip, we gon' get our drink on and have a few laughs tonight, and hopefully you can get back focused on the man who's currently holding you down."

Shayla sighed. "I hope you're right, Taj. I hope you're right."

King was dressed in his normal thuggish attire: saggy black True Religion jeans, a wife beater under a fresh white tee with some butter-colored Tims on his feet. Since he hadn't been out in a while he decided to pull out some of his jewelry. He put on his twenty-four-inch platinum chain with his diamond crown pendant hanging from it. He then added a platinum and diamond ring on each of his pinky fingers. Last, he put on his Hi-Tek platinum and diamond watch around his wrist. After one last look in the mirror he smiled at himself. Satisfied, he left his home.

"Where you at, nigga?" asked Tippi over the phone as she sat inside of her truck smoking a blunt. "I've been here for close to twenty minutes waitin' on your ass."

King laughed. "I had to make a quick stop. I should be there in like five minutes."

"A'ight, I'll see you when you get here. I'm parked right in front of the entrance to the club."

"Is the line long to get into that bitch?"

"Kinda."

"Go get at one of the bouncers in the front and let them know that the King is on his way and I'm not tryin' to be waitin' in no damn long-ass line. Slide that nigga a note if you have to."

"Whatever, nigga, just hurry yo' ass up!" She hung up, hit her blunt one last time, and put it out in the ashtray. She checked her appearance quickly then hopped out of the SUV. All eyes were on her as she walked toward the club's entrance. Tippi wasn't dressed in her normal tomboyish way. She was in a feminine mood and was definitely looking good. The low-rise jeans she was wearing fit her like a glove, and her cropped wife beater exposed her tight stomach and the piercing in her navel. Her hair was braided straight to the back, hanging way past her shoulders. On her feet were a pair of D&G sandals. As she stepped to the front of the club, two of the bouncers smiled at her as they inhaled her scent. She smiled because she knew that they were loving that Goddess by Kimora Lee Simmons she was wearing.

"What's up, fellas?"

"Hello to you, lovely lady," said one of the bouncers.

"I was wondering if it was possible for me and my people to avoid waiting in this long line to get into the club tonight," Tippi said as she stared at the first bouncer who had spoken to her. Before he could answer she reached two fingers inside of her tight jean pocket and pulled out a hundred dollar bill and gave it to the bouncer and said, "A li'l somethin' for you and your friend."

The bouncer accepted the money and asked, "Where's your people?"

On cue, King stepped next to Tippi, put his arms around her waist, and said, "Here I am." The smile left the bouncer's face as he stepped aside and let the couple enter the club. Once they were inside of the club King was pat searched by another bouncer and Tippi was also being searched by a female security guard. After paying the admission they went inside of the crowded club. King led Tippi to the back of the club and found them an empty table and took a seat. King smiled at Tippi and asked, "What the hell done got into yo' ass?"

She batted her eyes and said, "What, you forgot I'm a fuckin' lady? I wanted yo' ass to see what you've been missin', nigga. I may not look like it all the time—"

"I know, I know, you're a fuckin' lady!" They both started laughing. King put his hand on top of hers and said, "Seriously, though, you lookin' real good tonight, baby."

"Good enough to eat?" she teased.

"Fuckin' right!"

A waitress came to their table and asked them if they would like anything to drink. "Do you have any Gran Patrón?" asked King.

"Yes, I believe we do," answered the waitress.

"Cool. Bring me a bottle." The waitress was about to tell King that a bottle cost at least $500 in the club. She stopped herself when she focused on all of the expensive jewelry King was wearing.

"Would you like anything?" the waitress asked Tippi.

"Yeah, bring a bottle of Grey Goose, too. Make sure you bring some lime slices and some salt, too," Tippi said as she smiled at King. After the waitress left to get their bottles she told King, "Looks like we're about to get blasted tonight."

"Don't overdo this shit. You know how you are when you get bent," he warned.

Tippi smiled and said, "I'm not in the mood for any violent shit tonight."

"What are you in the mood for?"

"You already know. Once that Patrón and Goose gets to kickin' in, it's really gon' be on," Tippi said seductively as she squeezed his hand.

"Mondo gon' be in trouble tonight," he said as he stared into her brown eyes.

Tippi returned his stare and said, "Uh-uh, no, Mondo; it's all about my King tonight. No strings, no problems afterward, my word," she said as she licked her pouty, glossed lips.

King kept his cool and calmly replied, "We'll see."

The waitress returned with their order, setting the bottles of liquor onto the table. She smiled brightly when King gave her a fifty dollar bill for her tip. She knew when he ordered the most expensive tequila on the market he was going to be a big tipper. After the waitress had set them up with lime slices, salt, and napkins, King grabbed the bottle of Patrón and poured them both a shot of the potent liquor. They each licked some salt from the back of their hands and then quickly downed the tequila, followed by a lime slice inside of their mouths. They repeated this process two more times before they poured themselves a glass of Grey Goose. After they had downed another shot of Patrón, King said, "Whew! That shit is the bomb right there!"

"I know," Tippi agreed as she fanned herself with her hands, trying to cool off the heat that was generating through her body from the liquor.

"Well, I'll be damned."

"What?" asked Tippi as she instantly became alert.

King stared at Tippi and said, "Promise me you're goin' to be good tonight."

"What's up?"

King gave a nod of his head toward his right and said, "A part of my past just came into the club."

Tippi turned her head and followed his gaze. When her eyes landed on Shayla she said, "Aww, hell nah! I know that ain't your ex-bitch Shayla."

King stared at his ex, poured himself another shot of Patrón, downed it quickly, and said, "Yep, that's exactly who that is."

Chapter Eight

Shayla and Taj both saw King at the same time. Before either of them was able to react, King saw them too. "Oh, shit, girl, he's looking dead at me," Shayla said nervously through clenched teeth.

"You might as well go on over there and speak and get this shit over with. Ain't no need to be standing there staring at the man," Taj said logically.

"Uh-uh, I'm not goin' over there. If he wants to talk to me then he's goin' to have to come over here," Shayla said as she turned her back toward King.

"Looks like that's not going to be a problem. Here he comes now."

Shayla took a deep breath and turned around and watched as King walked confidently over to where they were standing and said, "What's good, Shay? I see you're still hangin' with good company. What up, Taj?"

"Hi, Trevor," said Taj.

"So, it looks like we were destined to see each other after all, huh, Shay?" he asked with a grin on his face.

Shayla was so stunned by how good he was looking that she was momentarily speechless. She stared into those intense brown eyes of his and felt as if she was about to melt. Right then and there she realized that she was still in love with King. After a few more seconds had passed she smiled weakly and said, "I guess so. How are you, Trevor?"

That put a smile on his face as he answered, "I'm good. I'm eatin' and so is everyone around me."

"I'm happy for you, Trevor. You finally achieved the success you've always wanted," she said sarcastically.

"Not really, but I'm well on my way. Anyway, let me buy y'all somethin' to drink."

"We're fine."

"No, we're not!" interrupted Taj. "It's not polite to turn down a free drink, Shayla. We'll have a glass of Cîroc."

King turned and waved a waitress over and told her, "Please make it a point to make sure that these two lovely ladies are taken care of for the rest of the night. I'll be sittin' right over there so bring me their tab, okay?"

"No problem," replied the waitress as she took Shayla and Taj's order.

After the waitress left, King smiled and said, "Time has been good to you, Shay. You're lookin' delicious. Your dude is a lucky man."

"Thank you, Trevor. I know Lawanda is happy that she finally has you all to herself." *Dammit, why in the hell did I say some shit like that?* she scolded herself.

King ignored her comment, smiled again, and said, "Y'all be good." *Damn, she looks better than ever,* he thought as he went back to the table with Tippi.

As soon as he was out of earshot Taj shook her head and said, "That comment was definitely uncool, girl. You could have come better than that."

"I know, but that was the first thing that came to my mind. Damn, why did he have to be here tonight of all nights? You know we have to get outta here right?"

"Wrong! Girl, we got action and free drinks all night long. Ain't no way in hell I'm letting you ruin this for us. You better sit back and try to enjoy the rest of the night 'cause we ain't going nowhere."

"But, Taj—"

"But my ass! I mean it, Shayla. That nigga is back at his table doin' him with his friend over there. Why are you going to ruin our evening worrying about his ass and he ain't paying you any attention? That don't make no damn sense, no sense at all."

Before Shayla could respond the waitress came back with their drinks. After she left Shayla said, "Humph, that's no friend; that's Shelia. They've been together for years. She's his partner in crime. Shit, she probably hurt more niggas in this city than Trevor."

"She don't look like no killer to me. As a matter of fact, she's over there looking nice in those jeans. Look at those Dolce & Gabbana sandals she's rockin'. Sista girl got it goin' on."

Shayla started laughing and said, "Leave it up to you to identify some expensive-ass clothes. Girl, I'm tellin' you, Shelia is one of the roughest females on the north side. Trust that."

Taj shrugged and said, "So what? It don't really matter anyway. They're enjoying themselves and we're about to do the same damn thang. Now come on!"

Shayla stole another glance at King and Tippi then reluctantly followed her friend to the other side of the club.

The lights inside of the club came on, signaling that the club was closing. Even though he couldn't pay attention to her like he wanted to, King couldn't believe how good Shayla was looking. Tippi was on him, though, and he wasn't trying to get her riled up. That would be too dangerous for everyone involved. *I can't believe I'm lettin' this crazy-ass girl dictate my moves. This shit is gonna have to stop,* he thought as he scanned the club, hoping to get one last glance at Shayla. When he finally spotted her his heart skipped a beat when he saw her smiling at him. *She still loves me. I can see it in her eyes.*

"Damn, nigga, you can take that silly-ass grin off your face. I'm sure it won't be the last time you'll be seein' Shayla," Tippi said sarcastically.

King turned to face her and said, "Kill that shit, Tippi. I'm not in the mood for any of yo' bullshit."

"What are you in the mood for?" she asked, hoping that he'd answer her question the way she was desperately wanted him to.

He didn't. "Let's hit the block and make sure everything is everything; then we can go get our eat on."

"And then?"

He sighed and said, "Come on, Tippi, let that shit go!"

"You got that! But I'ma tell yo' ass this one time and one time only. I'm accepting your terms because I care about yo' ass that much. But if I find out you're back fuckin' that bitch Shayla, it's on. And you know what I mean when I say it's on!"

"Do you really think I'm gon' sit here and let you threaten me? Who the fuck do you think you're talkin' to?"

Tippi stared directly into his eyes and said, "The man I'd die for."

Her statement stopped the anger that suddenly had taken over him. Once again he sighed and said, "Come on, crazy girl, let's get up outta here." He stood and grabbed her hand as he led her out of the club.

Shayla watched as Trevor left the club with Shelia and frowned. They looked almost as if they were a couple. *I know he ain't messing with Shelia now, uh-uh, that can't be,* she thought as she waited patiently for Taj as she gave her phone number to some wannabe baller sporting a white gold chain while telling anyone who would listen that it was platinum.

After Taj was finished, she came to Shayla's side and said, "All right, girl, let's go. I don't know 'bout you, but I'm starving. Let's go get something to eat."

"Yeah, I could go for some Denny's. How about you?"

"I don't care where we eat, just as long as we hurry our asses up and get there!"

By the time they made it out of the club Shayla saw Shelia and Trevor talking to a few guys. *Damn, he's so fine.* She quickly headed in the opposite direction. Shayla knew for certain that some drama was definitely waiting for her down the line because there was no way she was going to be able to get Trevor off of her mind. She still loved him. *Damn.*

They got lucky when they arrived at Denny's. They beat the club crowd and were able to get a table as soon as they got there. While they were eating their food Taj was yakking up a storm about how they should get out more often. "I'm telling you, girl, you have to tell Flamboyant that you can't be all cooped up in that big-ass house all the time. You got to breathe. I mean, damn, you need to enjoy yourself more often."

"What makes you think I don't be enjoying myself while I'm with my man? I mean, it's not like we don't be having fun with each other."

"You know what I mean. We don't get to kick it like we used to, unless we go out shopping or something. You're too damn young and pretty to be sitting up under a nigga all day. Yeah, I know you're in school now, but that shit gets old too. You got to live, girl."

Shayla sipped her glass of orange juice and said, "You are too crazy, Taj. I'm . . ." She stopped midsentence when she saw Trevor and Shelia enter the restaurant. "Damn, can't we go anywhere tonight without bumping into them?" Shayla said, frustrated. Frustrated because just as she temporarily had him off of her mind, here he went and showed up again. *Shit!*

"Girl, I don't know about you but it looks like y'all bumping into each other like this is happening for a reason. Flamboyant better watch out. Looks like he's in jeopardy of losing his position and he don't even know it," Tajanaye said and giggled.

Shayla rolled her eyes and said, "Girl, please, Marco ain't nowhere near losing me. As for Trevor, humph, been there done that."

"You can save that shit for somebody who believes it. I know Trevor is on your mind."

"How in the hell do you know that?"

"If he wasn't you wouldn't be blushing like a li'l school-girl. The love is still there, girlfriend. You might as well admit it."

"Fuck," Shayla whispered as she continued to watch Trevor and Shelia.

King felt someone staring at him. He raised his head and turned to his right and saw Shayla quickly drop her head. He smiled and continued to look her way until she raised her head again and tried to peek to see if he was still looking at her. When she saw that she was busted she smiled shyly. *That smile, damn. She still can break me down with that pretty-ass smile of hers,* he thought as he gave her a slight nod. He turned his attention back to Tippi. Tippi hadn't seen Shayla yet and King hoped it would stay that way as a waitress led them toward a table on the other side of the restaurant. After they were seated Tippi said, "That nigga Flex be actin' like he's the king of the block whenever I'm not around."

"He's in charge whenever neither of us are there. He's doin' what he's supposed to."

"That's not what I'm talkin' 'bout. He's startin' to run his mouth a li'l too much. Talkin' 'bout he's about to blow up and get his own shit crackin'."

"That bothers you?"

"Yeah, we ain't got room for that nigga to be takin' any food off of our plate."

"As long as he spends his chips with us he won't do us any harm. Plus, it looks like Boleg, Cuddy, and Nutta have added more to the kitty anyway. Don't pay Flex any attention, I'll holla at him and see where his head is at."

"You should just let me handle it my way."

"Nah, he's been good people for too long. Ain't no need to be that cold. If the need arises, you will be called upon. Now come on, let's order. I'm hungry like a mothafucka," King said as he picked up his menu.

Shayla gave a sigh of relief when she saw that Trevor and Shelia were being led to the other side of the restaurant. She couldn't believe how fast her heart started beating when their eyes met. *I have to get this man out of my head before a whole lot of mess gets started.*

Taj smiled at her friend and said, "Earth to Shayla, can you hear me, Shayla?"

"Huh? Oh, what were you saying, Taj?"

"Damn, girl, it's like that? That nigga gon' get you in some deep shit with your man if you don't get your mind right."

"I was just thinking the same thing. You finished yet? I gotta get out of this place."

"Mmm hmm, I'm good. Go on out to the car while I take care of the bill."

"Thanks, Taj. I got you on the next one," Shayla said as she quickly stood and left their table. When she made it to the door she couldn't resist taking one last peek in her ex-boyfriend's direction. Instead of seeing him, her eyes locked with Shelia. They frowned at each other for a few seconds before Shayla turned and left the restaurant.

By the time Taj had dropped Shayla off at home she was dead tired. She went into the bedroom, took off her clothes, and then went and took a hot shower. While she was showering, she began to wonder why Marco hadn't called home. He hadn't called since he had been in Miami. *I know his ass bet' not be fuckin' up,* she thought as she stepped out of the shower. After drying off and slipping into one of Marco's T-shirts, she grabbed the cordless phone and checked the voice mail to see if he'd called while she was out. When she heard that there were no messages she became upset all of a sudden. Since she made the reservation for their trip she knew where they were staying. She got up, grabbed her purse, and pulled out a copy of their itinerary for their trip. She then dialed the number to the Hotel Victor in Miami. Even though it was close to four in the morning Florida time, she was determined to hear her man's voice before she fell asleep. She needed to hear her man's voice for more reasons than she cared to admit.

When the phone was answered Shayla hesitated then asked the hotel clerk, "May I have Marco Freeman's room please?"

"One moment please," replied the clerk.

There was a pause and then the phone started ringing again. She inhaled deeply and waited for Marco to answer the phone. She smiled when she heard him pick up the line and sleepily say, "This better be a fuckin' emergency whoever the fuck this is."

Sitting on top of the bed with one leg up under the other, Shayla smiled and said, "It is an emergency. Why haven't you called me, Marco?"

"Shayla? Wha . . . what time is it, babe?"

"It's a little after three here so it should be after four there. Now answer my question."

After wiping sleep from his eyes, Flamboyant answered, "I'm sorry, babe, we been rippin' and runnin' these streets all day. Then we went clubbin' and got to drinkin' and stuff. You know how I get when I go out."

"Umm hmm, I know. I also know your ass better be by yourself right now."

He laughed. "You know I'm lyin' here wishin' you were beside me. Wait a minute, what the hell are you doin' up this late anyway?"

Dammit, he's not supposed to be asking me questions, she thought as she tried to think of something to tell him. She decided to go on and tell him the truth. "Me and Taj went to that club on Tenth."

"Déjà Vu?"

"Yeah, that one. After the club let out we went to Denny's and got something to eat. I just got home about thirty minutes ago. I was about to go to bed until I realized that I hadn't heard from you all day."

"Was you worried about your man?" he teased.

"Humph. I was worried that I was going to kill my man for being so damn inconsiderate."

"My bad, babe. If it will help any, I did think about callin' you once I got back to my suite, but I figured that it was too late and I didn't want to get you started by waking you up. You know how cranky you be acting." He laughed.

"I guess I'll let you make it up then, boy. Go on and go back to sleep. I'll talk to you tomorrow."

"You still love me?"

"Yes, Marco, I still love you."

"I love you too, baby."

"Bye," she said as she hung up the phone. She set the cordless onto the nightstand and said, "I love my man. I. Love. My. Man." *If I love my man so much why in the hell am I still thinking about a man I haven't seen since I was eighteen? Ughhhhhhh!*

Chapter Nine

After spending the entire day with his kids, King felt that it was time for him to hit the block. Even though it was a holiday, he wasn't letting anything interfere with his money. Fourth of July or not, he was going to get his. When he brought li'l Trevor and Tandy back home he knew Lawanda was going to give him some grief when he told her he was leaving; so instead of walking the kids into the house, he waited outside in his car and watched as they went inside the house. Just as he was getting ready to put the car in reverse, Lawanda came to the front door waving her hands, signaling for him not to leave. He sighed heavily as he turned off the ignition and climbed out of his car.

"Where are you going? I've been barbequing while y'all were out poppin' them fireworks. I got all of your favorites, too: chicken as well as some ribs," Lawanda said.

"That's cool, but I got some shit to get into. If I can, I'll come back later on and get my eat on."

"That's fucked up, King. It's the Fourth and you can't even spend it with us."

"What you talkin' 'bout? I've been with the kids all damn day. I gots to do me, so don't be givin' me no shit right now, Lawanda. I'm not really in the mood."

"Yeah, you've been with the kids; but what about me? Don't I deserve some of your time too?"

"Like I said, I'm not in the mood for this shit. You know what time it is with us, so don't be trying to make it seem

like we're some happy fuckin' family. I'll hit you later on,"
he said as he turned around and went back to his car.

"That's fucked up, King. You didn't even have to go
there!" she yelled as she stormed back into her house.

As King pulled out of the driveway, he knew he was
wrong for saying what he said but, hell, it was the truth.
Lawanda had tricked him into getting her pregnant and
she knew damn well that he wasn't feeling her like that.
Not only did he fall for that, "I'm on the pill" shit once,
like a straight sucker he fell for it twice. His lack of dick
control when it came to her ass was the reason why he
had two kids. He loved his shorties dearly, but he felt
they were brought into this world by the wrong woman.
*Damn, if I would have held on to Shayla like I was sup-
posed to, none of this shit would be goin' on,* he thought
as he headed toward the block.

The block was popping and everything looked to be
going smooth as King pulled his Magnum in front of
the main trap. Tippi was sitting on the porch listening
to some music on her iPhone. When she saw King she
pulled out her earplugs and asked, "How was family
time?"

"Don't start with me, Tippi. I'm tellin' yo' ass, don't
start."

"Damn, nigga, all I did was ask a question."

"What's up out here? Is everything good or what?"

"Yeah, we straight. 'Em bad-ass li'l kids down there got
them bitch-ass black and whites comin' through every
twenty minutes or so though."

"Why, 'cause the fireworks and shit?"

"Yeah, you know that shit is illegal within the city
limits. They just riding through to make the kids stop,
but you already know as soon as they leave they got they
li'l asses right back out there poppin' away."

"Where that nigga Flex at?"

Tippi shrugged and said, "Ain't no tellin'. Probably somewhere tryin' to do him. I told you that nigga got somethin' else poppin'."

"Yeah, we'll see," King said as he pulled out his cell and dialed Flex's cell number. When Flex answered he told him, "Meet me at the 7-Eleven off of Fortieth on Scott Street."

"What's up?" asked Flex.

"I'll get at you when I see you." King ended the call and told Tippi, "I'm puttin' that nigga out in Del City by Keko's new spot."

Tippi laughed and said, "He's not goin' to like that shit."

"If he has somethin' else poppin' then this will be his chance to bring it to the table. If not, then he's goin' to work that spot with Keko's people. It's either that or he's off the squad."

"You need me to roll wit' you?"

"Nah, do you. I'll be back in a li'l while," King said as he stepped off of the porch. He got into his car and just as he was turning the ignition one of the kids who lived on the block came running toward his car, waving his hands. King rolled down his window and said, "What's good, li'l man?"

"We don't have any more for any more firecrackers. Can you look out for us, King?"

"How much y'all need?"

The little boy thought for a minute then held up both of his hands and said, "Ten dollars."

"Ten dollars? That's gon' be enough to last y'all?"

"Uh-huh."

"A'ight. Here, take this and make sure that everybody gets some," he said as he gave the little boy a C-note.

"Thanks, King!" The little boy smiled.

"A'ight, li'l man, y'all be safe," he said, returning the smile.

"We will!" yelled the little boy as he ran off to show his friends how much money King had given him.

By the time King arrived at the 7-Eleven, he saw Flex standing next to his Navigator smoking a cigarette. King parked next to Flex's SUV, jumped out of his car, and said, "Take a walk with me real quick." Flex fell in step with him and they strolled toward an apartment complex down the street from the 7-Eleven. "So tell me, what's poppin', Flex?"

"Same old shit, my nigga, just tryin' to get 'em dollars."

"Yeah, I see. What you got crackin', dog?"

"I'm makin' a few moves tryin' to get a li'l extra somethin', you know how it is. Just grindin' for real."

"I feel you, but peep this, I was thinkin' 'bout puttin' you out this way with Keko and his people. Would you have a problem wit' that?"

"It depends."

"On what?"

"On whether this will interfere with what I'm tryin' to get poppin'," Flex said seriously.

"What exactly are you tryin' to get jumped off?"

"I've been lightweight fuckin' with this white broad out on the far north side behind Quail Springs. She's been hookin' a nigga up with these high-powered crackas. Doctors, lawyers, and shit like that. They be spendin' like a mothafucka. But they ain't fuckin' with the hard; all they want is the soft. I be delivering it to them whenever they get at ol' girl. It's been lovely for me so far. I was hopin' to be able to buy three or four bricks of my own; then I'd be bringin' in more chips for the squad as well as myself."

"That's cool. For a minute there I thought you was tryin' to shake us. That's the reason I was gon' put you over this way."

"Come on, King. You know I ain't wit' no faulty shit. I'm tryin' to make as much paper as I can, but I'd never cross you, my nigga. Real talk."

"Good lookin', Flex, but I had to holla at you, you know what I'm sayin'?"

"I ain't fucked up 'bout it. It's all good."

"Come on in here with me. Let's see what Keko got crackin'. You might still want to come out this way," King said as he led Flex past a small security office and into the Summit apartments. Before they were all of the way inside of the apartment complex, they heard Keko yelling at someone. King smiled and said, "That nigga Keko runs a tight ship wherever he gets down."

"Yeah, but he be on some bullshit sometimes, though. If I do come out here, I'm not gon' be goin' for that punk shit, dog."

"Don't worry 'bout it. I'll make sure that everything is straight."

Keko saw King and Flex when they entered the apartment complex and watched them as they came toward him. Keko was twenty-eight years old, a year older than King. He was well known throughout the north side from his old gangbangin' days. He gave up being a Blood for gettin' money with King and the squad. They first met each other when they were doing time in prison. Keko was a slim, light brown–skinned brother with a chipped front tooth. His choice of hairstyles varied from week to week. Either he had his hair cut bald, or kept cut low with designs shaved all over his head. He was known around the north and was a top earner for the squad. He was also well known for busting his gun. His knuckle game wasn't that great, so he made up for the lack of fighting skills with pulling out his pistol. He not only pulled it out, he used it quite effectively.

King observed how the smokers were purchasing their drug of choice from Keko's hand-to-hand man. He also noticed that after every sale was made Keko's workers would then go to the back of the apartments for a few minutes then return to the front to wait for the next sale.

"Don't you think you're a li'l too obvious with your workers takin' the ends straight to the back after every sale?" asked King.

Keko smiled. "Don't miss a thang, huh? Don't trip, my nigga; looks are deceiving. When they go to the back they take the chips to my girl, Neecy. Neecy then takes the chips to my apartment where I keep all the ends. No one knows about this apartment but me and Wifey so, believe me, it's all good. I've locked this apartment complex down tighter than Nino did the Carter building, dog!"

King laughed. "But is the money flowin' like it was in *New Jack City?*"

"You fuckin' right! I've gone through a half unit in less than two days out here. And it's only gon' get better as time goes on. As you can see, I got a straight line on all incomin' traffic. So if the Ones come, they'll be spotted way before they can do any damage. I got the manager in my pocket as well as the rent-a-cops who call themselves security guards. You did notice that they didn't say anything to y'all when y'all walked by 'em, right? That's how Keko gets down. Ya know!"

"You are the man, my nigga," King said as he gave Keko a pound.

"That I am; but I do have one problem, though."

"What's that?"

"I got word from a few cluckheads that there's a spot on the other side of the highway that's competin' with a nigga. So far they haven't been able to do any harm, but the word from the clucks is that they're about to step up their game."

"Do you know who's runnin' that shit over there?"

"Nah, not yet. I'm checkin' on that shit now. The thing is, we don't control shit out this way like we do on the north. I might have to get a li'l physical in order for my presence to be felt. Cool?"

King understood what Keko was asking him and answered, "Do what needs to be done in order for you to be able to do you. Just make sure you don't overdo it, Keko."

"Gotcha." Keko smiled.

"We're outta here," King said as he turned and was followed closely by Flex out of Keko's gold mine. When they made it back to the 7-Eleven, King took a look on the other side of the highway. He saw what looked like several crackheads walking in and out of the Candlewood apartment complex.

"Do you want to come out this way and get a part of Keko's spot, Flex?"

"Nah, I'm good. I'll do better if I stay where I'm at, dog. I would like some more room to get down, though. I need to get my roam on a li'l bit more. When I'm stuck on the block I be missin' more than I should."

"A'ight, then, do you. Tippi can handle the block for now. If you're needed, you'll be called."

"I ain't trippin'. You know I'll be there, G."

"I'll holla at ya later," King said as he got into his car and drove away.

As King was on his way back to the block he was thinking about giving Shayla another call. He couldn't believe how funny style she acted toward him. *She has to know how much she still means to me,* he thought as he turned onto the highway. He grabbed his cell and called his aunt. "What's good, Aunty?"

"Nothin' much, boy, just sittin' here feelin' real good right about now."

He laughed and said, "Yeah, I bet you are. You need to stop smokin' so much of that bud. That shit can't be good for you."

"Believe me, boy, ain't nothing wrong with smokin' weed, especially weed that's this damn good. Now, what you want, boy? You messin' with my high!"

"That's cold. I just wanted to see what you were up to. I see a brotha can't even check on his peoples from time to time."

"Yeah, yeah, save all of that shit for someone who believes it. If you checkin' to see if Shayla has called back, you're wasting your time 'cause she hasn't."

He started laughing again and said, "You really think you know me, huh?"

"Am I right?"

"Kinda," he admitted and started laughing.

Doris May's tone turned serious as she said, "I raised you, boy, and I know when you're worried about something or someone. I can hear it in your voice. Don't be goin' out of your way for that girl. If it's meant for y'all to be together it'll happen sooner or later."

"I feel ya. Are you good or do you need me to slide by there and bring you some more medicine?"

"I'm cooool, boy, reallll coooool." She giggled, high as the clouds in the sky.

"You're outta there, Aunty, but I love your crazy self."

"I love you too, boy. Bye," she said as she hung up the phone.

As he drove on he continued to think about Shayla. *Fuck it, Aunty's right. If it's gon' happen it's gon' happen. I got way too much money to make to be trippin' off of a broad from my past,* he thought as he pulled back onto the block.

Chapter Ten

Shayla was sitting in the living room watching television when she heard Flamboyant pull his car into the garage. She couldn't help but smile; her man was home and she needed him like bad! She jumped off of the sofa and ran into his arms as soon as he came inside of the house.

"Damn, if I knew it would be like this I'd go out of town without you more often, babe," he said as he returned her tight embrace. After sharing a tender kiss he released his hold of Shayla and said, "You know I need some right?"

She stared into his brown eyes seductively and said, "I need some too, babe, come on." She pulled him into their bedroom and quickly undressed. As soon as he saw those firm D cups of hers his hard-on seemed to become even harder. Shayla was normally submissive while making love, but for some strange reason she was in a real aggressive mood. She grabbed Flamboyant by his waist and pulled him on top of her. While he was busy kissing her neck and chest she held on tightly to his ass. She slid her hand in between them, grabbed his dick tightly, and gave it a squeeze as she guided it into her sweetness. As soon as he felt her wetness at the tip of his dick he gently slid inside of her love walls. Shayla wasn't trying to have nothing gentle about this session. She wrapped her legs around his waist tightly, clamped her legs against his back, and started bucking like a wild bull. She was bucking so hard that she made that super bull Bodacious proud of her moves. "Give it to me, bae. Give me that dick!" she screamed.

Flamboyant didn't know what had gotten into her but he loved it! Somehow he pried her legs loose, grabbed each of them by her calves, pushed them all the way back to her shoulders, and started pounding away inside of her. "Is this how you want it, babe? Huh? Is it?"

"Yes! Yes! Fuck me good, Marco! Fuck me good!"

He pulled out of her abruptly, turned her onto her knees, and reentered her from the doggie style position. As he was hitting that piping hot pussy from the rear he started slapping her on the ass asking her, "Whose pussy is this? Who's is it, babe?"

Shayla was biting the right corner of her bottom lip, enjoying the pleasure Flamboyant was giving her body. Her answer to his question was a few grunts as she was trying to match his intensity by bucking her rear right back into him.

Shaking his head from side to side as if she could see him, he once again slapped her on her ass and asked again, "Whose pussy is this, Shayla? Whose is it?"

"Yours, Marco, yours!" she screamed out.

"Uh-uh, wrong answer," he said and continued to go hard at her.

Shayla was enjoying their lovemaking tremendously, but every time he asked her that question she felt her guilt override the pleasure she was feeling at that moment. Every single time he asked her, "Whose pussy is this?" the first thought that came to her mind was Trevor. *This can't be good,* she thought as Flamboyant continued his onslaught on her sex.

"Whose it is now, Shayla?"

"Marco's!" she grunted as she felt her orgasm mount-ing.

"Whose?"

"Flamboyant's!" she screamed as she realized that's what he wanted to hear. They came at the same time in one blissful motion.

He slid out of her and collapsed next to her on the bed. "Damn, babe, what in the hell got into you?"

She put her index finger to her lips and said, "Shh, let's relax for a minute and enjoy the afterglow of that good sex, babe."

He smiled and did as he was told. Whatever had gotten into her he damn sure didn't want to mess up the mood she was in.

While they were lying side by side, Shayla felt the sudden urge to cry. *I love this man, I really do, but I just can't get Trevor off of my mind. God, please help me make it through this,* she prayed silently.

Flamboyant turned on his side and said, "Come here and let me hold you, babe." He grabbed her and gave her a hug and held her tightly in his strong arms, not knowing that's exactly what she needed. They fell asleep in that exact same position.

The next morning when Shayla got up she showered and got dressed. She was rushing for two reasons: one, she wanted to get away from the house because she had some serious thinking to do; and two, she didn't feel like talking to Marco. It would only confuse her more at this point, she thought as she slid on her Nike running shoes. Just as she was grabbing her purse Flamboyant said, "Come back to bed, babe. Fuck school today; come kick it with your man."

She smiled and said, "Uh-uh, I'm not lettin' you put that big old thang inside of me for a few days. I'm still sore from last night's workout. It's a miracle I'm able to go to school this morning."

He smiled and said, "That's your fault! You was the one on some aggressive shit. You got a nigga fired up like crazy."

"Whatever, I'll see you later," she said as she stepped to the bed and gave him a quick kiss.

"Do you wanna have lunch later on?"

"I'll call you when I get out of class, you never know what you're going to be into by that time."

"A'ight, love you, babe."

"Love you too," she said as she grabbed her purse and book bag and walked out of the bedroom.

Since he was up so early in the morning, Flamboyant decided to get dressed and go check out how his money was flowing while they'd been in Miami. Once he was dressed, he called Prince and asked, "Have you holla'd at Gunna yet?"

"Nigga, it ain't even nine o'clock in the mornin' yet and you callin' me askin' me some crazy shit. You must have forgotten that we just got back a few fuckin' hours ago," Prince said, highly agitated.

"Well, get the fuck up! Playtime is over; it's time to get that fuckin' money! Get at Gunna and see how his peoples did out there in Del City while we were gone."

"A'ight, anything else, you fuckin' slave master?"

"Nah, that's it for now, so get on it, nigga," Flamboyant said as he hung up the phone. He went into the kitchen and poured himself a glass of grape juice. He was sipping his juice when he had another thought cross his mind. He grabbed the phone and dialed Ken.

When Ken's wife, Javon, answered the phone she said, "He's still 'sleep, Flamboyant."

"Hello to you too, Javon. Can you wake that nigga up for me? It's kinda important."

"Can't I have a little bit more time with my man, Flam? Damn, y'all just got back."

"I promise I'll let you have him all day if you put him on the line real quick." He laughed.

"Whatever," she said as she gave the phone to her man.

Ken accepted the phone from Javon and said, "What it do?"

"I just wanted to get at you to see if you'd checked with them young ones about gettin' some more of that."

"Not yet. I've been kinda busy takin' care of Wifey. She thinks that if I can't break her off properly then that means I cheated on her while we were in the MIA."

Flamboyant started laughing when he heard Javon in the background yelling, "And yo' ass ain't proved shit to me yet! That's why yo' ass ain't leaving the house today!"

"Damn, my nigga, it's like that?" Flamboyant joked.

"Don't pay that girl no attention. I'll get at ya later after I had a chance to get at them young'uns."

"A'ight, nigga, tell Javon I said to take it light on our ass."

"Man, fuck her. I'm 'bout to wear her ass out so she can leave me the fuck alone," Ken said and started laughing.

"Get at me," Flamboyant said as he hung up the phone.

Shayla felt like she wasn't focused enough for school, so she went over to Taj's house instead. When Taj opened her door she said, "I hope your ass don't have anything serious to talk about 'cause I'm going back to bed." She turned and started walking sleepily back toward her bedroom.

Shayla smiled as she stepped inside of the house and closed the door behind her. She went into Taj's kitchen and made herself some tea. She was sitting down at the dining room table sipping her tea when Taj came into the room with a frown on her face.

"All right, what's wrong?" Taj asked as she sat down across from Shayla.

Shayla signed heavily. "Girl, can you believe I still can't get Trevor off of my damn mind? I mean, damn, all I keep thinking 'bout is his touch and smell, how he used to make love to me so tenderly. Girl, I was actually thinking 'bout his ass last night when me and Marco was doin' it."

"What? Damn, girlfriend, you got it bad. When you start thinking about another nigga while you're gettin' your swerve on with your dude, anything is capable of happening. What if you would have screamed out Trevor's name in the heat of the moment? You'd be up shit's creek for real."

"I know. It's worse than that, Taj. Trevor has consumed my every thought. I don't know why, but I can't get him off of my mind. I've been honest with myself. I still care about him; hell, I still love him. But I'm in love with Marco."

"Are you sure you're in love with Marco and not Trevor?"

"Marco is my heart, Taj. I'd never hurt him. I know my love for him is real."

"Uh-uh, don't be evasive, Shayla. Answer the question."

With her eyes watering, Shayla stared at her best friend and said, "I honestly can't answer that question. I really can't."

"Damn."

Milo smiled when he saw Flamboyant's 600 pull into the southeast apartment complex. "What it do, dog?" asked Milo after Flamboyant stepped out of his car.

"Ain't shit. What's up with you? Ain't your ass tired?"

"Nope. I came straight over here last night and checked all my traps to make sure the ends were in order. After that I went to the pad and got some Zs. I'm good now. What's up with you rollin' through this early?"

"Just makin' sure everything is everything. I'm waitin' on Prince to get back at me so I can see what's what with that setup out in Midwest City and Del City."

"Yeah, Gunna told me 'bout that shit. He's got an apartment out there in Del City rollin' like a mothafucka. He called me last night and told me that when we got back he went over there to check his ends and they dumped damn near two birds over the weekend."

"That's cool. Did he say anything 'bout Midwest City?"

"Nah."

"So, what's your plan for the rest of the day?"

"I'm 'bout to sit here and get this cock-suckin' paper, my nigga. I'll be needin' some more work around the evening time. Is that cool with you?"

"Yeah, give me a holla when you ready." They were interrupted by Flamboyant's cell ringing. He pulled it out of his pocket and saw Prince's number on the screen. "What's good, my nigga?"

"I'm over here in Del City at Gunna's spot. He told me that things are extra lovely out this way."

"I heard."

"From who?"

"Milo just put me up on everything."

"You with that nigga right now?"

"Yep."

"Good. I need y'all to meet me and Gunna out in Midwest City in 'bout thirty."

"What's poppin'?

"I'll put you up on it when we meet. Meet us at that McDonald's on the corner of Twenty-third and Douglas."

"Ain't there a li'l breakfast spot across the street from there?"

"I think so, why?"

"Let's meet there instead. I'm hungry as fuck."

"Okay, that's cool," Prince said as he hung up the phone.

Flamboyant told Milo, "We got to go meet Prince and Gunna out in Midwest City."

"What's up?"

He shrugged. "We'll find out when we get there. Go get your soldiers and let them know we'll be out for a li'l while."

"I hope this shit is about some fuckin' money, 'cause I ain't got time to be wastin' fuckin' around with Gunna's wild ass."

"If Prince wants to meet with us then it's definitely about some ends." He laughed. "Go handle your business so we can bounce."

By the time Prince and Gunna arrived at the small breakfast restaurant, Flamboyant and Milo had already placed their orders and were sipping two cups of coffee. Gunna had a smile on his face as they sat down at the table.

"Check it: I really don't got that much time, but shit is poppin' off the hook in Del City. I gots to hurry up and get some more work out there. I can't handle shit out this way and maintain what I've put together out there. Do you think you can handle this shit, Milo? I got it all set up; all you have to do is move in some of your team and everything else will fall right in place."

"Run it down to me before I commit to this shit, dog," Milo said as he sipped some more of his coffee.

"It's like this: I got a trap set up down the street from this park where all the Bloods from the Murder One hang at. Ain't really no hand-to-hand gon' be needed. They just want to be able to cop from us. After that, they do the hand-to-hand shit on their own blocks. The park is where they hang, get high, and clown and shit. Plus, they'll be gettin' bud and probably some X from you."

"What about that water?"

"That ain't really poppin' too hard over this way. But it is poppin' over in the Panic Zone. I got a broad who lives over there on Sycamore. She'll be hittin' you whenever some of that is needed. She will also get at you from time to time for some X. I'm tellin' you, dog, this shit is gravy over this way. If I could handle it I'd run all this shit myself, but I can't take care of my end of the south as well as Del City, too. I got my team spread out thin enough as is."

"I could probably send about five of my niggas out this way."

Shaking his head no, Gunna said, "Dog, it's gotta be you for maybe the first couple of weeks. Ain't no room for mistakes. If 'em Blood niggas sense any weakness they will try your team. Once you set the pace and they see a real nigga on deck then you could send some of your boys."

Milo turned toward Flamboyant and asked, "What you think, Flam, should I fuck with this?"

"It sounds pretty straight to me. Give it a try and see how everything falls. You might have just been handed a blessin'."

"Fuck it, I'm wit' it."

"Cool. How long will it take for you to get over here and get it crackin'?"

"Take me to that trap you was talkin' 'bout and let me peep it out. Then I'll make a call and have my people out here with me within the hour."

"That's straight. What 'bout the work?"

"I'll have some brought when my team gets here."

"Okay, that's that then," said Prince. "Since this shit has picked up so much we're goin' to need some more work, Flam."

"Don't worry 'bout that. I'll have y'all fully stocked within a few days," Flamboyant said, just as the waitress came to their table with their orders.

"One more thing, dog," Gunna said, turning toward Milo.

"What's that?" asked Milo as he slid a piece of bacon into his mouth.

"Ain't no need for you to be on no rah-rah shit with these niggas. These niggas ain't soft, so there's no need to be testin' 'em with the extra shit. Run your trap like a G and the real will recognize real."

"Gotcha, but if 'em niggas try to test my gangsta an example will be made. Real talk," Milo said in a calm but deadly tone.

Gunna grinned and said, "But of course! Now hurry up and finish eating that swine. There's plenty of money to be made."

Chapter Eleven

Nutta was loving it. He couldn't believe how much money he was making in Midwest City. *These Bloods be spendin' for real,* he thought as he counted out the $5,400 he just made. He jumped inside of his truck and picked up his cell to call Boleg. When Boleg answered Nutta told him, "Dog, you two fat fucks need to hurry up and get out here. I just finished the last of my pack and it's like seven niggas out here waitin' for some more."

"We're on our way, li'l nigga. Tell 'em niggas to hold what they got; we'll be there in like fifteen."

"A'ight, I'm 'bout to go gas up my truck. I'll get at 'em before I head toward the north. I'll get at y'all later on."

"A'ight, dog, be safe," Boleg said.

"Y'all too," Nutta said as he hung up the phone. Nutta started his truck and blew the horn a couple of times as he drove down the street to where some of the Bloods were hanging out. He rolled the window down and told them, "The work's on the way. My people should be here in about fifteen. They'll meet y'all at the park."

"A'ight, but 'em niggas need to hurry the fuck up, dog. It ain't like we got to be waitin' for they ass. We can go right up the street and get some work from them south side niggas," one of the Bloods replied.

"South side niggas?" asked Nutta.

"Yeah, my li'l homeboy's relative got a spot set up down the street. But 'em niggas' zips are seven, but since you and your peeps got 'em for six we gon' keep fuckin' wit' y'all."

"That's right. I'll get at y'all later," Nutta said as he rolled his window back up and pulled away from the gang members. He picked his cell up and called Boleg. "Dog, did y'all know it was some south side niggas out there gettin' their serve on too?"

"Nah," answered Boleg.

"Well, there is, so make sure y'all watch 'em fools. Their ticket is a buck higher than ours, that's why them Damus are still fuckin' with us. It's only gon' be a matter of time before they drop their ticket so they can get some of this fuckin' money."

"Don't trip, we'll be up on that shit."

"Y'all strapped?"

"Cuddy is. Why, you think 'em niggas on some grimy shit?"

"Ain't no tellin'. Better to be safe than sorry."

"You strapped?"

"Always. I got two nines for they ass if they want some funk. But I'm on my way out so I'm good. Make sure y'all get at me before y'all get up outta that bitch."

"Fa' sho'," Boleg said as he ended the call.

King and Tippi were walking around Penn Square Mall doing a little shopping. Really it was Tippi who was doing the shopping; King was just carrying all of her purchases. "For a broad who likes to dress like a tomboy you sure are buying a lot of girly shit today," King teased.

"Don't start with me, nigga. If you took the time to look, you'd see that it's a whole lotta woman under these baggy-ass jeans. Now, come on. I want to go Bath & Body Works. After that we can get the hell up outta here."

"Good. It feels like we've been in here all damn day."

"Yeah, yeah, just come on, fool," Tippi said with a smile on her face.

When they entered Bath & Body Works King saw Shayla's best friend, Taj. He quickly let his eyes roam all over the small store. He knew if Taj was inside of the store the odds were high that Shayla was too. His heartbeat increased as he continued to look around the store. Since Tippi didn't remember Taj from the club the other night, he chose not to inform her wild ass. After confirming that Taj was alone in the store he watched as she went and paid for a few items. Taj saw him staring at her and smiled. He returned her smile and followed Tippi to the back of the store.

"Smell this," Tippi said as she rubbed a little fruity-smelling lotion onto her wrist.

"It smells like peach."

"I know. You like?"

"It's cool." He then grabbed one of the other small bottles of lotions and began dabbing himself on the wrist to see how they smelled. After testing a few more he told Tippi, "You know what, I think I'm gon' get me a few of these. This apple and strawberry smells good. The peach is cool, too." He smiled at her as he grabbed several different bottles of lotion.

"Look at yo' ass. I done got you showin' your feminine side, huh?"

He frowned, but before he could respond to Tippi's joke his cell rang. He pointed his finger at her nose and said, "You have just been saved by the bell. Here, go pay for all this shit and I'll meet you outside." He then accepted his call. "What it do, Keko?"

"Same old shit, my nigga. Remember that small problem I told you 'bout when you was out at my new spot?"

"Yeah."

"It looks like it's startin' to become a larger problem. My shit has actually slowed down in the last couple of days."

"I thought you were gon' do you."

"I plan to, but it looks like it's gon' be a li'l tricky."

"Say no more; me and Tippi will be over there in twenty. We're out here at Penn Square. I'll holla at ya when we get there."

"Uh-huh," Keko said as he ended the call.

Tippi came out of the store and fell in step with King. She could tell by the way he was walking that something was up so she asked, "What's goin' down?"

"I don't' know yet. We got to bounce out to Del City and get at Keko. Looks like he's got a problem with a li'l competition."

"Yeah? He's ready to go to war, huh?"

"You know how he gets down. Keko's always tryin' to go to war."

As they left the mall and got into King's car Tippi asked, "What is your gut tellin' you at this very moment?"

"That I should close that spot down and make Keko stand down. Ain't no need to get crazy over this shit. It ain't like that's his main spot."

"You trippin'! Didn't you tell me that he had that shit over there poppin' off like crazy?"

"Yeah, but—"

"But my ass! Get yo' mind right, nigga. What the hell's gotten into you? You know how we get down. Just 'cause we ain't on the north don't mean we gon' let some fluke-ass niggas get in the way of us makin' this fuckin' money. If Keko wants to go hard, then let him move 'em niggas like we've always moved niggas who get in our way."

"Don't get it twisted, it is what it is. I'm more concerned about the fact that we're not protected in Del City like we are on the north."

"Why don't you handle that shit then?"

"It's not as easy as that, Tippi. I got to get at Charlie and see if it can be taken care of. First, I want to see what's what with Keko before I make that call."

"I feel ya."

When King and Tippi arrived at the Summit apartments, Keko was handling business as usual. There was a steady flow of traffic from the crackheads. King stepped to Keko and said, "Shit don't look no different to me, nigga. What's good?"

"Dog, 'em niggas across the highway are on my dick bad. They not only servin' the clucks, they got weight, too. Once they found out I was over here servin' these niggas zips for six, they started servin' they shit for five-fiddy. I lost like seven to eight of my best weight customers. I could match that shit, but why do that when I can cross the highway and move 'em niggas? I wanted to give you the heads-up before I made my move."

"When you gon' get at 'em fools?" asked Tippi.

Keko checked the time on his watch and said, "As soon as the sun sets."

Taking a look at his own watch, King said, "Like I told you before, this is your thang so I'm not gon' interfere with you doin' you. We don't have a blanket around us out this way so you got to make sure that you safe. I'm 'bout to make a call to see if I can get some coverage on you out this way."

"Dog, that shit don't mean nothin'. I gots this shit! I know how to put in work, nigga! Them niggas got to be moved, G! This money is too fuckin' good to just let go."

"I feel ya and I'm not trippin' wit' you. But I'm still gon' try to cover your ass. You're no good to the squad or yourself if you get knocked from some rah-rah shit. Feel me?"

"Handle your end, dog, 'cause I'm handlin' mine in about three hours," Keko said with a determined look on his face.

"Girl are you sure Trevor's not messing with that girl he was at the club with?" asked Taj.

"I'm positive, why?"

"I just saw them at Penn Square and, girl, they looked like a couple to me. They were testing and buying all kinds of stuff outta the Bath & Body Works store."

"Just 'cause they were shopping together doesn't make them a couple, Taj."

"I know, silly. I'm just saying, they looked real comfortable with each other, ya know, like a couple. She didn't look as good as she did the other night, though."

Shayla laughed. "What was she wearing, Ms. Fashion Police?"

"She had on some baggy-ass jeans with a wife beater. Girl, you could even see that she was wearing a pair of men's boxer shorts! T-a-c-k-y! The only good thing about her outfit was the jeans."

"What can be good about a pair of jeans?"

"The girl was rockin' some jeans that looked like they cost a grip! Shit, I don't even have a pair of 'em bad boys yet and you already know!"

Shayla started laughing and said, "Girl, you are way out there for real. But, look, Marco just came in. Let me call you later."

"All righty, then, holla," Taj said as she hung up the phone.

By the time Boleg and Cuddy made it to the park they could tell the Bloods were kind of riled up. Boleg told Cuddy, "Watch my back, dog, these niggas look a li'l salty."

"Don't trip, I'll blast all they ass if they even look like they wanna get outta line," Cuddy said as he pulled out his heat: two twin Glocks. He flipped one off the safety position and racked a live round into the chamber. He was ready for whatever.

Boleg climbed out of his Chevy Suburban and calmly approached the small group of gang members. "What it do, my niggas, y'all good or what?"

"Nah, we need to holla, but some shit went down with some of the enemies a few minutes ago. The Ones are gon' be rollin' through any minute. Let's get this shit outta the way real quick," said one of the Bloods, who was obviously the top dog of the group.

"That's cool. Who needs what?"

HK, the head Blood, said, "I got everybody's money, dog. We need like ten zips."

Boleg stepped back to the truck and grabbed the purple Crown Royal bag. He came back to the group, gave HK the bag, and accepted the $6,000 HK gave him. HK emptied the bag in his hand and passed it back to Boleg. Boleg then put the money inside of the bag and said, "Y'all be safe out here, dog."

"You ain't gon' count your ends, G?" asked HK.

"It's right ain't it?"

"Yeah, it's straight."

"I know how y'all get down. I don't think you would try some sucka shit like shortin' a nigga. That's for weak niggas."

HK smiled at the compliment and said, "Ya know that's right, dog. We'll get at y'all when we ready for some more work."

"Fa' sho'," Boleg said as he climbed back into his SUV.

As they were leaving the park Boleg noticed three dudes standing next to an emerald green Chevy Tahoe staring at them real hard as they drove by. "You see 'em niggas, Cuddy?"

"Yep. I peeped them bitch-ass niggas."

"Must be 'em south side niggas Nutta was talkin' 'bout."

"Fuck 'em. If they get outta line they can get whatever," Cuddy said as he relaxed in his seat and fired up a Black & Mild.

King and Tippi were back in his car headed back to the block. Tippi was sitting silently listening to King's conversation with Charlie. "Yeah, I need to see you as soon as possible."

"Is there something wrong?" asked Charlie.

"Kinda, sort of, in a way," replied King.

Charlie laughed. "Where are you?"

"About to get off of the Forty, headed north."

"Okay, meet me in the parking lot of the Homeland grocery store on Twenty-third and MLK."

"I'm not alone, Charlie. Tippi's with me."

"That's fine. You'll see my car parked in front of the liquor store right next to Homeland. Come and join me and tell me about your problems."

"I'll be there in less than ten minutes."

"Good, 'cause I'm here already," Charlie said as the line went dead.

When King pulled into the parking lot of the grocery store he parked his car several cars back from where Charlie's car was parked. He got out and casually strolled toward Charlie's vehicle. Once he was inside of the car he said, "What up, Charlie?"

"I guess that's what I should be asking you, Mr. King. You're the one who seems to have the problem."

"It's not really a problem yet, but then again it could definitely become one."

"Please explain."

"A member of my squad has made some aggressive moves out in Del City. It's been very profitable for us all out that way, but now there's some other niggas tryin' to compete around my people's way. Before I let my man handle the situation I wanted to know if you could wrap that blanket you got on the north side around my mans out in Del City?"

"Del City? I thought you were solely working the north side, King."

"I do, but my man saw somethin' he liked out that way so I gave him the green light to do him."

"Has it been prosperous?"

"Definitely. And it's only going to get better from what I can tell."

"Do you expect a lot of violence from your man?"

"It depends on what you mean by a lot, Charlie. My man gon' do what he feel he has to. Once he moves the crowd, everything should go back to normal."

"What about retaliation?"

King laughed and said, "When the squad puts it down it's very unlikely that there will be any retaliation, Charlie."

"King, still confident as ever, I see." Charlie chuckled.

"Always."

"Violence—or, should I say, war—is never good for business, but in most cases it is necessary. I understand that fact. I want you to understand that I can have you protected in Del City with a phone call. But before I make that call I need your assurance that you will keep the violence to a minimum."

"I can only assure you that my man's moves will be swift and hard, Charlie. This shit is too unpredictable for me to put my stamp on it any more than that. My man will handle up. After that, everything should be everything. Like I said, there won't be any retaliation or any shit like a comeback. The shit will be dealt with."

"Fine. It's done, you're protected. Is there anything else I can do for you, Mr. King?"

"I need to get with you in a day or two for some more work. I'm down to my last twenty birds of the yay. I'm also gon' need some more bud; that's movin' faster than normal all of a sudden. I'm cool on everything else right now."

"Will Friday be sufficient?"

"Yeah, that's cool."

"I'll call you on Friday at noon. Be ready."

"Fa' sho'," King said as he climbed out of Charlie's car. Charlie watched as he went back to his vehicle and left the parking lot.

"Be careful, King. You're playing a very dangerous game now," Charlie said aloud.

Chapter Twelve

Flamboyant and Shayla were enjoying a very romantic evening together. Shayla went all out to ensure that their evening would be perfect. She made a layered lasagna, along with some baseball-size Italian meatballs. After eating her Caesar salad she served her man the main course. She knew how much Flamboyant loved her lasagna; that's why she chose to have an Italian meal this special evening. It was special to her because she was determined to get her mind and heart back on track. She loved Flamboyant and she didn't want to be the one to screw up their relationship. She was not about to let her past interfere with her future.

Shayla smiled as she poured Flamboyant some merlot. *Everything is just perfect.* Flamboyant sipped his drink and said, "Mmm, this is the perfect touch for this meal, baby. You need to let me buy you an Italian spot so you can sell this good-ass lasagna, for real! You'd straight make a killin'."

"Stop playing, Marco. You can't open up an Italian restaurant and just sell lasagna. That's crazy."

"Not really. All we'd have to say is that our Italian spot only served lasagna. That would be your specialty. We could call it the Lasagna Spot."

She shook her head and said, "Sometimes I really think you be letting this money interfere with your common sense. You are too crazy!"

"Baby, all I'm sayin' is, it's all 'bout you. Ain't nothin' wrong with a man havin' confidence in his woman's abilities. That's all I'm doin' here, baby. I love you and want to do whatever it takes to make sure that you are happy and will always remain that way."

"I'm happy with you, Marco, because I love you just as much as you love me. You make me happy in more ways than I can even put into words, but wanting to buy me a restaurant is going a tad too far, baby." They laughed as they continued their meal. When Shayla heard Flamboyant's cell ringing back in the bedroom she said, "Marco, let that go to voice mail, please."

He checked his watch, shook his head no, and said, "Can't, babe, this has to be important if someone is calling me at this time. Excuse me real quick. I'll be right back." He got up from the table, went into the bedroom, and answered his cell just before it rolled over to his voice mail. "What's up, Prince?"

"Dog, we got problems out in Del City."

"What happened?"

"It's Gunna and his niggas."

"Shit, did they get cracked?"

"You're askin' questions I can't answer, G, at least not on this line. We need to meet like right now."

"Fuck! This shit can't wait 'til the morning?"

"You obviously didn't understand what I said. We need to meet now, Flam!"

He sighed heavily. "I'll be outside your pad in fifteen." He grabbed his car keys off the dresser, prepared himself for Shayla's wrath, and went back into the dining room. Before she could go off he said, "Something serious has happened to Gunna and his team, babe. I got to go check on this shit real quick."

"Why can't Prince take care of whatever is going on, Marco? We're in the middle of our meal."

"I know, babe, you already know if it were something that Prince could handle alone I wouldn't even be thinking about leavin' this hell of a meal you made for me. Like I said, it's something serious. I'll be back as soon as I can, 'kay?"

"No, it's not okay, Marco. I went out of my fucking way to make sure that we had a very special evening and you and your damn dope dealing has fucked it up! Go on and do whatever the fuck it is that you have to go do!" She stormed from the table, went into the bedroom, and slammed the door, yelling, "I'm sick of this shit! Sick of it!"

He started to follow her but thought better of it. *I'll make it up to her when I get back.*

When Flamboyant made it to Prince's home he saw Ken's Navigator parked in the driveway, so that meant that Wave was inside of the house, too. *Something real fucked up has gone down,* he thought as he knocked on the door.

Prince opened the door with a grim look on his face. "Come on in, Flam," Prince said as he stepped aside.

Just like he thought, Wave was sitting down next to Ken and both of them had the same grim look on their faces as Prince. "A'ight, what the fuck happened to Gunna?" Flamboyant asked as he sat down next to Wave on the sofa.

"Some crazy mothafuckas ran up in the Candlewoods and dropped like seven mothafuckas. Two of Gunna's people are outta there and the other five people who got hit were crackheads," Prince said from the other side of the room.

"Where's Gunna?"

"He went out to Midwest City to get with Milo and his peoples. That nigga is on the warpath, dog. The only reason he didn't get got was because he was across the highway at 7-Eleven gettin' him something to drink."

"Does he know who did this shit?"

"That's the fucked-up part, dog. He doesn't know exactly who 'em niggas are who done this shit, but he knows where they came from."

"Explain."

"Like I told you, he was across the highway gettin' him somethin' to drink at the 7-Eleven. When he was goin' inside of the store he saw four black trucks, 'Burbans I think, pull out of 'em apartments. He told me that by the time he came outta the store he heard all of the fuckin' shootin' goin' on over at the Candlewoods. By the time he jumped into his shit and got back to the apartments he saw those same four black trucks punchin' it away from the apartments."

"So, some of them Del City niggas did this shit?"

"That's what it looks like, Flam. And that nigga Gunna is ready to take it to they ass like right now."

"As soon as he calls and lets us know that's he's ready I'm rollin' right along with his ass, my nigga, real talk!" said Wave.

"Me too," added Ken.

Flamboyant shook his head and said, "Y'all are trippin' the fuck out. Didn't you tell me that there are seven bodies over that way?"

"Yeah, and?" asked Ken.

"And? And that means that the fuckin' police are all over that fuckin' place right now. Ain't no way in hell y'all are goin' to be able to move on 'em fools tonight. Hell, you might not be able to make a move on 'em niggas this month! That spot is gonna be hot as hell. Think, niggas; don't go out there all cock fuckin' diesel and get your fuckin' selves cracked. What good will y'all be to the team then? Get that nigga Gunna on the phone and tell him that I said to get his ass over here. And make sure that you tell him to leave Milo and his people right where they are."

"I'm tellin' you, G, that nigga ain't gon' be tryin' to hear that shit," said Wave.

"I don't give a fuck what he's tryin' to hear! Call his ass, Prince!"

"So, how are we gon' play this shit, Flam?" asked Ken.

"Right now, I don't have a fuckin' clue. But I do know we're goin' to wait 'til we can come up with a proper way to destroy them niggas who did this punk shit," Flamboyant said as he sat back down on the sofa.

It took close to an hour before Gunna finally arrived at Prince's house. As soon as he came inside of the house Flamboyant saw the look on his face and said, "I know you hurtin', my nigga, but you gon' have to suck this shit up before you get yourself caught up. We got to think before we move on this shit."

"I know, Flam, I know. But we have to move on 'em niggas, dog. We got to hit 'em fools real hard. I don't want them bitch-ass niggas to think they got away with a gotdamn thang!" Gunna yelled angrily.

"I feel ya, dog, and I give you my word we will. Nobody gets away with doin' shit like this to us. But for now I need you to go get at your nigga's people and make sure they know that everything will be taken care of as far as funeral expenses and whatnot. Let them know no amount is too much; whatever they want, they will have." Flamboyant paused and stared at the members of his team for a few seconds before he continued. "This is an ugly situation that's only going to get uglier. We will come out on top though, my word."

"How long do you think we gon' have to wait?" asked Wave.

Flamboyant frowned and said, "As long as it takes for this shit to cool the fuck down. I gotta make some calls in the morning to make sure that our ass is covered out in Del City. 'Em niggas obviously got more nuts than you thought they did, Gunna."

"Yeah, I know, and that fact alone is what's killin' me, dog. I should have run a better check on my surroundings. I didn't, and for that mistake I lost two thorough niggas. I swear on everything that I've ever loved in this crazy-ass life of mines, 'em niggas gon' pay for this shit. I lost two niggas; they gots to lose ten times as many."

Shayla pulled out of the garage and sped off down the street. She didn't have any particular destination in mind, she didn't know where she was going, she just knew where she didn't want to be. And that was nowhere near Flamboyant. Even though she knew what she was about to do was wrong, Shayla let her anger control her actions. She grabbed her cell phone and dialed King's number as she drove toward the north side of town. When King answered she asked, "Can you meet me somewhere so we can talk, Trevor? It's kinda important."

King was smiling from ear to ear when he answered, "Anytime, anyplace, Shay, you know that."

"Take that damn smile off your face, boy, and meet me at that little park on Sixty-third."

"The one down the street from Broadway Extension?"

"Um hmm."

"How long will it take you to get there? 'Cause I can be there in less than five."

"Well, get to movin' then 'cause I'm on the Broadway Extension now. I just passed Twenty-third Street exit."

"I'll see you in a minute then," he said then hung up the phone.

As nervous as Shayla was she was still excited about meeting up with King. *I have to see if what I'm feeling is real or if I'm just tripping.* After making a right turn onto Sixty-third Street, she drove a couple of blocks and turned into the park. By the time she parked she saw a dark-colored car pull into the park and pull right beside her. "Okay, you wanted this; now you got it," she said aloud as she got out of her car.

King smiled as he climbed out of his Magnum looking thuggish as ever, sporting a pair of saggy jeans with a wife beater and Tims on. *Damn, she looks good,* he thought as he strolled casually toward her. Shayla smiled shyly as she stared at her ex. "What's good, Shay?" he asked as he leaned on the front of his car.

Even though it was dark in the park the streetlights seemed to have a direct aim at the jewelry that King was wearing. It seemed as if the lights made all of the diamonds he had on glisten even more than they normally did. She inhaled deeply and said, "Nothing much, Trevor. Come on, let's walk," she said and led him away from their cars. She made him follow her to the sandbox and swing area of the park. She sat in a swing and said, "I really shouldn't be doing this."

"Doin' what?" he asked as he sat down on the swing next to hers.

"Meeting you like this. This is wrong."

"If it's so wrong then why are you here, Shay?" Before she could answer his question he said, "Look, I know you got a man and all of that, but you can't deny the fact that there's still some love for me left in that sweet heart of yours. Fuck, I feel exactly the same way. Time has kept us apart but our hearts still feel the same as they did back in the day."

Shaking her head no, she said, "Time didn't keep us apart, Trevor, you did. I can't believe you did me dirty like that."

"Come on with that shit, Shay. I was lookin' out for the both of us for real. I didn't want you to be out here havin' to wait on a nigga. That shit wouldn't have been right. Like I told you before, I was bein' selfish, too. I wouldn't have been able to take it if you started out ridin' with a nigga and then shook me after a while. That shit would have killed me. Real talk. Lookin' back now, though, I wish I would have at least tried."

"Okay, I understand your reasons, but why didn't you get in contact with me when you got out?"

"I was only out twelve days, Shay."

"Twelve days? What did you do in twelve days to get sent back to prison?"

"Some stupid shit. I never reported to my parole officer. I went straight to the north and startin' gettin' my serve on again. You know I was on that paper chase for real. I didn't want to come get at you without bein' able to take care of you properly."

She put up her hand and said, "Uh-uh, don't even try that shit. You know damn well that money don't have anything to do with how I felt about you, Trevor."

He smiled and said, "Yeah, I know. You know how I am. I had to get my money right. Before I could make that happen I got violated and sent back to the pen for another two years."

"Two years for a violation? Man, they socked it to you for something that trivial?"

"Not really; they gave me a year for the violation. While I was down I kept fuckin' up, gettin' into it with niggas. You know how 'em gangbangin' niggas be tryin' to act all hard and shit. Since I wasn't down with no particular set them niggas thought they could get at the King. And you know I wasn't havin' any of that shit."

"Um hm. So, you were only out for twelve days and you couldn't give a sista a call. But you were out long enough to stick your thingy inside of that tramp Lawanda? Not only did you have a baby by that slut, you had the nerve to have two! Uh-uh, I should be forever mad at your ass for that fact alone."

"I ain't even gon' try to play you, Shay. I fucked up on that for real. I let her get to me and fell for the ol' okey-doke like a sucka. When I was in the pen and she told me that she was pregnant, I was like, by who? When she said she was pregnant by me, I was like, get the fuck out of here! But seven months later when she brought my daughter to see me I knew she was mine as soon as I saw her pretty brown eyes. She's my heart, Shay, for real."

"What's her name?"

"Tandy," he said proudly.

"How old is she?"

"She turns seven in November."

"Okay, so when you got out after doing the two years why didn't you get in contact with me then?"

"Same reason: I had to get my money right. I went back to hustlin' and doin' me around the north. Shit was comin' along slowly but I was makin' some progress. Then I met some people and thangs popped off for me in a major way."

"I bet, 'cause then you went and had another child by loose drawers," Shayla said sarcastically.

He started laughing and said, "Yeah, I fell for the same shit twice." Making his voice sound like a female he said, "'I'm on the pill, King. You ain't got to worry, nigga. I ain't gettin' pregnant by your ass again.'"

"But she did."

"Yep. She gave me a son."

"How old is he?"

"He turns five in March."

"What's his name?"

King smiled and said, "Trevor."

"How sweet," she said as she got off of the swing. "Let's take a walk while I try to digest all of this information."

"Shay, you—"

She turned and faced him, put her index finger to his lips, and said, "Shhhh, let me think for a minute. Come on," she said as she pulled him out of his swing. He smiled and followed her.

It was close to midnight when Flamboyant made it back home. He was hoping and praying that Shayla was sound asleep when he came home because he wasn't in the mood to hear her bitching at him. When he pulled into the garage and saw that her car wasn't there he said, "Aww, shit, she's really mad." He went inside of the house and everything was as it was when he left a few hours ago. Shayla didn't even clear off the dining room table.

After clearing off the table and putting away what was left of their food, he went and took a shower. After he finished he climbed into the bed and grabbed the phone to give Shayla a call. When she answered the phone he could hear cars as they passed wherever she was. "When you comin' home, babe?"

"When I feel like it, Marco."

"Come on, you know when I get business calls I have to be on deck at all times. Don't be like this, babe; come on back home."

"I'll be there when I get there! Bye, Marco!" she yelled as she hung up the phone.

"Fuck it. Do you, crazy girl," he mumbled as he set the cordless phone back on its base. Fifteen minutes after his head hit the pillow he was sound asleep.

After she had hung up the phone on Flamboyant, Shayla turned to King and said, "Don't you say a thing either, mister."

He smiled and did as he was told. Before either of them could speak he got a call on his cell. "Excuse me real quick," King said he answered the call. "What it do, Tippi?"

"Your boy handled his BI."

"Yeah? How bad is it?"

"Pretty bad actually. To be honest, I'm kind of proud of ol' boy."

"Where he at?"

"Back on this side of the north."

"Call him and tell him I said to stay on the low-low until I can get with him and see what's what."

"A'ight. Where you at?"

"Takin' care of some shit. I'll get with ya later," he said quickly and ended the call. He turned toward Shayla and said, "Look, I gots to go. Some shit went down and I have to make sure that my peoples are straight. Can we do lunch or something tomorrow?"

"For what?"

"So we can finish what we started."

Shayla smiled and asked, "And exactly what have we started, Trevor?"

"I hope some sort of reconciliation."

"I still got a man, Trevor. I can't just up and leave him."

"Lunch. Tomorrow. Your choice. What time?"

She always did love it when he took control of a situation. That used to turn her on, as it was doing at that very moment. With a loud sigh she said, "The Outback in Edmond. I'll meet you there at noon."

He smiled confidently and said, "See ya then, Shay. Now, come on, let's raise up outta this cold-ass park."

Chapter Thirteen

By eight o'clock King was on the block waiting for Tippi to arrive. It was a chilly morning so he decided to wait inside of the main trap. Flex was busy inside of the dining room counting the money that was made the night before. Two more of King's young hand-to-hand men were sleeping soundly on the couch and loveseat in the living room. King stepped into the dining room and asked Flex, "How did y'all do last night?"

"Around the same. 'Em young niggas don't be playin' when it comes to servin' them rocks. If it gets slow on the block they take that shit on the road and go get theirs for real. They dumped close to half a brick between the two of them, and that was all rock for rock."

"Yeah? No weight at all?" King asked, impressed by his young squad members.

"Yeah, they dumped some weight too, about a bird and a half. They gettin' that money, dog."

"That's right. When they get up tell 'em I said to take a night off and chill and enjoy themselves. They earned that."

"Right," Flex said as he put the last of the money he counted inside of a duffel bag and set it on the floor next to his feet.

"So, how's your thang comin'?"

"It's gettin' better and better every day. I'm tellin' you, that white broad has hooked me into some heavyweight crackas. They be snortin' that shit so damn fast that it don't make no sense. And they some crazy crackas, too."

"What you mean?"

Flex started laughing and said, "Man, they get all coked up and start gettin' on some freaky-ass shit. I mean, I sat there and watched them freak with ol' girl for over an hour. Puttin' line after line all over that broad and snortin' off of her and lickin' her ass and all kinds of freak shit."

King shook his head from side to side and said, "'Em some nasty-ass white people."

"I don't give a damn. As long as they keep spendin' 'em chips I'm good."

"I feel ya." King checked his Cartier and said, "Damn, where the fuck is Tippi?"

"Ain't no tellin'. When was the last time you holla'd at her?"

"I called her an hour ago and told her to meet me over here. She should've been here by now—" He was cut off midsentence by Tippi blowing the horn of her H2. King stepped to the front door and saw two black and white police cruisers parked right behind Tippi's truck with their sirens silently flashing. "What the fuck!" he yelled as he stepped outside of the trap.

When Tippi saw King come outside she smiled and climbed out of her truck. She turned and faced one of the four police officers who were walking toward her and said, "I don't know what the problem is, but y'all really need to get the fuck away from me!"

"Could you please step back next to your vehicle, ma'am?" one of the officers said calmly.

Tippi stopped and watched as King came and stood next to her side and asked, "What's the problem, Officer?"

"We've been trying to pull this lady over for over a mile and a half now. She refused to respond to any of our warnings. And for that, she's going to jail, sir. Now, would you please take a step back so we can do our job!"

King turned and faced Tippi and whispered, "What the fuck have you done? You dirty?"

She shook her head no. "Nah, I was in a rush. Hell, I was already late enough as it is. Fuck these clowns!"

King sighed and said, "Shut up." He turned back toward the officer who informed him of Tippi's behavior. "If you could, may I have a word with you, Officer? I give you my word you won't have any problems from her."

"As soon as the lady takes a few steps back toward her vehicle like she was instructed to, then you can have a word with me, sir."

King turned and faced Tippi. "Do what this fool says so I can see if I can get you outta this stupid shit." She did as she was told and frowned as she watched King step toward the police officer. They talked for about ten minutes and then King shook hands with the officer and came back to Tippi's side. "Get your ass in the truck so we can roll," he said as she stepped around to the passenger's side of her H2.

When they were inside of the truck, Tippi asked, "What did you tell 'em fools?"

He smiled and said, "None of your fuckin' business. Now drive; we got to get at Keko and find out exactly what's what with this shit out in Del City."

They arrived at Keko's trap on the northeast side to see Keko sitting on the hood of his old-school Chevy. He smiled when he saw them pull onto his block. King jumped out of the truck and said, "Don't look like your ass is over here sweatin' shit to me. What's good, cra-zy-ass nigga?"

Keko shrugged his slim shoulders and said, "Same old shit, G. You know I ain't gon' let somethin' like a li'l work bein' put in stop me from doin' me."

"That's right. So, what's the deal out there? Is it still poppin' or what?"

"Nah, I had to shut that bitch down; the spot is way too hot right now. Don't trip, though. I'll have that bitch back up and runnin' by the end of the week," Keko said confidently.

"What makes you think you'll be able to get it right back crackin'?" asked Tippi.

"Trust, Keko knows what he's doin', li'l lady," he said as he lit a Newport.

"Fuck you."

They laughed and then King said, "Look, I don't want this shit to turn into more than it has to. When you get back out that way make sure you handle that shit right."

"Don't sweat it, dog, I will."

"What if 'em fools get it back on and poppin'? Then what yo' ass gon' do?" asked Tippi.

Keko stared at the both of them for a few seconds before responding. "Whatever it takes to maintain my spot. If they think about openin' back up then they'll have to get served again. If I have to put another demo down it will be way worse than the first one."

"I hope it won't come to that, I don't know how long I'll be able to keep a blanket on your ass with all of this gunplay. So try to chill the fuck out, my nigga," said King.

"I got ya, dog. But, look, Del City ain't the only spot crackin' in this fuckin' town. I need some more wiz for my shit out this way. Spook mad at a nigga 'cause he thinks I've deserted his ass. I gots to make sure that we're stocked nice for the weekend. 'Em young gangstas been spendin' more and more lately. So I'm gon' need more ya-yo than usual. As for the X and that water, keep it the same."

"You got some chips for me?"

"Do I? You better fuckin' believe it!" Keko said as he stepped to the back of his Impala and popped the trunk. He pulled out two duffel bags full of money and gave one to Tippi and King. "That's everything right there. I took care of my people over this way as well as my niggas who put in that work with me."

"Cool. A'ight then, my nigga, we're out. Keep me informed on that shit in Del City, Keko."

"Gotcha." As he watched King and Tippi walk back toward Tippi's H2 Keko yelled, "Hey, Tippi!"

Tippi stopped, turned and faced his direction, and said, "What, nigga?"

"Did the work I put in impress your wild side?"

Tippi started laughing and said, "Fuck you, Keko!"

Keko laughed too and said, "You wish!"

When Tippi and King made it back to the block King told her, "Go get them chips from Flex and meet me at my pad at two."

"At two? What you 'bout to get into?" Tippi asked as she climbed out of the H2.

"I got a meetin'."

"With Charlie?"

He frowned and asked, "What's with all these fuckin' questions? I'll meet you at my spot at two. We got to get all of the ends counted and stacked."

"A'ight, I'll get wit' you in a li'l while," Tippi said as she started walking toward the trap. Before she made it to the porch her cell phone rang. "What it do?"

"We got a problem out here in Midwest City," said Boleg.

"Hold on," she said as she took her phone away from her ear and called out to King, who was just about to get into his car. "Hey, King! Come here real quick!" She turned and went back to him. "You might want to hear what Boleg got to talk 'bout," she said as she gave him her phone.

King took the phone and said, "What's poppin', dog?"

"Some niggas from the south side got at Nutta in the wee-wee hours."

"What? Is he a'ight?"

"Yeah, he straight, just mad as hell. He peeped 'em comin' and was able to shake the spot before they could do him any damage. But peep this, he heard one of them Blood niggas from the Murda One say something 'bout how 'em south side niggas' spot got shot up out in Del City."

"South side? Yeah? Where you at right now?"

"Me and Cuddy are on our way over to Nutta's spot."

"Me and Tippi will meet y'all there in about fifteen."

"Cool," Boleg said as he hung up the phone.

King told Tippi, "Go get 'em chips from Flex and put 'em in your shit. Some shit has happened to Nutta. We got to go check on him at his spot." Tippi didn't respond; she did as she was told. King got in his car. He checked the time and saw that it was a little after eleven. "Fuck!" he yelled as he grabbed his cell and dialed Shayla's number. When she answered the phone he took a deep breath and said, "What's up, Shay?"

Shayla didn't like the sound in his voice one bit. She knew him too well; something was wrong. "You're not going to be able to make it for lunch, are you, Trevor?"

"Nah, baby. I got to check on somebody real quick. After I make sure everything is good with my man I'll hit you up and we'll do lunch. Cool?"

Shaking her head no as if he was right beside her she said, "No, it's not cool. This whole thing is wrong and this proves it. It's not meant for us, Trevor. Take care of yourself," she said then hung up the phone on him before he could say something to change her mind.

King sat there for a minute and stared at his phone. "Fuck!" he yelled again just as Tippi came and got inside of the car.

"What happened to Nutta?" she asked as she strapped on her seat belt.

"Some south side niggas tried to get at him out in Midwest City early this morning."

"Did he get hurt?" Tippi asked as she felt herself starting to get angry. Very angry.

"Nah. Boleg said Nutta saw them comin'. Before they could get him he shook the spot. What's fuckin' wit' me is that Nutta heard one of 'em Blood niggas say some shit about the south side niggas gettin' shot up out in Del City last night."

"I thought 'em was some Del City niggas' spot."

"I did too," King said as he started the car and pulled away from the curb.

They saw Boleg's Suburban parked next to Nutta's Dodge Nitro in Nutta's apartment building. King parked and they quickly got out of the car and went to go check on the youngest member of the squad.

Nutta opened the door to his home and said, "What's good, King? What up, Tippi?" He turned and they followed him inside of the apartment.

King saw Boleg and Cuddy sitting down on the sofa and said, "A'ight, explain to me what the fuck happened, Nutta."

Nutta sat his thin frame down next to Cuddy and said, "I was out there gettin' my late night on and I heard one of them Blood niggas talkin' 'bout how his cousins from the south side spot got blasted out in Del City. That raised my radar 'cause Boleg told me about Keko's mission. Anyway, 'em fools was bumpin' they gums and shit talkin' 'bout how 'em south side niggas are plugged real heavy with the work and shit. I wasn't trippin' off that shit until I heard them say something 'bout how they tryin' to get money out they way too. I peeped 'em niggas earlier before I left to go get some rest."

"Yeah, we saw them niggas when we rolled through after you left," said Cuddy.

"I was strapped so I wasn't trippin' too much. But when I heard that nigga say somethin' 'bout how the south side niggas are hot and might start trippin' I decided to get the fuck on. I had a zip sale around the corner so I was like, I'm gon' go on and dump this ounce and call it a night. I gets in my shit and roll around the block. When I get there I see 'em south side niggas parked across the street. I don't pay 'em too much attention as I climb outta my shit and go into the spot to make that zip sale. When I come out, one of 'em niggas asked me where I'm from. I thought they was on some bangin' shit, so I said, 'I don't bang. I'm from the north side, though.' They like, 'This the south side, nigga!' I don't give 'em a chance to make a move. I pull out heat and stare them down as I climb back in my shit and shake the spot."

"You think they was gon' try?" asked Tippi.

Nutta nodded. "You fuckin' right! I could see it in they eyes; they was lookin' for some drama. Probably 'cause they people got served out in Del City. I don't know. I wasn't 'bout to get fucked up tryin' to find out, though."

"I know that's right, my nigga. Y'all gon' have to fall back off that Midwest City blast 'til we can check into this shit further," King said as he pulled out his cell and called Keko. When Keko answered the phone King told him, "Dog, I need you to come over to Nutta's pad. We need to talk."

"I was just 'bout to hit you. This shit done got a li'l flipped. 'Em niggas ain't from Del City; they from the south side," said Keko.

"Yeah, I know."

"Yeah? But did you know that they're supposed to be plugged with some nigga they call Flamboyant? He's supposed to be high powered or some shit. From what

I've learned he's just as strong on the south as you are on the north."

"Is that right?"

"Yep. So, you know what that means, huh?"

"Yeah, looks like we're about to go to war. Get over here, dog. We got a lot to discuss."

"I'm on my way," Keko said as he ended the call.

King turned toward Tippi and said, "Call Flex and tell him he needs to get here as soon as possible."

"What's up?" asked Tippi.

King sighed and said, "The niggas Keko got at belong to some nigga from the south who's supposed to have some weight behind his name. We might have to prepare for war."

"Might?" asked Tippi.

"That's what I said. We can't rush into this shit and get caught the fuck up. We still got a business to run. Money before bullshit. You know how I get down."

"Yeah, I know how you get down, but you know how I get down too. If it's time for war let me do me. You worry 'bout the business and I'll handle everything else," Tippi said in a deadly tone. She switched to kill mode and that meant a lot of people's lives were in jeopardy.

Chapter Fourteen

Flamboyant was sitting at the table waiting for Toni to arrive. This meeting was going to be very important. He had to make sure that he had protection for his people out in Del City. There was no way in hell he could let something happen to any of his team members without some form of retaliation. But before he got violent he had to make sure Toni would back his play. As he sat and sipped on a flute of Krug, he thought about how mad Gunna and Wave were. *I won't be able to contain those two fools much longer,* he thought as he sipped some more champagne.

Toni strolled into the restaurant and joined Flamboyant at his table. "How are you doing today, Mr. Flamboyant?"

"I'm good, and yourself?"

"As long as I wake up every morning I know I'm in the best possible position. I'm very proud to say that I am blessed. Now, what's with this emergency meeting?"

"I got a few problems that I might have to deal with violently. I wanted to make sure that you can still protect me and mines before I make my move."

"I assume that this problem is above being resolved peacefully? If I remember correctly, you only resort to violence when it's absolutely necessary."

"Correct. One of my team members lost two good men last night. If I said he was upset that would be putting it mildly. He's ready for war."

"I see. How can I be of service?"

"I've moved a li'l outta the south. This particular move is out in Del City."

"Del City? This problem has something to do with that shooting that happened last night?" asked Toni.

"Yeah. My man Gunna made some moves out that way and was doin' lovely until some of those Del City niggas pulled that bullshit last night."

"And you feel you have to retaliate?"

"Definitely."

"I understand. I can protect you out there. I'll make the arrangements when we're finished here."

"Thanks, Toni."

"It's business, Flamboyant. I understand that some-times these things are going to take place in the game. I don't really like the violent aspect of this but it is what it is. You have to remember that you have to know when and how to distribute violence without letting it interfere with your business. If you don't, then you've let the violence become a liability instead of an asset. I say this because I want you to be careful going into this, Flamboyant. Too much violence will attract the attention of people we don't want looking into our lives."

"Who? The feds?"

"Exactly. My people and I have pretty much free rein with the locals. If the FBI becomes involved that's an entirely different ballgame. So be careful, and always remain in control of this situation."

"I got you, Toni. Good lookin'," he said as he downed the rest of his champagne.

"Now, is there anything else we need to discuss? I have a busy day ahead of me."

"Nah, I'm good for now. I should be gettin' at you within a week or so to get hooked back up."

"No problem. So, until we see each other again, take care of yourself, Mr. Flamboyant."

"You too, Toni," Flamboyant said with his normal cocky smile on his face.

"I'm telling you, girl, it was a sign for real. Take it for what it's worth. It's not meant for y'all to get back together," Taj said as she relaxed on Shayla's bed.

"I know, girl, but for a minute there I really felt like it was going to happen again. I was feeling him more and more. It was like Trevor had consumed my every thought. And when Marco pissed me off I was damn near positive that I was about to do something way the fuck out," Shayla said as she sat down on the end of the bed next to her best friend.

"Thank God you didn't do something you would regret."

"You're right. All that nigga had to do was ask me once to go back to his place. If he would have I swear it would have been on and poppin' for real!"

"You mean to tell me that you were actually that mad at Marco?"

"Now that I think about it, I wasn't that mad at him. I was really trying to find a reason to get back with Trevor. I know I still care about him. Hell, I can honestly say that I still love the damn man. The fact remains, though, I'm in love with Marco. Even though he pisses me the fuck off with all of that dope dealing shit, he's my boo and I won't be the one to fuck up our happy home."

"Good for you, girl. I wish nothing but the best for you and Marco. But I want you to be absolutely positive about the decisions you're making."

"I am."

Shaking her head no, Taj said, "I don't think you are." Before Shayla could interrupt Taj continued, "The next time Marco pisses you off, I mean really gets under your skin, are you going to go running out late night to meet Trevor in a park for a talk? And if you do and he does suggest something sexual, are you going to fall weak and go off and fuck him 'cause you mad at your man?"

Shayla was sitting next to her friend, shaking her head no as she listened to Taj speak.

"You're shaking your head, but that's exactly what you did last night. If Trevor wouldn't have called and canceled that lunch date y'all might be somewhere fucking right about now. Look, I'm not trying to check you or anything like that. Like I said, I just want you to be happy, whether it's with Trevor or Marco. You are the only person I'm concerned about here. You get mad at Marco about his drug dealings and whatnot; you act like you forgot what Trevor does. Right now it's like you're giving Trevor all of the slack instead of your man. Remember, I'm looking at the game from the outside, so it's clearer to me, girl. You're like the chess player who's about to miss a crucial move. I see it, but I can't tell you because it's your game. I love you, Shayla, and I know you're a good person. I also know that you don't want to hurt nobody. The only way that's going to happen is if you choose to stay with your man and continue to make the best of y'all's relationship."

"How can you say that, Taj? What about Trevor? I could be hurting him by not seeing him anymore. I could be missing something that's really special by not giving him a chance."

"A few minutes ago you were sitting there telling me that you weren't going to be the one to fuck up y'all's happy home. Now here you are telling me that you could be hurting Trevor by your decisions. In all honesty, you don't know what you want or who you want to be with. For real, I think a part of you wants to have them both."

Shayla smiled sadly and said, "Now wouldn't that be like having the best of both worlds."

***

After meeting with Toni, Flamboyant went back to the south side and met with his team. They were gathered back at Prince's house waiting for their man to give them the green light to go defend their man Gunna. Flamboyant came inside of the house, faced his team, and said, "Gunna, Wave, and Ken, find out what needs to be learned then go handle this shit fast and furious like. I don't need this shit to be lingering after the work's put in. I got y'all protected, but only for so long. If this shit goes on too long then sooner or later them alphabets gon' come into play, then we lose. I'm not tryin' to lose."

Gunna smiled at his man and said, "I got this, my nigga. 'Lose' ain't a word any of us understand, you know that."

"It is what it is! Let's get at them niggas and dead this shit so we can get back to makin' this fuckin' money!" Wave yelled excitedly.

Flamboyant stared at Prince for a few seconds. When Prince gave him a slight nod of his head he smiled and said, "Handle this shit then, my niggas. I'm outta here."

When Flamboyant made it back home he smiled when he saw Taj's Cherokee parked in his driveway. That meant his baby was home. Through all of this drama he was still worried about how upset he had made Shayla. Now that everything was in order all he wanted to do was make up with his girl.

He parked his car in the garage and went inside of the house. He heard Shayla and Taj talking in the bedroom as he entered the house. "Hey, what y'all doin' in there, plannin' my funeral or somethin'?" he joked as he entered the bedroom.

Shayla frowned and said, "I should be, but it looks like I'm going to have to keep on dealing with your ungrateful ass."

Before he could respond Taj said, "Well, boys and girls, that's my cue to skedaddle. Y'all be good. Call me tomorrow and tell me all about how he makes up for his boo-boos, girl."

"I will." Shayla laughed.

Flamboyant walked Taj to the door and asked, "I'm in the dog house big time, huh?"

"It's not as bad as you think. Pay more attention to your girl, Marco. She needs that more than you think."

"Good lookin' out, Taj," he said as he closed the door behind her. He went back into the bedroom to see Shayla lying on the bed. He sat down next to her and asked, "How was your day, babe?"

She shrugged and said, "The same. I went to school and then I hooked up with Taj and we came over here and kicked it. What about you? Did you get all of your business taken care of?"

"Yeah, some foul shit went down but everything is everything for the moment. Look, babe, I know you hate it when I have to get in 'em streets or have to go take care of some business, but that's what I do. That's how we eatin', babe. You know I try my best to not let that street life interfere with our time together, but sometimes that shit is unavoidable. I'd rather be with you twenty-four hours a day, seven days a week if I could, but that shit ain't gon' happen. I've set the bar way up, babe, so in order for us to continue to maintain this type of lifestyle I've got to stay on top of everything at all times."

"I understand, Marco, but sometimes I want you to say 'fuck that money for now; I'm trying to be with my girl.' It seems like you can't do that, though. It's like money runs your life. When you don't have any drugs you're making calls, and setting up meetings with that Toni person. When you do have drugs you're making sure that Prince, Milo, Wave, Gunna, and Ken are, as you like to say, 'properly stocked.' While they're making the money you still find ways to be involved in everything except for me. That shit has really started to bother me. I love you and I know you love me, but you're going to have to find some ways other than buying me shit to show me and make me feel wanted. Show me that I'm special to you. Show me that I mean more to you than that money. Show me that it's all about me sometimes and not all about the flossing and that money!"

The pain and sincerity in her voice damn near broke him down. He slid next to her and said, "I won't lie to you and say that I'm gon' make everything better in a day, babe, but I will promise you that I'll try my very best to pay more attention to you and your needs. Believe me, I love you more than anything in this world, Shayla. I'd kill for you; I'd die for you. I won't lose you over some stupid shit. You're right, I'm that nigga so I can run shit my way and not let the streets run me. From this point on I'm going to do just that, but there will be times when I will have to go make some moves. Times when we might have something planned. That is a part of the game, babe; it's unpredictable. Gunna lost two of his peoples. Some niggas came and shot up his spot out in Del City. Shit like that ain't a part of our day-to-day operations, babe, you know what I'm sayin'? Shit like that gots to be handled with the quickness."

"I understand, Marco, and I would never purposely or selfishly get in the way of you taking care of your business. It's when it becomes excessive that fucks with me. Your people don't be getting shot every day, do they?"

He laughed and said, "Nah, but I feel ya. From this moment on shit's about to change."

She smiled lovingly at her man and asked, "You promise?"

He returned her smile and said, "Promise."

***

When Toni arrived at Charlie's home, Charlie was sitting down, watching television. "How was your meeting with your man Flamboyant?" Charlie asked as Toni sat down and got comfortable.

"Everything is good, I guess."

"You guess?"

"Yeah. Remember when you told me about King asking you for some extra protection?"

"Yeah, out in Del City. Why?"

"Flamboyant just asked me for the same thing. Seems like that shooting that happened out there last night has something to do with the both of them."

Charlie stared at Toni for a minute and said, "Maybe it's a coincidence."

"Come on with that shit. You don't believe that shit and neither do I. I think we're going to have to pay a li'l more attention to our ponds, Charlie," Toni said seriously.

"I agree. We can't let them fuck thangs up for us. Them *chicos* would shit out all them damn beans they be eating if this money slowed up."

"The question is, how long are we going to control this situation?"

"I'll get at King in the morning and set up a meeting. After I've finished feeling him out I'll figure out how we'll deal with this mess."

"Do you really think it'll be that easy?"

Charlie smiled. "Nothing is ever easy. We have two of the most money-gettin' niggas in this state on our line. They're dependent on us. If we don't supply them with what they need, they don't eat. Don't forget, we're the ones runnin' this shit, not them."

"I know, I'm just sayin'."

"Relax and let me take care of this. I'll get at you after I've gotten at King."

Toni stood up and said, "Yeah, you do that. In the meantime, I'm keeping everything strictly business as usual."

Charlie smiled at Toni again and said, "I wouldn't expect anything different."

Chapter Fifteen

Though it had only been a couple of weeks since the incident in Del City, Keko felt it was necessary for him to get things right back poppin' at the Summit apartment complex. His motto was "there is money to be made." King was against Keko making his move so quickly, but he chose to keep his mouth closed and sit back to watch what would go down. Everywhere else on the north side was business as usual. The money was coming in and everyone was eating good. *Flex seems to be eating exceptionally well,* King thought as he watched as Flex pulled onto the block in a brand new Lincoln Navigator.

"Look at that nigga, big old flossin' like he the shit," Tippi said as she stared at Flex as he climbed out of his new SUV and came and joined them on the porch of the trap.

"What it do? Y'all good?" Flex asked as he sat down on the third step of the porch.

"Yeah, we straight. What's up wit' you?" asked King.

Flex shrugged and said, "Same ol' shit, just tryin' to eat like everybody else."

"Looks like to me you eatin' way better than everybody else," Tippi said sarcastically, staring at Flex's new truck. "What happened to your other Navi?"

"Man, that shit was two years old. It's that time I had to come new. I got this plug with this cracka who gets powder from me. He owns a spot out in Bethany and he hooked me up with that bad boy. He even has the plug with a finance company, so it's like all of my paperwork is straight legit. I got a payment book and everything. But you know a nigga ain't payin' no notes; that bad boy is straight paid for," Flex boasted.

"Good for you, nigga," Tippi said as she stood and stepped off of the porch.

Flex waited until she was out of earshot and asked, "Damn, dog, why she hatin' on a nigga?"

"Don't pay her no mind; you know how she gets at times. Tell me, thangs done got that better wit' your white girl, huh?" King asked as he relaxed back in the chair.

"Yeah, they been spendin' like a mothafucka, dog. She done got 'em crackas turned on to that pipe now. They startin' to smoke like crazy! In a minute I'm gon' be able to go through a whole brick just fuckin' wit 'em!"

"That's straight, but make sure you don't get too comfortable with 'em mothafuckas. Anything can happen when you fuckin' wit' fools who fucks wit' that hard. Don't take shit for granted, feel me?"

"Got ya. I'm 'bout to head back out that way. I'll be back this way for the late-night hype. Cool?"

"Yeah. Be safe, fool."

"Fa' sho'," Flex said as he left the porch and got back into his brand new Navigator and sped off the block.

Tippi came back to the porch and said, "I don't give a damn what he say; that nigga needs to be kept on a short leash, King."

"Why?"

Tippi tapped her stomach lightly and said, "I can feel it in my gut."

He laughed and said, "Don't trip. He's doin' him right now. As long as he keeps the ends comin' ain't no need to be mad at him."

"Mad at him? I ain't mad at his ass. I don't trust that nigga like I used to. He's up to more than he's tellin' yo' ass."

"Maybe, but as long as he doesn't come short wit' 'em chips or crosses me, let that nigga be."

"Oh, I ain't trippin', 'cause sooner or later that nigga gon' show his hand. Then I'm gon' be right there. Dead on his ass."

King smiled at his number one killa and said, "You need a role model."

Tippi laughed and said, "Nah, I need some dick."

Before King could respond to her statement his cell phone rang. "What it do, Charlie?"

"We need to get together. I have some things I want to discuss with you. Meet me at that Chili's out on Northwest Expressway in thirty," Charlie said and hung up the phone.

King stared at his phone for a few seconds then shrugged his shoulders. Tippi noticed his strange look and asked, "What's wrong with you?"

"That was Charlie. That fool has never came at me on no order type shit. All of a sudden it seems like there's been a change in the program."

"What you mean?"

"Nothin'. Look, I got to go get wit' Charlie. I'll be back in a li'l while. You good?"

"Always. Be careful, nigga."

He smiled at Tippi and said, "Always."

Charlie was sitting in the back of the restaurant when King entered Chili's. He saw Charlie and quickly stepped toward the rear of the restaurant and joined Charlie.

After King was seated, Charlie asked him, "Are you hungry?"

"Nah, I'm good. What's poppin'?

"That's exactly what I wanted to ask you." Charlie saw the confused expression on his face and said, "It seems like there's a problem out in Del City that you need to tell me about. An associate of mines has relayed some information to me and I need for you to confirm it for me, King."

"Such as?"

"Did that shooting that took place a couple of weeks ago have anything to do with you asking me for protection in Del City?"

"Yeah."

"Enlighten me, please."

"My nigga Keko opened up a spot in Del City at the Summit apartments. He got it jumpin' off real quick like and the money was lovely and gettin' better and better each day. Some fools on the other side of the Forty decided to open up a spot of their own in the Candlewood apartments. That caused my man's business to slow up a li'l. He wasn't trippin' at first 'cause his shit was still doin' good. But when he heard 'bout 'em fools on the other side droppin' their ticket in order to compete with him, he felt it was necessary to make a move. So he got at me wit' it."

"And you gave him permission to shoot up that apartment complex?"

Shaking his head no, he said, "Nah, not at first. I came and got at you to make sure that you would be able to blanket him if he got into any shit out that way."

"Then you gave him the go-ahead?" Charlie asked with a frown.

"Yeah," he answered sheepishly feeling like a little kid again.

"Do you know who the guys are who were trying to compete with your man?"

"At first I thought they were some Del City niggas, but since then I found out it's some niggas from the south side."

"So, you authorized a hit without knowing anything about the people you ordered to be moved on? I never thought you'd get down like that. Tell me, have you gave any thought about those guys retaliating?"

"Yeah, that's why I had my man back off of Del City for a minute. I wanted shit to die down before I let him go back out that way and get it back poppin'."

"You're not worried about your man gettin' hurt?"

King shrugged and said, "To be totally honest with you, Charlie, nah. Keko knows how to do him. He's no rookie when it comes to the gangsta shit."

"Gangsta shit? Shooting up an apartment building full of crackheads ain't gangsta, King! It's stupid! If I'm not mistaken, seven people were killed that night. That kind of heat ain't cool. When there's violence in the hood behind drugs the local officials catch a lot of heat from higher-up officials. Mainly because the people above them are on top of their asses. If shit don't cool down then the feds get involved. When that happens everything is fucked. Do you hear what I'm saying, King? Because we can't afford to get fucked with by the feds. I need you to be smarter with your decision making. You made a mistake that could become fatal for us all."

"I feel you, Charlie, but damn, neither me or my man can afford to let niggas think they can do what the fuck they want to when it comes to us gettin' this money. You didn't trip out on a nigga when I had Tippi and my mans and 'em smash 'em niggas who was tryin' to get in on my groove on the north side. Or the time when 'em Cali gang niggas came to the north trippin' out like they was gon' take shit over. You let me bust my gun then. You wasn't worried about 'em alphabet boys back then, so why are you trippin' out on me now for handlin' shit like I've always done? I'm holdin' down what's mines, at whatever fuckin' cost. I've kept this money comin' and comin' since you started fuckin' wit' me. I can't let you put restraints on me and how I get down just 'cause there's been a few bodies. That's how this game is played, real talk."

I've created a fucking fool, thought Charlie. "Listen, King, I can't afford for you to be involved in shit that can be avoided. You didn't think this one through clearly enough for my taste. If you had, I feel you would have never given your man the green light to do that shit. What's done is done, though. When are you going to let your man go back out there and open back up?"

King smiled and said, "I let him get back crackin' earlier today. The spot should be fully operational as we speak."

Charlie returned the smile and said, "You're something else, King."

"Nah, I'm just doin' me. My squad trust my judgment just as I trust theirs. I won't fuck this shit up, Charlie. I can't. Too many people are eatin' off of this plate of yours. It's my job to keep that plate full and I'm gon' do that no matter what it takes. I don't give a damn who I gots to lay down in order for us all to continue to eat this damn good."

"Understood. But in the future, before you choose violence of this nature, give it deeper consideration before you go off all cock diesel, a'ight?"

"You got that, Charlie," King said and smiled.

After their meeting concluded, Charlie called Toni and said, "I've just finished gettin' at King. You need to have a sit-down with Flamboyant as soon as possible."

"Why, what's up?"

"I'm pretty confident that those people who got shot up in Del City a couple of weeks ago were his people."

"So, that was his reason for asking me for protection out that way. He's about to retaliate," said Toni.

"Exactly."

"But what does that have to do with your man King?"

Charlie sighed heavily and said, "King's people were the ones who shot up that apartment complex."

"Oh, shit!"

"Exactly."

Tippi was sitting on the porch of the trap watching the block as the squad's hand-to-hand men made that money. It amazed her how automated their moneymaking was. She loved this game. When King pulled back onto the block she could tell that whatever he'd been told at his meeting with Charlie was something good. He had a big smile on his face as he came toward the trap.

"I guess everything is everything, huh?" asked Tippi after he was seated.

"Yeah. Charlie was on some bullshit at first, but after I gave it to that fool raw it was all gravy." King then went on and explained everything that was said during his meeting with Charlie.

When he was finished Tippi said, "Damn. Charlie actually thought a nigga was just gon' let 'em fools get in the way of us gettin' this money?"

"Yeah, but not no more. So it is what it is. Have you heard from that nigga Keko?"

"Nah, that nigga Boleg called and told me that they back out in Midwest City."

"Yeah? What about 'em south side fools?"

Tippi shrugged and said, "He didn't say. He said they were strapped and that they brought along some extra wolves."

"Why is that?"

"He wanted someone up there to watch Nutta's ass after they shook the spot."

"That's right. Damn, I got to piss," King said as he stood and stepped toward the front door of the trap.

Tippi smiled and asked, "You need some help in there with that big old thang?"

He shook his head from side to side but didn't respond to her joke. After he handled his business he was washing his hands when he heard Tippi scream out his name. He ran back to the front and said, "What the fuck are you screamin' for?"

Tippi was holding her cell phone, trembling and shaking her head as she listened to whoever was on the other line. She took a deep breath and in a controlled and deadly tone said, "A'ight, listen: King wit' me now. We'll be over there in a few minutes. Make sure that you keep that nigga under wraps 'til we get there, Spook. Don't let him get caught the fuck up. We on our way," she told him. She turned to King. "South side niggas hit the Summit. Obviously they been waitin' for that nigga Keko to open shop back up. As they were settin' everything up four niggas ran into the apartment complex blastin' everybody and everything in sight."

With a grim look on his face King asked, "How many got hit?"

Tippi shook her head and said, "Only one."

"Who?"

"Keko's wife, Neecy."

"Awww, fuck no! Come on, let's roll!" King yelled as he stepped off of the porch and ran toward his car. The game was about to get real bloody now.

Chapter Sixteen

Flamboyant had dropped Shayla off at home when he got the call from Prince informing him of what Gunna, Milo, Ken, and Wave had done in Del City. "From what Gunna told me, they shot up everybody and everything that was movin', dog. Ain't no tellin' what the body count gon' be. That nigga Gunna gon' have to fall back from out there for a minute," said Prince.

"Oh, that's fa' sho'. Where they at now?" asked Flamboyant.

"They didn't want to take the chance of tryin' to make it all the way back south so they went to Midwest City to Milo's new spot to lay it down for the night."

"That was good thinkin'. Where you at? I'm 'bout to come scoop you so we can go holla at 'em niggas."

"I'm on the block."

"A'ight, I'll be there in twenty," Flamboyant said as he ended the call. He then called Shayla back at the house and told her, "Looks like some shit has come up, babe. I got to go out to Midwest City for a li'l bit. Ain't no need for you to wait up; ain't no tellin' how long I'm goin' to be."

"All right, Marco, be careful. I'm about to take a shower then lie down and watch a li'l TV."

"A'ight, babe. I'll see you when I get home," he said as he ended the call.

After hanging up with Flamboyant, Shayla changed her mind. Instead of taking a shower, she chose to take a nice, long, hot bath. While she was running her bathwater she turned on the television that was mounted right above the Jacuzzi tub. She sat on the edge of the tub and watched as the news reported a story about a shooting in Del City: "In what seems to be a related case, there has been yet another brutal shooting here in the city of Del City. Approximately twenty-five minutes ago, four gunmen ran into the Summit apartment complex and proceeded to shoot several rounds of automatic gunfire. So far there has only been one casualty reported. Neecy Gipson was fatally shot twice in the chest. As you can see behind me, there seems to be quite an uproar from family and friends of Ms. Gipson."

Shayla's mouth was wide open in shock as she stared at the television and continued to listen to the news reporter: "Just two weeks ago there was a similar shooting right on the other side of Highway Forty at the Candlewood apartments. Seven people were shot down by gunmen of this same type. Was this some form of retaliation? Are these two shootings here in Del City related at all? These questions have yet to be answered. This is Bobby Joe Trent, reporting live for Channel Five's *Five Alive*. Back to the studio, Linda."

Shayla continued to stare at the television in complete shock. She saw King crying while holding on to a guy who looked familiar to her. *Probably a guy from the north side.* She put her hands on top of her head and said, "Oooh, what was that boy's name?" She snapped her fingers after a few minutes and yelled, "Keko! That's that Blood boy who used to go to John Marshal." She went into the bedroom and grabbed the cordless phone. She paused for a few seconds then said, "Damn, I almost fucked up." She grabbed her purse and pulled out her cell phone then nervously dialed King's cell phone. When King answered the phone she asked, "Are you all right,

Trevor? I just saw you on the news. What's going on out there?"

"Look, Shay, shit is kinda thick for me right now. My nigga's girl just got killed. Let me get back at ya later, okay?"

"Is that guy Keko okay?"

There were a few seconds of silence before King answered her question. Finally he said, "He's a rider. He'll be good in a li'l while. I got to go. Thanks for checkin' on a nigga, Shay. It's good to know that you still care."

Before she could respond to that statement King hung up the phone. She set her phone down on the bed and started to undress. After she had taken off her clothes, she went and climbed into the warm water of her bath. As she relaxed in the tub she thought about King's last statement to her. *Damn, when I saw Trevor crying like that on TV my heart skipped a thousand beats. I still love that man. Oh, God, I still love him.*

Flamboyant and Prince arrived at Milo's trap in Midwest City to find the mood there quite festive. Gunna was laughing and joking around with Milo, while Ken and Wave were sitting on the other side of the room smoking a blunt, getting very high. Flamboyant stared at the bottles of Moët and Dom P. and said, "You niggas are somethin' else. Y'all act like y'all just won the fuckin' lotto or some shit, instead of puttin' in some work."

Wave shrugged his broad shoulders and said, "It is what it is, dog. Niggas fuck wit' the team they get dealt wit'! We figured since we're holed up here for the night we might as well get bent and kick it."

"I'm surprised y'all ain't got no hoes over here," Prince said as he sat down on the couch next to Gunna.

Wave smiled and said, "We do! They should be here any minute!"

Flamboyant shook his head again and said, "A'ight, then listen: you know that ain't no way in hell you're goin' to be able to go back out to Del City anytime soon. So you might as well get used to doin' your thing back south or out this way with Milo."

"Yeah, I feel you," said Gunna.

"Good. Next, we got to keep our eyes open 'bout this shit to make sure that everything is good. The streets will be talkin'."

"Dog, after the work we put in tonight 'em Del City niggas ain't gon' be tryin' no shit wit' us no more," Milo said confidently.

Prince frowned and said, "Never underestimate, nigga; that's how niggas get done. Even a gangsta-ass nigga like yourself. That spot is gon' be hot and the Ones is gon' be gettin' at snitch niggas, smokers, and everybody around there tryin' to find out who is responsible for all of that chaos."

"Exactly. Like I was sayin', I want y'all to stay on point and make sure that y'all don't be slippin' and shit."

"What you mean by that?" asked Ken.

Flamboyant pointed toward the bottles of liquor as well as the weed on the table and said, "Y'all niggas are gettin' blowed and fucked up tonight. That's cool; I'm not trippin' on that bullshit. What I'm concerned about though is how y'all will be actin' once 'em females arrive. Y'all can't be runnin' your mouths 'bout what was put down. Some stupid shit like that could get us all fucked up."

"Come on wit' that shit, Flam, you know damn well we don't get down like that," Wave said as he took a swig from a bottle of Moët.

Slightly disgusted with his man's arrogance, Flamboyant said, "I hope not." He turned toward Gunna and said, "You got your man; now get back focused on this fuckin' money."

Gunna nodded his head solemnly and said, "Fa' sho', my nigga. Fa' sho'."

Toni saw the news that evening. After hearing about the shooting and seeing King on TV, Toni quickly called Charlie and said, "There's been another shooting in Del City. And guess who I just saw on the fuckin' news holding on to one of his friends, crying like a baby?"

"Who?" asked Charlie.

"Your man."

"King?"

"None other."

"Shit. Did you get a chance to speak with your man today?"

"Nope. I had to drop off that package of change for Eduardo, remember? That took up most of my day."

"This shit is about to erupt into a fuckin' war if we don't hurry and get a grip on this. Get at your man as soon as you can and I'll do the same. We have to put a stop to this shit before they fucking kill each other and completely fuck up everything we've put together."

"All right, I'll give you a call later after I've spoken to Flamboyant," Toni said and hung up the phone. Toni sat there for a moment, decided to hell with it, picked the phone back up, and quickly dialed Flamboyant's number. When he answered the phone Toni said, "I know it's late but we have to meet immediately."

"Where?" Flamboyant asked nervously.

"Meet me in the parking lot of the Pizza Hut on Lincoln. I'll be there in about thirty."

"I don't do the east side too often. Is there any place else we can meet?"

Highly irritated by this statement, Toni yelled, "No, there isn't! So have your ass at the Pizza Hut before I get there!"

Flamboyant stared at his phone after Toni had hung up on him and thought, *oh shit. I bet this shit has something to do with Del City.* He turned toward Prince and said, "I gots to bounce. I'm 'bout to make a run to the east side real quick. When I'm finished I'll come back and scoop you."

Prince frowned and asked, "You sure you don't need me to roll wit' you?"

"Nah, I'm straight. It shouldn't take me too long."

"Toni?"

"Yeah," Flamboyant said as he turned and walked out of the trap in Midwest City.

Flamboyant made the twenty-minute ride to the east side in fifteen. He parked his truck close to the front of the Pizza Hut and waited for Toni's arrival. Toni pulled into the parking lot fifteen minutes after Flamboyant. Flamboyant hit his light switch so Toni could see where he was parked. After Toni parked next to him, Flamboyant got out of his truck and got into Toni's car. As soon as he had the door closed, Toni pulled out of the parking spot and left the parking lot. Toni remained silent and drove for about ten minutes before speaking. Finally, after turning onto the Broadway Extension Toni said, "I see you had your team retaliate like we discussed the other day."

"Yeah. I told you it was a must that my man got back at 'em dudes who did that bullshit."

"In two weeks, there have now been eight murders in Del City. There is no way I'll be able to keep the heat off this one if you choose to continue to let your team work out that way."

Flamboyant heard what Toni said but something didn't sound right to him. He asked, "Eight? What you mean by eight murders?"

"The seven who were killed two weeks ago and the lady who was murdered this evening equals eight, Flamboyant. What's wrong with you, you can't count now?"

"You mean to tell me that only one lady was killed tonight?"

Toni laughed and said, "Obviously you don't watch your local news, huh? There was a lot of shooting but, yes, only one person was killed and I'm sad to say that it was in fact a woman."

"Damn. 'Em niggas went through all of that shit and didn't even get their man. Ain't that a bitch."

"Yes, it is. Now you have to fall all the way back from this."

"I know. I was just telling the team that when you called."

"Not only that, but in case of any form of retaliation, I want you to make sure that your team is aware that for no reason whatsoever are they to strike back."

"What? You tryin' to tell me if those Del City niggas try to get back at us I have to have my people lie down and do nothin'? Come on wit' that shit, Toni."

Toni stared at him and said, "I want you to listen to me and I want you to pay very close attention to every single word I speak. The people who shot and killed your people were not, as you said, Del City niggas. They have just as much strength as you do, Flamboyant, if not more. I'm in the process of getting in contact with them now, so it's imperative that you do exactly as I say. I—no, we—cannot stand for a war. War costs and I don't have the time nor the energy to be dealing with something so silly as this shit. Do you understand me?"

"I hear what the fuck you sayin' but this shit ain't really registerin'. You know the niggas who got at my man and

'em and you tellin' me to fall back 'cause you don't want
a war 'cause it could be costly? What 'bout my man's
people? Don't you think their lives were costly, Toni?
This is some straight-up ho shit you're askin' of me."

"No, this is business I'm informing you of. Don't get
this mistaken. I'm not asking you for a mothafuckin'
thang, Mr. Flamboyant! You are going to do exactly as
you're fuckin' told! If not, then you and your team will
simply have to be dismantled. Am I understood, Mr.
Flamboyant?"

He couldn't believe how Toni was getting at him. He
felt like a complete coward. A coward because he knew
that without Toni's help he would be completely out of
the game and that was something he wasn't ready to deal
with. He sighed and said, "Yeah, I understand. But tell
me something, Toni."

"What?"

"Who is these niggas who's supposed to be so high
powered?"

Toni smiled and asked, "Have you ever heard of somebody by the name of King? He runs the north side of
Oklahoma City just as tight as you run the south side."

King . . . King . . . Yeah, I heard 'bout that nigga,
Flamboyant thought. To Toni he said, "Nah, I don't think
I have. So, he's the nigga you're protectin' from me and
my team?"

Toni pulled back into the parking lot of the Pizza
Hut and parked next to Flamboyant's truck. "What
makes you think I'm protecting him from you? Why
can't I be protecting you and your team from them, Mr.
Flamboyant? After all, I don't have any business dealings with King or his crew. You're my breadwinner. I'm
just making sure that you stay in a position to continue
being my breadwinner." Before he could say a word,
Toni said, "Have a good evening, Mr. Flamboyant. This
meeting is over."

Chapter Seventeen

King couldn't believe what he was hearing. *Is he actually sitting across from me talkin' like I am some little kid or some shit?* he thought as he silently fumed. When Charlie paused for a brief moment he used that opportunity to get a word in. "My man's girl, his woman, his significant other was murdered, Charlie. There is no way in hell I'm gon' hold him back from doin' whatever he feels he has to do to get his revenge for his wifey. To be totally honest with you, I don't think I would be able to stop my man even if I wanted to."

Charlie sighed and said, "You don't get it, King. I'm not asking you to make this happen. I'm telling you to! This isn't up for any debate, nigga. You do what needs to be done or—"

"Or what?" King asked with rebellion in his voice.

Charlie smiled. "You think you can buck at me, King? Do you honestly think that if you disobey my orders you will be able to continue to live the way you've become accustomed to? Better yet, live at fucking all! Don't let this smooth face fool you. I can end your existence with a fucking text message. Don't you dare sit there and try to act like you're running shit anywhere else. If I let you go to war behind this mess I'll lose money. I'm not in this business to lose anything, let alone my fucking money. I admire your strength; that's one of the qualities you possess that led me to you in the first place. But don't ever think you're stronger than me. Because when you start thinking foolishly, you're being borderline suicidal. Get your squad to lie back and chill; this shit will soon pass. When it does, maybe, and I do mean maybe, you'll be able to let your man get revenge for his wife. Until then, you have to get your mind right as does the rest of your squad. Get back to business, get that money, King, and get rich. That's the ultimate goal here, right?"

"Yeah, you right. I feel everything you sayin', Charlie. But check this out, I told you I'm not a nigga who is used to havin' restraints. I'll continue to get this money like I been doin', believe that, but ain't no way in hell you can expect for me to lay it down if 'em niggas keep gettin' at me and mines. I'll do as you've asked me to, 'cause I don't do what I'm told. I do what the fuck I want to. Yeah, you the boss 'cause you got that sack, but don't ever think you can treat me like a punk peon-type nigga. Once you've made that mistake there's only one thing left for us to find out."

Charlie smile and asked, "And that is?"

King returned Charlie's smile and simply said, "To see who is going to actually end whose existence."

Charlie burst into laughter and said, "Understood. Now, I can guarantee that you or your squad won't have any further problems."

"How can you be so sure? That nigga Flamboyant has shown me that he wants to play. What makes you think he won't get at me again?"

"Trust me, King, I got this. If he does, which he won't, I give you my word that I'll give you all of the assistance necessary for you to make him and his entire family disappear. So back off and get that money, and keep the reins held on your man, a'ight?"

"Yeah, I got you."

"Oh, and for the record, King, you will lose if and when you ever decide to go up against me. If I were you I'd

erase all thoughts of ever trying to go into a battle that
you have absolutely no chance of winning. This meeting
is over unless you have anything further to add."

"Nah, I'm good. I'll be gettin' at you in a few days for
some more work, probably after Neecy's funeral."

"Call me when you're ready. And please send my
deepest condolences to your man. This is a tragedy, but
those in the living must continue to live. Feel me?"

"Yeah, I feel ya, Charlie," King said as he slid out of the
booth. As he left the Applebee's restaurant he was trying
to figure out a way to tell his squad that they weren't
going to be able to retaliate on them south side niggas.
*How in the fuck am I goin' to be able to hold Keko and
Tippi back? Shit!*

When King made it to the block he saw Flex's Navigator,
Boleg's Suburban, Nutta's Nitro, and Tippi's H2 lined up
in front of the trap. He sighed as he got out of his car and
went inside of the house. As soon as he was inside of the
trap Tippi asked, "What did Charlie have to say 'bout this
shit?"

"Charlie wants us to fall back. The heat from this will
hurt our ends and we can't afford to go to war wit' 'em
niggas, not right now anyway."

"What? I know you told Charlie to eat a dick, right?
Right?" yelled Tippi.

King frowned and said, "If you shut the fuck up and
listen I'll tell you what's what. We are goin' to fall back
'til this shit can cool down. I'm not lettin' Keko open
that trap back up, at least for a minute. We're going to
bury Neecy, then get back to what we do best. When the
time is right we'll get them soft-ass south side niggas.
'Til then, we got to get back to doin' what it do."

"Bullshit! That ain't how you get down, nigga, and you
fuckin' know it! That may be how Charlie gets down, but
not you! I can't believe you gon' let Charlie make the call

on this shit! That's some fucked-up shit, King!" Tippi screamed as she stood and left the trap.

King ignored her outburst and continued as if she hadn't even been inside of the house. "Where's Keko?"

"He spent the night with Neecy's mom. She's taking it real hard," Boleg said as he lit a Black & Mild.

"Yeah, and that nigga ain't gon' be tryin' to hear that shit you just shot at us, nigga. Real talk, that is a fucked-up move," said Cuddy.

"I know, but that's how it gots to be. We'll move on 'em fools when the time is right," King stated firmly.

"I know it's hot and shit, but it's hot in Del City, not the south. Why can't we go look at 'em niggas real quick like?" asked Nutta. "I mean, it ain't like it's gon' take much to go out there and let 'em cowards have it."

"Yeah, we could get Spook and some extra wolves and go do 'em niggas on some late-night shit. Once that's that then we could fall back in the cut. The heats gon' be out that way, not over here," added Flex.

King shook his head from side to side and said, "Y'all don't get it. If we move on 'em niggas when we're finished they'll try to move right back on us. The heat will not only be on the south side, but the north as well. The entire fuckin' town will be on fire. That means no money will be made and shit will get real fucked up. We wait. We fall back 'til I say so. I don't want to hear anything else on this shit. If you ain't wit' what I'm talkin' 'bout then get to fuckin' steppin' right fuckin' now!"

"Dog, you know we ain't goin' no-fuckin'-where so you can kill that shit. But real talk, you gon' have one hell of a time tryin' to stop Keko from doin' him. His wifey just got took on some foul shit, my nigga. If the shit was the other way around would you be able to fall back if your man told you to stand down?" Cuddy asked as he stared at King.

"I know this shit is fucked up, Cuddy, but we all have to eat. We can't let our emotions take control of our common sense. Fallin' back is the best move for now. I know it's gon' be hard for Keko to understand that, but on the real, dog, he don't have a fuckin' choice!" King said fiercely.

Tippi was driving around aimlessly, thinking about what King told her and the others. *I can't believe that nigga gon' let Charlie put him on some bitch shit like that. One of ours gets hurt, twenty of theirs must die. That's the code we always lived by. I don't see why that shit has to change now,* she thought as she pulled into a 7-Eleven so she could get her a pack of blunts. She wanted to get high. When she got back inside of her truck she grabbed her cell and called Mondo. "Where you at?"

"I just got off work," answered Mondo.

"Are you tired?"

"A little."

"How fast can you meet me at the Fifth Seasons?"

"I'm almost at my house, so I'd say about thirty."

"Thirty? You don't stay that damn far; why that fuckin' long?"

"Since I'm almost home I might as well go take a shower real quick and clean myself up."

"Fuck that. Take a shower at the room. I'll see you in a li'l bit," Tippi said. Before she could set the cell down, it started ringing. When she saw King's number on the caller ID she started to let it roll over to her voice mail. She went on and answered it instead. "What, nigga?" she asked, still highly pissed off at him.

"I can't have you out there trippin' the fuck out tonight. We can't move on 'em niggas, Tippi. If we do, Charlie will cut us off. Without that plug or protection, all of this shit will have been for nothin'. Don't go left on me when I really need your ass to be at ease," he said seriously.

Tippi thought she heard a little desperation in his voice and figured she'd use that to her advantage. "Nah, fuck that shit! I'm damn near on the south side now," she lied. "I got to do 'em niggas for my nigga Keko."

"Come on wit' that shit, Tippi. You know damn well you don't even know where that fool Flamboyant rest his fuckin' head. If you can't get him, it ain't worth the risk. He'll try to bounce back and get at us, then we'll have to war, and then everything will be straight fucked up. Come on back to the block and fall back for me, baby."

Got ya, Tippi thought as she told him, "You want me to fall back? How bad?"

"What you talkin' 'bout?"

"I'm sayin', if you want me to fall back I want to know what you willin' to do to get me to do that."

"Come on wit' that bullshit, Tippi. That shit you thinkin' ain't even cool right there."

"Nah, if you want me to fall back then you need to meet me at the Fifth Seasons in thirty. It's time you gave me what I been wantin' for years. It's either that or I'm on my way to cause some havoc on the south side. What's it gon' be?"

He sighed and said, "You've wanted this dick for years, huh? A'ight, you got it. I'm gon' hurt you, Tippi. I'm 'bout to stuff this dick so far up in you you're goin' to feel it deep in yo' chest cavity."

"Umm, that's what I'm talkin' 'bout. Hurry yo' ass up!" After Tippi ended that call she quickly called Mondo back and said, "Change of plans. Go on home. I got some business to take care of."

"Come on, Tippi, I just pulled into the parking lot of the hotel," whined Mondo.

"So what? Go home!"

Tippi smiled as she turned onto the highway headed for the Fifth Seasons. She was finally about to get what she'd been desiring for years: King.

By the time King arrived at the hotel, Tippi sent him a text message informing him of the room number. He couldn't believe he was actually about to fuck her. After all of these years of shaking her, here he was finally about to see how good that pussy really was. He couldn't help but smile at that thought. Even though he had chosen not to look at Tippi in that way, he knew that she was sexy as hell and this sex session was about to be intense, to say the least.

When he made it to the door of suite 567, he knocked and waited for Tippi to open up. Tippi opened the door and he damn near fell back when he saw her standing there dressed in only a transparent thong. Her firm C cups stood at attention as she stood there looking fucking edible. He stepped into the room and closed the door behind him with a smile on his face. As soon as the door was closed Tippi wasted no time. She dropped to her knees and began unbuckling King's Louis Vuitton belt. Once that task was taken care of she pulled his jeans down to his ankles and greedily began sucking his dick. His eyes rolled in the back of his head as he enjoyed her head game. "Damn, baby . . ." He reached down and used his right hand to guide her.

"Mmmmmm hmmm," she mumbled as she continued to suck away. She let his shaft slide out of her mouth with a pop as she quickly began sucking his balls. She began to hum lightly as she savored the flavor of his testicles. She grabbed his shaft and began stroking him slowly as she continued to hum and lick his balls. That combination was just too much for him to take. He pulled away from her slowly and scooped her into his arms before she could say a word. He kicked his legs all the way out of his jeans and carried her into the bedroom of the suite and gently laid her on the bed. She frowned and said, "Dammit, King, this is my moment, not yours! Let me do this my way!"

"If I let you do it your way a nigga will be 'sleep right now. You had a nigga 'bout to bust too fuckin' quick."

"Ain't like we got somewhere else to be. We got all fuckin' night!"

He smiled at her pretty face and said, "You got that right." He then reached down and pulled her transparent thong off and said, "Now it's my turn to do the tastin'." He dipped his head between her legs and began licking her sex. Her nectar tasted so sweet that he felt as if he'd lost all control of his tongue. He slid it all over her pussy lips, inside and out. It was as if his tongue had a mind of its own at that moment. Tippi moaned and squirmed all over the bed as he performed what seemed to her as the perfect form of cunnilingus. Before she knew what was happening she started climaxing. Her moans quickly turned to screams as her orgasm rocked her entire body.

"Oh! My! Fuckin'! God! That! Shit! Feels! Soooo! Gooooood!" Tippi screamed at the top of her lungs.

Before her orgasm ended, King got on top of her and slid his dick deep inside of her, stroking her slowly. She automatically wrapped her legs around his waist and matched the pace that he'd set. They were in complete harmony with one another as they made love for what seemed like hours. King came several times but he refused to stop. *This pussy is too damn good to stop,* he thought as he continued to stroke harder and deeper inside of her.

Tippi, on the other hand, felt exactly the same. *Ain't no way I'ma let this nigga stop. He bet' not stop; this shit is feelin' too fuckin' good,* she thought as she continued to bump and grind with King. Before either of them knew it they were once again cumming simultaneously.

"Shit! Here I go again, Tippi! Here I go!" he screamed.

"Me too, baby! Me too! Harder, nigga! Harder!" Tippi screamed as she emphatically felt his dick way up inside of her chest cavity, just like King said she would. *Wow!*

Chapter Eighteen

Two days after the funerals of Gunna's men, Flamboyant got a call from Prince informing him that they needed some more work.

"It's time, my nigga. Everybody is on their last leg. I'm talkin' 'bout a complete reload."

"You slippin', dog. Where you at right now?" Flamboyant asked as he checked himself out in the mirror of his bathroom.

"I just made it to the block."

"A'ight, then, I'll be over there in twenty," he said and hung up the phone. He stepped out of the bathroom and smiled at Shayla as she sat up in bed. "Good morning, sleepyhead."

"Good morning," she replied as she slid out of the bed and stepped into the bathroom. While she was relieving herself she asked, "So, what are your plans for the day?"

"I have a few errands to run real quick. After that I'm free. What 'bout you?"

"I'm meeting Taj at the nail shop at two. Other than that, I don't have anything else planned."

"I'll hit you when I'm through running around. Maybe we can do lunch or something."

"Okay," she said as she started brushing her teeth.

By the time Flamboyant made it to the block Wave and Ken had joined Prince. Flamboyant got out of his 600 and confidently strolled over to his team members. "What it do?"

"Ain't' shit, dog. Waitin' on yo' ass for real," Wave said as he lit up a blunt.

"Yeah, niggas is out of everything. Shit gon' get back to crackin' in a minute, so we needs to get back on as soon as we can," said Ken.

"Yeah, I feel you." Turning toward Prince, Flamboyant frowned and said, "You gots to watch your mouth when you be flappin' on that phone. You have gotten way too comfortable wit' that shit."

"My bad, dog. I wasn't even payin' that shit any attention for real."

"I know! You got the ends ready?"

"Yeah. Hold up, I'll be right back," Prince said as he stepped away from the group to get the money from the trap house.

While he was waiting for Prince to return, Flamboyant told Wave and Ken, "I don t know how long it's going to be exactly, but y'all will be straight within a couple of hours. I already made the call while I was on my way over here."

"That's cool. 'Em youngstas hit me up and they want a couple of gallons of that water," said Ken.

"I got a few hits for some X as well as a few pounds of that indo, too. Looks like we're 'bout to be busy than a mothafucka," Wave said as he inhaled deeply on the potent marijuana he was smoking.

"What up with Gunna? He good?"

"That nigga a'ight. He still trippin' off the fact that we only got a broad after the work we put in. He felt a li'l better when he found out it was that nigga's broad, though. He ain't too much trippin'. He's back to gettin' money as usual."

Flamboyant shook his head and said, "That's good, real good."

"You ain't worried 'bout 'em north side niggas tryin' to get back at a nigga? Especially since that nigga lost his bitch? I know if that was me I would have already been over this way tearin' shit up," Ken said seriously.

"Me too," added Wave.

"Nah, we good. 'Em niggas ain't gon' make no moves, so stay focused on this money, a'ight?"

"How can you be so sure, Flam?" asked Prince as he rejoined the group with two Louis Vuitton duffel bags full of money in each of his hands.

Flamboyant smiled and said, "Trust me. Now look, I'm 'bout to go make this shit happen. Stay ready and be waitin' on my call. I'll hit y'all up in a li'l bit," he said as he grabbed the bags from Prince and got inside of his car.

As they watched him leave the block Wave shook his head and said, "I'm still not feelin' that shit with 'em north side niggas, though."

"Me either," Ken chimed in.

Prince shrugged and said, "It is what it is. If Flam says we shouldn't trip on 'em niggas then to me it's all good. If they do get outta line then we'll give 'em fools the bidness for real."

"Now that's what I'm talkin' 'bout," Wave said as he took another long drag of his blunt.

After dropping the last of the work off to Prince, Flamboyant felt like he'd been working all morning. *And mothafuckas think selling dope is easy. Humph, this shit ain't no fuckin' joke,* he thought as he pulled his car out of Prince's driveway. Now that every one of his team members was restocked, he could play. He grabbed his cell and called Wifey. When Shayla answered the phone he told her, "I'm done doin' me, babe. You ready to get something to eat?"

"Sure. Taj is with me. Is it a'ight if she joins us?"

"Of course. What y'all tryin' to eat?"

"Hold on for a minute while I see what Taj is in the mood for." Shayla put her phone to her chest and asked Taj, "Girl, what you want to go eat?"

Taj was inside of the dressing room of the Gap trying on a pair of jeans that she knew were way too tight. "It don't matter to me; y'all choose. Shit, a beggar can't be choosy!"

Shayla shook her head as she put the phone back to her ear and said, "It doesn't matter, bae. You choose something."

"Where y'all at?"

"Quail Springs."

"A'ight, meet me at the Golden Corral on NW Expressway. I should be there in 'bout twenty."

"Okay, we're on our way." When Taj stepped out of the dressing room wearing those extra tight jeans Shayla shook her head. "Uh-uh, you know you need to hurry up and take off those tight-ass jeans."

Taj laughed and whined, "But, Shay, they make my booty look big." They both laughed as Taj went back into the dressing room.

Flamboyant was sitting at a table in the rear of the all-you-can-eat restaurant, talking to Milo on the phone as he waited for Shayla and Taj to arrive. "So, you good, my nigga?"

"Yeah, I'm straight. I'm 'bout to make a run out to Midwest City and take care of some thangs out that way. After that I'm comin' back over here to do me," said Milo.

"Has everything been cool out that way?"

"Yeah, it's straight."

"Make sure you keep your eyes open for any of 'em north side niggas. We ain't tryin' to make no noise right now, but we ain't duckin' nothin' either."

"Oh, fo' sho'. A'ight, dog, I'll holla," Milo said as he hung up the phone.

Flamboyant smiled when he saw Shayla and Taj enter the restaurant. *Damn, my baby is lookin' good as fuck!* He stood up so they could see him.

Shayla saw him first and led the way toward his table. "Hi, baby," she said as she gave him a kiss and sat down.

"What's up, Marco?" Taj said as she too took a seat.

"Ladies. So, tell me, how much of the mall did y'all get to buy this mornin'?"

They laughed. "We didn't do too much damage," Taj said as she sipped a glass of water. "I don't know about y'all, but I'm not even trying to be cute. I'm hungry and I'm about to get my eat on. So y'all can sit and have small talk. I'm about to eat!" Taj got up from the table and made a beeline for the buffet.

Flamboyant and Shayla laughed as they too got up to go fill their plates.

Shayla was piling some Italian meatballs onto her plate when she saw King and Tippi enter the restaurant. *Shit! Shit! Shit! Why in the hell are they here?* Though she remained calm on the outside, she was actually a nervous wreck on the inside. *Why am I trippin'? I haven't done anything wrong.* She looked up from her plate and stole a glance King's way. *Look at his ass. Always got to look so fucking good!*

"Damn, girl, you ain't that hungry?" asked Taj once she was seated.

"What makes you say that?" Shayla asked as she started cutting her meatballs into small pieces.

"All you got on your plate is a few of them nasty-look-ing meatballs and some bread. I know you a lasagna freak. Why didn't you get none of that lasagna they got up there?"

"Are we in a rush? I didn't know there were rules on how to eat when one came to the Golden Corral."

"Well, excuuuse me!"

Flamboyant started laughing and said, "You two kill me. Y'all be beefin' sometimes like y'all ain't been best friends for years."

"I don't even pay that girl no mind. She can be too silly sometimes," Shayla said as she stole another glance in King's direction.

Taj was pulling her fork out of her mouth when she noticed who Shayla had taken a quick peep at. She damn near choked on her food when she saw King and Tippi piling food on their plates at the hot bar. *Oh, shit!* After swallowing her food she said, "I may be silly sometimes but you're the one with the crazy streak."

"Crazy? Girl, you know you need to quit it. Don't even get me started."

Amused, Flamboyant shook his head and laughed again. "Excuse me, y'all, but I got to go get me some more of those buttery-ass rolls. Them thangs are good!"

"Bring me back a few, baby," Shayla said sweetly.

As soon as Flamboyant was out of earshot, Taj said, "Girl, have you lost your mind? You better watch your step. You're playing a little too dangerously."

"What am I doing? I'm not playing any games. It's not my fault that Trevor and that bitch are here. I don't have any control over that."

"That may be true, but you ain't got to be sneakin' peeks at his ass, either."

Shayla smiled and said, "I know, but I couldn't help myself. Look at that fine-ass man. Damn, he's looking good!"

"Um hm, yeah, he's looking real good. As a matter a fact he's looking so good that your man is standing right next to him as we speak."

Shayla almost choked as she took another look toward King and saw Flamboyant standing right next to King at the hot bar. Each of them was piling food onto their plates. "This is a little too close for comfort," Shayla said as she stared at the both of them. King raised his head and they locked eyes with one another. He smiled and Shayla quickly dropped her head and whispered to Taj, "Girl, Trevor just saw me staring at his ass. Please tell me that he's not still looking over this way."

Taj turned her head and locked eyes with Trevor and said, "I wish I could tell you that, girl, but I can't. He's looking at the both of us."

"What is Marco doing?"

"He's not paying any attention. He's too busy fixing his plate." Taj watched as King gave her a nod of his head. She returned the gesture and then quickly lowered her head. When she took another peek his way she was relieved to see that he had gone and joined Tippi at their table on the other side of the hot bar. "The coast is clear, girl; he's gone."

Shayla raised her head and said, "We have to hurry up and get the hell outta this place. I'm a nervous wreck right about now."

"Why? You ain't done nothing. Or have you?"

Shayla frowned and said, "Of course I haven't done anything. I just don't want to feel uncomfortable when I'm with my man. If Marco picks up on my mood then he's going to ask questions that I don't have answers for."

Before she could continue, Flamboyant came back to the table and said, "Here you go, babe." He gave her some of the hot rolls and said, "These things are the bomb for real." As he ate he couldn't help but notice how the mood seemed to have changed since he left to go get more food. "Is everything a'ight with y'all? Y'all seem spooked or some shit."

"Spooked? Spooked of what?" Taj asked.

"You're tripping, Marco," Shayla added as she ate some of her meatballs.

He shrugged it off and continued to get his eat on. While they finished their meal, Shayla couldn't stand the fact that she was letting King indirectly dictate her lunch with her man. *Fuck this shit.* She smiled and asked, "Are you full, baby? Do you want some of that dessert they got over there?"

"I am full, but I could do for a li'l of that vanilla ice cream with some of that caramel sauce they got."

She smiled and said, "Look at you, just greedy. I'll be right back, boy," she said as she stood with Taj staring at her as if she'd lost her damned mind. When she made it to the dessert buffet area she made Flamboyant a caramel sundae and a strawberry one for herself.

Just as she was turning to head back to her table King said, "You always did love strawberries."

Shayla refused to be rattled. She turned and looked at him and said, "Hi, Trevor, how are you today?"

"I'm good. I'd be better if you explained to me why you shook me like you did."

"Shook you? You're the one who canceled our lunch, not me." Before he could respond she said, "Look, as you can see this isn't exactly a good time for us to be having this conversation."

King smiled and asked, "So, that's your dude over there sitting wit' Taj?"

"Duh. Bye, Trevor," she said as she started to walk away from him.

He reached out and grabbed her lightly by her arm and said, "Call me, Shay. We need to talk."

She looked at his hand on her arm and said, "We don't have anything to talk about, Trevor. Now please let go of my arm." He did as she asked him to and watched as she went back and joined her man and Taj. He had a sly grin on his face as he went back and joined Tippi at their table.

After Shayla was back seated Flamboyant asked, "Who was that guy you were talkin' to, babe?"

Without any signs of nervousness she straight lied, "His name is Trevor. He's in one of my classes at school."

"Oh," he said as he got busy eating his sundae.

On the other side of the table Taj looked as if she was about to pass out. She stared at her girl, who seemed to be all cool and calm like nothing was wrong. Taj grinned and gave Shayla a look of admiration that silently said, "You go, girl!"

Chapter Nineteen

"You got some huge nuts, nigga! I can't believe you actually went over there and got at that broad wit' her nigga sittin' right on the other side of the room," Tippi stated angrily.

"All I did was speak, damn. It ain't like I tried to get at her or nothin'. Besides, if that nerdy-lookin' nigga would have said some slick shit I would have let you deal with his ass," replied King.

Shaking her head no, Tippi said, "Uh-uh, nigga, you would have been on yo' own with that one. You was bad for leavin' me to go talk to that bitch in the first place. Especially after all that dick you been servin' me."

Ever since their first sexual encounter it seemed as if King couldn't get enough of Tippi. They made love damn near every night since. Lawanda had been calling King, trying her best to get him to come over to her house so he could break her off. He refused because, for some reason, he just couldn't get enough of Tippi. All of that was momentarily forgotten as soon as he saw Shayla. Tippi may have had his body locked down for the moment, but Shayla still had total possession of his heart. *Damn, and I can't even have her. Ain't that a bitch!*

"You need to get that bitch off your mind and get yo' head right. We got a funeral to go to in the mornin', nigga."

"Yeah, I know. That shit gon' be crazy. I hope that nigga Keko don't lose it."

"Don't lose it? Nigga, that was his wifey! That nigga is gon' be mad hurt once we lay her in the ground. All we can do is stand by his side and try to help him through this shit. I think he'll be a'ight during the funeral, though. What you should be worried 'bout is how he's gon' be once it's over. So far you've been able to hold his ass back, but I doubt if you'll be able to put any of that shit down after we bury Neecy. That nigga is gon' flip the fuck out," Tippi said seriously.

"I know, but I got something for his ass."

"What's that?"

King smiled and said, "He's goin' on a vacation and a business trip all at the same time."

"What the fuck are you talkin' 'bout?"

"I'm sendin' his ass out to Cali to take care of somethin' for me and to rest his mind a li'l bit."

"Some rest? Nigga, if you think that Keko gon' go for some shit like that then you're outta your fuckin' mind!"

"Wanna bet?"

"You fuckin' right! How much you tryin' to lose, nigga?"

"A stack."

"Fuck that! Make it ten stacks!"

"Bet."

"Bet," Tippi replied. She noticed that Shayla and her companions were leaving the restaurant and said, "Your bitch is leavin'. You don't want to run over and say good-bye to her and her man, do you?"

He frowned and said, "Fuck you."

Tippi started laughing and said, "Maybe later on, Mr. Big Dick."

Neecy's funeral was one of the saddest moments King had ever experienced. Keko took it harder than he had expected. He threw himself over the closed casket and screamed out Neecy's name over and over, begging

God to bring back his wifey. It took King, Flex, Spook, and Tippi to finally get him back to his seat with the rest of Neecy's family. Not only was the funeral extremely sad, during the final prayer at the cemetery Keko and Neecy's mom went ballistic. Which in turn had everyone else crying their eyes out. King included. By the time the preacher finished with the final rites, there wasn't a dry face in the entire cemetery. As they were walking back toward the small fleet of limousines that King rented for Neecy's family, Keko stepped up to King and said, "I need to holla at ya for a minute, dog."

After leading King away from the rest of the family, Keko told him, "I know you want to fall back and let this shit die down. I respect that 'cause I respect the rules of the game. I've tried not to let my anger and pain cloud my judgment, G, but it just ain't workin' no more. I got to have 'em niggas, King. I'm not tryin' to fuck up yo' money or put anyone else in the way. This is all 'bout me. My wifey has been laid down now, dog. I got to do what I got to do. 'Em fools gots to die by my hand."

Staring his man directly in the eyes, King said, "No question, G. But there's a time and a place for everything. Charlie has my hands tied for the moment 'cause of all the work and shit. Charlie keeps the blanket around us. If we lose that protection then we're open game for the Ones as well as 'em alphabet boys. I'm not tryin' to go back to nobody's jail, dog, and I know you ain't either."

"Jail is the last thing on my mind. All I want to do is get each and every one of 'em niggas. Once that's a done deal I can have some kind of peace with myself. We buried that girl today 'cause of me. Me and my greed. That's what hurts me the most. I gots to do what I gots to do, King. Please, don't get in my way, nigga. I'm beggin' you, dog, let me do me," Keko pleaded.

Once again King stared at his man and said, "Check it, in order for this to be put down, it has to be put down right. I need you and Spook to fly out to L.A. and hook up with my peoples. They gon' hook us up with the right equipment to do this thang right."

"What are you talkin' 'bout?"

King then went on to explain, "Some of my peoples from Compton are gon' give us some heavy, and I do mean heavy, firepower. I'm talkin' 'bout hand grenades and some mo' shit. Y'all gon' have to drive them shits back out this way. When you get back, then we'll handle them clowns. And I promise you with all of that shit we gon' have, we won't miss, real talk."

Keko stared at King for a few seconds and asked, "This shit on the up and up? You ain't tryin' to shake a nigga, are you?"

"Come on wit' that shit, dog, you know I don't play games with real niggas. I'm not gon' lie; I'm also bankin' on the time you're out that way you calm down a li'l bit. Regardless, it is what it is when you get back. My word."

"How long is it goin' to take to put everything in motion?"

"Everything is everything already. Y'all flight leaves in the mornin' at ten. When y'all make it to the West my niggas will be there to take y'all to get a suite at the W 'til everything is put in order for y'all return."

"What you mean by that, dog?"

"I'm havin' someone drive a Suburban out to Cali for y'all to use for the drive back out here. I don't want y'all on that highway wit' all of that shit driving a vehicle with Cali plates. It'll look better if y'all had a ride wit' Oklahoma tags. Feel me?"

"Yeah, I feel yo' slick ass," Keko said with a smile on his face.

King returned his man's smile and said, "Come on, let's go chill wit' the fam. We'll talk 'bout the rest of the details while we get our eat on."

Later that evening, while King and Tippi were lying next to each other on King's California king-sized bed, he told her, "I'm gon' need you in the mornin'."

"What's up?" Tippi asked as she turned and faced him.

He smiled and said, "I want you to take Keko and Spook to the airport. Their flight leaves at ten, so you're goin' to have to get up early in order to have 'em there on time."

Tippi smiled and punched him lightly on his chest and said, "You sneaky-ass nigga, how you do it?"

"Do what?"

"You know what! How did you get Keko to agree to that California shit?"

He laughed and told her about his plans for Keko and Spook to acquire some weapons for them. What he didn't inform her of was the fact that his people in Compton were not really his people at all; they were Charlie's. When Spook and Keko arrived in California, Charlie's people would take them to their hotel suite and lead them on a nice long run-around. By the time they did get the weapons that they came for, a minimum of thirty days would have passed. That's how long King figured he'd need. Hopefully, by then Keko would have calmed down. If not, then he'd have to think of something else. There was no way he was going to mess up his plug with Charlie. No way.

After he was finished he said, "Okay, this is what we're goin' to do 'bout what you owe."

"What I owe? Nigga, I know you ain't gon' take no ten stacks from me! Not after all of this good pussy I've been given yo' ass," Tippi said as she reached under the covers and gently fondled his nut sack.

"Hmmmm, that shit feels good right there, baby, but you are in the red and I could use some extra chips to blow. You know my birthday is comin' up. Ouch! Girl, what the fuck you doin'?"

Tippi laughed and started back rubbing his balls after she had given them a real hard squeeze for his slick remarks. "Yeah, I know your birthday is comin' up. What you wanna do? Fly somewhere real fly and kick it this year or what?"

"I was thinkin' 'bout throwin' a party at Déjà Vu. You know, get real flossy wit' it and clown a li'l bit. It'll be fun for everyone to come out and get they shine on."

"That li'l nigga Nutta gon' love some shit like that."

"Boleg and Cuddy too."

"Do you want me to start hookin' that up?"

"Yeah, get on top of that for me."

"A'ight. Now, I'll pay you what I owe you."

"You got my money on you?" He smiled.

"Uh-uh. I thought I'd start payin' you back like this," she said as she ducked her head under the covers and started sucking him off.

"Mmmmmm, that's a damn good way to start," he moaned.

"What are you going to do for your birthday this year, girl?" Taj asked.

"I don't know. I'm tired of going out of town, so I hope Marco doesn't come up with any surprise trips this year. We've done that way too much. It's gettin' old," said Shayla.

"Leave it to your ass to say traveling is old. Girl, it ain't like you been all around the world yet. There's plenty of exotic places y'all can go."

"I know, but I'd rather stay here and do something in the city. It's been a minute since I spent my birthday at home."

"Why don't you throw a party then?"

"Come on, that's so corny."

"No, it's not! Especially if you let your man take care of it. Shit, you can have the most talked-about party this city has ever seen."

"You think so?"

"Do I? Run it by Marco and see what he says. You know how that nigga gets down. Shit, he might even fly in Diddy or some wild way-out shit like that."

Shayla laughed and said, "Marco has a li'l pull, but I doubt he got it like that!"

"That nigga has chips, and with the right amount of chips anything is possible, girl, even here in li'l old Oklahoma City."

"Whatever. I'll talk to him about it when he gets home, though. It might be fun to have a party. God knows it's been a long time since I've had one."

"All right then, girl, give me a holla when you've talked to him about it."

"Okay, bye, girl," Shayla said as she hung up the phone. *September seventh I'll be twenty-six years old,* Shayla thought as she relaxed on the bed. She rubbed her stomach and said, "Twenty-six years old and still no direction with my life. Ugh!"

Tippi was gone the next morning when King opened his eyes. He climbed out of the bed and got dressed. He had a busy day ahead of him. After he was dressed and inside of his car he called Lawanda, who had been blowing up his phone all damn night. "What you want?" he asked as soon as she answered the phone.

"I need to talk to you. Why haven't you returned any of my calls, King?"

"I been busy."

"When can you come over here?"

"Why you ain't at work?"

"I took the day off. If your ass wouldn't have called me back I was coming to the north to find you today."

"Yeah? Is somethin' wrong with the kids?"

"Nah, this ain't 'bout them."

"Well, what's it 'bout then?"

"You."

"Look, I don't have time for games, Lawanda. What the fuck do you want?"

"You comin' at me foul and all I'm doin' is lookin' out for your best interests. You need to calm the fuck down. When can you get over here? 'Cause what I got to say can't be said over no damn phone."

He checked his watch, sighed, and said, "I'll be there in 'bout twenty."

"A'ight."

"Oh, and, Lawanda?"

"What's up?"

"If this is some bullshit you on, I'm gon' slap the shit outta yo' fuckin' ass. Do you hear me?"

"Yeah, nigga, I hear yo' ass," she said and hung up the phone.

Twenty minutes later King pulled into Lawanda's driveway. He jumped out of the car and strolled toward the front door. Lawanda opened the door before he made it there and said, "Well, well, look at the father of my children lookin' dope boy fresh as ever."

"You better fuckin' believe it. Now, what's up?"

Once he was inside of the house she closed the front door and joined him in the living room. She sat next to him on the couch and said, "I do expect to be blessed if what I tell you turns out to be important. Agreed?"

"Yeah, yeah, I got ya."

"Your man, Flex, is making some power moves. He's even thinkin' 'bout shakin' you and your peoples."

"Where did you get this from?"

"He's fuckin' a friend of mines. She turned him on to some white boys who be spendin' a lot of money. He's made a whole bunch of money off of her and her people. At first he was breakin' her off lovely, but now he's on some grimy shit, shakin' her ass off and not kickin' it like he was. She called me and told me of his plans of doin' him. She even told me that he's thinkin' 'bout gettin' with some nigga you got beef with out on the south side. Flamboyant, I think is his name."

King really wasn't paying any attention to Lawanda at first, but at the mention of that nigga Flamboyant's name, she now had his undivided attention. "Look, do me a favor and have your friend get at me. Let her know I'll break her off for everything she does for me. She won't have to worry 'bout that nigga Flex no more 'cause now she'll be plugged in wit' the King. Real talk."

Lawanda smiled and said, "A'ight, but what about me? Don't I get some kind of blessin' for passing along this information?"

He smiled at her and said, "Don't trip, you know I got you. But right now shit needs to be handled. Hit me after you've gotten at ol' girl. What's her name anyway?"

"Karmen."

"After you've holla'd at her, give her my number and tell her I said to get at me. After I've handled my business we'll hook up and do us. Cool?"

"Mmm hm," she answered with a smile on her face as she watched King leave.

As soon as he was back inside of his car he picked up his cell and called Tippi. When she answered the phone he told her, "Looks like you get to loot at that nigga Flex."

"You lyin'! What that fake-ass nigga do?"

"I'll put you up on it when we get together. Did you get 'em niggas on that flight?"

"Yeah, they made it. That nigga Keko was bitchin' the whole damn time, too."

King laughed and said, "He'll be a'ight. Meet me on the block. Looks like we're 'bout to be busy today."

Tippi smiled into the receiver and said, "Good. I've been waitin' for this shit for a long fuckin' time."

"I know," King replied as he ended the call.

Chapter Twenty

"So, you want to have a party this year, huh, babe?"

"Mmm hmm, it might be fun. At least it will be something different this year. I'm tired of going out of town every year for my birthday," Shayla said as she sat down next to Flamboyant on the sofa. "So, what do you think?"

"It's cool with me. I'll have Prince get at 'em New York niggas and set everything up. Since your birthday falls on a Friday this year everything should be all good. We'll turn a regular club into one hell of a Friday night in Oklahoma City."

"Come on now, Marco, there's no need to get too crazy with this."

"You know how I get down, babe. If I'm gonna do this it has to be top notch all the fuckin' way. So make sure that you tell everyone you invite that it's going to be on and poppin' for your twenty-sixth birthday party," he stated proudly.

Shayla rolled her eyes slightly and said, "Oh, God."

When Milo saw Nutta hopping out of his truck at the McDonald's in Midwest City, he couldn't resist the urge to see what that little north side nigga was about. Though Milo was just a little shorter than Nutta at five six, he was confident that if they got into a fight he'd come out victorious. He sat back in his seat and watched as Nutta entered the Mickey Dee's.

While Nutta was paying for his food he noticed Milo sitting at his table grilling him. Alarm bells went off inside of his head. *South side nigga! Shit, I left my strap in the truck!* He took a look in Milo's direction. Milo smiled at him and slid to the end of his seat and raised his shirt so that Nutta could see the butt of his pistol. Nutta stared at him for a moment as he tried to figure out what he was going to do. He turned back and faced the counter and waited for his food. When his food was ready he took a deep breath, grabbed his Big Mac combo, and started for the front door. Milo watched him stiffly walk out of the fast food restaurant and began to laugh. Milo's laughter infuriated Nutta. Once he was outside of the McDonald's he ran to his truck, opened the door, and quickly grabbed his gun. He stepped back into the Mickey Dee's with his weapon in his hand and glared at Milo, who was still sitting in his seat inside of the restaurant. When he saw that Nutta had pulled out a gun his smile quickly departed.

"Shit!" Before he was able to say another word Nutta began unloading his 9 mm in Milo's direction. Milo was missed by centimeters. He dove to the ground and was luckily able to avoid being shot.

After the last round from his gun had been fired, Nutta smiled and yelled, "Bitch-ass nigga! This the north!" He then ran out the restaurant and jumped into his truck and sped out of the parking lot.

"Babe, I'm about to go get with Prince for a li'l while. I'll be back shortly," Flamboyant said as he stepped toward the front door.

"Bring me back something to eat!" Shayla yelled from their bedroom.

"What do you want?" he yelled back.

"It doesn't matter, you choose!"

"A'ight!" As he stepped out of the house his cell phone rang. "What's up?" he answered.

"Dog, you ain't gon' believe this shit, but some north side nigga just tried to take Milo," said Prince.

"What? Where?"

"Out in Midwest City at that McDonald's on Twenty-third and Douglas."

"Where that nigga at?"

"He's on his way to my spot now, and he's mad as fuck. You know you gon' have to calm that li'l nigga down. 'Cause if you don't, it's about to be on with 'em north side niggas for real."

"Yeah, I know. I'm on my way; be there in twenty," he said as he turned around and went back into the house. He stepped into the bedroom and told Shayla, "Babe, I'm goin' to be gone longer than I thought. Somebody tried to shoot Milo."

"What? Is he a'ight?"

"I think so. I'll know more when I get to Prince's house. Can you order some pizza or somethin'? 'Cause I got to get over there in a hurry."

"I'll be okay. Don't worry about me, baby. Go on and handle your business."

He smiled at her as he bent and gave her a quick kiss. "Thanks, babe."

By the time Milo made it to Prince's house he was in a murderous state. All he wanted to do was kill somebody, preferably 'em north side niggas. Prince opened the door and said, "Come in, dog."

Milo quickly said, "Dog, I can't believe that li'l nigga really tried to get off at me! That fool was bustin' his gun like he a G for real!" Milo screamed with admiration in his voice.

"Damn, nigga, you sound like you proud of that fool or some shit."

Milo smiled and said, "I am. 'Cause now it's on and ain't nobody gon' stop me from gettin' at 'em niggas. I'm 'bout to tear the north side up. First, I'm gon' start on the east side, then I'm gon' hit the northwest, and then—"

"Hold up, nigga, you know damn well Flamboyant ain't gon' be tryin' to hear no crazy shit like that. You got to think 'bout this shit, dog."

"Think? Not gon' be hearin' no crazy shit? Dog, Flam ain't gon' be able to stop me from doin' what needs to be done. He wasn't the nigga dodgin' shells inside a mothafuckin' McDonald's a few fuckin' minutes ago!"

"I know, dog, but you got to be careful right 'bout now. A lot of shit will be put at stake if you go all out on 'em niggas right now. Especially after what popped off out in Del City. Come on, my nigga, calm down and chill for a minute. Flam's on his way. Let's be rational, my nigga."

"Rational? I need a drink."

"Help yourself," Prince said as he pointed toward the bar in the corner of his living room.

Flamboyant arrived just as Milo was pouring himself a stiff drink. After Prince let him inside, he wasted no time gettin' at Milo. "I know you hot, my nigga, and I'm not gon' even fake this shit wit' you, but we can't move on 'em niggas. We can't stand that type of heat. You gon' have to trust me and fall back 'til a better time."

Milo downed his glass of Hennessy in one gulp and said, "When will there be a better time, Flam? When have you ever known a good time for killin', dog? It is what it is. Any day is a good day to kill. I'm not gon' sit here and argue with y'all all night. I feel what you sayin', though. I'll fall back for a minute, but if 'em niggas get at me again and don't take me, I swear on my mama I'm gon' ride on they ass 'til I'm stankin' or stuck in somebody's jail! Real talk!"

"Let me make a call real quick. I was told this kind of shit wouldn't be goin' down," Flamboyant said as he pulled out his cell quickly and dialed Toni's number. As soon as Toni was on the line he said, "We need to talk."

"What's wrong?"

"A member of my team just got blasted at by one of 'em north side niggas. You told me that if I didn't war there wouldn't be any aggressive moves made toward me and mines. What's up wit' this shit, Toni?"

Toni sighed heavily. "Let me check into this, I'll call you back." Toni hung up on him before he had a chance to respond.

Flamboyant stared at his phone for a few seconds. "This shit is fuckin' crazy."

"What?" asked Prince.

"How can Toni control or know what's what wit' 'em north side niggas? Somethin' ain't right wit' this shit."

"Maybe Toni fucks with 'em niggas too," said Prince.

"Nah, I doubt it. Toni's too fuckin' smooth to waste time with some foul niggas like 'em cowards."

"You sure?" asked Prince.

Before he could answer the question, he was interrupted by the ringing of his cell. He checked the caller ID and saw that it was Toni calling him back. "We're 'bout to see now," he said to Prince. He answered the phone, "What up?"

"Meet me at Pearl's on the Lake in thirty."

"A'ight, but I need to know—"

"Your questions will be answered when we meet," Toni cut him off angrily. "Don't waste your time questioning me right now, Flamboyant."

"Whatever. I'll see you in a few." He faced Milo and Prince and told them, "Hold it down, my niggas. I'm 'bout to go find out what's what. I'll holla back at y'all later on."

"Want me to roll with ya?" asked Prince.

"Nah, you know how Toni gets down. I'm good. I'll get at you after this meet."

"A'ight, be safe," Prince said as he walked Flamboyant to the door. After Flamboyant left the house, Prince turned toward Milo and said, "This shit is 'bout to get ugly."

"What makes you say that?" Milo asked.

Prince tapped his right hand on his stomach a few times and said, "I can feel it in my gut."

Toni was talking to Charlie on the phone when Flamboyant entered the restaurant. "Look, he's here now. I handle this end; you make sure you get control of your man. That nigga is trying to fuck up our money in a major way."

"Don't worry about King. I'll take care of his ass. You just keep that nigga Flamboyant in check," replied Charlie.

"Got it." Toni set the cell phone on the table just as Flamboyant approached. "Good evening, Flamboyant, have a seat." After he was seated Toni said, "First off, let me apologize for my tone earlier. I was out of line. It's just that when I get news of that nature I tend to lose my composure."

"That's cool. I was trippin' a li'l bit, but it was nothin' for real. What I am trippin' off of is how are you able to know and basically control what 'em north side niggas be doin'? You fuckin' wit' 'em niggas too?"

Toni smiled and said, "Of course not. You are my only concern. I deal only with you. Rest assured of that fact. My hand is all over this town, though. There won't be much going on that I won't know about. When it comes to you and your team's well-being, I will make sure that I hold nothing back to ensure that everything is all good for you. I made a few calls and some inquiries about what happened with your man. I'm waiting for some answers now. So you'll have to be patient for the time being. I can tell you with the utmost confidence that you or no one on your team will have to worry about getting shot at again. At least not by any of those gentlemen from the north side."

"What makes you so sure? You told me that I didn't have shit to worry 'bout before. I can't hold these sharks back for too long. They ain't no punks. When they feel challenged the only thing they know how to do is step up and face their challengers head-on. On top of that, holdin' 'em back compromises my position."

"I understand, but you're going to have to stand firm and hold them back. We cannot afford a war between you guys. Continue to get that money and I'll handle everything else. My word."

"You better, Toni, 'cause if you don't, this town is 'bout to turn red."

Shayla was sitting down watching TV when she got a call on her cell from King.

"What's up with you, Shay?"

"Why are you calling me, Trevor? This shit ain't even cool."

"It ain't, huh? Well, how come you ain't got back at me then?"

This nigga got some fuckin' nerve, she thought as she said, "Look, I already told you I have a man. Why can't you accept that and chill?"

"Accept it? I have accepted it. You must have forgot that you called me. You initiated all contact, Shay. If you wouldn't have got at my aunty then we wouldn't have holla'd at all. Come on with the bullshit; you know what it is just as much as I do. You're still feelin' me."

"Nigga, please. Don't flatter yourself and let all of that newfound money fuck your head up, Trevor. You've never been the conceited type."

He smiled and said, "You right, ain't nothin' conceited about the King. I know what I want and I'm confident that my feelings are on point. As a matter of fact, I'm sure of it. So stop playin', Shay."

"Bye, Trevor, and don't worry about calling me back 'cause I'm about to turn off my phone for the night. And when I get up tomorrow I'm changing my number. I've moved on with my life, Mr. Confident. I advise you to do the same." Shayla was shaking slightly as she pressed the end button on her phone. She couldn't believe how upset King made her. Not only was she upset about him calling her phone, she was extremely pissed off at the fact that he had the nerve to be laughing at her as she hung up on his ass. He knew she still cared for him and that shit spelled danger with a capital D. *Fuck,* she thought as she stared at the television screen.

Chapter Twenty-one

King was sitting back in his room chilling, waiting for Tippi to arrive. He was still smiling because he knew for a fact that Shayla was still feeling him. "I'm playin' a dangerous game now," he said aloud as he thought about Shayla and Tippi. *I shouldn't have never started fuckin' with Tippi's crazy ass. Ain't no way I'm gon' be able to fuck with the both of 'em. Tippi would kill Shayla before she would let me kick it with her. Fuck, what was I thinkin' 'bout? I care about Tippi; fuck, I love her ass. I just don't love her like I love Shayla, though. Shit, I don't even know if I'm gon' be able to take Shayla from her nigga any-fuckin'-way. So why the fuck am I trippin'? I got mine and she got hers, so be it.*

He went into the kitchen and was getting himself something to drink when he heard Tippi pull into his driveway. He stepped to the front door and smiled when he saw her sexy tomboy-looking ass climb out of her H2. *Damn, she's fine as fuck,* he thought as he continued to watch her walk toward the front door.

Tippi had a smile on her face as she came into the house and said, "It's all set. That nigga Flex is meeting us on the block for the late night 'round one in the mornin'."

"Cool. Did you make sure that everybody knows to meet us at the trap? I want everyone there when we expose that nigga."

"Yeah, Boleg, Cuddy, and Nutta will be there. Have you talked to Keko and Spook?"

King smiled and said, "Yeah, and that nigga is salty for real."

"He ain't no dummy. You should have known he was gon' figure out you was shakin' his ass to the left."

"I know, but he's good, though. He told me that he'll handle what needs to be taken care of out that way, but as soon as he gets back home he's gon' be on one for real and I won't be able to tell him a damn thang."

"So you lied?"

He stared at Tippi for a moment before answering her question. "If Keko still wants to get at 'em niggas when he gets back, then it looks like we gon' have to get at 'em south side niggas. I love that nigga. He's remained loyal to me so I have no choice but to return that loyalty to my nigga."

"What about Charlie? What 'bout all the work and all of this money? I thought that was the number one priority. You gon' fuck it up for some loyalty bullshit?"

"What other choice do I have? He lost his wifey, Tippi. I can't expect him to fall back and accept some shit like that."

"True, but you gon' have to find a way to be able to deal wit' this shit in a way that can satisfy Keko's hunger for revenge wit'out pissin' off Charlie at the same time."

"That's easier said than done. Hopefully I'll be able to come up with somethin'. You know damn well I'm gon' give it my best shot. 'Til then, it's business as usual."

"I know that's right, and since it's kind of early, we might as well handle some BI right 'bout now," Tippi said as she pulled off her black wife beater and exposed her firm set of C cups with a smile on her pretty face.

He shook his head and said, "It was a major fuckin' mistake ever givin' your ass some of this dick. You done got sprung on a nigga now."

As she stepped toward him she said, "Baby, I've been sprung on yo' ass. The love is real, nigga; you and I both know it. Now, come here. I want to suck that dick!"

King had a satisfied smile on his face as he climbed out of his bed and went to the bathroom. Even though he knew he wasn't in love with Tippi, he loved the way she handled her business in the bedroom. *Shit, she might just could be Wifey,* he thought as he finished relieving himself. He washed his hands and stepped back into the bedroom to see Tippi still sleeping soundly. He stared at her for a minute and smiled again. *Damn, she looks so damn good. Who'd ever believe that she was a damn fool?* He shook his head and said, "Wake up, girl! Time to get some fuckin' work done!"

Tippi opened her eyes and smiled lazily at the only man she truly loved. "Damn, nigga, you could have let me get a li'l more rest, especially after that fuckin' workout."

"Rest? My number one soldier is supposed to have the stamina to be able to deal with anything. What, you fakin' on me now, Tippi?"

She laughed and threw a pillow at him and said, "Fuck you, fool! You know how I get down. My work speaks for itself."

"Yeah, well, get your ass dressed so I can watch you earn your money tonight."

Her smile turned into a determined grin as she said, "You got that."

When King and Tippi pulled onto the block they saw that everyone who was supposed to be at the trap was there. King noticed Flex's new truck parked right next to Nutta's Dodge Nitro. *I think I'll give that clown's truck to Nutta,* he thought as he climbed out of Tippi's H2. They went inside the trap and saw everyone sitting in the living room, chilling. Boleg, Cuddy, Nutta, and Flex were passing a blunt back and forth among them, getting nice and high.

"What up, my niggas, y'all good?" asked King as he went and joined the group in the living room. Tippi came in behind him and sat down next to Cuddy on the couch, right on the opposite side of where Flex was sitting.

"Everything is everything, my nigga," replied Cuddy.

"Yeah, we good. What up with you, though?" asked Boleg.

King stared at Nutta for a minute and wondered why his little partner was looking so uncomfortable. "What up, Nutta, you good?"

"Yeah, I'm straight. I . . . I need to holla at you though, King. I may have fucked up a li'l bit."

King frowned and said, "Holla then." Nutta then gave everyone a recap of what had gone down at the McDonald's out in Midwest City earlier that day. After he was finished, King asked, "Why in the fuck you didn't get at nobody, Nutta? What was you thinkin' 'bout?"

Nutta shrugged his slim shoulders and said, "I was 'bout to get at you when Tippi called me and told me 'bout this meet here tonight. So I was like fuck it, I'll get at you when I see you. I was still a li'l spooked so I went to the pad and tried to chill and not think 'bout that shit. I'm tellin' you, King, that nigga shouldn't have showed me that heat and didn't use it, dog. That shit got me hot, so I handled up."

"You did what you was supposed to do, li'l nigga," said Tippi. "As a matter of fact, I really think it's time we come up with a plan to deal with 'em south side niggas. We got to get 'em out of our fuckin' way for real."

"Tippi! What the fuck did we just finish talkin' 'bout earlier? That shit ain't gon' happen right now, so kill it!"

"I know what we spoke on, nigga. Remember, I was the one tryin' to look at the bigger picture. But that was before I knew that those fools did some more goofy shit with one of ours. There has to be a way to deal with 'em niggas wit'out fuckin' up everything else. It looks like we gon' have to do somethin', 'cause these niggas ain't fadin' away, King."

King stared at Flex and asked him, "What you think 'bout that, Flex? You think we can move 'em niggas wit'out fuckin' up our ends?"

Tippi smiled as she stared at Flex.

Flex thought about King's question for a second before answering. "On the real, anythang is possible. But I think the best way to deal with 'em niggas is to go for the kill shot on our first move. Knock the head off and the body falls."

"Real talk. But how can we get that close to that nigga? It ain't like he not knowin' 'bout us."

Flex smiled and said, "I think I can take care of that part, my nigga."

"Yeah, how?"

"Remember I told you 'bout that broad I was fuckin' with who plugged me wit' 'em crackas and shit?"

King shot a glance toward Tippi and answered, "Yeah, but what does that got to do wit' this shit?"

"One of 'em crackas I be servin' used to get his work from one of 'em south side niggas. He told me that they work is just as tight as ours. Anyway, we got to choppin' it up one night and he told me that he was damn near positive that our work came from the same peeps. I thought he was on some smoker shit, but somethin' told me to check this shit out. Don't ask me why, I just did. So I shot him some shit like, I'm tryin' to get a new plug and come up on my own and asked him if he could hook me up wit' 'em south side niggas. I even told the broad who hooked me up with the crackas that I was 'bout to do me and if she wanted to continue to ride wit' me she should convince that fool to help me get in wit' 'em niggas from the south. That was a week or so ago. It's been poppin' so hard that I haven't had the time to push that shit any further, though. But now I see how we can use that shit to our advantage."

"I can't believe that nigga, Flamboyant, gets down like that. Servin' his own shit makes him an easy target for real," said King.

"You never know, that nigga just may be on some sucka shit like that," said Boleg.

"Nah, I don't think he gets down like that. I told the cracka that if I got down wit' the fool I wouldn't fuck with no flunkies. He told me that he only dealt with the second in charge, some nigga they call Prince. If he could hook me up wit' that nigga then it shouldn't be too hard for me to get in wit' the other nigga. Then we can do 'em both," Flex said as he relit the blunt that had gone out while they were discussing the termination of Flamboyant and Prince.

King stared at Tippi and they both started laughing.

"What the fuck is wrong with y'all? Y'all act like y'all been smokin' some of this good shit too," Cuddy said as he inhaled deeply on the blunt Flex had passed to him.

Before either of them could speak, King's cell started ringing. He checked the caller ID and saw that it was Shayla. He smiled as he checked the time on his watch and saw that it was close to two in the morning. *Hmm, this gots to be some good news,* he thought as he answered with, "What up?"

"We need to talk."

Staring directly at Tippi he asked, "When and where?"

"Tomorrow, Tony Roma's on Meridian. I'll be there no later than one," Shayla said seriously.

"See you then," he said and ended the call.

"Say, King, what was this meetin' supposed to be 'bout? I'm missin' mad money. I gots to go do me," said Nutta.

"Yeah, we been here for damn near an hour and we still haven't gotten to your shit yet. What's up, King?" asked Boleg.

"I wanted to touch base wit' my niggas, that's all. Tippi felt it was best that we got together to make sure that we were all on the same page," he lied. "Now, tell me, how's thangs lookin' wit' the work? Y'all good or do I need to make that call and get us stocked properly?"

"We're gettin' low on the bud," Cuddy said with a high-ass smile on his face.

"And it looks like we're goin' to need some more water, too. 'Em young niggas been actin' a fool for that shit over in the North Highlands," added Boleg.

"How's the yay holdin' up?" Tippi asked.

"We're good for the time bein'. Check wit' me in a day or so, though," said Flex.

"A'ight, then, y'all go on and do you. Be safe and get at me tomorrow some time. Flex, get on that shit and get back at me wit' what you come up wit'. It looks like we're definitely goin' to have to move on 'em south niggas."

"Gotcha," Flex said as he got to his feet.

"Before y'all bounce, y'all niggas need to leave the seventh open 'cause we gon' do it real big for this nigga's birthday this year. I've hooked it up for us to have his party at Déjà Vu. So make sure y'all get real flossy wit' it 'cause it's gon' be on and crackin'," Tippi said with a smile on her face.

"Is that right? I'm wit' that shit. Fuck, we ain't did no shit like that since Cuddy's party last year," said Nutta.

"I know, it's 'bout time we clowned a li'l bit," added Boleg.

"Yeah, I'm wit' that," Cuddy replied.

"Me too," said Flex.

"A'ight, then, y'all. I'll holla," King said as he and Tippi left the trap. When they were back inside Tippi's truck they both started laughing again. They laughed so hard that tears fell from their eyes. "That would have been real fucked up if you would have done that nigga, Tippi."

"It wouldn't have been on me, nigga. That shit was your call, not mines!" Shaking her head from side to side she said, "You and that damn baby mama of yo's. She damn near got that nigga Flex wig split for nothin'."

"I know, huh? Damn."

"You might as well send for Keko and Spook. Ain't no need for 'em niggas to be way out West when it's 'bout to go down out here."

"You right, and Keko loves to get his floss on like everybody else."

"I doubt flossin' is gon' be on that nigga's mind once he touches back down."

"You're right."

"Let's get back to your spot. I'm tryin' to get back to sleep," Tippi said as she started her truck and pulled off the block. As they were headed toward King's home, his thoughts were of Shayla. He had a funny feeling that shit was about to get thick. Some major decisions were about to get made concerning his relationship with Tippi and Shayla. *Damn, it's hard bein' the King!*

Chapter Twenty-two

Shayla tossed and turned all night. After getting maybe a couple hours of sleep, she climbed out of bed and showered. After she was dressed she left the house and made a beeline directly to Taj's home. After ringing the doorbell repeatedly, Taj finally came to the door, screaming, "What the fuck are you ringin' my doorbell like you crazy for, fool! It's fucking eight o'clock in the fuckin' mornin', Shayla!"

Shayla ignored her and walked right past her and into the house. She plopped herself down on Taj's cream-colored sofa and said, "I think I still love Trevor."

"What else is fuckin' new? You came over here to wake me up for that shit? Girl, you must have lost your damn mind! You know damn well I'm no good to you or the world until after ten o'clock!"

"Come on, Taj, this is serious. I don't know what to do. Here I am still in love with my ex, while I'm involved with Marco. This shit ain't right."

"It ain't right, but it's life. Shit happens."

"I can't hurt Marco, girl. I just can't."

"Sooner or later you're going to have to make a decision. If you continue to be with Marco then you're only prolonging the inevitable. You may be doing more harm than good by staying with him. Sit Marco down and explain that you're still in love with Trevor and that it has nothing to do with him; it's all about you and how you're feeling."

"And you think he'll accept it that easily? Girl, that nigga gon' go ballistic on my ass!"

"I didn't say he would like what you've told him, but he would at least respect your honesty. A nigga like Marco hates to be played, more than anything. At least this way he can save face in the situation."

"Marco adores me, Taj. I can't do him like that. He hasn't done a damn thing to deserve some shit like this, but here I am actually thinking about doing this to him. He's treated me like a damn queen and look how I'm going to repay him. This is really fucked up."

"You're going to have to do something. Look, while you sit there and decide who will be your future mate in life, I'm about to go back to bed. Wake me up around eleven. No, make it twelve."

"All right. I'm having lunch with Trevor at one."

"Lunch?"

"Mmm hmm. I have to talk to him before I make my decision. I'm hoping he's not feeling me; that'll make my decision that much easier."

Shaking her head no, Taj told her best friend, "No, it wouldn't. If anything, that would make you want that nigga even more."

Shayla slapped her hand to her forehead, lay back on the sofa, and softly moaned, "I know."

Flamboyant got dressed a couple of hours after Shayla left, and went to meet Prince at his home. Prince was waiting for him to arrive. They went to their main trap on the south side and collected the money that was made the previous evening. After they picked up the cash they went back to Prince's house to make sure the count was correct. Today was re-up day, and that meant today was going to be hectic for Flamboyant. He was going to have to make sure everything was right; then he was going to be constantly moving around town, picking up and dropping off their new batch of works. Flamboyant hated days like this. All he really wanted to do today was scoop up Shayla and take her somewhere to hang out. He smiled as he thought about his girl. *I'm 'bout to make her a very happy woman,* he thought as he watched Prince put the last stack of money into his Louis Vuitton duffel bag.

"That's it, dog, the rest is on you," Prince said as he relaxed back in his chair in front of the dining room table.

Flamboyant pulled out his cell and called Toni. When Toni answered he said, "I'm ready."

"Good. Meet me at Mickey Mantle's in an hour. We'll have an early lunch, on me."

"Cool," Flamboyant replied as he hung up the phone. He smiled at his right-hand man and said, "Everything is everything. Did you take care of that thang for me yet?"

"Yeah, Mista Tricky, I got you. You love that broad for real, huh?"

"Wit' all of my heart, nigga, wit' all of my heart. When will it be ready? I want Shayla's birthday to be the best one she's ever had wit' me."

"The dealership in Dallas told me that it'll be here on the seventh, just like you wanted. I'm havin' it delivered over here."

"Right. I'll have you drop it off at my spot some time that night. I want my babe to wake up and see her brand new BMW 355i parked in our driveway. She's been lightweight sweatin' me for a new car for a minute now. What 'bout the party? Have you taken care of that, too?"

"Come on, Flam, when have I not taken care of the shit you ask me to take care of? Everything is good, dog. The caterer has already hooked up wit' 'em New York niggas, so the food is a go. I also told 'em East Coast fools to see if they could get Jim Jones to come perform that night.

They told me they didn't think that would be a problem. I've gotten at all of the team, so they already know what time it is for the seventh. We're good."

"That's straight. Shayla loves that nigga Jim Jones's shit so it'll be a perfect night for my wifey. Just fuckin' perfect. Let me roll. I'll get at you when I'm ready to drop."

"I'll be ready," Prince assured him.

Shayla arrived at the restaurant ten minutes after one on purpose. She had hoped to piss King off a little before she arrived. When she walked into the restaurant and saw a smile on his handsome face she knew she'd failed at her attempt at getting him angry. After she was seated King said, "What up, Shay, you good?"

Sighing heavily she said, "Actually I'm not. Let me get right to it. What do you want from me? Sex? Do you just want to hit it again for old times' sake or do you want something more?"

Trevor smiled confidently and asked her, "What do you want, Shay?"

She frowned. "Stop it, Trevor, this isn't funny and it damn sure ain't a game! Answer my question!"

"A'ight. I want what I've always wanted, Shay: you. I love you, Shayla, always have and I always will."

"Then why did you do me the way you did me when you went to prison? Why? I would have waited forever for you!"

"I already answered that question, Shay. Blame it on a nigga not wantin' to take a chance on gettin' his heart broke."

"That's so damn wrong. You can be so selfish at times."

He gave her that confident smile again and asked, "But you still love me, right?"

She stared at him before answering him. "I'm really not sure. I know I still care deeply for you. And I know that fact will never change. We've been through too much for me to sit here and say that I don't care about you."

"Care? Fuck care! I didn't say shit 'bout no damn care! I asked you if you still loved me, Shay. Now answer the question."

"Yes. Yes, I still love you. But you and I both know that there's a difference between being in love and just plain old loving a person. I can't honestly say if I'm still in love with you, Trevor." Before he could say a word she raised her hand and continued, "Please don't try to force that answer out of me. I'm going to need some time to think about all of this."

"Think about what? You still love me so you can't be all in love with that nigga you wit'. If you was, you wouldn't be here right now. Come on, you know don't no nigga in this world know you better than I do. You're here 'cause I've been on your mind nonstop, just as much as you've been on mine. Stop wastin' time so we can go on and do this."

"Do what? What are we going to do, Trevor, if I do decide to be with you? How is it going to be? I move in with you and live the life of a baller's wifey? Or are you willing to make that major commitment and wife me for real? Are you willing to do that, Mr. Big Time?"

Whoa! He sat in silence while everything she said to him digested.

"Ahh, so the cat has your tongue, huh? Well, while you're sitting over there pondering my words, let me give you something else to think about. If, and I do mean if, I do decide to be with you again the only way it's going to work is if I'm Mrs. King. I'm turning twenty-six in a few weeks and I don't have time to be wasting sitting around being the girlfriend of the town's big baller. It's either wife me or nothing whatsoever, Mr. King."

He smiled and said, "You do still love a nigga! You got to if you wanna be Wifey."

She shook her head and said, "Didn't you hear anything I just told you? God! I swear, you still can get on my last damn nerves if you want to. If! If! If! 'If I decide' does not mean I'm going to be your wife, Trevor!"

"You know what?"

"What?"

"I love when you call me by my government name. You are the only person I let get away wit' that shit. Tippi be tryin' to say it on the slick and I be havin' to check her ass. But, for some reason, I've always allowed you to get away wit' that. Why do you think I let that happen?"

"I dunno, why?"

He stared directly in her brown eyes and said, "Because I've never loved a woman the way I love you, Shay. I've loved you ever since the first day I met you. I know that's some corny shit, but it's true so fuck it. We have history, Shay. We've shared each other's pain over the years. We've been there for each other when no one else was. This is meant to be, you know it just as well as I do. So it's not on me right about now, Shay; it's all 'bout you. 'Cause I don't have a problem makin' you Mrs. King. Real talk!"

Shayla was sipping a glass of water and damn near spit a mouthful of water all over him. She grabbed a napkin, wiped her mouth, and said, "I'm going to need some time to think about this, Trevor. Please don't rush me. Give me some space."

"I'll give you all the time you need, baby. I ain't going nowhere. You must have forgot, I'm the King in this town."

She shook her head and watched him as he signaled for the waiter to come to their table. After they gave their orders she asked, "Why didn't anyone come to us sooner?"

That confident smile returned as he said, "When the King speaks, his subjects listen!" He laughed. "Nah, I told 'em I'd let 'em know when we were ready to order. I knew this shit was gon' be deep and I didn't want us to be disturbed."

"You've matured, Trevor. I like that. I like the fact that you seemed to have grown in a positive way. Back in the day you would have never thought of something as simple as that. You would have been rude and tried to bully the situation and basically act like a complete asshole."

"Yeah?"

"Yeah."

"But you liked that shit, too, huh?"

She started laughing and answered him honestly. "Yeah!" They started laughing as the waiter returned with their order of ribs and French fries.

As they were finishing their meal, King received a call on his cell. "What's up, Charlie?"

"We need to talk. I just got back in town and I've been informed that there's been some more violence out in the streets."

"Contrary to what people think, Oklahoma City is a violent spot, Charlie. You really need to be more specific."

"Don't fuck with me, King! You want specifics? All right, have your ass at the Elephant Bar in twenty!"

He stared at his phone after Charlie had hung up on him. *Fuck!* "Check it, Shay, I got to roll out. Some shit has come up. Get at me when you know what's what. I ain't goin' nowhere." Before she could say a word, he slid out of his seat, came to her side of the table, and gave her a quick kiss on her lips. "Don't you ever forget that we were born to be together."

She stared into his brown eyes and nodded. Just as he was about to walk away she grabbed his hand and said, "That reminds me, what are you getting into for your birthday?"

He laughed and said, "Probably party like it's 1999; ain't no tellin' wit' the King. Now let me go. I'll holla."

She sat back in her seat and munched on a French fry and watched King leave the restaurant. As she sat there thinking about what her next move was going to be she prayed that God would guide her in the right direction. "God, help me, please!"

Chapter Twenty-three

King pulled into the parking lot of the Penn Square Mall and parked his car in front of the Elephant Bar. He entered the restaurant and saw Charlie sitting at the bar. He took a deep breath and went and joined Charlie. As soon as he was seated, Charlie said, "You must have lost your fuckin' mind. I can't believe you would let your people get down on some stupid shit like shooting up a fuckin' Mickey Dee's." Though Charlie's tone was harsh, the words spoken came out in a firm whisper.

"I just found out 'bout that shit last night. It ain't like you think."

"Enlighten me then."

King gave Charlie Nutta's version of what happened at the McDonald's out in Midwest City. "If that nigga from the south wouldn't have showed Nutta his strap my man wouldn't have got off on his ass. He felt threatened, Charlie, so he did him. It's as simple as that."

"Understood. I can't be mad at you if that was what happened. But you have to get control of your squad, King. You have to let them know that they are to avoid any and all conflicts with these south side guys."

"Come on wit' that shit, Charlie. Do you know what you're askin' me? That shit ain't cool at all. Now, I will pull 'em back; that's no problem right there. But if confronted or put in any position like it's 'bout to go down, there is no way in hell I can tell any of 'em to stand down. It is what it is and if it's war, then so be it."

"War hurts pockets. I'm not trying to lose any of my money over some petty-ass war between the north and south sides of Oklahoma City. I can't tell you to tell your squad not to defend themselves. I'm not crazy, King. But I can tell you to advise them to avoid any drama if it's at all possible. If they see the south side guys coming their way, turn around and head in the opposite direction. Avoid any confrontations and there won't be any."

King shook his head. "You just don't get it. If anyone shows any type of weakness the other side will eat the other alive. We're sharks in these streets, Charlie. Sharks prey on the weak. I don't expect 'em to turn the other cheek so neither will my squad. We ain't lookin' to war 'cause we want to continue to get that money. But we ain't duckin' nothin' or nobody, either. Real talk. You need to get word to 'em fools out south to fall back and we'll do the same."

"It looks like all of this shit is coming from either Del City or Midwest City. Why don't you pull your men back and let that shit out that way cool off for a minute?"

"And let 'em fools eat off that plate?" King asked angrily. "Sorry, Charlie, that ain't happenin'."

Charlie took a deep breath and said, "Control this situation, King. I don't give a damn how you do it, but you need to make sure that all of this damn shooting comes to a fucking cease. Understood?"

King slid off of the stool he was sitting on and said, "Gotcha."

King and Tippi made it back to the block at the same time. Tippi was smiling as she climbed out of her truck and met King on the porch of the trap. "What up, baby?" she asked.

"Same ol' shit. Look, we got to make sure that everybody understands that we can't be gettin' into it wit' 'em south side niggas."

"Charlie tripped, huh?"

"Yeah. We can't lose this plug, Tippi, so make sure that you handle this shit for me."

"I got ya. I'll make sure that your words are understood, don't trip."

"Good. I'm 'bout to go holla at my aunty. Get at me later."

"What's up with Keko and Spook?"

"They're on the way. They should be back in a day or so."

"So they gon' be here for the party?"

"Yeah, they'll be here," he said as he turned and went back to his car.

Tippi pulled out her cell and dialed Boleg's number as she went inside the trap. "What up, Boleg?"

"What's up wit' you?"

"Bidness, nigga. Check it, make sure that you tell Cuddy and that li'l nigga Nutta, King said to duck any and all drama wit' 'em niggas from the south."

"What? What's up wit' that shit?"

"It is what it is, nigga. That's the way King wants it to be, so that's how it's gon' be, at least for now. Make sure you pass the word."

"Whatever."

"Y'all good on that end?"

"Yeah, we straight over here. You might want to check with Nutta, though. We ain't heard from him since last night. He might be ready for some more."

"A'ight, holla back," she said as she ended the call. Just as she was about to call Nutta, Flex came inside the trap.

"What up, Tippi?" he asked as he went into the kitchen. A moment later he came back with a can of Bud Ice in his hand. "Where that nigga King at?" he asked as he sat down on the couch.

"Gon' over Doris May's house. What's up?"

"'Em fools tryin' to give me the run-around. They spooked 'cause I'm from the north so they playin' games wit' a nigga."

"You told 'em you was a north side nigga? That was dumb."

"Not really. I figure it would be better for me to tell 'em from jump instead of 'em findin' out later on and really trip. At least this way they already know what time it is."

She shook her head and said, "I'm feelin' that. Do you think they gon' fuck wit' you?"

"Yeah, they want to do business, but they playin' it safe for now. It'll probably go down in a day or so."

"Good. Make sure you keep me posted. I got some runs to make. I'll holla at yo' ass later," Tippi said as she left the trap with her cell phone in her hand. By the time she was inside of her truck she had Nutta on the line. "What's up, li'l nigga, you good?"

"I'm straight. What's up wit' you?"

"Just checkin' on yo' li'l ass."

"I'm good. Shit was slow last night but it's pickin' up now."

"Cool. Look, King wants us to fall back on 'em south side niggas. I already got at Boleg and Cuddy, so now I'm tellin' you. If 'em niggas come around you or you happen to bump into one of 'em fools, fall back."

"What if 'em niggas try to look at me? You tellin' me that King wants me to duck some rec?"

"If you think 'em niggas is gon' look at you then you already know you got to do what you got to do. But if you can, shake that shit and just bounce."

"That's some bullshit, Tippi."

"That's the way it has to be for now, young'un, so stay down and play it like this for a minute."

"Gotcha."

King was sitting next to his Aunt Doris May, watching as she inhaled deeply on a blunt. He shook his head and said, "Damn, Aunty, you don't be playin' wit' that shit, huh?"

Doris May smiled and said, "Boy, this here is what keeps me sane. Now tell me what's on yo' mind before you blow my high."

He sighed and said, "I had lunch with Shayla today. I think she's tryin' to get back wit' a nigga."

"You think?"

"She asked me what I wanted from her. If I wanted to just do it or did I want her to be my girl again. Before I could answer her she told me that if she did get back wit' me she would have to be Mrs. King. She actually wants to be Wifey. That shit fucked me up right there."

"I know how you feel about that girl, but are you ready for something as deep as marriage?"

"I can see me and Shayla married. I mean, that's all we used to talk 'bout back in the day."

Doris May shook her head as she took a small hit of her blunt. "Uh-uh boy, this ain't back in the day. This is a new day and the both of you have changed. Y'all ain't the same two lovebirds y'all used to be. Yeah, y'all still got all them feelings for each other; that's because y'all been separated for so long. The question is, are them feelings y'all sharin' strong enough to keep y'all happy? Happy enough to marry each other?"

"The love is real, Aunty, that's not what I'm worried 'bout. I know that girl and I know she would never play games wit' my heart."

"Never say what a woman will or won't do, boy. I know I taught you better than that."

"I know, but I know how I feel, and you know Shayla. She don't play games."

"So what is it that has you so worried, boy?"

"Tippi."

"What about her?" Before he could answer her question she put her blunt in the ashtray and said, "I know you ain't done stuck that li'l thang of yours in that girl!" She stared at her nephew for a few seconds, shook her head again, and said, "You damn fool! You know damn well that girl has been lovin' you just as long as Shayla. Hell, probably longer! I thought you were goin' to keep that bidness."

"I meant to, but we kinda put that down for a minute."

"I've never tried to tell you how to run your bidness, boy, and I ain't about to start. But you know just as well as I do that Tippi is a loose cannon. The only reason you've been able to control her for this long is because she's so gone over your silly ass. Now that you done went and stuck that li'l thang inside of that girl you done created some shit that's gon' get way too thick."

"I know. Ain't no way in hell I can shake Tippi for Shayla. You know she'll do some ol' crazy shit."

"Boy, you done put Shayla in harm's way."

King sat back on his aunt's couch, sighed heavily, and said, "I know."

Chapter Twenty-four

Flamboyant was excited; he felt as if it was his birthday instead of Shayla's. He reached over and gently shook Shayla and said, "Wake up, baby, it's your birthday! It's your birthday!"

She opened her eyes slowly, frowned at him, and said, "I'm up, Marco, you don't have to scream. I hear your crazy butt."

He smiled and said, "Get up so I can give you your first present."

"First? How many am I getting?" she asked with a smile.

He shrugged and said, "You know me, babe. When it comes to you, ain't no tellin'. Now hurry up and get yourself right. We're goin' out to breakfast."

She wiped an eye booger from her eye and saw that he was already dressed. She smiled again because he was looking good as ever in a pair of jeans with a sky blue striped Polo shirt. She climbed out of the bed and went into the bathroom to handle her business.

Thirty-five minutes later she came out of the bedroom dressed comfortably in a pair of yellow Capri pants with a matching top and some white and yellow sandals on her tiny feet. Flamboyant was sitting in the living room watching the early edition of *SportsCenter* on ESPN when she came into the room. He smiled when he saw her and quickly jumped to his feet and said, "Come give me some love, birthday girl." She stepped into his warm embrace and sighed as he gave her a tight hug and another kiss.

She pulled from his embrace and asked, "Where are we having breakfast? I'm starving."

"You're takin' me to Jimmy Eggs."

"I'm taking you? I thought since this is my birthday that my man is supposed to be taking me wherever. What are you up to, Marco?"

He smiled at her lovingly and said, "I thought you'd want to drive, that's all. I mean, you're the one with the brand new whip and thangs."

"New whip? Wait! Ooooooh, no, you didn't, Marco!" she screamed happily as she ran toward the front door. He laughed as he followed her. As soon as she opened the door and saw her brand new BMW 335i she let out a scream so loud that Flamboyant was certain the entire neighborhood heard her. She ran outside and was hopping up and down like a little girl, screaming, "I love it! I love it! I love it!"

Flamboyant held the keys to the Beemer in his hand and asked, "Well, don't you want to drive it?" He tossed her the keys and said, "Let me lock up the house and I'll be right back."

Shayla quickly opened the car and hopped inside. By the time Flamboyant came back outside she had the car running and a gigantic smile on her face. Once he was inside of the car she leaned to his side and gave him a kiss with a whole lot of tongue and said, "Thank you, baby! Thank you so much. I don't know what I've done to deserve a man like you in my life. I love you, Marco."

After saying those words to him she realized right then and there that there was no way she could ever hurt him. She still cared for Trevor, she couldn't deny that, but she loved her Marco and she was going to remain loyal to her man. With that decided, her smile broadened as she put her new Beemer in reverse and pulled out of the driveway so she could go enjoy a good breakfast with her man.

"Wake up, nigga, it's your birthday!" Tippi said as she stood over King. He opened his eyes and stared at her like she was crazy and rolled to the other side of his huge California king-sized bed. Tippi laughed as she jumped onto the bed and started singing the beginning of 50 Cent's song, "In da Club." "Get up, nigga. 'It's yo' birthday! It's yo' birthday! We gon' party like it's your birthday!'"

He sat up slowly and let his head rest on the headboard and said, "Why in the fuck are you so damn energetic this mornin'? Today ain't nothin' but another day."

"G'on wit' that shit. You're a year older, you got way more money than you did this time last year, and hopefully you're a li'l more smarter, nigga."

He smiled and said, "I know that's right. But look, since it's my birthday, can I start it however I want to?"

Tippi pouted and looked absolutely adorable while doing so and answered, "I guess."

"Good. This is how I want to start my day." He pulled the comforter off of himself so she could see his huge erection sticking up under his boxers. He smiled again and said, "Come and suck this big ol' thang. He's a year older too."

She laughed, smacked her lips together loudly, and said, "Yeah, he's a year older and I'm lovin' him somethin' awful."

King sighed loudly as she put his manhood inside of her mouth and began to suck him slowly. "Yeah, that's what I'm talkin' 'bout. That's how a King is supposed to start his birthday."

***

After they finished eating breakfast, Shayla made Flamboyant go with her over to Taj's house so she could show off her new car. When they pulled into Taj's driveway, Shayla began blowing the horn like she'd lost her mind. Taj came running outside, screaming, "Oh, my God! Oh, my God! Girl! You got a Beemer!"

Shayla smiled proudly as she got out of her car and gave her best friend a hug. "I'm the shit, huh?"

Taj smiled at her, shook her head, and said, "Hell fucking yes! Girl, this bad boy right here is like that!" Taj began walking around the BMW, checking it out as if she was a car inspector or something. When she opened the passenger door, she told Flamboyant, "You sure know how to treat a lady, Marco."

He smiled and said, "Whatever will keep a smile on my babe's face, I'll always make that happen. You know how I get down. What up, y'all want to go rollin' for a li'l while or what? You can drop me back off at the house, babe. I got some shit to take care of anyway. I know you tryin' to go shoppin' for the party tonight anyway."

"What, you don't want to spend the day with me, Marco?" Shayla asked with her bottom lip stuck out.

"Come on, babe, you and I both know you want to roll out wit' your girl for a li'l while. G'on and do you. I ain't trippin'."

She smiled brightly and said, "Okay! Go on and get dressed, girl! I'll be right back after I drop off my baby."

Taj stared at her friend for a few seconds then said, "All right, girl, hurry yo' ass up!"

"I will." Shayla laughed as she started the car and quickly pulled out of the driveway.

By the time she returned to Taj's, Taj was standing outside of her house waiting for her. As soon as she was inside of the car she asked, "What kind of games are you playing? You know damn well shit like this can be hazardous to a woman's health."

"I'm not playing any games, girl. I love Marco and that's that. I'm not going to mess up what I have just because of some old feelings."

"Old feelings? Shayla, you know I love you no matter what you do. I'll always have your back. I just want you to be absolutely sure about this. Dope boys can be real unpredictable. Hell, any man can when it comes to his heart and his pride."

"Don't sweat it, Taj. I know what I'm doing. I'm not going to hurt Marco. He's been too damn good to me."

"All right, girlfriend. Come on, let's get our roll on!"

After having an extremely long sex session with Tippi, King was in a very good mood. He sat up in the bed, grabbed the phone, and made a few calls to make sure that everything was in order with his kingdom. After that he turned and woke Tippi up.

"Girl, get yo' ass up. We got shit to take care of today."

"I thought you was gon' lie back and chill all day."

"Nah, fuck that shit. I'm gon' hit Charlie and load us back up so we can be ready for whatever. Plus, I got to make sure that Keko's head is in the right place."

"They back?"

"Yeah, that nigga called me last night. So get yo' ass up and go take a shower."

She smiled seductively and said, "Come take one wit' me?"

He shook his head no and said, "Uh-uh, then we'll be caught back up longer than necessary. Go on, we got the rest of the day for that freaky shit." He grabbed the cordless phone and started dialing another number as Tippi climbed out of bed and went into the bathroom.

When Keko answered his phone, King asked him, "What it do, my nigga, you good?"

"Yeah, I'm straight, fool. What's up wit' you? How ya feelin' on your birthday?"

"Just another day, dog, just another day."

"I heard that. So what, it's gon' be on and poppin' tonight, huh?"

"Yeah, we gon' floss a li'l bit and let the town see how the north gets down."

"Baaalllinn'!"

King laughed and said, "Fa' sho'. Meet me on the block in about an hour. I need to holla at ya."

"Right. I'm 'bout to roll to the northwest to see how everything has been since you sent me on that wack-ass mission."

"Boleg and Cuddy have made sure that everything was straight while y'all was out the way. Dog, you needed that break, for real."

"I know, and on the real, that was good lookin' out, my nigga. My head is a li'l clearer now, but I'm still on some murda shit the first chance I get to look at 'em south side bitches. Real talk!"

"That's what I want to talk to you about, so do you. I'll see you in an hour or so."

"Gotcha," Keko said as he hung up the phone.

When King and Tippi pulled onto the block King noticed a charcoal gray Lexus GS 350 parked in front of the trap. He frowned when he saw a few youngsters standing around the brand new luxury vehicle like it was the shit. "Who the fuck car is that, Tippi?"

Tippi parked her truck directly behind the Lexus, smiled at King, and said, "How the fuck should I know, nigga? You act like I ain't in this damn truck with yo' ass."

He stared at her for a second and was about to say something about her smart-ass mouth but thought better of it. He then climbed out of the truck and asked the youngsters who were checking out the new Lexus with twenty-four-inch chrome rims, "Do y'all know who whip this is?"

"Nah, it's been here since early this mornin', King," one of the youngsters replied.

"Is that right? Y'all ain't seen who drove it here?"

"Nope."

King stared at the vehicle for a few more seconds then walked up to the trap. When he was inside of the house he asked Keko, who was sitting down in the dining room smoking a blunt, "Dog, do you know who Lexo that is outside?"

"Nah, I thought you done went and got real flossy on a nigga since I've been out in Cali."

"That's a bad whip, but I ain't got down like that."

Tippi came inside of the house behind King, smiled, and asked, "Why you so worried 'bout that damn car? You trippin' the fuck out."

"What? A brand new fuckin' Lexus is parked in front of my main mothafuckin' spot and you askin' me why I'm worried 'bout it? You on some stupid shit today or somethin' Tippi? Huh? You know fuckin' better!"

Tippi didn't respond to his outburst; instead she smiled lovingly at him. That seemed to piss him off even more. "Why the fuck are you smiling at me? You think this is a game, Tippi? You need to get on top of your fuckin' shit if you gon' continue to be my—"

"Aww, shut the fuck up wit' that shit, nigga, damn! You know damn well I ain't gon' let nothin' happen to yo' ass, fool. Come on, I'll show you what the deal is," she said as she turned around and walked out of the trap.

With a puzzled expression on his face King followed her outside, followed closely by Keko. As soon as he stepped onto the porch Tippi, Boleg, Cuddy, Nutta, and Flex all yelled, "Happy birthday!"

Tippi stepped to him and gave him a kiss on his cheek and whispered in his ear, "You know I'd die before I'd let anything happen to my King. Now here, nigga, happy birthday," she said as she gave him the keys to the Lexus.

He stared at the keys in his hand for a second because he was trying his best not to let any tears fall from his eyes. He couldn't let the squad see him like that; it wouldn't be a good look. He raised his head and smiled at his peoples. He stepped off of the porch and shook hands with his niggas and thanked them for his birthday present. "I can't believe y'all done went and copped a nigga a brand new Lex."

"Dog, we ain't get this shit for you. Tippi did this shit for yo' ass. A nigga got mad love for ya, baby, but I ain't got it like that to be droppin' no seventy-plus Gs on yo' ass," said Nutta. Then everyone started laughing.

King turned toward Tippi and asked, "You did this for me?"

"You're my King, aren't you?"

With a sincere smile on his face he told her, "You better fuckin' believe it!"

Chapter Twenty-five

It was party time and King couldn't believe how good he was feeling. Everything was going right for once and he was loving it. His money was right, his squad was good, and all was fuckin' well, he thought as he dressed for the club. Though he was pushing a brand new Lexus, he still didn't feel the need to get too dressed up; that wasn't his style. He was on that rugged look for real, but tonight he chose to tone down his thuggish style just a little. He had on a pair of True Religion jeans with a black vest and a wife beater. Since they didn't allow sneakers inside of Déjà Vu he threw on a pair of butter-colored Tims.

He went and stood in front of the mirror and smiled at his reflection. He grabbed a brand new platinum Jacob that Boleg and Cuddy gave him earlier and fastened it to his wrist. The diamonds all around the bezel sparkled as they reflected off of the lights in the bathroom. He then grabbed his next gift: a platinum chain and crown medallion. He smiled as he thought back to earlier when Nutta put the chain around his neck and told him, "Now, the King has been properly crowned." It felt good to have been shown that kind of love on his birthday. No one other than his aunt had ever made him feel this special. No one but Shayla.

Damn, I haven't even called her. It's her birthday too, he thought as he grabbed his cell off of the dresser and dialed Shayla's number. When he got her voice mail he left a quick message: "Hey, you. Happy birthday, baby.

Hope yours has been as cool as mine. Holla at me when you can." After he ended the call he grabbed the keys to his Lexus and went to go meet the rest of the squad on the block so they could head out to the club. It was time to have some fun.

When King made it to the block everyone was there waiting for him, everybody except for Tippi. He jumped out of the Lexus and said, "What it do? Y'all ready to do this or what?"

"Nigga, we been over here waitin' on yo' ass for the last hour! Of course we ready," said Keko.

"Where Tippi ass at?"

"She said she was gon' meet us there. She had to take care of some shit," Flex said as he stepped off the porch.

"Everythang a'ight?"

"Yeah, she's good."

"A'ight, then, let's roll." King went and got back into his car while Boleg and Cuddy climbed into Boleg's Suburban. Flex and Nutta were riding with each other in Flex's Navigator while Keko and Spook followed them in Keko's old-school Impala. As the small caravan left the block King was wondering what was up with Tippi. *She didn't tell me anything 'bout taking care of any business.* He shook his head and said, "Fuck it, tonight's my night to have a ball. Tippi gon' be a'ight!"

By the time they arrived at the club the parking lot was packed. King could tell that all of the teenyboppers were out in full blast. *Everyone came out to see Jim Jones do his thang tonight,* he thought as he parked his car. Just as he was getting out of the car he saw Tippi pulling into the parking lot bumping some Lil Wayne. He smiled and shook his head as he watched her park her H2 right next to his Lexus.

His eyes grew wide as saucers when he saw what Tippi was wearing. She was looking extraordinarily good in a pair of black shorts with a black bra, covered by a black feathered open vest by D&G. On her feet were a pair of stiletto heels that had to be at least four inches high. But what really had him mesmerized was how sexy she was looking. She had her hair put in a style that he'd never seen before. It was sort of like a bun, but then again it wasn't. Her long black hair was now dyed a light brown and it was piled on top of her head, being held together by what looked like two oriental type of stick pins. She had several strands of her hair falling lightly from the right side of her head, giving her a look that screamed sexy!

Tippi smiled shyly at King and asked, "Why are you staring at me like that, baby? You don't like what you see?"

Before he could answer her Nutta came over to them and said, "Gotdamn, Tippi! What the hell you done did?"

She frowned at him and said, "Shut the fuck up, nigga. Just 'cause I'm lookin' feminine tonight don't mean I won't come out these heels and kick yo' li'l ass."

"I'm just sayin', you lookin' good as fuck for real."

That put a smile on her face. "Thanks. Now, are we gon' stand out here all night or are we goin' inside of the club and clown?"

King grabbed her by her hand and said, "Yeah, let's go get our clown on."

"That's right! The squad is in the mothafuckin' hizzhouse!" screamed Nutta as they headed toward the entrance of the club.

Shayla was impatiently waiting for Taj, sitting inside of her car in Taj's driveway. She couldn't believe that after all of the rushing Taj did she had the nerve to have her sitting outside, waiting for her ass. Just as she was about to get out of the car to go see what was taking her so long, Taj came out of her house looking gorgeous as ever. She was wearing a gold form-fitting dress by Max Mara that left very little to the imagination. To say she was looking sexy would be an understatement. She looked too damn good!

Taj opened the door of the car and said, "Sorry, girl, but my mother called and had me on the phone and wouldn't let me go."

Concerned, Shayla asked, "Is everything okay?"

"Yeah, she's fine. She's bored out of her mind, that's all. She actually thought she was going to get me to come over to chill with her tonight. Uh-uh, sista girl is on her own tonight!"

Shayla laughed and asked, "What did you tell her, Taj? I know you weren't mean to your mom."

"I told her I had a hot date and there was no way I was going to cancel. She sounded disappointed but when I told her we could get together tomorrow or something she seemed cool. Anyway, I'm ready to get my swerve on tonight. Girl, hit that light and let me see how that dress looks." Shayla did as requested and Taj smiled as she gave her friend a nod of approval and said, "Yep, you're wearing that there dress, girlfriend. It fits you perfectly."

"Thanks." She cut off the inside light, started the car, and pulled out of the driveway. "Girl, that dress was made for you."

"It's off the hook, huh?"

"Um hm. You're going to have your hands full tonight."

"I hope so! But for real, Shay, I'm kinda hoping to impress that nigga Gunna."

"What! You never told me you were feeling him. When did this come about?"

Taj shrugged her slim shoulders and said, "I saw him a couple of weeks ago at the mall and I was like damn, that nigga is cute."

"Why didn't you tell me so I could have Marco hook y'all up?"

"I wanted to wait until tonight. I knew he was going to be at your party so I decided to wait. Girl, I'm telling you, it's something about him that gets me wet!"

Laughing, Shayla said, "Hopefully you'll be able to do something about that tonight."

"And you know it!"

King and the squad were all sitting around the VIP area, downing shots of Gran Patrón. At $300 a bottle, King told their waitress to keep them coming every time she noticed they were running low. King was proud of the way Tippi had everything laid out for his birthday party. She had the people at the club rope off a section of the VIP area with what looked like yellow and black crime scene tape the police use whenever there is a murder. But instead of having CRIME SCENE written on it, it read, HAPPY BIRTHDAY! PARTY IN SESSION! in bold, black lettering. To top everything off, she had a cake made with a picture of King on the front of it. He was touched so deeply by her efforts that he couldn't resist giving her a passionate kiss in front of everyone.

"I knew y'all was gon' get together sooner or later!" Flex laughed.

"Me too. Tippi too damn overprotective of that nigga for her not be in love wit' his ass," added Cuddy.

"It's all good, baby. We all family so it ain't nothin' but love!" yelled Nutta.

Tippi smiled shyly and said, "I love you, King."

He returned her smile and said, "I love you too, Tippi. Thank you for what you done for me today. It really means a lot to a nigga."

Before she could respond Nutta said, "Aww fuck nah! That's that nigga from the south who I blasted in Midwest City!"

"Where?" asked King.

"Right there," Nutta said as he pointed toward Milo, who was standing next to Gunna on the other side of the club.

King followed Milo and Gunna with his eyes and watched them sit down with a crowd of other niggas. As he continued to stare in their direction his heart skipped a beat. There was obviously another birthday party being given at the club tonight, and it was Shayla's. He read a bright pink banner that said, HAPPY BIRTHDAY, SHAYLA, and he felt sick to his stomach. *Man, shit gon' get crazy tonight. What the fuck is Shayla doin' fuckin' 'round wit' 'em south side niggas? Shit!*

He turned back toward everyone in the squad and said, "Listen, ain't no need to get wild. We gon' fall back and continue to have a good time. Y'all already know what time it is, right?"

"I'm good," said Nutta.

"I'm straight," said Cuddy.

"Whatever, dog," added Boleg.

"Gotcha, King," said Flex.

King stared at Keko and Spook and asked, "Y'all gon' hold me down or what?"

Keko was staring at the people over at the other party and asked, "Do you think that's 'em niggas over there, King? Do you really think that's 'em fools who took my wifey?"

"Come on, Keko, this ain't the place nor the time, my nigga. You got to stand down."

Spook put his hands on Keko's shoulders and whispered, "We'll get 'em niggas, dog, just not tonight. Don't fuck up our people's birthday love."

Keko smiled suddenly and raised his shot glass in the air and said, "To the King!"

Everyone raised their glasses also and repeated the toast: "To the King!"

King downed his shot of Gran Patrón and sighed. *Tonight is gon' to be a long night. Fuck!*

Chapter Twenty-six

When Flamboyant saw Shayla and Taj enter the club he quickly went to meet them at the entrance. He wanted any- and everybody inside of the club to see that Shayla belonged to him. He smiled brightly, gave her a hug, and said, "You're lookin' beautiful, babe. Happy birthday."

She smiled at her man and said, "Thank you, Marco."

"Come on, I got the other side of VIP reserved for us," he said as he led the way toward their tables. As he led them over to the far end of the club they walked right by where King and his squad were enjoying themselves. Flamboyant didn't pay any attention to the stares he received from the squad as he passed them. Shayla, on the other hand, locked eyes with both King and Tippi. *Oh. My. God,* she thought as she let Flamboyant pull her toward their table.

After they were seated Shayla turned toward Taj and whispered, "Did you—"

Taj cut her off and said, "I saw. Keep your cool and pray to God that Trevor doesn't decide to come over and wish you a happy birthday."

"I need a drink."

"A strong one," added Taj.

On cue, Flamboyant popped a bottle of Cristal and said, "Nothin' but the best for my queen, y'all. Now fill y'all glasses so we can toast to the birthday girl."

Flamboyant's team were all looking dapper for tonight's party. Every member of the team was suited and booted.

They were wearing everything from tailor-made suits and alligator shoes to Armani slacks and Italian loafers.

Gunna, who was looking extremely handsome to Taj, was distracted by the stares he was receiving from across the room. Just as he was about to speak to Flamboyant about it, Taj slid next to him and said, "Hi, Gunna."

He returned her smile and said, "What's up, Taj, you good?"

She stared into his light brown eyes and said, "Mm hmm, you?"

"Always."

"Am I going to be able to get a dance out of you tonight, Mr. Gunna?"

Damn, this li'l broad is right! "Yeah, that could be arranged."

"Is that right? What else can you arrange, Mr. Gunna?"

"Why don't we discuss that a li'l bit later on?"

Taj placed her hand on top of his and said, "Certainly."

On the other side of the club Flex damn near spilled his shot of Patrón when he saw Prince tap glasses with Flamboyant. "Dog, that is 'em south side niggas! That's that nigga Prince right there. And that nigga he's standin' next to got to be that fool Flamboyant."

"Who, the one wearin' the blue suit?" asked King.

"Yeah, that's him."

"Fuck 'em. We doin' us over here so let 'em do 'em over there," he said as he poured himself another shot. As he downed his drink he noticed Flamboyant give Shayla a kiss on her lips. Not only did the expensive liquor burn his insides, watching that take place infuriated him. *Ain't that a bitch! She's fuckin' wit' my enemy and had the nerve to try to get at me. I'll kill that bitch,* he thought angrily. *Hold up, ain't no way Shayla would do me that. Fuck, she don't even know 'bout this beef. I'm trippin' the fuck out,* he thought as he continued to stare at her from across the room.

Tippi was watching King as he watched Shayla and she was getting angrier and angrier by the minute. *I know this nigga ain't sittin' here sweatin' that bitch! Don't make me act a fool in this bitch tonight, King, 'cause you know damn well I will,* she thought as she continued to watch him watch Shayla. *Fuck!*

Gunna and Taj were getting along just fine and the evening was progressing nicely until Jim Jones finished his set. The club was hyped, everyone kept screaming out "Baaallllinnn'!" The Dipset Capo did his thing big time. Even though Shayla was uncomfortable because of the constant stares she was receiving from King, she refused to let him spoil her party. After all, it was her birthday too. But then she overhead Gunna tell Milo, "Dog, that's 'em north side niggas over there on the other side of the club."

"Where?" asked Milo.

"Right there, nigga, look," Gunna said as he pointed in the direction of King and the squad.

Milo stared at the group for a few seconds and said, "Ain't that 'bout a bitch! There's that li'l nigga who blasted at me! That is 'em north side niggas!"

Oh, God, please let me not be hearing what I think I'm hearing, silently prayed Shayla.

Wave came over to Milo and Gunna and asked, "What's poppin'? You two niggas look like you got somethin' on y'all mind. What's up?"

"'Em north side niggas are on the other side of the VIP. Look," Milo said as he pointed directly at Nutta. "That's that nigga who got at me out in Midwest City."

"Yeah? What, y'all want to look at 'em niggas or what?"

"Look at who?" asked Flamboyant as he came and stood next to Wave.

"'Em north side niggas. They over there in the VIP."

Flamboyant turned and faced the other VIP section and watched King and his squad as they enjoyed themselves. "Are you sure that's 'em fools, Milo?"

"Positive."

"Shit. I'm not tryin' to ruin Wifey's party on some bullshit, but this shit needs to be addressed. Come on," Flamboyant said as he led the way toward King.

Shayla watched in horror as her worst nightmare came true right before her very eyes. Taj saw it too and whispered, "Oh, shit!"

When Flamboyant, Milo, Wave, Ken, Gutta, and Prince made it in front of King's table, Flamboyant said, "Excuse me, dog, can I have a minute? You are King right?"

King sized up Flamboyant for a few seconds before answering. *So this is the nigga Flamboyant. Humph, straight soft.* "Yeah, I'm King, what up?"

"They call me Flamboyant."

"And?"

"I think we need to have a talk."

"'Bout what?"

"Let's not play games. You and I both know what it is. Ain't no need for this weak shit to continue. It's really a waste of time and energy. Y'all gettin' y'all money, we gettin' our money, why do we have to beef?" Flamboyant asked logically.

King, on the other hand, wasn't in the mood to be logical. He was too upset at the fact that Flamboyant had Shayla. "Check it, homes, y'all niggas took the life of my man's wifey. Do you really expect not to have beef?"

"If I remember correctly, y'all hit up my man's spot first. That's what started all this drama. But, peep this, there's no need to go back and forth with this shit. I'm here tryin' to dead this shit for real. My man Milo got blasted by your man. Luckily, no one was hurt. Before someone does get hurt again, let's do what's good for all of us and kill this shit. What you say?"

King turned slightly and stared at Keko for a moment. He was thinking about Charlie and how he couldn't fuck up his money. The pain and hurt in Keko's eyes on top of his anger over Shayla made him tell Flamboyant, "Dog, you need to take your weak-ass crew back on where y'all came from. If you don't, it might just get ugly over here."

Tippi smiled and so did Keko. *That's my nigga!* Keko thought.

Wave stepped forward and said, "You tried to be the bigger man, my nigga, now let me speak for a minute."

"So, it's beef then, huh?" asked Flamboyant.

Keko stepped next to King and said, "You fuckin' right it's beef, clown. You niggas took Wifey. For that, death is on the way. Real talk!"

Before Wave could respond, Gunna eased his way to the front of the small crowd and said, "Let the record reflect that I'm the one who took your wifey, nigga. What?"

King put his arm in front of Keko's chest to stop him from rushing Gunna and said, "This ain't the time or place for this shit. We'll have our day wit' these niggas."

"Oh, that's fa' sho'," Wave said as he turned toward Flamboyant. "Come on, dog, 'em New York niggas is tryin' to ear hustle. We'll look at these niggas another day."

"Yeah, listen to yo' man. Go enjoy the rest of your evening, chump. And tell Shayla I said happy b-day," King said with a smile on his face.

At the mention of Shayla's name Flamboyant's anger rose to a new height. "Keep my girl's name out yo' mouth, nigga."

"Or what, fool? You better go ask her 'bout the King. I'm sure she'll properly inform you of my tendencies." The squad started laughing.

"Keep on thinkin' I'm pussy 'cause I tried to be a real nigga 'bout this business. I got somethin' for yo' ass, nigga."

"You know where to find us, fool, just like we know where yo' ass at. So, 'til then, get the fuck on!"

Flamboyant smiled and said, "We'll be seein' you sooner than you think, clown-ass nigga. Let's get back to the party," he told his squad.

As Flamboyant led his team back to their section of VIP, Tippi asked King, "What happened to that 'fall back' shit you was talkin' 'bout?"

He ignored her question and told Keko, "'Em niggas ain't 'bout no drama for real. They too flossy wit' it for any real gangsta shit. They straight soft."

"Maybe, but we can't afford to be fakin' wit' they ass, either. We move, we move hard."

"No question," King replied as he poured himself another shot of Patrón.

As soon as they made it back to their tables Flamboyant sat down next to Shayla and asked her, "Do you know that nigga King?"

"Why?"

He gritted his teeth and said, "Don't fuckin' question me right now, Shayla. Do you or don't you know that nigga?"

"Yes, I know him, Marco."

"From where?"

"Does it matter?"

Trying his best to remain calm he inhaled deeply and said, "'Cause me and that nigga got beef, and I want to know what the fuck's goin' on wit' my wifey and my enemy."

"I had a life before you, Marco. I know a lot of people. Just because I know him doesn't mean I'm against you. I don't appreciate you talking to me as if I've done something wrong."

"I have a good heart, babe, you know this, but this heart can get ugly, so please don't sit there and get slippery lip wit' me. That nigga is a threat to my well-being as well as the rest of the team. All threats to us have to be dealt wit'. Do you understand what I'm sayin'?"

"That's your business, Marco, not mine. Why are you telling me this stuff?"

"'Cause if there's anything you need to tell me 'bout that nigga, you better tell me now. I'm not tryin' to be hearing no bullshit later on in the game. Do you understand what I'm sayin', Shayla?"

The tone in his voice scared her. She couldn't believe he was speaking to her so harshly. This wasn't the Marco she was accustomed to. "I understand, Marco."

"Good." He turned toward Wave and said, "We'll meet at Prince's spot tomorrow at noon."

"Gotcha."

Then, as if nothing had changed, he told everyone, "This is a party. Let's get back to partying!"

"So, it's on then?" Tippi asked.

"Yeah, it's on. I'm gon' get at Charlie in the mornin' and explain that some shit just can't be ignored," replied King.

"You think that's gon' work?"

"I doubt it."

"But fuck it?"

He smiled at Tippi and said, "Yeah, fuck it."

"Good. I'll be right back," she said as she went toward the bathrooms.

After relieving herself, Tippi came out of the bathroom and saw Gunna as he went into the men's room. She quickly scanned the area and saw that it was pretty dark in that part of the club. She stepped into the corner next to the men's entrance and pulled out her two oriental stick pens from her hair, which were actually two ice picks without handles. Her hair fell down across her face. She moved several strands of hair from her eyes so she would be able to see what she was doing.

"Come on, come on before someone comes and I miss, nigga," she said as she waited for Gunna to come out of the bathroom.

On cue, Gunna came out of the bathroom, wiping his hands on a paper towel. He never saw Tippi as she hit him twice in his neck and once directly in his heart. He died before he was able to make a sound.

Tippi was walking back toward their table in the VIP before his body hit the ground. When she was back at their table she whispered in King's ear, "I'm outta here. Don't forget, you said it was on."

Before he could say a word she was walking out of the VIP toward the exit in a hurry. "Now what the fuck has she done did?"

Chapter Twenty-seven

What's taking Gunna so long? Taj asked herself as she once again scanned the club to see if she could spot him. After a few more minutes of waiting for him to return to their table, she decided to go look for him. "I'll be right back, Shay. I'm about to go find Gunna."

"Damn, girl, like that?" Shayla asked playfully.

Taj gave her friend the hand and said, "Don't you even try that shit with me. But for the record, yeah, like that!" They laughed as Taj left the VIP. After checking the DJ booth and both bars she went toward the restrooms. When she made it to the restroom area she saw a man kneeling over someone. As she was easing by, she saw that the man on the floor was Gunna. "Oh, my God! Gunna, are you all right?" she screamed.

The man kneeling over Gunna turned and asked her, "Do you know this guy?"

"Mm hmm, he's a friend."

"You need to go get some help, 'cause I don't think this cat is breathing."

In a daze, Taj turned and ran quickly as she could back to the VIP to get Flamboyant and the others. When they returned, the club owners as well as some security guards had the area blocked off. Flamboyant and Prince forcefully shoved their way through the security. "That's my man right there! Get the fuck outta my way!" screamed Flamboyant.

Ricky, one of the club owners, said, "Chill out, yo, ain't nothin' we can do for your man. He's gone, son."

"What? How the fuck this happen?"

"Noooo!" screamed Taj. Shayla grabbed her and led her back to their table away from the gruesome scene.

"Looks like someone stuck your man in the neck and chest," Ricky told Flamboyant as he pointed toward Gunna's wounds.

"Ain't this a bitch! It had to be 'em north side niggas!" yelled Wave as he turned and ran toward King and his squad.

"Come on, son. Get your man, Flamboyant! I'm not tryin' to have that shit pop off like the last time. I'm tellin' you, son, he's goin' to jail this time around. We've already called Jake. They should be here any minute," warned Ricky.

King saw Wave rushing toward them and said, "Watch yourself. It's 'bout to go down, y'all."

"What?" asked Keko.

"Look," King said as he pointed toward Wave as some security guards grabbed him. King smiled and said, "It's on fa' sho' now, my nigga."

"What you mean by that shit, King?" asked Cuddy.

"Tippi made some kind of move."

"Where she at anyway?" asked Nutta.

"She shook the spot 'cause she knew it was about to get crazy."

"What happened?" asked Boleg.

King shrugged and said, "Ain't no tellin', but we 'bout to find out."

Flamboyant and Prince rushed over to King's table, followed closely by Ricky. "So, this is how it's gon' be, huh, nigga?" Flamboyant said with tears streaming down his face. "You wanted this war, nigga, now you got what you asked for."

"What the fuck you talkin' 'bout?" King asked.

"Don't play no games, nigga! Y'all took our man Gunna out so we gon' take all you niggas out! Real talk!" screamed Prince.

King stared at them for a few seconds like they'd lost their minds and then told Rick, "Look, dog, you need to get these crazy mothafuckas away from me. I don't know what the fuck they talkin' 'bout."

King's calm and cool attitude drove Prince over the edge. "Fuck you, nigga!" he screamed as he rushed King. Before he could get close to King, Cuddy stepped in front of him and pulled out a chrome 9 mm and pointed it directly at Prince's head.

"You tryin' to die tonight, nigga? Huh? 'Cause if you is I ain't got a problem layin' yo' punk ass down. My man told you we don't know nothin' 'bout your man, so y'all need to get the fuck on before niggas start catchin' cases in this bitch for real!"

Flamboyant pulled Prince back and said, "Come on, dog, we know what we gotta do." He turned back toward King and said, "I got somethin' for yo' ass, nigga. I promise you that."

Before King could respond the club lights were turned on and the club was quickly filled with policemen. King groaned when he saw Officer Don walking his way. When he made it to King's table Officer Don said, "Now, why did I know you'd be here tonight, King? This has your name written all over it."

"Come on wit' that shit! If I'm gon' do somebody ain't no way I'd still be here. I would have been long gone before yo' ass got here."

"Is that so? Tell me, King, where's your right-hand man? Or should I say, woman?" asked Officer Don.

King smiled knowingly and said, "Tippi wasn't feeling good, so she went home to lay it down for the night."

"I bet. Well, you guys may as well get comfortable. The entire club is a crime scene now and there's going to be a nice long wait before any of you are gettin' outta here."

King shook his head as he poured himself another shot of Patrón and said, "What a fuckin' birthday!"

On the other side of the club Ken was telling Wave and Milo, "I don't give a damn what Flam says, we're movin' on 'em fools tomorrow. Fuck this shit, 'em niggas got us fucked up!"

"Exactly. But I don't think Flam is gon' keep the reins on us now. He's just as fucked up 'bout this shit as we are," said Milo.

"Good. 'Cause I'm 'bout to get my man. I want that nigga King's head like a bad dog," said Wave.

"Not more than me," Flamboyant said as he came to the table and joined his team. "We gon' do what needs to be done. Ain't no need to discuss what's gon' pop off right now though, feel me?"

"Yeah, I feel ya," said Wave.

Flamboyant turned toward Shayla, who was still trying to console Taj, and asked, "Are you okay, babe?"

"No, I'm not okay, Marco! This stuff is crazy! I knew I shouldn't have gone along with this party shit! Dammit, I can't believe this shit happened!" she screamed as she rocked back and forth with Taj in her arms.

"I told you that nigga King was the enemy! What fucks me up, though, is how in the fuck did they get that close to Gunna to do him wit'out nobody seein' shit? I mean, we been right here wit' 'em niggas in our sights all fuckin' night!"

Shayla knew the answer to his question but she refused to say a word. She continued to gently rock with Taj in her arms. *This murder scene got Tippi written all over it! If you have beef with Trevor, then you have beef with Tippi, and that's not good. You better be careful, Marco.*

Watch your every step, Shayla thought as she tried her best to console Taj.

It was close to five in the morning when everyone was able to leave the club. Once they were outside of the club, King told his squad, "Look, y'all go on and get some rest. Looks like we're at war, so prepare for it. Meet me on the block 'round one."

"Bet," said Flex.

"Gotcha," said Nutta.

"Fa' sho'," added Cuddy and Boleg.

As they climbed into their respective vehicles and pulled out of the parking lot King saw Flamboyant and his team staring at them. He smiled and waved at them as he turned into traffic. *The war has begun,* he thought as he headed home. *Shit!*

By the time he made it to his house he was dead tired, but when he saw Tippi lying on top of his bed completely naked, his fatigue seemed to vanish. He undressed as quietly as he could and then slid into the bed next to her. She opened her eyes when she felt his tongue on her good spot. "Hmmmm, eat that shit, baby, eat it good," moaned Tippi as she gyrated her pussy against his face. After bringing her to a satisfying orgasm, he climbed on top of her and slid himself as deep as he could inside of her piping hot sex.

"Damn that feels good," he said as he started stroking inside of her nice and slow. "You love me, don't you, Tippi?"

She opened her eyes and stared directly at him as she answered his question. "You know damn well I do."

"Is there anything in this world that you wouldn't do for me?" he asked as he continued to stroke deeper and deeper.

She shook her head from side to side and said, "Baby, I love you! I love you! I'll do whatever you want or need me to do! Please, please stop fuckin' talkin' right now. You're fuckin' up my nut!" she screamed as she came hard again. Her orgasm kicked his into gear and he came too with tremendous force.

As he slid off of her and tried to catch his breath he smiled and said, "Damn, that was the shit!"

Out of breath herself, Tippi smiled and said, "Yeah, it was. Now why were you askin' me all that shit?"

"'Cause I wanted to know. I mean, you've shown me over the years that you don't have a problem killin' for a nigga, and I know that you're loyal and shit. I just wanted to know if your love had any limits."

"Absolutely none. Anythang you want from me, King, I'll give you. I'd give my life up for you if it meant that you would be happy and safe."

"That's deep, Tippi. What have I done to deserve such devotion from you?"

She shrugged sleepily and said, "Just bein' who you are, I guess."

"Who am I? Who am I, Tippi?"

She stared into his brown eyes and said, "My King."

Chapter Twenty-eight

Flamboyant arrived at Prince's house at exactly noon. Every member of the team was already inside waiting for him. As soon as he entered the living room he said, "It's like this: 'em fools gots to pay for Gunna, period. Ain't no need for no plannin' or none of that shit. I want the work put in and I want it put in immediately!" Flamboyant sat down next to Prince and continued, "We need to find out exactly where 'em fools are doin' their thang on the north side. If we can, find out where any of 'em rests their head. 'Em niggas got to die for thinkin' we on some pussy shit!"

"I think we can make a quick move on one of 'em niggas," said Prince.

"What you mean?"

"One of 'em north side niggas has been tryin' to get close to me for some work. I peeped him at the club last night wit' 'em fools. He was trying to shade himself by playin' the background but I saw his punk ass. I'm glad I was shaking him left for a minute. My first mind told me he was a shady nigga."

"Is that right? What's that nigga's name?"

"Flex."

"You got a line on that nigga?"

"Yep."

"Good. Flex is our first hit then, but our ultimate move is to cut the head off so the body can fall. Get me a line on that nigga King," Flamboyant said angrily. "I want that nigga's life!"

"We gon' get 'em niggas, Flam. Don't trip, my nigga," said Wave.

"Don't trip? Wave, 'em niggas took Gunna right under our fuckin' noses! That shit right there is fuckin' embarrassing! Find that nigga Flex, Prince. Find him before he has his dinner, and take his life before I'm finished with mine!"

The next morning when King woke up, Tippi was gone. He smiled at the memory of the good sex they shared earlier that morning. But that was over; now he had business to take care of. *The war is officially on and there is no turning back now,* he thought as he grabbed the phone and dialed Charlie's number. When Charlie answered the phone, King said, "We gots to meet today."

Charlie sighed and said, "Please tell me last night's violence at that club didn't have anything to do with you and those south side guys?"

"If I told you that I'd be lyin', but it's not what you think, Charlie. They think we moved on 'em but we didn't," lied King.

"All right, meet me at Charleston's."

"You like that spot, huh?"

Charlie laughed and said, "Yep, they got the best baby back ribs in the city. And their liquor isn't watered down like most of the other restaurants around here. I got a feeling that I'm definitely going to need a strong drink for this meeting. Be there at one," Charlie said as the line went dead in King's ear.

After King was dressed he called the squad and told them to meet him on the block. By the time he made it there everyone was sitting inside the trap. Boleg smiled when King came into the house and said, "Man, Tippi's a fool wit' it, huh? I'm tellin' ya, she is straight-up gangsta."

King stared at Tippi as she played a game of chess against Nutta. "Yeah, she did that shit last night, but now we got to deal wit' the aftermath of this shit."

Tippi moved her queen that was protected by her knight in front of Nutta's king and said, "Checkmate, li'l nigga." She turned toward King and said, "Fuck it, nigga, it is what it is. Now we can stop playin' wit' 'em niggas and wipe they asses out. Did you see 'em fools? They on some soft flossy shit. They ain't 'bout no war for real."

"That's right, but we can't underestimate 'em just by how they look. They might not be killas, but what can stop 'em from hiring some wolves?" King said wisely.

"Yeah, they did move on Keko's spot, so they can't be that fuckin' soft," added Cuddy.

"Exactly. That's why I feel we should be careful wit' these niggas. If we get careless wit' it we might just slip. I'm not tryin' to bury any of y'all. What up, Flex, you think you can get at that nigga Prince today or did he peep you last night?"

"I'm not knowin' for sure but, fuck it, it is what it is! No?"

"Right. Give that fool a call and try to feel him out, though. If you think you can set up a meet wit' his ass then get back at us so we can do that nigga."

"Have you gotten at Charlie 'bout last night yet?" asked Tippi.

"Yeah, I got a meeting set up at one. That's why I had y'all meet me here earlier than I said last night."

"What you gon' say?"

"That we didn't do nothin'. That it was a mistake on 'em south side niggas' part. What the fuck else can I say?"

Tippi started laughing and said, "Scary-ass nigga."

"Nah, not scary, smart. We can't lose that plug. We do and we're nothin' but some useless-ass street punks wit' no fuckin' pull at all. Officer Don and every fuckin' narc officer in the city would be all over our ass as soon as Charlie pulled our protection."

"That's real talk. So, we wait and see what's up with Flex and that nigga Prince first, huh? Then what?" asked Tippi.

"We'll take it one step at a time. I want all y'all strapped and ready at all times. 'Em niggas might be comin' to try to look at us so I want y'all prepared for whatever."

"What about you? Are you ready for this shit, dog?" asked Nutta.

"Li'l homie, it's just like that chess game you was just playin' wit' Tippi. I'm always ready as long as I got my queen."

Tippi smiled at the compliment and said, "That's right, 'cause his queen will always protect her King."

"Aww, both of y'all need to stop with that corny-ass shit!" said Keko and everyone in the trap laughed.

Taj spent the night at Shayla and Flamboyant's because Shayla wasn't comfortable with her staying at her house alone after what happened at the club. Plus, she wasn't comfortable being alone with Flamboyant. She felt that his anger about Gunna's murder might be directed toward her. That's why she slept in the guest room with Taj. After making them some breakfast Shayla told Taj, "Girl, I don't know what's going on but a lot of people are about to get hurt behind this mess. Did you see how angry Marco was last night? I've never seen him like that before."

"He has every right to be angry, Shay! They killed his man!"

Shaking her head from side to side, Shayla said, "Come on, Taj, how do we know that it was Trevor and his friends?"

Taj's look of disgust made Shayla flinch when she said, "Look, I know you still care for that nigga Trevor and all, but don't you dare sit there and try to play this shit off like you know they didn't have anything to do with what happened to Gunna. Don't you dare, Shay!" Taj screamed as tears started falling from her eyes.

Shayla grabbed her best friend, gave her a firm hug, and said, "I'm sorry, Taj. I'm just messed up behind this, that's all. I know how you was feeling Gunna. I'm really sorry."

Taj pulled from her embrace, wiped her face, and said, "It's all right, girl. Like I said, I know how you feel about Trevor. What are you going to do about this shit now that Marco knows you know Trevor?"

"What can I do? I told him last night that Trevor was a part of my past. That was the truth. Luckily, he didn't push it any further."

"He will, though. You can bet your ass on that."

Shayla sighed and said, "I know."

Flamboyant and Prince were having lunch when Prince got a call from Flex. Prince checked the number on his caller ID and told Flamboyant, "It's that south side nigga." He answered, "What's the bidness?"

"What it do, Prince, it's Flex."

"What up, baby, you good?"

"Not really. I'm needin' to holla at ya for real. You've been havin' a nigga in limbo way too long, dog. What's up, you ready to holla at me or what?"

"Bidness is bidness. I was just sittin' here talkin' to my man, tellin' him 'bout you. Yeah, I'm ready. When you want to get together?"

"That's all on you, dog. You the man wit' the big plate. I'm just tryin' to eat off of it."

"Let me get back at ya in an hour or so. You still tryin'
to get what we talked 'bout?"

"Yep."

"A'ight, then, I'll hit you back in a li'l bit."

"Fa' sho'," Flex said as he hung up.

Prince smiled and said, "Okay, this nigga has just
confirmed his date wit' death. How do you want to play
it, Flam?"

Flamboyant sat back in his seat and sipped on some
of his Krug. "What did he say?" After Prince repeated his
conversation with Flex, Flamboyant said, "That shit he
said don't make you think he could be settin' you up to
get smashed?"

Prince thought about that for a moment, then
answered, "I ain't even look at it like that, dog. That fool
could be tryin' to make a move on me, huh?"

Flamboyant smiled at his right-hand man and said,
"Could be. But this is what we gon' do. We're goin' to set
up a meeting and shake that fool to see if he's tryin' to
make a move on us. Once we see that it's cool, then we'll
take his ass."

"If he's on some grimy shit why don't we smash whatever he brings our way?"

"Ain't no tellin' how deep he'll come. This way we'll
know what we're up against. I'm not tryin' to lose any
more of the team on this bullshit. I want to dead this shit
as quickly as we can. 'Em niggas think we fear 'em and
that's gon' work to our advantage."

"How?"

"When there's beef in these streets your enemies look
for the fear; if they don't see any they hesitate. Their
hesitation will give us the advantage. That nigga King is a
street nigga no doubt, but he's too confident that he can
take us. That overconfidence is goin' to be the reason he
dies. Get at Wave and Ken and set this shit up. That nigga
Flex is 'bout to die today."

Chapter Twenty-nine

Charlie watched as King entered the restaurant right on time. After he was seated, King said, "Check it, Charlie, we didn't have shit to do wit' that fool gettin' killed at the club last night." He then went on to explain everything that had taken place the night before. After he was finished he relaxed back in his seat and sipped some of his water.

"So, you're telling me that this guy Flamboyant is accusing you and your squad of killing his man without any real proof?"

"Exactly. All we were doin' was celebratin' my birthday and chillin' at the club. They chose to come over and holla like they were checkin' somebody or some shit. And, we still didn't trip! After that fool left it was like whatever for real."

"Okay, I'll look into this later on. I'm glad you informed me of this first, because if I would have heard it from my other sources I would have really been pissed."

"I'm knowin'. I wanted you to hear it from me so you wouldn't be tryin' to check a nigga. I hate that shit," he said with a grin on his face.

"I know. How's everything else coming along? Any other problems?"

"Nope, everythang is everythang. As a matter of fact, everything is just fuckin' lovely." They were interrupted by King's cell phone ringing. He checked the caller ID and saw that it was Flex. "What it do, Flex?"

"I know you busy and shit. I just wanted you to know that I got at 'em fools earlier and they want to meet. They just got back at me and I'm supposed to meet 'em at Crossroads Mall in thirty."

"Yeah? A'ight, look, get at Tippi and have her put somethin' together for y'all. Keep me in the loop, though. You straight wit' this?"

"Fuckin' right."

"A'ight, then, my nigga, handle that shit."

"Real talk," Flex replied as he hung up the phone.

King ended the call and thought about how mad Charlie was going to be when the word got out that Prince got smashed. He sipped some more of his water and said, "Man, I'm kinda hungry. What's up wit' some of 'em baby back ribs you were talkin' 'bout?"

Charlie smiled and said, "I've already ordered some for us; they should be ready any minute. Tell me, do you think that Flamboyant will try to retaliate since he feels that your squad is responsible for his man's death?"

King shrugged and said, "Ain't no tellin'. I doubt it, though."

"Why is that?"

"That fool is a pussy for real. He ain't really 'bout no gangsta life. He on some flossy shit. I peeped that last night."

As the waiter came to their table and set their plates in front of them, Charlie said, "I hope you're right, because this shit has the makings of getting real ugly."

"I doubt it," King said as he started eating his baby back ribs.

"A'ight, this is how we'll handle this shit. We'll get to the mall first and peep how that nigga plays it. If he comes alone and seems to be straight up we'll go straight at this ass and take him. But if he's brought some help then you call his ass and change the location for the hookup."

"Then, what, we let him make it?" asked Prince.

"Nah, we send him and whoever is with his ass into the lion's den. I'll have Wave, Ken, and Milo waitin' on they ass somewhere," Flamboyant said as he drove toward the mall.

"This is how we gon' do this shit, fool. I'm on my way to the mall now. I should be there in about ten. Where did they say they was gon' be?" Tippi asked.

"They didn't. They told me to park in the back by Dillard's and they'd get at me," answered Flex.

"A'ight. What kind of whip does that nigga Prince push?"

"A black Escalade sittin' on some twenty-fours."

"Cool. By the time you get there I should have already peeped his ass. Once he approaches you I'll take care of everythang."

"What if he's not by himself?"

"Don't trip. I'm crazy strapped right now so if it gets too hot for me then you know what to do."

"Right."

"A'ight then, fool, I'll see you in a bit," Tippi said as she smiled and hung up the phone.

Flamboyant and Prince were sitting inside of Flamboyant's S600, waiting for Flex to arrive at the mall, when Tippi pulled into the parking lot in her H2. They didn't pay it any attention because they couldn't see anybody's face behind the dark-tinted windows of the truck. Flamboyant was sitting there thinking about Shayla. *Man, I tripped out on my babe last night. What the fuck was I thinkin' 'bout? I'll make it up to her later.*

"Dog, here that nigga comes," Prince said as he pointed toward Flex's Navigator as Flex parked in the back of the parking lot. "It looks like the fool is by himself."

"Good. A'ight, I'm gon' pull over in front of his shit. You jump out and serve his ass. Two to the head, my nigga, and we out."

"You gon' put this shit down out your own shit, dog? That could be dangerous."

"Nah, we good. Come on, let's do this shit," Flamboyant said confidently as he put the car in gear.

Tippi was too busy concentrating on any and every truck in the mall's parking lot that she didn't pay any attention to the off-white S600 as it pulled in front of Flex's SUV. By the time she realized that it was Prince, it was too late. She watched in horror as Prince got out of the Mercedes and unloaded his gun inside of Flex's SUV.

Stunned momentarily, she watched as Flex was murdered. She snapped herself out of it, grabbed her guns, and sped toward the fleeing Mercedes. There wasn't any use checking on Flex; she knew he was already dead. Her mission was to make sure that she got them niggas in that Benz.

As the Mercedes pulled out of the mall she was right behind it. She didn't want to give herself away so she eased back slightly and let a couple of cars come between them. "I'm gon' get you niggas the right way," she said aloud as she grabbed her phone and called King. When King answered the phone she told him, "They got Flex."

"What?"

"You heard me. They took Flex in the parkin' lot of the mall."

"What the fuck happened?"

"Flex had me lookin' for a black Escalade, but 'em niggas slid up on his ass in a off-white S600. By the time I realized what was what a nigga jumped out the Benz and started dumpin' on Flex. I didn't have enough time to get at 'em so I'm followin' they asses right now. Best believe they ain't gettin' away from me," she said angrily.

"Where are you?"

"They just got onto the highway, I-35 South. I'm 'bout three cars behind 'em."

"I'm too far out to catch up to you. Get at Cuddy and Boleg and see if they can hook up wit' you before you make a move on 'em niggas, Tippi."

"Fuck that! I got this shit. I'll holla at ya later on," she said as she ended the call.

King stared at his phone for a few seconds before his thoughts were interrupted by Charlie. "Is everything all right?"

"Huh? I mean, nah, Charlie, it's all bad right now. 'Em soft-ass niggas done did my man, Flex."

"What? Shit! I don't want you doing anything crazy behind this, King. Let me take care of this shit," Charlie said sternly.

"Let you take care of this? Come on, Charlie, you know what time it is now. Those niggas are for real, they ain't playin'! I underestimated that soft-ass nigga, Flamboyant. Now we got to retaliate the hardest! I'm outta here, Charlie," he said as he jumped out of his seat and left the restaurant.

Charlie called Toni and said, "Your guy has just taken out one of my guy's men."

"You sure? I got word that your guy took one of my guy's people last night at a club."

"That's questionable. You have to get a hold of your guy before he gets himself killed. King's on the warpath."

"This shit has gotten out of hand."

"That's an understatement, Toni. Get at your guy and I'll do the same. We have to somehow get control of this shit."

"I'll talk to you later," Toni said and hung up.

***

Tippi followed the Mercedes for another ten minutes before the driver of the car pulled into the driveway of a modest-looking home on the south side, on Shields Street. Tippi parked her truck down the street from the house and quickly climbed out of her vehicle and started walking back toward the house.

As she was approaching the house, the passenger's side of the Benz door opened up and she saw Prince get out of the car. She held her 10 mm cannon behind her back as she strolled slowly toward the house. Just as she made it in front of the house the Mercedes was pulling out of the driveway. She saw the vanity license plate that read FLAM 1.

Damn, I should have gotten that nigga, Tippi said to herself as she ran up on the porch of Prince's home. She said, "You thought you got away wit' that shit, nigga? Wrong!"

Prince turned around in horror and pissed on himself as Tippi shot him twice in the head. Before his body hit the ground she was already running back toward her truck. She was a long way from the north side of town, but she knew she had to hurry up and get as far away from that street as she could.

When she made it to the highway she grabbed her cell and called King. "I'm on the highway headed out toward Norman."

"Norman? Why the hell you goin' out that way?"

"I didn't think I'd be able to make it back to the north."

"You got your man?"

"Yeah, but I may have been seen. Come and scoop me from that Leo's Barbeque spot in Norman on Lindsey Street."

"I'm on my way."

"Hurry yo' ass up!"

Chapter Thirty

Flamboyant walked into his home and received two phone calls. The first call was from Toni. "Are you outta your fuckin' mind? Didn't I tell you that there was to be no fuckin' war on these streets? Huh? Didn't I?"

He sighed and said, "I know, but that was before they took my man Gunna. I couldn't let that shit ride, Toni. I just couldn't."

"From what I've been told, you don't even know for sure that they did that to your man. You're only assuming. Now your foolish assumption may cost you everything you got! Meet me at Ted's Mexican Restaurant on May off of Sixty-third Street in an hour and don't be late! It's time for this shit to stop!" Toni screamed and hung up on him.

Before he was able to sit down he received the second phone call with even more bad news. "Dog, they smoked Prince!" yelled Wave.

"What? Come on wit' that shit! I just dropped Prince off at his pad not even fifteen minutes ago."

"I'm tellin' ya, I'm over here now. The Ones are every-fuckin'-where. They said somebody ran up on him and dumped him on his porch. This shit has gotten outta hand, my nigga. We need to move on 'em niggas now!"

"We already did!" Not wanting to say too much over the phone, he told Wave, "Look, meet me on Southeast Fifteenth. Tell Milo and Ken to get there, too. I got a meeting to go to first, but I'll be through there in a couple of hours. Stand down 'til we can put somethin' right together."

"What you want me to do with Prince's wifey? She's real fucked up right about now, my nigga."

"Hold her down as best you can for now, dog. Tell her we'll be back by there after the Ones bounce." He hung up the phone and screamed, "Noooooo! No! No! No! Nooooo! I can't believe this shit! I swear to God, you a dead nigga! King, you are fuckin' dead!"

Shayla was sitting on the bed, listening to her man scream bloody murder on her ex. "This is so fucked up," she said softly.

Tippi was sitting inside of Leo's Barbeque Joint eating a barbeque chicken sandwich when King arrived. After he was seated he asked, "What the fuck happened?"

She quickly told him how everything went down and finished with, "We might as well take it to 'em niggas all the way now. They've shown they 'bout it. Ain't no need in playin' anymore."

"Playin'? You think we been playin' wit' 'em niggas? This shit ain't no game. The only reason I've taken those clowns lightly was 'cause of Charlie. You know that, Tippi."

"Yeah, I know that, and that's what I'm talkin' 'bout. Charlie may be the plug wit' the work, baby, but none of that shit will matter if none of us are here to move that shit. How the fuck are we gon' move when we got to worry 'bout 'em niggas poppin' up at any given time? We got to rid ourselves of the problem, King, once and for all. Come on, baby, let me get at some wolves I know and finish this shit. You know I can handle this shit."

Before he could answer, his phone rang. "Yeah?"

"Ted's Mexican Restaurant, one hour. This shit stops today," said Charlie.

"I'm out the way right now, Charlie."

"I don't give a fuck where you're at. Have your ass at Ted's in one hour! And make sure when you get there you remain calm, nigga. This is business."

"What you mea—"

Charlie hung up on him before he could finish asking his question.

Tippi noticed the strange look on his face. "What Charlie talkin' 'bout now?"

"I just left that mothafucka. Now I got to go to some Mexican spot to have another meetin'."

"About what?"

"Ain't no tellin' wit' Charlie. Probably somethin' to do wit' your handy work. Fuck it. Come on, let's bounce." They stepped out of the restaurant, walking toward King's Lexus, when he stopped and asked, "What you gon' do 'bout yo' truck?"

"Keko and Spook are comin' out here to get it later on."

"They know what's up with Flex?"

"Yeah, and so do the others. I called 'em when I was on my way out here."

"Fuck! How did this shit get so outta hand?"

"This is the life we live, baby, and the game we play. Don't trip. As long as I have a breath in my body your queen will always protect her King."

"Yeah, that's all good, but what 'bout everybody else, Tippi? We can't keep losing members of the squad."

"There's always gon' be casualties in war, baby. That's just the way it is. Come on, let's roll so you can see what the fuck Charlie wants."

Flamboyant pulled his Denali into the rather small parking lot of the quaint little Mexican restaurant. He didn't want to take the chance of driving his Mercedes, especially after what happened to Prince. *It is just too hot right now,* he thought as he got out of his SUV and entered the restaurant. Once he was inside, he took a look around until he saw Toni and another person sitting in the rear of the small restaurant. He took a deep breath and strolled over to their table. "What's up, Toni?" he asked as he sat down and joined them.

"Business," Toni replied crisply. "This is my associate, Charlie. Charlie, this is Flamboyant."

They shook hands and Charlie said, "I've heard a lot of good things about you. I hope after this meeting has concluded everything will be put into a better perspective."

Curious, he asked, "What do you mean?"

"You'll see," said Toni. "Do you want something to eat while we wait?"

"Nah, I'm good. What are we waiting for anyway?"

"We're waiting for a business associate of mine to arrive. He should be here any minute," replied Charlie.

As if on cue, King came strolling confidently into the restaurant. He saw Charlie sitting in the back of the restaurant with two people and headed in their direction. When he made it to their table he said, "What it do, Charlie?"

When he heard King's voice, Flamboyant stood slightly and looked into King's brown eyes and said, "Y'all on some bullshit for real, Toni, if y'all think I'm 'bout to have a sit-down wit' this nigga!"

King smiled and said, "I hate to say this, but I feel exactly the same as this clown. What's up with this shit, Charlie?"

"Sit your ass down, Flamboyant," Toni whispered in a no-nonsense tone of voice.

"Join him, King," Charlie said in a tone similar to Toni's.

They both glared at one another as they sat down like they were told to.

"Very good. Now we all know why we're here. This shit between you two has to stop. Nothing productive will come from you two beefing with each other. Flamboyant, King here does some very good business with me. I've heard all about the good business that you conduct with Toni, as well. As long as you two continue with this petty shit we will all lose money. I, for one, don't care to lose money; so, tell me, what has to be done in order for this madness to come to an abrupt halt?" asked Charlie.

"This nigga has to drop dead! He took two of my men, and for that this shit won't stop until he dies too." Flamboyant stared directly at King and said, "It's as simple as that, Charlie."

Before Charlie could respond, Toni said, "No, it's not as simple as that. Every action has a reaction. Your man got killed at the club the other night, right?"

"Right."

"And you hold King here responsible for that, right?"

"Exactly."

"You then retaliated this afternoon by taking out King's man, correct?"

Flamboyant smiled smugly toward King and said, "Yep."

"And if I'm not mistaken you then retaliated and took Flamboyant's man out a little bit afterward, is that correct, King?"

"You damn skippy."

"All of this is behind what took place a few months back out in Del City. You two are two money-getting men, and neither of you are smart enough to realize that this shit has been nothing but a bunch of bullshit from the beginning. Come on, gentlemen, let's look at the bigger picture. If this shit doesn't stop today neither of you will be making any more money. Either you'll be dead or in jail, because if we don't come to some sort of peaceful resolution in the next few minutes I'm personally pulling off my protection of you, Flamboyant. And Charlie here is going to do the same for you, King. Then neither of you will be able to do anything but continue to try to murder one another. Now, here are your options: call a truce and end this shit, or say fuck it and let the chips fall where they may. What is it going to be, gentlemen? Charlie and myself have other matters to attend to. We don't have all fucking day for this madness."

"To be honest with you, Toni, it don't even matter to me. Either way I'm gon' do what I have to do. This nigga took my man Flex today and I didn't even have shit to do wit' his man gettin' took at that damn club. So, I have no problems goin' to war wit' this clown and the entire south. But it's like you said, this shit is business and I do consider myself a hell of a businessman. I ain't tryin' to lose the plug I have with Charlie over some punk shit. I'd rather continue to get my money right, so it's whatever wit' me," replied King.

"What about you, Flamboyant?" asked Charlie.

"If I decide to truce wit' this fool, what guarantee do I have that he won't try to get back at me on some sneaky shit later on in the game?"

"Keep yo' ass on the south side outta my way and I'll do the same, nigga. And tell your men that if they bump into any of my squad members out in Midwest City or Del City, stand down. I'll make sure my side does the same. I'll honor this truce 'cause Toni's right; there's a bigger picture that we've been ignoring over this beef. Lives have been taken. It'll only get worse if we keep this shit up. So, I'm wit' it."

"If you would have been with this shit the other night my nigga Prince would still be alive."

"And so would my nigga Flex."

"Whatever. I'm tellin' all of y'all if I even think this nigga is on some sneak shit the truce ends at that very same moment. No more meetin', just straight war."

King smiled at Flamboyant and said, "Whatever you say, tough guy."

"Fuck you!"

"Kill that shit, you two! So, it's agreed, the beef ends today. Inform your people and let them know that this shit is over and it's back to business," said Toni.

"If there's any more problems make sure you contact us before you go off crazy and shit. Am I understood, King?" asked Charlie.

King shrugged. "I'm good, Charlie. You won't have anything to worry 'bout as long as this bad guy does what he's supposed to do. I'm gon' do me. I ain't trippin' for real."

"What about you, Flamboyant, you good?"

"Yeah, it is what it is, for now. Don't cross me, nigga, 'cause if you do, I swear it's on."

King laughed and said, "A'ight, dog, I got you." He then reached out to shake hands with Flamboyant and said, "Tell Shayla I said hello."

The grin King had on his face when he made that comment made Flamboyant feel as if there was some kind of subliminal message, and it pissed him off. "Keep. My. Wifey's. Name. Out. Of. Your. Mouth. Nigga. I mean that shit, King! She told me 'bout y'all's li'l past, so don't think you can shoot a lug at a nigga. That was then, this is now. It's a new day."

King raised his hands in mock surrender and said, "I ain't trippin', dog. All I said was to tell her what's up. It's all good, baby. I know that's your girl."

"Okay, kids, y'all can go back out and play now," Charlie said sarcastically.

King stood and said, "It was a pleasure meeting you, Toni."

"Likewise, King."

"I'll holla, Charlie," he said as he left the table without saying another word to Flamboyant.

After he watched King leave the restaurant, Flamboyant told Toni and Charlie, "I want to continue to get this money like we been doin', Toni, but I swear if that nigga goes anywhere near my wifey, I'm gon' kill him and his entire crew."

"What's the deal with him and your girl?" asked Charlie.

"They used to mess around back in the day, I guess. I really didn't get that deep into it wit' her. All I'm sayin' is that nigga bet' not go anywhere near her."

"Don't worry, Flamboyant. The truce has been made here today and I don't think King will break it. As a matter of fact, I'm sure of it, so hold your end of this and everything will be fine," said Charlie.

"I agree," added Toni.

"I hope y'all right, 'cause if not, that nigga is a dead man," Flamboyant said seriously.

"Where has all of this anger and violent behavior come from, Flamboyant? That's not your normal style," asked Toni.

"That nigga is responsible for the deaths of two members of my team, Toni. I don't give a damn what y'all think. I know that slick-ass nigga found a way to do Gunna. Prince was my man since we was in junior high, and now I have to bury him 'cause of that nigga. To top everything off, that nigga used to fuck wit' the woman I'm in love wit'. That alone can make me become the most violent man you've ever seen. Let's just hope that nigga keeps his word, 'cause if he doesn't—"

"We know, we know, he's a dead man," said Toni not wanting to go into it any further.

Chapter Thirty-one

It had been over two months since King and Flamboyant had made their truce. Everything seemed to go back to normal for the both of them. King and Tippi continued to get deeper into one another and the money continued to be made in abundance. All was definitely going well. That was, until King received a phone call from Shayla practically begging him to meet her.

"What's wrong, Shay?" asked King because of the urgency in her voice.

"I don't want to talk about it over the phone, Trevor! Are you going to meet me or not?"

"Where?"

"At your aunty's house in thirty minutes."

"A'ight, I'll see you then," he said and hung up the phone. He picked the receiver right back up and dialed his aunt's number. When she answered he said, "What's up, Aunty?"

"Hey, boy, I was just thinkin' about your ass. You know my medicine is runnin' kind of low; can you help me out?"

"Yeah, I can do that. As a matter of fact, I'm 'bout to come through there in a li'l bit. Shayla wants to talk to me so I'm meetin' her over there, is that cool?"

"You know I don't have a problem with that. You know how I feel about Shayla. But that other one, humph, she's somethin' else I tell you."

"Who, Tippi?"

"Nah, that damn Lawanda."

He sighed and asked, "What has she done now, Aunty?"

"Nothin' really, she gets on my nerves always tryin' to figure out what you're out there doin' through me. No matter how many times I tell her ass I don't get into your business, she always callin' or comin' over here tryin' to play me. That shit really irritates the hell outta me, boy. Especially 'cause she uses my babies as an excuse to call me or come over here. You know I love them kids of yours, boy, but that damn baby mama of yours is outta her damn mind."

He laughed and said, "Don't trip, Aunty. I'll check her silly ass. She won't be doin' that shit no more."

"Now don't you be hittin' on that girl, boy. Just have a li'l talk with her or somethin'."

"I got ya. Look, I'll see you in a minute."

"Don't forget my medicine!"

He started laughing and said, "I won't." After he got off of the phone with his aunt he went to the block and picked up an ounce of weed, and then proceeded over to his aunt's home so he could meet Shayla.

As he was driving toward the northeast side, he wondered why Shayla wanted to talk so suddenly. He knew she wasn't still on no shit about them hooking back up, especially after she found out about the beef with him and her man. *What if she does want to get back with me? Damn, that would throw a monkey wrench in the game for real,* he thought as he pulled into his aunt's driveway.

As he was getting out of his car Shayla pulled into the driveway behind him. He smiled at her as he started walking toward her car. When Shayla jumped out of her BMW and ran into his arms crying, he knew that the truce that had been made with Flamboyant was on the verge of being terminated. *Damn.*

"What's wrong, Shay? You a'ight?" he asked as he held on to her tightly.

"He hit me! He fuckin' hit me!" she cried in his arms.

"Calm down, baby, and tell me what happened," he said as he pulled from her embrace and led her toward the house.

Once they were inside and seated in the living room, King gave his aunt her medicine and said, "Excuse us for a li'l bit, Aunty."

Doris May shook her head but chose to keep her comments to herself. She left the living room clutching the brown bag that held her precious medicine; she was ready to get high.

When Doris May was out of the room King asked Shayla, "What made that clown put his hands on you?"

Shayla pulled off of the pair of Chanel shades she was wearing so he could see the black eye that Flamboyant gave her. She said, "Ever since Gunna's and Prince's funerals, things have been different between us. Marco started drinking more and more and started acting strange toward me. When he gets drunk all he talks about is you. Then he gets mad and starts asking me all kinds of questions about our past together. When I refuse to answer any of his questions he gets even madder and starts yelling at me. Up until now, that's all he ever did. Today I was so fed up with his shit that when he asked how many times I sucked your dick, I lost it."

Trying to suppress his smile, King asked, "He asked you some shit like that? That's some sucka shit for real."

"When I told him that I never kept count, he slapped the shit out of me. I couldn't believe it, Trevor. He's never done anything like this to me before."

"Check it, Shay, you know I'm the last nigga who'll come to that clown's defense, but he's stressed and trippin' behind losin' his mans and 'em. Let thangs cool down and he'll chill out. Shit should get back to normal wit' y'all in no time."

"Back to normal? Fuck that shit. Look at my face, Trevor! I'm not giving him the opportunity to get shit back to normal! It's over. I'm done with his ass!"

"So, you want me back now, huh? Is that it? That nigga fucks up and you think you can run on back to King and I'd accept you wit' open arms like it's all good? That's what you want, Shay?"

She dropped her head in shame and said, "Honestly, Trevor, I don't know what I want anymore. I just know that a man don't hit the one he loves."

Flamboyant sat on his bed missing Shayla something terrible. *I done fucked up this time! What the fuck was I thinkin' 'bout?* He replayed in his mind the argument he had with Shayla. *Why did she have to fuck wit' that nigga? Of all of the niggas in the city, she had to fuck wit' that fool! Fuck, this shit is fuckin' crazy for real!* He grabbed the phone and dialed Shayla's cell. When he got her voice mail he apologized and begged her to come back home, or to at least return his call. After he hung up the phone he called Ken and asked, "Is everythang straight out your way?"

"Yeah, we good. But on the real, Flam, niggas ain't really feelin' this shit wit' 'em north side niggas. Especially me and Wave. It's like we pussy or some shit!"

Flamboyant sighed heavily and said, "I know, but y'all know it ain't like that. This is business and there is no way we can fuck up what we got behind a war. What good would we be to Prince and Gunna's people if we got locked down or worse? Let's continue to get this money. You never know what might pop off for us later on in the game."

"You know we wit' you. A nigga just had to let you know what's on our minds, though. We gon' keep it one hundred wit' you at all times, my nigga, real talk."

"I appreciate that, G. What's up wit' that li'l nigga Milo? He good?"

"Yeah, he doin' his thang on the southeast, and out in Midwest City, too."

"A'ight, my nigga. Y'all hold me down. Get at me if y'all need anything."

"Fa' sho'," Ken said as he hung up the phone.

Flamboyant hung up the phone and said out loud, "Come home, Shayla. I'm so fuckin' sorry, babe. Come home."

Shayla and King were still sitting in Doris May's living room talking. Their conversation took a turn that neither of them expected. "I love you, Shayla. I always have and, no matter what happens, I don't think I'll ever stop lovin' you. The thing is, I'm caught up wit' Tippi now. I don't know how I let thangs get this deep wit' me and her. It kinda just popped off wit'out any real effort."

"Do you love her?"

Without any hesitation in his voice he said, "Not as much as I love you. I'm lovin' her, but I'm not in love wit' her. You and I both know how dangerous that can be though. I can't just get at Tippi and be like 'look, I'm 'bout to fuck wit' Shayla again so we gots to fall back.' She'd go fuckin' nutso and then you'd be in danger. Fuck, we both would!"

Shayla smiled and said, "Don't tell me that you're afraid of Tippi."

"Tippi's a cold-blooded killa, Shay, straight up. It has nothin' to do wit' fear 'cause we all gotta die someday. It's how you die that matters. Fuckin' wit' Tippi could be real fuckin' painful, real talk! I'd rather die laughing than walk 'round this city in fear of anybody, especially Tippi."

"So, what are we going to do, Trevor?"

"It depends."

"On what?"

"On what you really want, Shay. I can't go off all cock diesel 'bout us if I'm not one hundred percent sure that you're bein' real wit' a nigga. We can make some moves, but first I got to know if it's really me you want."

"I've never lied to you, Trevor, and I never will. I chose to stay with Marco because he didn't do anything to deserve being hurt by me. I care for him and I really thought I loved him more than I loved you. After he put his hands on me I knew that I was wrong. You'd never hit me no matter what; I know that. He made my decision easy today, Trevor. I want to be with you for the rest of my life. I want to be your wife, Trevor. That's all I ever wanted."

"So be it. But you gon' have to give me a minute to get thangs handled wit' Tippi."

"What are you going to tell her?" she asked nervously.

He smiled and said, "Don't tell me you're afraid of Tippi."

Shayla started laughing and said, "Hell yeah, I'm afraid of that crazy girl!"

"A'ight, how we gon' do this, Shay? Do you want to go back to y'all spot and get your shit or what?"

"Where am I going to go, Trevor? I can't go over to Taj's; that's the first place he's going to look."

"Nah, I'm gon' set you up wit' a suite downtown at the Skirva 'til I can figure out how we're goin' to do this shit."

"What's there to figure out?"

He sighed and said, "Tryin' to find a way to tell Tippi that I'm leavin' her for you is gon' be hard as hell, baby. Real talk!"

Chapter Thirty-two

"Come on, Taj, I know you know where Shayla's at. She wouldn't hide from you," Flamboyant said as he paced back and forth in Taj's living room.

"I'm telling you, Marco, I haven't heard from her since y'all's fight. All she told me was that she was leaving you. She brought her car over here and told me to make sure I called you so you could come pick it up. She wouldn't tell me where she was when I asked her so I let it go."

"Do you think she's messing 'round wit' another nigga?"

"Come on, Marco. You hit her, but I don't think she'd just go jump right into another man's bed because of that. My girl don't get down like that!" Taj lied. She knew Shayla was with Trevor, but she would never betray her friend. Never.

"Yeah, I know. I'm trippin' the fuck out and I deserve to; all of this shit is my fault. I fucked up and 'cause of my fuck up I've lost Wifey."

The sadness in his voice touched Taj, but she couldn't tell him where Shayla was because all hell would break loose. "Don't worry, she'll call you when she's ready to talk. She's still mad at your ass right now. I would be too if you hit me in my fuckin' face like that. What was you thinking about, boy?"

"I . . . I don't know, Taj. I kinda lost it when she got smart wit' me. I'm tellin' you, ever since we buried Gunna and Prince I've been really stressed."

"And you took out your frustrations out on my girl; that was smart," she said sarcastically.

"Look, when you hear from her tell I said to give me a call, or at least answer her phone so I can talk to her and apologize for my stupidity. And tell her I said I love her."

"If I hear from her I'll make sure she gets the message."

"Promise?"

She felt sorry so sorry for him. "I promise."

It had only been a couple of days but Shayla was kind of enjoying living in a nice hotel. She lounged around the room most of the day watching television and ordering food from room service. If she got too bored, she'd go downstairs to the hotel's gym and work out for a little while. She really enjoyed swimming in the heated pool located on the tenth floor. But what she enjoyed the most was making love to King.

He came over every night so far and made crazy love to her. Her body never felt as good as he was making her feel. She smiled at that thought because she knew she was in for another long sexing when he came to her suite later. And she couldn't wait.

She hated the fact that so far he hadn't spent the entire night with her. He blamed it on business to take care of in the late night, but she knew it was because he hadn't told Tippi about them yet. She wasn't mad at him, though. For now she was content living in the Skirvin and pampering herself. *The pieces will fall in place sooner or later.*

"So what's the bidness out here?" asked King as he got out of his car.

"Everythang is everythang, nigga. You know I got this shit on lock over here," replied Keko.

"Yeah, well, why haven't I heard from your ass in a week?"

"'Cause I've been doin' me, that's why. What up, though?"

"Shit, just checkin' this paper. You good out this way?"

"Yeah, I'm straight for now, but I'm gon' need some more yay for Del City, though. Ever since we opened that bitch back up it's been on and poppin' like we never shut it down."

"What's up across the highway? Any problems from 'em fools?"

"Nah, they doin' 'em but that ain't stoppin' nothing on my side. Believe me, the first sign of any drama I'm gettin' dead on they ass," Keko said seriously.

"G'on wit' that shit. I told you that shit wit' 'em fools is dead. Ain't no need for you to be still trippin'. Or are you just mad that Tippi handled up for you and you didn't get a chance to get yo' man?" King asked and laughed.

"Whatever, nigga. G'on and get yo' flossy-ass, Lexus drivin'–ass off my block before I take a look at that shit."

King smiled and said, "Look at who? Me? Nigga, this may be your block but it's still a part of my kingdom. Don't get it twisted, fool!" They both started laughing. "I'll holla at Tippi and have her get at you wit' some more yay later on."

"Right. I'll holla," Keko said as he turned and went inside of his trap.

After leaving Keko's part of town, King called Tippi and told her to meet him on the block. By the time he arrived, Tippi was already there talking to Nutta and Cuddy. "What's up, fool?" Cuddy asked King once he was out of his car.

"Ain't shit. Y'all good?"

"Yep," answered Nutta. "Everything is sweet as can be, big homie."

"That's right. Where that nigga Boleg at?"

"He went out to Midwest City to pick up some ends. He should be here in a li'l bit," answered Cuddy.

King turned toward Tippi and asked her, "What's up wit' you?"

"The same ol' shit, just tryin' to maintain all of this shit. Since they took Flex it's like I gots to do every fuckin' thang."

"Stop whining. You always wanted to run this side anyway, so why you trippin' now that you got it?"

"'Cause it takes up too much of my playtime. I've been movin' so much that I haven't been able to get broken off properly."

"Oh, shit, y'all need to hold the fuck up and let me and Cuddy roll out before y'all get to talkin' 'bout that freaky shit," Nutta clowned with a smile on his face.

"I ain't goin' nowhere! I'm tryin' to hear this shit," said Cuddy.

"Fuck y'all!" both King and Tippi said in unison.

"Speakin' of work, you need to get Keko's people some more yay out in Del City."

"A'ight, but when are you goin' to put in some work on this?" Tippi asked as she pointed toward her sex.

He ignored her question and told Cuddy and Nutta, "If y'all niggas need somethin' get at me or Tippi. I'm 'bout to go scoop my kids for a li'l while. Be safe." He turned and faced Tippi again and said, "I'll holla at you later on after I've dropped off the kids. We need to talk."

"Talk? 'Bout what?"

"You and your fuckin' mouth."

Before she could respond, Nutta said, "Oooh, checkmate, Tippi. I know you ain't gon' go out like that."

"Yeah, you ain't gettin' soft on us now that you're all in love wit' your King are you?" Cuddy asked playfully.

Once again Tippi and King yelled, "Fuck y'all!"

***

Flamboyant called Shayla's cell and left another message begging for her forgiveness. "Come on, babe, don't do this to me. You're killin' me. I'm sorry for the stupid shit I said and did. Call me so we can talk this shit out. I love you, Shayla. You're my queen."

He hung up the phone, sat down, and poured himself another shot of Crown Royal. Though Krug champagne was his preference, since his drama with Shayla he'd been drinking nothing but Crown Royal. He felt the need for something stronger in order to help him make it through the day without his queen in his life.

As he sat on the sofa and sipped his drink, a thought came to him: *Shayla has class tomorrow at Rose State. I can pop up on her ass at school and we can talk. She'll talk to me once she sees me face to face. I know she will.* He relaxed back on the sofa with a confident smile on his face.

When King pulled into Lawanda's driveway he saw Tandy and Trevor Jr. playing in the front yard. He smiled as he got out of his car and joined his children. "What's up wit' y'all? Y'all been good or what?"

"Hi, Daddy. I've been real good. Trevor Jr. hasn't, though," said Tandy.

"Is that right? What have you been up to now, li'l man?"

Trevor Jr. stood in front of his father with his head bowed and said, "I got in trouble at school today."

"For what?"

"For cussing."

"What made you do that?"

He shrugged his small shoulders and said, "I don't know. I was mad, I guess."

"Who made you mad?"

"My teacher."

"You cussed at your teacher?"

"Uh-huh."

"What did they do?"

"They called Mama and told her to come pick me up from school for the rest of the day."

"Come here, Junior." King wrapped his arms around his son and said, "You can't be cussin' at yo' teacher. That stuff ain't cool. You got to take care of business when you're at school. How else will you be able to follow yo' dreams? School is the most important part of your life right now. You have to stay focused while you're there and not let yo' anger get you into trouble, like it did today. You understand what I'm sayin'?"

"Uh-huh. I won't do it again, Daddy, promise."

King hugged his son and said, "That's my li'l man right there! I'm gon' hold you to that promise, too. Now, y'all run on in the house and get y'all's jackets. We're 'bout to go get somethin' to eat." He followed his children inside of the house. When he saw Lawanda dressed in a pair of jeans with a jean vest without a shirt on, showing much cleavage, he said, "Yeah? Like that, huh?"

She frowned at him and said, "What is that supposed to mean?"

"Nothin', just checkin' you out. Where you goin' tonight? Got a hot date?" he asked with a smile on his face.

"As a matter of fact, I do. So could you please keep your children for a li'l longer than we planned? Or is that too much to ask of the King?"

"How much longer?"

"I should be home around eleven or so."

"That's cool. Have fun," he said as he turned toward his kids, who had come back into the living room with their jackets on, ready to go. "Come, y'all, let's ride."

"Ooooh, I can't stand yo' ass sometimes! I swear you make me sick, King!"

"What the fuck are you talkin' 'bout? Hold up. Tandy, you and your brother go get in the car. I'll be there in a minute." After the kids walked out he turned back to Lawanda and said, "What the fuck is wrong wit' yo' ass?"

"I'm sick and tired of you and yo' bullshit. Why do I have to call you and ask you to come spend some damn time with your own children? Why can't you just come over on a daily basis and check on yo' kids? You be on some bullshit all of the damn time, King, and I'm sick of that shit!"

He smiled at her and said, "You right, my bad. I've been so caught up dealin' wit' all of the bullshit that I've been neglecting mines. I'll get better wit' that shit for real. But you gon' have to stop actin' up yo' damn self."

"What you talkin' about?"

"You know what I'm talkin' 'bout. Sweatin' my aunty 'bout me and my business. I don't be all in your mix so stay the fuck out of mine. You got you a li'l date and thangs; I'm happy for you. You need to go out more often and enjoy yourself," he said with a smile on his face.

"You're so wrong. That's why I can't stand ya ass."

"Stop it. You know damn well if I told you to shake whoever you're 'bout to go meet, you would. It's a difference from doin' wrong and bein' wrong, Lawanda. Do you and let me do me."

"Whatever, nigga."

He smiled and said, "Have fun!"

Chapter Thirty-three

Flamboyant woke up the next morning with a slight hangover. After taking a shower he felt slightly better. He got dressed and left to go see if he could convince Shayla to come back home. As he drove toward Rose State junior college, he hoped and prayed that he would be able to achieve his goal.

Shayla was sitting in class with a smile on her face. She was thinking about how much she enjoyed her evening with Trevor and his kids the night before. She was surprised when he came to her suite and told her that he was taking her out with his children. What touched her most was when he told her, "You might as well get used to them now, especially since you're about to become Mrs. King." That made her feel so good that nothing else seemed to matter.

They went to Bricktown and had a nice dinner. Afterward, they went for a walk along the river walk and enjoyed the evening playing around with each other. She was shocked at how smart and obedient King's kids were. She had no problems whatsoever accepting them into her life, and from what she could tell, the kids really liked her too.

After they dropped the kids back home, Trevor took her back to her suite and rocked her world for over an hour and a half. She hadn't realized that she could have so many orgasms in one sexual encounter. *God, Trevor is much more advanced than he was when we used to be together,* she thought as she blushed at the memory of what Trevor did to her body the night before. She actually started getting wet at the mere thought of his touch. She dried up instantly when she saw Marco standing in the doorway of her classroom, motioning for her to come outside and talk to him. She sighed heavily, grabbed her books, and left the classroom in the middle of her instructor's lecture on clothing designs.

Once she was outside of the classroom she asked, "What are you doing here?"

"I'm here to apologize, babe."

"You've already done that like a hundred times already. I check my messages," she said in a tone so sarcastic that it shocked Flamboyant.

"Why you bein' like that? You know I love you. You don't have to be so cold toward me. I know I was wrong. I made a mistake, Shayla. It'll never happen again, I swear."

"Oh, I know it won't, buddy. Believe me, I know."

"Come on, Shayla, let's go somewhere and talk this out, huh?"

"What is there to talk about, Marco? You put your hands on me. No man has ever put his hand on me! It's over! Do you understand me, Marco? O-v-e-r!"

Before he realized what he had done, he slapped Shayla so hard she almost passed out. Before she was able to get herself oriented he grabbed her and pulled her out toward the parking lot. By the time they made it to his car his mind was made up: he wasn't about to let her leave him. He didn't give a damn what he had to do.

"What are you doing, Marco? Kidnapping me? You are fuckin' crazy! Let go of me!" she screamed.

"Shayla, I love you and, no matter what, I know you love me too. We have to work this out. I'm lost without you. Can't you understand that? I'm lost without you!"

He sounded so pathetic and desperate that the fear factor of how he was acting finally registered. *Oh, shit, this nigga is really on some fatal shit!* She stole a few glances around the parking lot to see if anyone could help her. She let out a sigh of relief when she saw one of the campus security guards driving their way. She yanked her arm out of Flamboyant's grip and yelled, "Over here! I need help over here!" She continued to wave her arms frantically until she got the security guard's attention.

"Come on wit' that shit, Shayla. You want to get that fool smoked? You comin' wit' me whether you like it or not," Flamboyant said as he pulled out a chrome 9 mm from the small of his back. "Now, when that rent-a-cop comes over here you better make sure you tell him that everything is all good."

"Or what?" she asked defiantly.

"Or there's gon' be a lot of blood in this parking lot."

"You're bluffing."

"Am I?"

"Why . . . why are you doing this? Why can't you let me be?"

"'Cause I love you and I'm not goin' to give up on our future. You're all I got, babe. You mean the world to me."

Before she could say something the security guard pulled up and asked, "Were you trying to get my attention, ma'am?"

She thought about the gun Flamboyant was hiding behind his back and answered, "No, um, I was waving toward my girlfriend. She didn't see me, though."

"Oh, okay, have a nice day," the security guard said as he pulled away from them.

"Smart move, babe. Now, can we go somewhere and talk this out?"

With venom in her eyes as well as in the tone in her voice she said, "Do I have a choice?"

"I guess not. Get your ass in."

Tippi was pulling into King's driveway as he was pulling out of the garage. He stopped when he was right next
to her, rolled down his window, and said, "What up?"

"Where you goin' this early in the mornin'?"

"Trevor Jr. got into some trouble at school yesterday
for cussin' at his teacher. You want to come?" he asked
with a smile on his face. *Sometimes lies have to be told.*

"Yeah, I want to cum a'ight, just not wit' you to no
damn schoolhouse. Why you been shakin' me, King?
What's up wit' that?"

"Let's talk 'bout that later on. I got to get to the school."

"At least tell me what I done, nigga, damn."

"You ain't done shit, Tippi. It's all on me." He checked
his watch and said, "Meet me back here later on this
evening and we'll holla. I'm outta here," he said as he
pulled out of the driveway.

As he turned onto the highway he grabbed his cell and
called Shayla. He was running late picking her up from
school. He hoped she wouldn't be too mad at him for
being a little late. When he got her voice mail he left her
a message informing her that he was on his way. After he
closed his phone he started thinking about what he was
going to tell Tippi later on when they got together. *Ain't
no way in hell am I goin' to be able to tell her crazy ass
the truth. She'll go straight for my ass!*

"Where are we going, Marco?" asked Shayla.

"Home."

"I'm hungry. Can't we go somewhere and get something to eat first?"

"When we get to the house you can cook something to
eat if you want to."

"Why are you doing this? Can't you see that you're causing more harm than good? Do you really think I'll ever feel the same way I used to feel for you?"

That stung. "Babe, I messed up but it's like you're not even tryin' to forgive a nigga. I don't understand that shit. Haven't I always treated you right? Haven't I always given you whatever you asked for? I've shown you how much I love you. Why can't you forgive me for making one mistake?"

"One mistake? Marco, you put your hands on me! Not once, but twice! On top of that you pulled a gun on me, too! And now you're taking me back to your home against my will and you want me to forgive you? Nigga, please! You can make me stay at your home as long as you want, but I will never, and I mean never, forgive you for what you've done to me!"

He sighed heavily and realized that he was digging a deeper hole for himself. "Where do you want to go eat?"

"It really doesn't matter. I just want to put something in my stomach."

"A'ight," he said as he pulled off the highway and turned into a Waffle House parking lot. "Is this cool?"

"It's fine," she said as she got out of the car and walked inside of the restaurant.

After they were seated she told Flamboyant, "Order me a patty melt and some scrambled eggs, please. I'm going to the bathroom." Before he could say a word she was out of her seat and headed toward the bathroom. As soon as she was inside the bathroom she pulled her cell out of her back pocket and quickly called King. She really didn't want to involve him in this but she had no other choice. She was afraid Flamboyant was going to hurt her. Before that happened, she would let King hurt his ass!

"What's up, baby? Don't go left on my ass; I'm almost at the school now," King said when he answered the phone.

"Listen, Trevor, and please try to remain calm, okay?"

"What's wrong, Shay?" he asked, sounding worried.

"Marco came to my class and made me leave with him."

"What?"

"He hit me again, Trevor. He even pulled a gun when I tried to call for security to help me. He's lost his fucking mind and I think he's going to hurt me. Please come and get me."

"Where y'all at?"

"I asked him to take me to get something to eat. We're at Waffle House right off of the Forty."

"I just passed that spot a few minutes ago. I'll be there in less than five."

"Okay. Be careful, Trevor, he has a gun on him."

"I do too," he said as he closed his phone. As he got off of the highway and changed directions he picked up his phone and called Keko. "Where you at, nigga?"

"I'm on my way to Del City, what's up?"

"I need you to meet me at that Waffle House off of the Forty. You know the one I'm talkin' 'bout?"

"Yeah, right before you get to Rose State. What's poppin'?"

"Just get there and you'll see for yourself. You strapped?"

"Always," Keko replied.

"Good," King said as he closed his phone.

King saw Shayla sitting across from Flamboyant inside of the restaurant as he pulled into the parking lot of the Waffle House. He parked his Lexus right next to Flamboyan's S600. He inhaled deeply as he grabbed his .40-caliber Glock and racked a live round inside of its chamber. He picked up his phone again and pressed redial. When Keko answered King asked him, "Where you at?"

"I'll be there in about three minutes or less."

"When you pull into the parking lot stop right in front of the door and get out of the car wit' yo' strap ready."

"Where you gon' be, nigga?"

"Inside of Waffle House, takin' what's mines," King said as he ended the call and got out of his car.

When Shayla saw King pull into the parking lot she tried her best to remain calm, but she was a nervous wreck. She knew that both of these men were dangerous and she hoped and prayed that no one died today, especially her. She followed King with her eyes as he came inside of the restaurant. As he walked toward where they were seated, she told Flamboyant, "Look, Marco, I'm leaving now. Please don't try to stop me. I don't want anyone to get hurt in here."

"What? What are you talkin' 'bout, babe?" Flamboyant asked, confused. When he saw her looking over his shoulder he turned around and saw King. "Ain't that a bitch!" he screamed as he jumped out of his seat and faced King.

Shayla jumped out of her seat and quickly got between the two men before any blows could be thrown. "I don't want any problems here, Marco. I just want to leave."

"Leave? Wit' who, this nigga?" he asked, completely shocked.

"Yeah, nigga, wit' me. Now, if you'd excuse us, we have shit to do," King said as he stared Flamboyant down. Flamboyant was about to say something slick until he saw Keko pull in front of the entrance of the restaurant and jump out of his car with a pistol in his hand. King smiled and said, "See ya later."

Flamboyant stared at King and Shayla for a few seconds and said, "You better fuckin' believe the war is back on, bitch nigga. Oh, and ain't nobody gon' be able to save yo' ass this time." King ignored him and grabbed

Shayla's hand and led her toward the exit. That infuriated Flamboyant. "And as for you, you triflin' bitch, you're just as dead as that nigga!"

Shayla shook her head sadly and gave him the finger as she walked out of the restaurant with her hand firmly inside of her man's hand. *Ooooh, weeee! Shit! Thank God no one got hurt!*

Chapter Thirty-four

As they left the Waffle House followed by Keko, King grabbed his phone and called Charlie. "We need to meet, like right now."

"What's wrong?" asked Charlie.

King sighed and stared at Shayla and said, "I got the beef back crackin' wit' that nigga Flamboyant."

"What? Charleston's in twenty," Charlie said and hung up the phone.

"Who was that?" Shayla asked as she watched King close his phone.

"That was my peoples. We're 'bout to have a meetin' and discuss this problem."

"Why can't you just leave it alone? I don't want this to turn into something crazy, Trevor."

He smiled at her and said, "That, baby, is unavoidable. You heard what that nigga said. Hopefully Charlie will be able to take care of this. If not, then somebody got to die. It's as simple as that, Shay."

"Oh my God."

"Exactly."

Charlie was already seated when King and Shayla arrived at Charleston's. After they were seated King made the introductions. "Shayla, this is Charlie. Charlie, this is Shayla, Flamboyant's ex-girlfriend. My current fiancée."

"Shit," Charlie groaned.

"Exactly." King then went on and explained everything to Charlie. He started from the beginning back when he and Shayla had first met, and ended with what had just happened at the Waffle House.

Charlie attentively listened without saying a word, staring at him as if he'd lost his mind. After a few more seconds of staring at King, Charlie picked up the cell phone and called Toni. When Toni answered the phone, Charlie said, "You won't fuckin' believe what's happened."

"Why wouldn't I? I just got off of the phone with Flamboyant. I'm meeting him at the Red Lobster on the south side in thirty to discuss why he's in such a murderous rage. What the fuck is your man thinking about, Charlie?" Toni asked seriously. "This shit can fuck up everything."

"I know." Charlie stared at the couple sitting on the other side of the table and said, "They're in love, Toni. I can see it in both of their eyes."

King grinned slyly and told Shayla, "I should have taken you back to your suite."

"Why, are you ashamed of being in love with me?"

"Never that." King grabbed her hand.

"Call me when you've finished calming your man down. Don't worry, we'll work something out, Toni," said Charlie.

"I doubt it, but I sure hope you're right," Toni said and hung up the phone.

After setting the cell phone back onto the table Charlie said, "Okay, you two, what the hell are we going to do about this fucking mess y'all created?"

King shrugged. "What can we do, Charlie? It is what it is."

Shayla remained silent.

Charlie stared at the couple again and asked, "If this were the other way around, King, how would you feel? Would it be 'it is what it is' then?"

"On the real, I'd probably be on some murda shit."

"Exactly. So you can pretty much see where Flamboyant's state of mind is at this point in time. Especially with what's transpired with you two recently."

"Yeah, but—"

Charlie held up a hand to stop him and continued. "No buts, King. This shit is serious. I'm beginning to feel as if you're trying to fuck with my money. Is that what you're trying to do?"

"It ain't even like that, Charlie. You know you trippin'. I love this woman, always have." He smiled lovingly toward Shayla and continued. "We were born to be together."

Charlie watched as Shayla put her hands on top of King's and returned his loving smile, and he said, "Shit!"

On the south side of Oklahoma City, Toni was sitting at a table inside of Red Lobster, waiting for Flamboyant to arrive. The wait wasn't long. Before Toni could order a drink, Flamboyant came strolling into the restaurant with a murderous look on his handsome face. "Shit," muttered Toni.

With no preamble, Flamboyant sat down and said, "Fuck this money, this dope, this game; that nigga got to die, Toni. I mean that shit right there."

"Have a drink, Flamboyant, and try to calm your nerves. There's no need for you to get so crazy."

"Toni, you got to be out of your fuckin' mind! That nigga had the nerve to come into the Waffle House while I was with Wifey tryin' to work out our problems, and he took her outta there as if she belonged to him! He's crossed the line and ain't no deadin' this shit! He's got my woman, Toni! And it's fuckin' killin' me!"

Damn, if I would have known this nigga would fall this weak behind a bitch I wouldn't have ever fucked with his ass, thought Toni. "Let's look at this from another perspective. Obviously your wifey wants to be with King. After all, she did leave with him, right?"

Shaking his head violently, Flamboyant said, "Hell nah, she's still trippin' the fuck out right now 'cause I put hands on her a couple of times. She's hot and shit so she's tryin' to fuck wit' a nigga's head."

"It looks as if she's doing a pretty good job of it. Why don't you let things cool down a little then give her a call and see if y'all can work this out?"

"That's exactly what I plan on doin'. While I'm lettin' her calm the fuck down I'm also gon' be huntin' for that bitch-ass nigga King! Like I said, he has to die and I don't give a fuck what you have to say 'cause ain't nothin' gon' make me change my mind. I don't know why in the hell I let that nigga make it after he done Gunna and Prince any-fuckin'-way. Real talk, Toni, he's outta here."

"So, you're going to put everything we've put together in jeopardy because of your anger toward a man who your woman seems to have chosen? That's some bullshit and you know it. Shake that shit off and move forward and don't look back. There's millions to be made in this fucking town and you know it. I know you're hurting right now because you feel as if you'll never get over losing your girl. Her choosing King adds insult to injury, but that's still some small shit to stress. You have to look at the bigger picture. Keep your eyes on the prize. When it's all said and done you'll be on top and she'll be the one regretting the decisions she made. Think, Flamboyant. Don't let your emotions get you into something that you won't be able to get out of."

"What's that supposed to mean, Toni? You threatening me now?"

Toni sighed and said, "No, I'm not threatening you. I'm giving you my word that if you don't let this shit die then you lose. Period. And you're going to lose way more than you think. So sit your ass back and let this pass. Everything will be all good and you'll be the one shining in the end."

Flamboyant smiled at Toni and said menacingly, "King will die by my hand, Toni. Whatever happens after that I ain't even trippin'."

Toni stared at him for a minute before saying, "If King dies by your hand you will die a slow death by mine. I give you my word on that, Flamboyant."

He shrugged his shoulders, got up from his seat, and left the restaurant without saying another word.

Toni watched him leave and said, "Shit!"

King had just dropped Shayla off back at the hotel when Tippi called him on his cell. "Where you at, nigga?"

"Downtown, what's up?" he asked as he pulled into traffic.

"We need to talk."

"Yeah, I know. Meet me on the block in about thirty."

"Nah, let's meet at your pad. I'm not tryin' to have any of 'em niggas in our business. I'm on my way out there now," Tippi said as she hung up on him.

As King drove toward his house he wondered if he was going to have to kill Tippi. "God, I hope not," he said out loud as he turned his car onto the highway.

Tippi was already inside of King's house when he pulled into the driveway. "I got to make sure to get my fuckin' keys from her crazy ass after this shit is over wit'," he mumbled as he climbed out of his car and went inside of the house. When he stepped into the living room he couldn't help but smile at the sight before him. Tippi was sitting down on his leather sofa with her legs crossed at her ankles looking sexy in a matching panty and bra set. She smiled at him as she took her bra and thong off. "I thought we had somethin' to talk 'bout?" he asked, staring at her firm body.

"We do. I don't want to talk 'bout it 'til after you've made me feel special. I want, no, I need you to make me feel special, King. I know you don't love me the way I love you. I've always known what we've been sharing these past few months was only some temp time. I hoped and prayed for more but since you've been shakin' me I've realized that my time has run out. So, take off 'em clothes, baby, and come over here and make me feel special." She stared at him innocently and added, "Please."

Her tone touched him deeper than he ever imagined. Where was the hardcore Tippi he was accustomed to? Confused, yet aroused, he slowly started to undress. "Let's take it to the bedroom."

Shaking her head no, she said, "Uh-uh, I want it right here." She slapped the sofa and continued, "Your bedroom is for whomever you're fuckin' wit'. This couch is where I want—"

King cut her short and finished, "Me to make you feel special." He then stepped to her and dipped his head between her legs and started licking her sweetness.

Tippi moaned and said, "Umm, exactly."

Chapter Thirty-five

Flamboyant had a smile on his face when he saw Taj pull into the parking lot of the Skirva. His smile got even brighter when he saw Shayla, the love of his life, walk out of the hotel's lobby with her Gucci luggage in her hands. He knew that if he kept an eye on Taj sooner or later she'd lead him to Shayla. Ever since that incident at the Waffle House he'd been a total wreck. He wasn't sleeping right, his eating habits had become irregular, and he was drinking more and more. He knew he couldn't keep going the route he was going so he made up his mind to find a way to get Shayla back in his life. But first he had to find her. Now that he had her in his sights there was no way in hell he was going to let her get away from him again.

Taj jumped out of her car and helped Shayla with her bags. "Damn, girl, I didn't know you had this much stuff," Taj complained as she loaded two of Shayla's Gucci bags into the trunk.

"Stop whining and hurry up, girl. I can't wait to see where Trevor lives."

"You decided to be with this man and you don't even know where he lives? That's crazy," Taj said as she got back inside of the car.

After joining Taj, Shayla said, "He had some loose ends he needed to take care of before I was able to move in with him. He called me this morning and told me that he had taken care of everything and that it was time for me to come home."

"Hmm, so he had another broad he had to shake first, huh?"

Shayla laughed and said, "Something like that."

"Well, at least he didn't try to play no games with you and try to keep her on the side."

"That's not Trevor's style. He may be on some thug shit, but as long as I've known him he's never lied or played any games like that with me."

"What's up with Marco? Have you heard from him anymore?"

"Not since I got rid of that phone. Trevor bought me a new one and no one has the number except you and him."

"You know you got to be careful, girl. Ain't no telling what's going on in that man's head. You hurt him, Shayla, and when a nigga from these streets get hurt like that he can become very dangerous."

"Don't I know it! A few months ago I would have put my hand on a stack of Bibles that Marco would never put his hands on me. Girl, that man has slapped the piss out of me twice, and God only knows what he wants to do to me now that he knows I'm with Trevor. But I'm not worried. Trevor won't let anything happen to me," she said with a confident smile on her face.

"I hope you're right," Taj said as she turned her car onto the highway, headed toward Shayla's new home.

Both of the females were so busy chatting that neither of them paid any attention to Flamboyant's Denali following them.

Everything is finally in place. My money is right, I got the north locked tight, and the squad is gettin' paid, too. I got the girl I've always wanted back in my life and Tippi ain't trippin'. The only thing I got to worry 'bout is that nigga Flamboyant, King thought as he sat down on the bed. He was anxiously awaiting Shayla's arrival to his home, their home. Today was about to be the official beginning of their relationship.

He grabbed the phone and called Charlie. When Charlie answered he asked, "Have you heard anything on that fool yet?"

"As a matter of fact, I have. Watch your ass at all times, King. It looks as if that guy is going to try to bring the drama your way."

"You know what that means, right?"

Charlie sighed and said, "Do you, King? I can't be upset with you for defending yourself."

"Good lookin', Charlie. I'll holla." After he got off of the phone with Charlie he quickly made another call. Tippi answered the phone on the first ring. "Listen, you need to get a line on that nigga Flamboyant and his peoples."

"I got the green light?" asked Tippi.

"No doubt."

"Good. I'm on it."

"Get at me as soon as you know somethin'."

"What, you want a part of this?"

"You don't think I'm gon' let your ass have all of the fun."

She laughed and said, "Whatever, nigga."

"Get on that BI for me. I want that nigga done like yesterday."

"Gotcha."

Fifteen minutes after King had gotten off of the phone with Tippi, Shayla and Taj pulled into his driveway. Shayla jumped out of the car and happily ran toward the front door. When King opened the door and stepped onto the porch she ran into his arms and gave him a tight hug. "I'm home, baby! I'm home!" she screamed, and then kissed him tenderly.

He pulled from her embrace and said, "Come on, Shay, let me get your stuff. I don't need my neighbors all up in mines. Y'all go on in the house while I lug in all yo' shit."

"Okay, come on, Taj," she said as she let Taj inside of her new home.

Flamboyant watched from down the street as King grabbed Shayla's bags out of Taj's car. He was parked about four houses down from King's home. "Your ass is mines, nigga," he said out loud as he watched King go back inside of his house. He started his truck and left King's neighborhood with a deadly smile on his face. *Somebody 'bout to die and it ain't gon' be me!*

"I just got off the phone with the damn Chicos, Toni."

"And?"

"They know about our little problem," said Charlie.

"How did they find out about that shit so fast?"

"You know them mothafuckas got eyes and ears every-fucking-where."

"What did you tell them?"

"That everything was under control and there was nothing to worry about. You know what that bean-eating mothafucka Eduardo had the fucking nerve to say to me?"

"What?"

"That he never worried, because he was the boss. I swear I wanted to roast that illegal immigrant motha-fucka!"

"Calm down, Charlie."

"Calm down, my ass! Look, Flamboyant is most likely about to fuck up a large part of our monthly income. How do you expect for us to make up for what we're going to lose?"

"Lose?"

"Yeah, lose. If he is successful and takes out King, we're going to lose that money from the north side, as well as the south side. Because if he hurts my man, he's a dead man too, Toni."

"Why don't we cut our losses in half?"

"How?"

"Call in Teedo and have Flamboyant taken care of before he gets to King."

"Teedo? I don't know. I think King may just be able to handle that nigga."

"Why take that chance? If he doesn't, we lose all the way around. If we let Teedo come do what he's highly paid for, then we'll only lose half of our monthly money."

Charlie smiled and said, "You know what, you're absolutely right, partner. Make that call to Teedo and get his ass down here from New Orleans as fast as you can."

Toni smiled and said, "Gotcha."

Chapter Thirty-six

Flamboyant paced back and forth inside of his living room as he waited for his team to arrive. He was ready to strike King and his people a blow that should bring their little organization crumbling down. "That nigga crossed me out and took Wifey. For that, he has to die painfully," Flamboyant said out loud as he continued to pace the living room. He stepped to the bar and poured himself a stiff shot of Crown Royal. He was sipping his drink when he heard cars pulling into his driveway. The team had arrived.

After letting everyone inside, Flamboyant smiled and said, "It's like this, I know y'all been waitin' for the opportunity to handle 'em north side niggas ever since we buried Prince and Gunna. I thank each one of y'all for listenin' to me and not pressin' the issue. My first concern was gettin' that money for all of us. If we couldn't eat we wouldn't be able to get our revenge. Shit is 'bout to get crazy around here so I wanted to make sure that y'all were down for what I'm 'bout to put down."

"What's poppin', Flam? You gon' let us do 'em niggas now or what?" asked Wave.

"Yeah, 'em niggas think they got away wit' this shit! You need to g'on and let us put 'em down," added Milo.

Ken remained silent as he stared and patiently waited for what Flamboyant had to tell them.

"Once we move on 'em niggas Toni will cut me off. That means no more work and our protection will be snatched.

We'll be on our own as far as gettin' our money. I'm to the point where it don't even matter no more. I want that nigga King to die a painful death for the shit he's done to our niggas. So, if y'all ready to ride on 'em niggas we might as well get this shit started. I already know where that nigga King rest his head. I'm takin' care of that nigga myself."

"Right. And we'll take care of the rest of 'em niggas. They got right back comfortable out in Del City so it won't be no problem lookin' at 'em fools out that way," said Wave.

"Yeah, that li'l nigga be poppin' up out in Midwest City, too. You already know I got his ass," said Milo.

"Good. We still got to hit 'em niggas up on the north side. Not only are we puttin' 'em niggas down, we're 'bout to make a mark on the entire city. We don't need Toni's ass to get money. We 'bout to lock this whole mothafucka down by our gotdamn self!"

"That's real talk right there," said Wave. "So, when do you want us to move on 'em fools?"

"The sooner the better. I'm gettin' at that nigga King later on tonight."

"So be it! It's on!" said Milo as he got to his feet. "I'm 'bout to round up my gorillas and make this shit pop off."

"I'll make my moves later on too," added Wave.

"Be safe and get back at me and let me know what's what," Flamboyant said as he poured himself another drink.

As they were leaving Flamboyant's home, Ken stopped after Wave and Milo were outside and asked Flamboyant, "Are you sure you want to make this play, dog?"

"Yeah, it's the only way. 'Em niggas got to die."

"That's no question. But you know the streets are talkin', my nigga. The word is out 'bout Shayla, dog. Is that the reason you've made this call?"

"Too keep it one hundred wit' you, Ken, yeah, it is."

Ken nodded and said, "I can respect that. At least you're keepin' it all on the table. Fuck, I'd be on some murda shit too if that shit happened to me. You know you're puttin' everything we've worked for at risk if this shit goes left on us, right?"

Flamboyant downed the rest of his drink and answered his homeboy. "Yeah, I know."

"Teedo will be here tomorrow evening. He wants us to have his equipment ready. He doesn't plan on staying long," said Toni.

"What, that nigga don't like Oklahoma City?" asked Charlie.

"You know how he is. He wants everything nice and quick, in and out."

"Whatever," Charlie said and hung up. Charlie picked the receiver back up and called King. When King answered Charlie told him, "It would be wise for you to take Shayla out the way for about forty-eight hours."

"Why's that?"

"Flamboyant might be trying to make a move on y'all soon."

"Yeah, well, I can deal wit' that clown-ass nigga. I ain't runnin' from that coward."

"This isn't about you running away from him, King. Do what I've asked and everything else will be taken care of. Do you understand me?"

King smiled into the receiver and said, "Yeah, I got you. But you know you should've let me and my squad handle this shit."

"Forty-eight hours, King," Charlie said and hung up the phone.

After he got off the phone with Charlie, King told Shayla, "Baby, go pack a lightweight bag real quick. We're 'bout to hit Dallas for a couple of days."

Shayla smiled and said, "Okay. Do you have some business to take care of out there?"

"Nah, I just want to go do a li'l shoppin' and shit. I got a li'l spot out there that has the plug on some True Religion jeans and a whole bunch of other shit. I'm tryin' to get my winter gear in order, that's all. Plus, I figured you wouldn't mind gettin' your shop on too."

"You know it."

He watched as she went into the bedroom to pack. As soon as the bedroom door closed he picked up the phone and called Tippi.

"What up, nigga?" asked Tippi.

"Look, somethin' is 'bout to pop off wit' that nigga Flamboyant. Charlie wants me to shake the spot for a couple of days so I'm takin' Shayla to Dallas. Have you found anything on 'em clowns?"

"I was gon' to hit you up later and let you know that I got a line on 'em fools' spots on the southeast and southwest side. I've already got wit' my wolves and we gon' go look at 'em fools later on."

"Do you. Make sure you get at me and let me know what pops off."

"Mmm hmm."

"And, Tippi?"

"What?"

"Be safe."

"Whatever, nigga, like you really give a fuck."

"You know I give a fuck, so don't be on no rah-rah shit out there. Watch yo' ass," King said sincerely.

His tone of voice touched her where she didn't want to be touched. She sighed and said, "I will."

***

Boleg and Cuddy pulled in front of the trap on the block as Tippi was stepping off of the porch. She strolled over to Boleg's Suburban and said, "Y'all niggas are right on time. Y'all want to put some work in wit' me and my wolves?"

"What's poppin'?" asked Cuddy.

"I'm 'bout to go look at 'em south side niggas out on the southeast side first. Then I'm gon' ride on the southwest side and see who else we can smash. Y'all wit' that?"

"You fuckin' right!" yelled Boleg.

"A'ight, look, go on and strap up and meet me back here in about thirty. Where that li'l nigga Nutta at?"

Cuddy shrugged his broad shoulders and said, "Ain't no tellin'."

"Hit him up and let him know what's 'bout to pop off. Have y'all heard from Keko?"

"Yeah, I talked to that nigga about an hour ago. He's out in Del City doin' him," answered Boleg.

Tippi checked the time on her watch and said, "A'ight, let me bounce. I got to get my wolves. I'll see y'all here in a li'l bit." She stepped quickly to her truck and sped off the block.

On the southeast side, Milo was gathering his gorillas and preparing them for what he had planned for King's squad, preferably Nutta. Ever since that incident at that McDonald's, Milo had been waiting for the opportunity to hurt Nutta something terrible. And now that he was in a position to make his move, he couldn't wait.

"A'ight, my niggas, it's like this: I just checked wit' my peoples out in Midwest City. That li'l nigga I want to smash is out there gettin' his grind on. So we gon' ride out that way and handle that fool real quick. After that we'll come back over here and chill 'til it gets dark;

then we gon' go tear up the north side. We smashin' every nigga I think is affiliated wit' that nigga King's crew." Milo's men were ready. They all gave nods of their heads, letting him know that his gorillas were ready for whatever. He smiled and said, "let's ride!"

Nutta was sitting on the porch of a crackhead's home counting the money he had just made. He had a smile on his face because he was making more money out in Midwest City than he ever thought he would. *Yeah, this shit is lovely right here,* he thought as he put a rubber band around the large wad of cash he held in his hand.

Just as he was putting his money inside of his pocket he saw Milo turn onto the block in his Chevy Tahoe, followed closely by two other cars. *Three cars deep. I know these niggas ain't lookin' for no drama,* Nutta thought as he pulled his pistol from the small of his back and racked a live round into its chamber. His cell rang just as he locked eyes with Milo. "What's up, Cuddy?" Nutta asked as he continued to stare at Milo.

"Dog, we 'bout to move on 'em south side niggas. You tryin' to ride wit' us or what?"

"It looks like I'm 'bout to have some drama wit' 'em fools right now."

"What's up?"

Before Nutta could answer Cuddy, Milo jumped out of his SUV with two .40-caliber H&Ks in his hands and yelled, "My turn now, nigga!"

"Aww, shit!" Nutta yelled as he dropped his phone and raised his nine and started blasting away at Milo.

Milo smiled as he held his ground and returned fire at Nutta. He knew that he had Nutta right where he wanted him and there was absolutely no chance of Nutta getting away from him or his gorillas.

Outmanned and outgunned, Nutta refused to back down. He continued to fire his pistol until he was able to slip into the crackhead's house. Once he was inside, he told the crackhead, who was screaming hysterically, to shut the fuck up and call the police. While she was dialing 911, he was reloading his weapon and trying to figure a way out of this mess. Just as he racked another round into his nine, the front door was kicked in followed by a deadly volley of bullets from Milo's gorillas who joined the heated gun battle.

Nutta heard the crackhead scream as she was hit twice in her chest. He wasn't really concerned about her; he was too busy trying to blast anyone who tried to enter the house. Sweating profusely, Nutta realized that he had no win. *It is time to get the fuck on,* he thought as he slid on the floor toward the back of the house.

When he made it to the kitchen he got to his feet and smiled as he opened the door. As soon as he stepped into the backyard he was shot three times in his chest. He tried to raise his arms to fire his weapon at a smiling Milo, but he had no strength. Milo calmly stepped up to Nutta and said, "I knew I'd get your punk ass." Then he shot Nutta point blank in his forehead and turned and walked away as Nutta's lifeless body fell to the ground.

When Cuddy heard all of the shooting in the background he screamed, "Awww, shit!"

"What?" asked Boleg.

"Nutta's in some shit out in Midwest City. I hear a whole lot of blastin'. Let's get out there."

As Boleg drove toward Midwest City, Cuddy called Tippi and told her what was going on.

"A'ight, I'm on my way wit' my people. We'll meet y'all out there. Y'all hurry the fuck up before they get that li'l nigga!" Tippi screamed into the phone.

"We on it," Cuddy said as he hung up the phone.

By the time Cuddy and Boleg pulled onto the block where Nutta made his money, there were police cars everywhere. Boleg parked his truck and they got out of the SUV, looking for their homeboy. When Boleg saw the yellow crime scene tape wrapped all around the crackhead's front door, he knew that Nutta was dead. He stepped to one of the police officers and said, "My li'l brother was inside of that house, Officer! Could you please tell me what's going on?"

"We have two people dead. One female and one male. One is inside of the home and the other victim is in the backyard. Can you give me description of what your brother was wearing today, son?" asked the officer, concerned.

Boleg shook his head and said, "I haven't seen him since last night. But he's five eight, light brown skin, and keeps his hair braided toward the back. I know he's here 'cause that's his truck parked in front of the house." Boleg pointed toward Nutta's SUV as tears fell slowly from his eyes.

"Come wit' me," said the officer as he led Boleg toward the backyard. "I can't let you contaminate this crime scene, but you can be helpful with a positive ID." When they stepped into the backyard Nutta's body was covered with a white sheet. The officer stepped to the body, knelt down to it, and pulled the sheet back. "Is this your brother, son?"

With his tears flowing harder, Boleg gave the officer a nod yes, turned left, and left the backyard. As soon as he was back in the front he told Cuddy, "They got him, dog. They smoked Nutta."

"What? Aww, hell nah!" screamed Cuddy. "Come on, let's get the fuck outta here!" When they made it to the truck Cuddy grabbed his cell and called Tippi. "Where you at?"

"We should be there in 'bout five. Is Nutta a'ight?"

"Nah, 'em niggas got him. Nutta gone," Cuddy said gravely.

"Shitttt! Come on, y'all, meet us at that li'l gas station on the corner of Southeast and Fifteenth, right off the highway."

"We on our way."

"Hurry the fuck up!" Tippi screamed, anger pulsing through her every vein.

King and Shayla were just about to walk out of the door when his cell phone rang. He dug it out his pocket and answered, "What it do?"

"They hit Nutta. He's out of here," Tippi replied calmly. Before a stunned King could respond Tippi continued, "We're on our way to the southeast side to do some damage. Watch yo' ass, baby, 'cause these niggas is playin' for keeps."

"Where y'all goin' on the southeast side?"

"It don't matter; you too far away for us to be waitin' on yo' ass. Take care of your girl, nigga. I got this."

Before he could say another word Tippi hung up the phone. Shayla saw the pained expression on King's face and knew instantly that something was wrong. "It's Marco, isn't it, Trevor? What has he done?"

King stared at her for a few seconds before answering. He shook his head sadly and said, "He done fucked up for real, baby. He's goin' to die tonight."

They say that sometimes everything in life happens for a reason. Tippi believed that and took it to heart. That's why she smiled when she saw Milo's Tahoe pull into the same gas station followed by two other cars where she was waiting for Cuddy. Tippi turned around in her seat and told her wolves, "Look, there go 'em niggas we lookin' for. We ain't got time to wait for my niggas so it's gon' just be us. Y'all cool wit' that shit?"

The three coldblooded killers sitting inside of Tippi's H2 all gave her a nod yes of their heads and began to load their fully automatic assault rifles. When it came to playing the murder game, Tippi's wolves were not to be fucked with. They were the best at killing.

Tippi smiled and had a look of timeless evil in her eyes as she said, "Breezy, you and Harry take out 'em niggas in those two cars right there." She pointed toward the cars parked on the other side of Milo's SUV. "Me and Coop will hit those niggas in that Tahoe. Y'all ready?" Her question was answered by the sound of live rounds being chambered in each of her wolves' weapons.

They jumped out of the H2 with their guns blazing. This time Milo and his gorillas were the ones outgunned and outmatched. Once the gunfire erupted they didn't have a chance. Tippi and her wolves cut them down as if they were nothing. Just as quick as the shooting started, it ended. Tippi stepped to the driver's side of the Tahoe and smiled when she saw Milo's lifeless body sprawled over the steering wheel. She ran back to her truck and quickly pulled out of the gas station. She grabbed her cell phone and called Cuddy and Boleg. "Change of plans, nigga. I'm headed to the southwest side. They've been taken care of. Meet me at that Valero on the corner of Shields and Southwest Twenty-ninth."

"We're on our way."

After meeting up with Cuddy and Boleg, Tippi led the way toward Wave and Ken's turf. They rolled all over the southwest side and didn't see any of Flamboyant's team. "Damn, I wish I knew where that nigga Flamboyant lived. Fuck it," Tippi said as she pulled out her phone and called Cuddy. "Did y'all let Keko and Spook know what's been poppin' off?"

"Nah, I thought you had already gotten at 'em," replied Cuddy.

"Damn!" She hung up the phone and quickly dialed Keko's number. When Keko answered the phone Tippi told him what had happened to Nutta as well as what happened at the gas station. "It's a full-court press, baby, so watch yo' neck, fool."

"Gotcha, li'l mama. What's up with King? He straight?" asked Keko.

"Yeah, he's out the way."

"That's . . . Wha . . . what the fuck!" screamed Keko. Keko was standing in the back of the Summit apartments while he was talking to Tippi. Wave, Ken, and several of their men pulled into the apartment complex, jumped out of their vehicles, and began to spray every man in sight. Spook caught the first wave of gunfire and died instantly.

Keko saw what was happening and yelled into his phone, "'Em niggas are puttin' it down, Tippi. They got Spook! Get y'all asses out here now!" He dropped the phone and ran into one of the many apartments he had inside of the complex and grabbed an AK-47 with a couple of extra clips. Before he ran back outside he took a look out the window to see what was going on. What he saw scared the shit out of him. Wave, Ken, and their men were methodically moving from the front of the apartment complex to the back, blasting everything and everyone in their path.

Keko knew that he didn't have any win if he tried to go outside and confront them head-on. *The best thing to do is sit back and wait this one out,* he thought as he watched the bloodbath outside. He heard Wave screaming, "This the south side niggas! Fuck all you coward mothafuckas! This is for Prince and Gunna! Fuck the north!"

Keko shook his head and threw all caution out the window. "Fuck these niggas! This is the north!" He took a deep breath and eased out of the apartment and stepped into the war zone.

Wave saw Keko at exactly the same time Keko saw him. They both raised their weapons and began firing at one another. Keko smiled when he saw Wave go down because he knew that Wave was now a dead man. He turned his sights toward Ken, but was a split second too late. Ken sent a deadly volley of bullets from his assault rifle his way and caught Keko three times in his stomach. Keko fell back against the wall of the apartment building, slowly losing his life.

With tears sliding down his face, Ken stepped slowly toward Keko to make sure that the bastard who had just killed his best friend was dead. When he made it to Keko and saw that he was still breathing, he inhaled slowly and said, "Die, nigga!" Ken raised his assault rifle and pointed it toward Keko's head; but he wasn't paying any attention to Keko, who already has his AK-47 pointed directly at Ken's head.

They both pulled the triggers of their weapons simultaneously. Keko's head exploded from Ken's shot, and Ken's head was damn near decapitated by the round from Keko's AK-47. The bullet went straight through his neck and his head was barely attached to his neck as his life disappeared. The rest of Wave and Ken's men saw that they were down and immediately retreated to their vehicles and got the hell out of dodge.

By the time Tippi, Cuddy, Boleg, and Tippi's wolves arrived in Del City, Tippi knew they were too late. Police were everywhere and no one was allowed to enter the apartment complex. "Shit!" Tippi pulled out her cell and dialed King's number. When he answered the phone she told him about everything that had taken place since they last spoke to one another.

King was furious. "You mean to tell me that Keko, Spook, and Nutta got took? Come on, Tippi, tell me you lyin'!" begged King.

"This shit has gotten real bloody, baby. They took losses too. We smashed some of 'em niggas on the southeast side. And from what I can see, Keko and Spook got some of 'em niggas too."

"Y'all get outta the way. I'll hit you back in a li'l bit."

"I thought you was gone to Dallas."

"Nah, fuck that shit! I'm still at the house. Drop off your people and come out here. Tell Cuddy and Boleg to come, too."

"A'ight," Tippi said as she ended the call.

Tears were sliding down King's face as he paced back and forth inside the bedroom. He turned toward Shayla and said, "Shay, please understand that what I'm 'bout to ask you is very, very important to me. I would never ask you anything like this if it wasn't—"

"You want to know where Marco's house is." Shayla inhaled deeply and said, "Sky Island, baby." She then gave him the address to the place she once called home.

King came and sat down next to her on the bed and said, "Shay, that nigga has killed my people today. That means he plans on takin' me too. I got to end this shit 'cause ain't no way I'm goin' to let that nigga get away wit' this shit."

"I understand. Just promise me you won't miss his ass."

He smiled and said, "Don't worry, I won't. Now, look, I want you to call Taj and have her come and scoop you up. I want you to stay wit' her 'til I finish this shit."

"Why . . . why can't I stay here?"

"It's not safe, baby. Ain't no tellin' what's gon' pop off. I'd feel better if you were out of the way for a minute."

He was interrupted by his phone ringing. When he picked up the phone he heard his aunt's voice. "Boy, are you a'ight?"

He smiled and said, "Yeah, I'm good, Aunty. What's up?"

"I'm sittin' over here watchin' the news and I saw all of this damn killin' goin' on and somethin' inside me told me to call yo' ass. Are you sure you a'ight?"

"Yeah, I'm good. Whatever you saw on the news has nothin' to do wit' me."

"You sure?"

"Come on, Aunty, you know ain't nothin' gon' go on wit'out me lettin' you know what's the real," he lied.

"All right, now. You be careful out there, boy. Them damn streets seem to have gone plumb fuckin' crazy."

"Don't worry about me, Aunty. You know I'm the King of these streets."

She smiled into the receiver and said, "Whatever, boy. Bye!"

Chapter Thirty-seven

Flamboyant sat parked in the exact same spot four houses down the street from King's house as he sat the day before, surveying his number one enemy's home. He was waiting for the perfect opportunity to strike. His mind was made up: King was going to die by his hands tonight.

He checked his watch and saw that it was a little after nine o'clock. He wondered why he hadn't heard from any of his team members. He picked up his cell and called Wave. After not getting an answer he called Milo. When he got Milo's voice mail, he nervously dialed Ken's number. After getting Ken's voice mail he said, "What the fuck is goin' on?" He then sent text messages to each one, ordering them to hit him back as soon as possible. *They're probably out doin' their thang,* he thought as he focused back on watching King's house.

After about twenty more minutes of waiting he noticed three vehicles turn onto King's block: a Suburban, an H2 Hummer, and Taj's Mustang. *Looks like that nigga is havin' some kind of get-together,* he thought as he watched each vehicle park in the front of King's home. He reached and grabbed the two silenced P-89s that were on the passenger's seat. He checked and made sure that each gun had a live round in its chamber. "I'll wait, nigga, as long as I have to, 'cause yo' ass is mines tonight. One way or another, you're outta here, King," Flamboyant said out loud as he stroked each of his pistols lovingly as if they were his lover's arms.

Once everyone was inside of the house, King listened again as Tippi told him everything that had taken place in the last couple of hours. Tippi also told him about Ken and Wave being killed by Keko. King smiled sadly and said, "My nigga went out like that, huh? That nigga was a straight rider for real. A'ight, listen, Taj: I need for you to take Shay to your spot 'til I can get this shit under control."

"No problem," replied Taj.

"How long do you think it'll be before I'll be able to come back home?" asked Shayla.

Tippi frowned but remained silent as King spoke to his girlfriend. Both Boleg and Cuddy noticed she was heated, though.

"I can't really say right now, Shay. Believe me, I plan on makin' that happen as soon as I can. Go on and get your stuff." As Shayla went to do as she was told, King turned his attention to Boleg and Cuddy and said, "I want y'all to go post up over at that nigga Flamboyant's spot." He then picked up a pen and pad and wrote down the address to Flamboyant's house in Sky Island.

"Damn, nigga, how did you get that fool's hookup?" asked Boleg.

Before King could answer Tippi said, "From his li'l girlfriend. I'm glad to see she's wit' the program after all."

King ignored her and said, "Like I said, I want y'all to go sit on that nigga. If he's there when y'all get over there hit me and Tippi up so I can come over there to do that nigga. We've took too many losses! This shit has to end tonight."

Shayla came out of the bedroom followed by Taj. "I'm ready."

King stepped to her and said, "A'ight, let me walk y'all outside." When they were outside in the driveway he gave Shayla a hug and a kiss and told her, "Hopefully this shit will be over and done wit' tonight, Shay. I'll give you a holla a li'l later on either way, okay?"

"Okay, Trevor. Be careful."

"I will. I love you, Shay. You know that, right?"

"Mmmm hmm. I love you too. Don't forget."

"Don't forget what?" he asked with a puzzled look on his face.

She smiled at him and said, "We were born to be together."

He returned her smile and said, "Forever and a day, baby, forever and a day." He kissed her again and watched as she got into Taj's car and drove away.

Flamboyant was sitting inside of his car fuming as he watched the display of affection that Shayla and King were showing each other. That fueled his anger and he was almost ready to jump out of his truck and run down there to blast both of them. *Calm down, baby, it's all good. Shayla belongs to me! Ain't no way I'm going to hurt her; oh, but that nigga is goin' to die slow, real fuckin' slow,* he thought, patiently waiting for his moment of truth.

Back inside of King's house, King told Tippi, "We need to bend some corners to make sure everything is everything around the way."

"A'ight. I sent my wolves back to the northwest side and told 'em to stay on point 'til they heard from me. The block should be runnin' itself but, you're right, we do need to run, through."

"Cuddy, make sure y'all get at me soon as y'all get posted up in Sky Island."

"Gotcha, dog," Cuddy said as he left King's house, followed closely by his road dog Boleg.

After they were gone Tippi told King, "You know the spot is gon' be way hot after all of this shit that done went down."

"Yeah, I was just thinkin' 'bout that shit."

"Have you talked to that fool Charlie?"

"I was 'bout to make that call now," he said as he picked up the phone and dialed Charlie's number. After Charlie answered he said, "What it do, Charlie?"

"What it do? It looks like all hell has broken loose out there. Tell me you did as I told you and got out the way."

"Nah, I'm still in the mix. Ain't no way I can shake the spot when my squad is out here dyin' for a nigga. Don't trip, though. The hunt is on. This shit should be over in a minute."

"You are one hardheaded young man, King. Do you remember what I told you a war would bring?"

"Yeah, 'em alphabet boys. But this shit ain't on me, Charlie. That nigga brought the ruckus so it gots to be on."

"That's true, but then again it isn't. You took the man's woman, for God's sake! So, in essence, you started this shit! But all of that is irrelevant now; what's done is done. Flamboyant is the least of my concerns. I'm more worried about how we're going to continue to get our money."

"The heat will pass, Charlie. When it does we'll get right back to makin' that paper. As for that nigga Flamboyant, he should be a mama's memory by the time the sun comes up. Real talk," King said confidently.

Charlie smiled and said, "We shall see. Be careful, King." The line went dead.

As King placed the phone in the receiver he smiled at Tippi and said, "Come on, let's—" The front door was kicked in and King stood there, shocked, when he saw Flamboyant point his gun at Tippi and shoot her twice in her midsection.

"Aww, fuck nah!" King screamed as he went and knelt down next to Tippi.

Flamboyant smiled a deadly smile and said, "You take my niggas; I take yours. Now stand up and die like a mothafuckin' man!"

Tears slid down King's face as he got to his feet. *Ain't this a bitch. This punk mothafucka caught me slippin' at my own spot.* He wasn't armed and he knew that his chances of making it out of this alive were slim to none. He figured if he was going to die, he was going out swinging.

He lunged toward Flamboyant with every ounce of strength in his body. Flamboyant smiled and fired both of his pistols, catching King directly in his face, chest, and neck. King was dead before his body hit the floor right next to where Tippi was lying. Knowing that Tippi was King's number one killer, Flamboyant stepped over to her and shot her two more times directly in her pretty face. "Yo' ass won't be puttin' in no more work, bitch." He spit on both of them and walked out of the house with a smile on his face. *Mission complete!*

After checking on his team and hearing how Milo, Ken, and Wave were murdered, Flamboyant was miserable. He couldn't believe that even though he'd gotten rid of King, he had lost the last few heads of his team. "This shit is too fuckin' crazy!" he screamed as he drove toward his home.

When he turned onto his block he noticed that same black Suburban that had been over at King's house earlier. As he drove past the SUV and his home he realized two things: one, those were King's people waiting to kill his ass; and, two, the only way they could know where he stayed was if Shayla told them. *That bitch crossed me like that? She got to get it too!* He drove out of his neighborhood and headed toward Taj's house.

When he made it to Taj's home all of the lights were out. He got out of his truck and knocked on the door. After no one answered he went to the garage and looked under the door to see if he could see Taj's car. Once he realized that they weren't home he decided to go get a room and chill for the rest of the night. He suddenly felt very tired. *It has been a long mothafuckin' day,* he thought as he climbed back inside of his truck.

Taj saved both of their lives that night by wanting to stop for drinks at Pearl's on the Lake. If she would have gone straight to her house, both she and her best friend would have been murdered. Everything in life does happen for a reason; most times people don't know it.

The next morning Flamboyant was awakened by the ringing of his cell phone. He grabbed his phone and smiled when he saw that it was Toni calling. "What's good, Toni?"

"I wanted to check on you to make sure that you were all right. I saw the news and this fucking city is on fire."

"Yeah, I saw it too."

"Where are you? We need to talk."

"I'm at the Fifth Seasons."

"On the north side?" Toni asked incredulously.

Flamboyant smiled and said, "Ironically, yeah. Why not? I don't have shit to worry 'bout. That nigga King is outta here."

"Really?"

"Oh, fa' sho'," he said arrogantly.

"Like I was saying, we need to meet, but you're too hot to meet me so I'll come to you. What's your room number?"

"I'm in suite 2671."

"I'll see you in a couple of hours, say eleven o'clock?"

"That's cool," he said, and hung up the phone, and went back to sleep thinking about Shayla and how he was going to take her life.

Teedo, Charlie and Toni's hired gun, arrived at the Fifth Seasons hotel thirty minutes after Toni had spoken to Flamboyant. When he made it to the door, Teedo pulled out a blank key card and inserted it into the door's keypad. He then pulled out a small cell phone–looking device and attached two magnetized wires, one to the keypad, and the other to the device in his hand. He pressed a three-digit code and the green light on the door keypad flashed, indicating that the door to the suite was unlocked.

He turned the knob gently and quickly pulled the wires free from the door. He stepped inside of the suite and closed the door gently behind him. He then pulled out a silenced Sig Ruger 9 mm pistol, his favorite weapon. When he entered the bedroom part of the suite where Flamboyant was sleeping soundly, he shook his head. It never ceased to amaze him how easy it was for him to do what he was so damn good at. He saw Flamboyant's guns resting on the nightstand next to him and wondered if he should give him a chance at fighting for his life. After a few minutes of debating with himself, he decided not to play any games.

He stepped next to the bed and gently tapped Flamboyant on his forehead with his Sig. Flamboyant opened his eyes and saw the barrel of Teedo's gun pointed directly at his head and said, "What the fuck is this shit?"

Teedo smiled, shrugged his shoulders, and said, "Toni said you got to go bye-bye." He then pulled the trigger twice and Flamboyant's head exploded all over the covers of the bed. Teedo turned and left the suite just as silently as he'd entered it.

Epilogue

After Shayla and Taj attended all the funerals for King and his squad, they both were questioned by the FBI and local police, and cleared of any involvement. Shayla and Taj knew if any one of them said anything close to the real story, their asses were next. It was already bad that they both had to move out of Oklahoma City to keep the rest of Flamboyant's goons at bay. The rest of King's people let it go and continued to get their money how they could now that their King was no longer. Tippi's wolves were another story. They were hunting for them both and needed revenge in the worst way. That was the only way Tippi would have wanted it, like a true killa.

Aunt Doris May buried her only nephew, who was the only child she could call her own. It was hard for her to look at Shayla when she showed up for the funeral, but she knew the life her nephew led and only regretted not opening her mouth when Shayla and King were in her living room that day rehashing their past.

A few days after the funeral, Shayla had stopped by her house, but she refused to open the door. She wasn't ready to face the reason her nephew was murdered. Doris May continued to medicate herself and looked after King's kids as much as she could to keep a piece of her nephew close.

Lawanda was a wreck. She had lost the father of her children and the love of her life. Although she never knew about Shayla or Tippi, she had heard rumors, and they confirmed her suspicions. After a couple of weeks of not working, she finally went back to work. At first it was hard to go back to normal, but she had to for her kids. As she continued to push forward, she met someone who filled the void King had left.

As for Toni and Charlie, they searched for their kingpins of Oklahoma City, but this time they decided to lay all the cards on the table. Both north and south side heads would know of each other to avoid any and all incidents that could be deadly. Toni and Charlie kept the money as their number one priority and made sure the new kingpins of Oklahoma City kept it that way, no matter the situation that arose.